SOULTRAPPED

SOULTRAPPED

DREW STOCKWELL

Copyright © 2017 by Drew Stockwell.

Library of Congress Control Number:		2017910494
ISBN:	Hardcover	978-1-5434-3497-2
	Softcover	978-1-5434-3496-5
	eBook	978-1-5434-3495-8

All rights reserved. No part of this book may be reproduced or transmitted in any form or by any means, electronic or mechanical, including photocopying, recording, or by any information storage and retrieval system, without permission in writing from the copyright owner.

This is a work of fiction. Names, characters, places and incidents either are the product of the author's imagination or are used fictitiously, and any resemblance to any actual persons, living or dead, events, or locales is entirely coincidental.

Any people depicted in stock imagery provided by Thinkstock are models, and such images are being used for illustrative purposes only.
Certain stock imagery © Thinkstock.

Print information available on the last page.

Rev. date: 08/17/2017

To order additional copies of this book, contact:
Xlibris
1-888-795-4274
www.Xlibris.com
Orders@Xlibris.com

To my father, Ronald, and my grandfather, John.

Still missed. Still with me.

Chapter 1

There are many evils that can be laid at the feet of Adolf Hitler. So many, in fact, that at his final judgment, it was likely that he soon became inured to his own atrocities, both personal and directed, and merely wished to get on to his final destination rather than endure the recounting. If Hell were to be merely boring, he would have sooner entertained Russian soldiers than have swallowed his pistol and bit down on the cyanide tablet. After all, many of these acts he had done with much pride. They were done in service to the German people. Was it his own fault they had proven too weak to be worthy of him and so doomed him to this eternal fate? Such thoughts may have crossed his mind if ever he was given the opportunity to offer them as a defense.

And yet among these sins, still, the other evils he had unleashed had possibly escaped his notice. The summary being total, the Fuhrer may have heard a number for which he could not account. One such instance, for example, came after he failed to bring the Royal Air Force (RAF) down during what became known as the Battle of Britain. Hitler, in a common bout of bilious rage, ordered a bombing campaign against the civilian population of London. If he could not force the island's military to yield through superior strength, he would do so on the backs of their people. Such suffering would cause the Brits to bend the knee on the grounds of humanity's sake.

The bombing began on September 7, 1940. Luftwaffe bombers dropped their payloads onto the city and its outskirts day and night for a grand total of fifty-seven days. This, of course, was a terrible evil in and of itself—the destruction incalculable, the terror insurmountable—or so the Fuhrer hoped. The noble isle, under the leadership of the squat English bulldog, Churchill, again failed to bow. In fact, Britain gave as good as it got, returning the favor with its own bombing raids in Berlin. But back in England, as the British fire brigades sifted through the rubble and the sirens signaling the coming storms wailed into the night sky, something crawled out from under the cement and ash.

It was old, much older than its bent and black-garbed form appeared. It shielded itself well in the darkness from distracted and inattentive eyes, flickering in and out of sight in the raging flames. It tilted its head toward the sky and cursed the Fuhrer for his boorishness, for destroying the obscure and secluded warehouse that it had used, uninterrupted until then, to accomplish some fine work and study. Its second, a hulking brute, bald, and silent, clothed in a tattered brown suit, gathered up what supplies could be salvaged and loaded the boxes onto a dark horse-drawn carriage. The pair headed north, where the Luftwaffe bombers could not reach for lack of fuel. The carriage, draped in black, was pulled by two steady horses, their coats a striking shade of luminous gray. The brute took the reins as the wiry man in dark Victorian garb many years out of date climbed into the back of the carriage. With a grunt and snap of leather straps, the hooves sounded their way slowly through the rubble.

This was the evil Hitler unwittingly released. He hadn't created it, nor could he have created it. This evil existed long before he had ever drawn breath. But it was the Fuhrer who had drove it underground to England. Once again, the price of even the briefest of contact with humanity, and that, in the low form of Adolf Hitler, was a heavy burden for the old sorcerer. For the Fuhrer, the pursuit itself had likely been ordered and forgotten, along with many other casual dismissals of consequence. With this minor act, among his many other greater and well-known monstrosities, Hitler had created the impetus for an ill-fated alliance, one that he would be far too long dead to suffer the result of birthing but, nonetheless, one for which he could be held accountable.

This was, of course, of no importance to the pale, thin creature riding silently in the black carriage. He turned his black speck eyes down at an old and tattered leather-bound book as the sound of the hooves softened from the paved roads of the city to the cobblestoned and beaten paths of the English countryside. The book was plain and silent in his lap, yet it was filled with an old, forgotten language. The knowledge in this tome made it a prized possession for its owner, and he ran a long and withered hand across weathered pages, looking for a passage he was sure existed but had yet to find.

The bombings had doubtless created new circumstances, circumstances that required a sacrifice to his solitude yet again, and that fact did vex him. But he was in possession of certain talents for which payment could be implied to the right purchaser. And so north then, he resigned himself, to the estate of a minor lord. There, his needs could be accommodated for the present. It was only that he would have to prostrate himself before lesser characters that made his old guts roil. But it must be so that the final work could be accomplished. He closed the book and sat back and gave a silent, wordless command to Mr. Warren, his loyal servant, an unspoken desire to make the journey last a while longer than the distance demanded.

Thankfully, at the pace of the horses, the journey did take an excess of time. Dawn would come before they arrived, and Malcolm Schreck, as he had taken to calling himself for some while now, had little tolerance for daylight. It was not harmful, truly, merely unpleasant. His natural constitution took sustenance in the dark of evening, which came early and lasted long in the recent weeks of Hitler's bombing campaign. It was provident then that Schreck and Mr. Warren found themselves deep in the woods, where the full complement of trees and low valleys shaded them from the blight of the overcast English sky. They chose such a place to rest the horses and for their own comfort.

Schreck had weeks before posted a letter in his own flourished hand as a reply to Lord Vaughn, as the gentleman still wished to be addressed despite the weakening of such titles in recent years, in case some event as the destruction of his current residence should happen to force a meeting of similarly interested agents. And Lord Vaughn had indicated in his own correspondence that he was such a similarly interested agent, though to what capacity Schreck hesitated to contemplate. Most men, Herr Hitler included, had not the experience or the fortitude to choose the path Schreck had long walked. "Again, no matter," he told himself. The situation tasked it to be so. This was perhaps an avoidable nuisance for Schreck, yet it was also a rather obvious means to which he could be supplied with enough comfort to complete his work.

The response from Vaughn petitioning Schreck for such a meeting came quickly enough, considering the catastrophic interruptions overhead and the secretive manner of its passage. Schreck hoped the lapse in time since it arrived had not caused the invitation to be invalidated. As the day approached, he watched as Warren gathered woods and built the fire to heat water and some meats they had retrieved—an old routine, perfected in an old quarter of an old country, now utilized once again as Schreck set his mind to a much-needed rest. A damp fog had settled on the rising field as he again climbed into the back of the carriage to let the day pass quietly, the commotion of the heavy ordinance well behind them.

As dusk fell again, the two resumed the trek and not long after returned to a cobblestoned roadway that led to the estate. Gently, Warren charged the horses to lumber forward as the formidable walls of the main building began to loom before him. Large oaks guarded and obscured the structure, but before long, glass windows and chiseled stone faced them in the drive as electric lamplights flickered behind heavy curtains. Motor vehicles—large bulbous steel structures with rounded hoods and shiny chrome bumpers—were parked in a gravel lot to the right of the building. Warren ignored them as he passed. Such machines held as much interest for him as they did his master. They were of the new time. The smell of horseflesh and the rhythmic beating of hooves were all that he cared to acknowledge. He pulled the reins to halt the beasts at the stoned arch leading to the main door.

"Here," Warren blurted out, his voice thick with the fact that it was so infrequently employed.

Schreck sighed in the back of the coach. His eyes closed under their heavy lids and dark brows as if to gather what strength as he may for a final exertion.

"Yes" was his only response as his gangly legs and buckled shoes swung to the open door. He exited to stand next to Warren, who dutifully held the door open like a proper manservant. Schreck rubbed his hands together as he looked up and around, surveying the mansion and the gray clouds that passed above its sharp peaks. He turned to Warren, who, in expectation, had Schreck's black beaver hat already in his hands. Schreck took the hat in his long fingers and nodded his approval.

"Stay close, Mr. Warren," he said in a velvet Eastern European accent. He donned the great chapeau, adding a full foot to his slender frame. "I am not at all certain how we will be received." Schreck's acknowledgment of this was merely admittance of the pair's unusual appearance and of their reluctance in accepting the company of other men. Warren grunted his assent of this fact and reached back into the carriage for Schreck's great leather bag. It was filled with as much of his supplies as its ample depth could receive. It also contained the old and heavy leather-bound book Schreck had been perusing during the journey. An average man would have strained to carry its weight. Warren took the curved wooden handles in one great fist and hefted it with little perceivable effort. At this moment, an older man with gray hair appeared in a traditional butler's attire, a starched white bow tie covering his thin throat.

"Sir," the butler said blankly as his eyes focused on Schreck, "your carriage was spotted coming up the drive by a stable hand. May I state to Lord Vaughn who calls?"

"You may," Schreck replied. "Malcolm Schreck. I believe your master is expecting me, although I gave no firm date for my arrival."

"Of course, sir," replied the butler. "We've had numerous visitors since the bombing began, though, I must say, you are the first to arrive by horse-drawn carriage. London must be pure hell."

Schreck stared coldly back at the man, studying his face with dark pinpoint eyes. Warren shadowed him close behind. He too showed an impassivity that unsettled the manservant. "In this grand estate, sir, what could you know of London or Hell?" Schreck asked.

The manservant ruffled a bit but composed himself quickly. "Quite, sir," he said. "I will inform Lord Vaughn of your arrival. Shall I have a boy take your carriage to the stable?"

"I prefer the carriage remain where it is."

"May I take your coats then?" The butler made as if to assist Schreck out of his garment. Schreck's look hardened even more profoundly. "As you wish, sir," the butler said as he drew his hand away from the strange man. "If you'd like to sit for a moment, I will return presently."

Schreck nodded. This was as he expected. It was why he had deliberately avoided such encounters. Warren was all the personage Schreck found necessary. Should supplies be needed, Warren had little trouble in acquiring them, either through stealth or force, if needed be. And London, even with the blitzkrieg falling around them, had been an ample supplier of materials. Truth be told, the bombings had made foraging much simpler. A large haggard man groping through rubble was not as odd a sight as it may have been previously. Warren had even procured more sentient subjects whose disappearance could be accounted to burning buildings and fallen arches. But one of those damnable weapons had dropped too close, and now Malcolm Schreck was forced to solicit another to assuage his needs. Again, he cursed the Fuhrer. *Damn that little fool.*

Schreck squinted against the glare of the small room's lights. A slight moment of thought and a gesture of his left hand took the liberty of dimming them to a more acceptable level. His skin was taught over the bony prominences of his pale cheeks and jutting nose. His dark hair matted against his skull from the weight of his hat. Many years under the shroud of darkness had totaled this effect. He was not an attractive man; he knew. And harsh light only made this more evident. He recognized it as a weakness. Men shied as much from him because of it. It made such occasions where he was forced to be in their company a very anxious time.

Eventually, the butler, James, returned. If he took notice of the newly darkened atmosphere or the fact that the man he had greeted at the door had sunken into the shadows, he gave no sign of it.

"This way, gentlemen," he said, turning back down the hall. Schreck took note of floral arrangements that sat on small tables every forty feet or so as they wound left and right toward a set of steps leading down from the main floor. Roses and chrysanthemums brightened the hallway as they turned the first corner, and new lights from crystal chandeliers shone down upon him as he passed under. A woman's influence was present, no doubt. It was yet another assault on his senses, keen as they were to this new ambience. Warren bent over for a large snort of the flowers as his heavy steps went by. An absentminded smile cracked the large moon face, only to drop suddenly as his master turned to look at him. Then after descending a wide set of carpeted steps and turning right down yet another hallway, in the middle of the final wall, a great black curtain hung ominously from the ceiling. A large gold rod and holder suspended it from the wall. From behind the curtain, music could be heard, and voices with some jolts of laughter mingled in the din.

James turned to them and said, "A moment, sir, while I announce your arrival." The servant drew the heavy curtains to either side and opened one dark-brown rectangular door. Schreck bent slightly to peer into the room, but the butler's narrow back obscured his view. The murmuring in the room quieted to acknowledge James's presence.

James stepped forward and drew his right arm back to beckon the visitors into the room. "Mr. Malcolm Schreck and associate," he said formally. Schreck instinctively took his cue and walked slowly into the opening to stand just beside James's outstretched arm. He removed his tall beaver hat and placed it against his chest as he bent his bony hips forward in a quick jerk of a bow. He took an exceptional amount of time to survey the room. Ten to twelve men stood about the back of the candlelit space, smoking cigars and cigarettes in their dark formal wear. One, a rather large rotund man, around fifty years old, with a brown handlebar mustache and a heavy gold band around the third finger of his left hand, stepped forward.

"Mr. Schreck?" the man offered dubiously. This was the lord of the manor, Brendan Vaughn. He took a puff from his fat cigar and, with his left hand, removed it from his hair-hidden lips. Vaughn studied the figure of Schreck for a moment, attempting to reconcile the man before him with the image he had formed in his mind of a fellow occultist. His German friends had, before the unfortunate hostilities, made some mention of Schreck's adherence to the theatrical, but they had not painted quite the full picture. Vaughn held out his right hand to Schreck as he approached the man. Schreck grimaced slightly and demurred from his grasp.

"I do not wish to express discourtesy, sir," Schreck said, "but I am not one who regards that custom as a necessary function of greeting."

The large man looked back toward his companions. He returned his gaze toward Schreck, looking him up and down a moment, and said, "No matter. I'm happy to make your acquaintance finally, Mr. Schreck. I am Brendan Vaughn, lord of the house, and these fine fellows you see before you are part of the group I mentioned in my letter, the Black Orchid Society."

Schreck nodded his head and pressed his lips together in something of a smile. "Gentlemen," he said as his survey of the room took scant notice of them. Instead, his dark eyes had focused sharply on the many female forms who were gathered about among the sofas and the bar tables. About half again the number of the men, they were all elegantly dressed and seemed to glow like angels in the darkness. But as Malcolm Schreck eyed them sternly, they grew noticeably flustered. They closed in together to form a larger group, all averting their eyes from his gaze. Warren took a step forward. Schreck thrust a hand back to halt him and inhaled sharply.

"You have women in this society of yours, Lord Vaughn?" he asked curtly. "Your letter made no mention of women."

At that, another gentleman came forward. He was roughly of the same height as Schreck and thin with rather striking features for a man, although age had begun to diminish them. Light-brown hair swept back off a smooth forehead, and when he spoke, it was with the air of an educated English aristocrat.

"The ladies are under my care, Mr. Schreck," he said. The man kept his hands firmly in the pockets of his dining jacket. "Arthur Drake, at your service."

Schreck looked the man over. "Under your care," he repeated, emphasizing each word short, cutting them off like a carrot on a cutting board. "May I presume then that they follow your commands?"

"Commands?" the man said quizzically. "I don't co—"

"Mr. Drake!" Schreck interrupted sharply. He was becoming irritated. "They serve some function here, no? You say they are under your care? Then they do as you tell them, yes?"

Arthur Drake's eyes narrowed. His right hand drew the impression of a fist in its pocket.

Schreck looked directly into Drake's face for a long moment. Then Malcolm Schreck's features softened, if it could be described as such. He let out a slight chuckle. "That is not necessary, Mr. Drake," he said. "Please forgive my ill manners. It is just . . . I would prefer the females not be present . . . for the demonstration I have planned. You see, I find them . . . a distraction. I am not practiced in such company. I fear it would affect my performance. I meant no disrespect to you or . . . your charges."

Drake seemed to consider this a moment and then took a quick glance in Lord Vaughn's direction.

"As you wish, Mr. Schreck," he replied as Brendan Vaughn stood, somewhat transfixed between them. "Ladies," Arthur called out, still returning Schreck's gaze, "I must agree with our new guest. You are a distraction, a very pleasant one, but still . . ." Drake turned toward the women, who seemed, as a group, to be relieved at the coming request. "If you wouldn't mind retiring to your rooms," he continued. "I'll be with you presently."

The women, all to a one, to Arthur's unspoken pride, did not rush out of the back doorway to escape but, with orderly steps, left the smoke-filled room to the men, who stood at some distance from the visitors with their own looks of discomfort and unease. It would seem that they too had not expected an arrival quite like the one Malcolm Schreck and his hulking companion presented.

After the women had left, Schreck stepped toward Arthur Drake with a wry smile on his face, which Arthur found unnerving. "I see they are under your care, Mr. Drake. You handle them well. And I must say the blade you carry just there"—Schreck's eyes went to the pocket of Drake's jacket—"is a display of wisdom I gather the rest of your . . . society is none too familiar. Again, I assure you it will not be necessary."

Brendan Vaughn stepped forward at this instant. "I believe some demonstration was mentioned, Mr. Schreck. Since you've deprived us of our distractions, perhaps we may see what you have to offer."

"Quite," Schreck responded. "A table . . ., a small table is all I will require." He gestured toward Warren, who then lifted the bag as a table was set beneath it. Warren then silently stepped back away from it as Drake and Vaughn rejoined the rest of the Black Orchid Society among the living area.

Schreck looked at them all once again with what could only be described as bemusement. "Gentlemen," he said, "it has been made known to me that the Black Orchid Society is a gathering of men of standing here in England. It has also been reported that you have an interest in darker knowledge than perhaps your more formal education has prepared you to receive. Such work has been my entire life. I carry the scars of it throughout my journey in this world and the other."

With that, Malcolm Schreck reached into his large leather bag and removed the ancient heavy book from the opening. It fell loudly to the tabletop, and his long fingers gripped the edge and slithered down the pages to splay it open. "Here," he said ominously, "is where it begins."

Schreck's voice, which had seemed low with an undefined European quality, now took on a deeper resonance. At times, it sounded Germanic and then, without warning, a guttural Latin. But it was a dark language none of the men in that room had heard before. It was a rather frightening sound to their ears. A couple of them took the nearest seat as if an illness had suddenly overtaken them, but everyone in the room was affected. Vaughn, Drake, even Warren, who had no doubt seen and heard such things before, stepped back with his eyes widened in expectation.

Suddenly, at the end of one of these unrecognizable phrases, Malcolm Schreck coughed forward a bluish-gray smoke from his throat. It fell forward with a thickness that threatened to encompass his entire form and began to emanate from the ends of his sleeves. He aged in that moment; his hair whitened, and bluish veins drew out on his marble face like a city map.

"My god, Brendan!" someone rang out. "You've invited Spring-heeled Jack into the house!" Spring-heeled Jack was the English boogeyman whom legend told accosted weary travelers in the dead of night. Jack had been known to belch blue smoke out of his mouth before he attacked. He had long been in danger of fading into obscurity in the modern twentieth-century world. Rarely was he used as a warning to small children to mind their manners and heed their elders. Malcolm Schreck brought all those forgotten childhood fears charging back with a sudden ferocity to the men in that room. They were perhaps the last generation of men to have heard this legend. The men of the Black Orchid Society, a ragtag group who fancied themselves modern-day practitioners of the occult, now made acutely aware that their real knowledge ended at the limits of their own feeble imaginations and even feebler theatrics.

But the demonstration was far from over. As the smoke grew in thickness, an electrical pulse emanated from it, and in its obscurity, a form began to take shape. In that heavy plume, a thing of some unknown origin appeared. It slithered at first with an unthinking purpose, for it, as yet, had no recognizable features. It was merely a cylinder of bumps and boils, which then bulged out slowly and singularly with huge effort. Great muscled legs then formed out of the cylindrical torso. A head and neck also birthed out from that grotesque body, and the face that appeared was a mush of teeth and eyes. It screamed out in either rage or pain a wordless fury but remained where it presented, head turning back and forth, teeth and maw jutting forward. The room itself seemed to shake in thunderous appeal of the beast's presence. And then slowly, the thing turned its myriad of eyes toward Schreck's audience. Someone there screamed in pitiful fright as the demon seemed to take a step out of its smoky cage and move toward them. Schreck may have called this creature from hell's domain itself, but did he have control of it? Had he brought the beast here to this room or rather them to the beast? If unleashed upon them, what defense would they have? These men craved sin of a different sort; evil was a game to be played for a lark. Here was no lark. Here was evil in its basest form, and the puppeteer, if that was what he was, seemed oblivious to the danger. The room was now dark, and the doors of the hall seemed miles away and blocked from access.

As if suddenly aware of the rising terror of the occupants of the room, Schreck fell forward, clamping down heavily on the open book as the beast turned its eyes toward him, its intent toward its keeper pure and entirely malicious. It had laid eyes on its first victim.

Schreck's upper torso suddenly collapsed on the book, and in that act, the smoke seemed to retreat upon itself as rapidly as it had been conjured. The beast then disappeared with it but not without echoing shrieks of rage. There was a stunned silence, except for a soft whimper from one of the members of the Black Orchid Society.

Schreck looked up, sweating profusely. If his age had been unaccountable before the demonstration, he now seemed as old as Methuselah; his hair frayed and gone white; his skin pale, dry, and wrinkled. It was a visage, only slightly less frightening than the one it had replaced. Schreck heaved breath after breath until finally, he calmed.

Arthur Drake looked toward Vaughn with a look of white shock. Brendan Vaughn returned the look and slowly began clapping his hands together. The other men unenthusiastically joined him.

"Remarkable!" Vaughn exclaimed. "Simply remarkable, I must say! Bravo, sir! Bravo!"

Schreck stood weakly, smoothed himself down his front, and stepped out from behind the table toward the group. Arthur Drake noticed that his face was ever so subtly returning to its former state, and his hair was also darkening as he approached. Whatever pains Schreck had gone through for his "demonstration," they didn't appear to have a long-lasting effect. Still, Schreck seemed somewhat winded, and he kept a few steps between himself and the group. Mr. Warren instinctively drew near him as Brendan Vaughn began to regain his own composure.

"Wondrous!" he bellowed. "You must share with us these secrets you possess!"

Schreck grimaced. "This is a knowledge for which most men have no capacity, Lord Vaughn," he said haltingly. "And I am, unfortunately, not well suited to the role of instructor."

Vaughn's gaze took a downward turn at this like a child being told he was not worthy of a promised gift. In response, Schreck smiled as best he could. "Although there are certain areas which I would be most pleased to pass on to a distinguished student such as yourself and your, um, colleagues."

"Excellent!" Vaughn returned. "Now then, Master Schreck, you look as though you might profit from a drink. What is your pleasure?"

"Water only, if I may. I never drink, sir. And a glass for my servant, if it is not inconvenient."

Vaughn pulled a tasseled rope that hung nearby, and shortly, the butler, James, reappeared. "Take Mr. Schreck and his assistant to the study, James," he said loudly, "and give them each a tall glass of water." He turned toward Schreck. "Mr. Schreck, if you don't mind, our little group has a new discussion on the table. Would you excuse us while you refresh yourselves?"

Malcolm Schreck bowed curtly, motioned for Warren, and followed James out of the dark room into the hallway. As the door closed behind him, Vaughn stared at the empty space Schreck had just occupied. The recent memory of what had occurred there seemed to affect him more now that Schreck was gone. It assaulted his senses and the senses of all the men there. Vaughn attempted to light his cigar, his hands visibly shaking. Arthur saw his struggle and steadied them.

"My thanks, old man," Vaughn said. "Did you see that?!" He was almost giddy with excitement, faltering between the emotions of fear and wonder. This man, Schreck, was truly a conduit to the unknown. Following his path could lead to great power.

Arthur took a drink of bourbon. "Yes," he replied. There was not much more he could add under the circumstance. He had seen illusionists and magicians before, traveling the circuits, both high end and low, to give a crowd of people a quick thrill. He knew the illusions as tricks and had never been fooled into thinking them any more than a clever use of distractions that caused a moment of inattentiveness so the illusion could work its will on the audience. This display of Schreck's, however, was quite different. Did the smoke hide some projection? Could it have been produced from a sleeve or from the end of his trousers? It had just suddenly billowed out of him. Was the huge idiot somehow a part of it? Did he control the projection from where he stood back in the room? It didn't seem that he had, yet Arthur and presumably the rest of the men had not paid attention to him once Schreck began speaking in that strange tongue. But most of all, the question that held the most weight for Arthur was how and why did the illusion, if that was what it was, take such a toll on Schreck?

The other men gathered around at the bar, all seeming to have some nervous sense of what Vaughn would soon propose: allowing Schreck entry into their group. An intense discussion ensued regarding just that idea. The obvious knowledge of the man, the artistry, and the excitement that he brought were thought to be a positive. Knowledge of what though? None had any answer to that. It was only Schreck's grotesque appearance and the presence of his hulking bodyguard that proposed any reticence on their part. It was befuddling then to Arthur Drake that he would be the one to raise the single objection. They all felt the danger in the room during the demonstration. Hell, he thought, one of them, he wasn't sure who, had screamed out like a frightened girl. And yet inexplicably, they were still attracted to it. Only after, when they had all nodded or muttered their assents, did Arthur feel compelled to speak.

"Brendan," he said calmly. He knew to broach the objection with passion would only serve to strengthen the lord of the manor's resolve against him. He was not an actual member of the little cult after all. "Do you think it wise to allow a man such as this into your home? Think of the future for a moment. The country is at war. Bombs are dropping in London. If it continues, refugees from the city will likely start seeking sanctuary in the country. Don't you think Parliament will be requesting aid from a man of your means? How would you explain his presence here? How would you clean him up?"

Brendan Vaughn smirked. He took a puff from his cigar and allowed it to rest in the corner of his mouth. "Arthur, the bombs have been dropping for some time. No refugees, aside from Mr. Schreck and his man, have entered the estate. We're too far removed from the city. And besides, my own groundskeepers have been instructed to discourage any forays onto the property."

"So," Arthur said directly, "this creature, crawls out from under a fallen rock, does a little magic trick for you, and you decide to invite him into your home? What price are you willing to pay for him to keep performing for you?"

"Magic trick?" Vaughn said dubiously. "Magic trick, you say? You saw what he did, Arthur," Vaughn said sternly. "We all saw it, did we not, gentlemen?" Vaughn surveyed the faces of the other minor lords and landowners, the former Parliament member, and the fallen clergyman. If he felt inclined to the truth, he would admit that it was his enthusiasm for the occult and their enthusiasm for hedonism that brought them here. But here they were, for the weekly gathering, the gathering that he had bestowed the name the Black Orchid Society.

These men would follow his lead. They all waited expectantly for him to reply to his own question. *They know who holds sway in this house,* Vaughn thought. But Arthur . . . he had different ideas and no great passion for the movement. He was merely the house pimp, and he saw fit to question. He had grown familiar in his time at the estate. He had cultivated a posh accent and a finery of clothing he would never have acquired in his cheap quarters in the East End. But he would have to learn his place here. Nasty business, putting a man he considered a friend down, and Arthur had become that in time. In fact, of all his acquaintances, Arthur was the one man he felt almost a familial affection toward, almost as a brother despite his low background. But it had to be done, he supposed.

"You call it a magic trick, Arthur?" Vaughn said. "Pick a card, any card. That's the beginning for a magic trick. This was a revelation. And Mr. Schreck, whatever else he may be, is an obvious guide and source of great knowledge, the kind of knowledge I've been seeking for many years. How can I refuse such an opportunity?"

Arthur Drake turned to the bar, began walking away from them, picked his drink from the far end of the mahogany tabletop, and brought the glass to his lips. He downed the rest of his bourbon and water in one swallow. "I don't know, Brendan," he said, turning to the large man at the center of this group of ne'er-do-wells and stuffed shirts. "But I would seriously consider it were I you. This Schreck character could bring all this crashing down on your head. If not that, the best he could do is fuck up a pretty good thing we got here. But I've said my piece. Do as you please. It's your house."

"Thank you, Arthur, for realizing that." Vaughn called for his butler. "James, have the gentlemen come back, please." And with that, Arthur Drake, who held no strong opinions on religion, politics, or the future itself, had a sudden premonition of doom. *The war,* he thought, *if we're lucky, may never get so close. But we've just traded one known horror for one made of nightmares.* As he watched the thin, odd, malformed man in the Victorian dress and the tall beaver hat reenter the candlelit room, that feeling hit Arthur with a force that made him turn away from the sight of him.

After some time devoted to niceties that neither Schreck nor his companion were obviously well accustomed to, the strange man stepped toward the lone individual at the bar. This was the wench herder who kept a knife in his pocket. *A man,* Schreck thought, *with some experience behind him.* Schreck wedged himself by the barstool next to Arthur and placed his tall hat on the countertop between them. Arthur noted it and studied it for a moment as if waiting for it to sprout legs like Schreck's demon and move across the bar.

"I understand," Schreck said casually, "you had objections to my presence here, Mr. . . . Drake, is it?"

"It is," Arthur replied. "And I do."

"May I inquire as to their source?"

Arthur tapped the ash from his cigarette into a green-hued glass ashtray. He looked at Malcolm Schreck's face. Arthur found even that an unpleasant experience. There was also a smell that had a slight effect of repulsion to the pale man. Was it a chemical? Formaldehyde perhaps?

"The girls don't like you," Arthur said finally.

Schreck seemed confused by the statement. He pursed his thin bluish lips as he mulled it over. "I fail to see the relevance," he said.

Arthur could not suppress a smile at the remark. "Of that, I'm quite sure, Mr. Schreck. Quite sure, indeed. But you see this lot over here?" Arthur gestured toward Vaughn and his followers, smoking and drinking, murmuring their banalities as if at a garden party. "They would . . . see the relevance, especially if they traveled here some dreary night, away from their wives and their pestering children, and found that, lo and behold, the lovely dreams they dream about in their own cold beds . . . were gone."

Schreck smiled. He looked at Arthur from under his brow and rested his elbow on the bar, leaning over his hat. "And this would be inconvenient for you as well, Mr. Drake?" Schreck shook his head absently. "Fear not, my young friend," he said. "I would not lay hands upon any of your stock. And I certainly would not presume to thwart your esteemed function for Lord Vaughn."

Arthur caught a glance of Mr. Warren, who wandered the perimeter of the room, looking at the paintings of Vaughn's forebears and bending to smell the flowers. Not one of the other men seemed interested in starting a conversation with the great bald brute, and he gave no indication that he knew they were also in the room.

"And him?"

"Warren?" Schreck answered. "Harmless, I assure you. He does nothing without my word. And so his interests are in keeping with my own, not to include your ladies. I will see to it. As I've stated to Lord Vaughn, Warren and I do not require the genteel pleasures of his estate. We merely have need of a place of seclusion and privacy in which I can continue my work in relative peace."

"Where'd you find him?"

Schreck's smile dropped. "In the hold of a ship," he said blankly. Before he could continue, Vaughn came forward, hands held up as he greeted the two at the bar. He almost clapped one of those big hands down on Schreck's bony shoulder but seemed to quietly think better of it; instead, he clapped them together and gave them a vigorous rub.

"Mr. Schreck!" he offered. "Shall I have James show you to your rooms? The group here will be up for some time yet, but you've had quite a long trip and must be tired. I can assure you of the privacy you seek. We have many unoccupied rooms in the west wing of the house. You shan't be disturbed."

"Thank you, Lord Vaughn, but no. Mr. Warren and I are quite accustomed to living in the elements. If you have no objections, I was hoping for a building away from the main house. I am afraid my work must needs seclusion from any possible disturbance."

Vaughn rubbed his beard and thought about this for a few moments. "Hmmm, well . . .," he said. "I certainly wouldn't wish you to be disturbed as your work is quite fascinating. There is an older structure up the hill about a kilometer down the path. It used to be for our horses, but I converted it to a garage. It has a few of my older vehicles in it, but there's still ample space despite that. No electricity, though, I'm afraid. There is an old stove for heat . . . I'm not sure of its current condition. Haven't been there for over a year now . . ." Vaughn continued to consider this absently as both Schreck and Drake looked at him.

"It sounds perfectly acceptable, Lord Vaughn," Schreck said. "And to assure my new young friend," he said, turning his attention to Arthur, "it will be as if we were not even here." Schreck retrieved his hat from the bar, bowed to Arthur, and turning to the master of the house, said, "You are quite correct in your observation, Lord Vaughn. Both Mr. Warren and I are quite spent for the evening. And it will take some time to make our arrangements in your building. We should be about it then."

With that, Schreck motioned to Mr. Warren and strode rather quickly out of the room, glancing at the others gathered about the fireplace and nodding curtly in their direction. James could hardly keep up with the man's pace, and he was gone.

Brendan Vaughn smiled. "I think we've just turned a page here," he said. "Obviously, Mr. Schreck has a deep understanding of the dark arts. I'm excited, Arthur! For the first time in quite a long while, I'm excited at our prospects."

"Rather a moot point," Arthur replied as the other men came up to them at the bar, "especially if we're invaded by the Germans."

This was answered with a few nervous bouts of laughter. "Doubt that rather. Bloody unlikely. Let them come." Then Vaughn muttered some agreement and chortled, "I shouldn't think that would affect our situation even if they did invade. Our boys would put up a hell of a fight as the air force proved, and if they lost, well . . . I'm sure Mr. Hitler would allow the noblemen to keep their standing in the community relatively whole. He would need such patronage, not being of our kind." There were subtle nods of agreement in the group to this statement, at least of the hopeful variety. Someone, possibly the ex-Parliamentary member, mentioned America as seeing an invasion of England as a reason to enter the conflict.

"I haven't heard much out of them," Arthur said. "Mr. Kennedy was quite condoning of Herr Hitler whilst he was here."

"That was then, Arthur," Vaughn replied. "Kennedy has been sent home. Besides, what else will Roosevelt do with America's abundance of niggers, dagos, and Irishmen? War is the only proper way to trim the fat from the land, eh?" He laughed, and the rest, beside Arthur himself, laughed with him. "No offense, of course, Willy."

William Shaughnessy grinned foolishly. "None taken," he said jovially. "Where'd our ladies get off to?"

"Yes, Arthur!" Vaughn shouted. "By god! Get the women back! The boogeyman has gone!"

Chapter 2

Malcolm Schreck was at the least true to his word. In the coming weeks, as the bombing of London waned and no new stragglers seemed to be appearing at Vaughn's door, few sightings of the man in the odd costume and his silent companion were reported to Arthur Drake. Once or twice, he had seen them himself late at night when all the servants were sleeping, milling about the kitchen, looking for a stray pot or spice it would seem. But it was a quick vision as they did not tarry for long. Neither engaged him in a conversation, although Malcolm Schreck would suddenly stop, look at him, and smile that leering smile of his. Then he would be gone out into the darkness.

His silence, along with his steadfast unwillingness to seek out his host, was beginning to pester Brendan Vaughn. The self-styled lord showed signs of frustration toward his distant guest. He told Arthur Drake he felt ill-used, to be perfectly frank about it. "Damned rude, I say," he huffed. "You'd think the man could show some common courtesy."

But common was not a word Arthur would have used when speaking of Schreck. Drake came at it from a completely different outlook. "I'm not sure he is a man, Brendan," he said. "And damned lucky is what I'd call it. Whatever Mr. Schreck is doing out there, better to know as little as possible. This sorcerer can bring nothing but trouble. Tried to tell you, but you wouldn't listen. Your best course now is plausible deniability. Start thinking of your excuses while you have time."

"To hell with that." Vaughn stood from behind his desk to look out his study window. The sun was setting as he gazed out upon the hill. Just over the rise, Malcolm Schreck and that mute ape of his had set up a shop. *It is well past time to pay a visit,* Vaughn thought. *My goddamn property after all.*

Arthur Drake watched his host carefully. "What are you going to do?"

"Nothing, Arthur," Vaughn replied. "Nothing. I'm just going to stand by and be disrespected! If you have no objections!" Brendan Vaughn gathered himself with a deep inhalation. He blew it out slowly. "Sorry about that, old chap," he said quietly after a few moments. He never apologized with as much force as he attacked, but then again, any acknowledgment of a given slight was unusual for a man of noble birth like Brendan Vaughn.

"Perhaps you're right, Arthur," he said. "We should be thinking of our escape route with Mr. Schreck at hand. Lord knows what he's been about there. My field hands won't go near the place anymore, and a few of them are quite rough. He's gotten entirely too comfortable on my good will, and I've seen nothing of what's been promised me."

Arthur stood and went to Vaughn's side. They both looked out of the large expanse of glass as the red sun inched closer to the hillside. "Brendan," Arthur said with as even a voice as he could muster, "you are an English lord. You have a grand estate with a grand manor, and all your friends, me excluded, of course, are among your peers. Now let's admit, you've dabbled in some less than lordly escapades to be sure. But a pastime is all it was. It's entertainment. The debauchery, the opium, the occult—it's all an act for you. And them. It really doesn't mean anything." Arthur turned to the large desk and retrieved their drinks. He handed Vaughn his glass.

"But this Malcolm Schreck," he continued, "from him, I don't get that impression at all, Do you? No. Malcolm Schreck is an entirely different animal. It's not an act. It's no mere pastime. It is his world. Now I'm far from religious, Brendan. You know that. But he makes me a believer in something I've always taken for granted—true evil. Some would say we're evil men. You and I. But this is a thing I've never encountered before. I dare say neither have you. You'd do better to give him a wide berth for now. Kick him out when winter comes, when that barn becomes too cold and he has to come to you."

Vaughn said nothing. He merely nodded and looked sadly down into his drink in the dimming light. Then he looked at Arthur and smiled. "All right, Arthur," he said finally, "consider it settled. So what are we going to do tonight?"

Brendan Vaughn quickly shed his gloomy mood and became the jovial host who had once greeted Arthur Drake at a bar and asked a question he knew full well the answer. Could the young man find him some companionship that evening? Realizing at the outset who he was dealing with, Drake was all too happy to comply. As that evening turned into the next and the next, Lord Vaughn would become his sole customer. To provide the utmost discretion, Arthur and his women were soon transported from an East London pub to a North England estate, and Arthur found the parties to whom he was offering his services grew. So also did grow the strangeness of the requests from these so-called gentlemen. Arthur had only one rule: the ladies were not to be hurt or otherwise damaged. Incredibly, with all the illicit drugs and alcohol consumption, that had yet to become a concern.

"It's acting," Arthur told the girls after a few had voiced fears that they were doing "the devil's work" as they said. *Strange attitude for whores to take,* Arthur thought, although this was a bit of a first for him as well. But the pay was well above what he could get for them on the street, with plenty leftover for him. Their wardrobe doubled in quantity and class as soon as they had set foot in the mansion. It was amazing the amount of excess a lord obtained just through day-to-day existence.

And Arthur found he was quickly gaining the lord's confidence in other matters as well. If a thought ever came to him to steal what he could and make a quick getaway, Lord Vaughn's generosity made the risk completely unnecessary. It was as if through a twist of fate, he had become the brother Brendan Vaughn had never had. Arthur enjoyed the luxury of this life. Why throw it away? So the girls had to degrade themselves in slightly different ways from what the average John required—garish costumes, incense, and a few paeans to strange idols. The men when they were spent were still spent, just like other men. Few, if any, needed another go round right away to appease their silly ghoulish statues. It was all a theatrical buildup leading to the same payoff. Once they saw the cash, the girls were more easily convinced. They would play the game for the comfort of living in a mansion, wearing fine clothes and jewelry. Vaughn called it Sex Magick, the orgasm as a metaphysical gateway to other dimensions. To Arthur, it was merely sex. The magic came with the money.

And Vaughn had plenty it would seem. He kept his wife and young son in comfort twenty kilometers away from the main house. Visits were frequent but planned. An older son had joined the army once the war began, which Vaughn had encouraged. "Bloody good for public relations," he said. He made the usual pronouncements of English spirit when called upon to do so. Privately, he thought Hitler made a lot of sense. Arthur himself cared nothing for politics, and since he was a nonentity as far as England was concerned, he thought only of a necessary move should the Germans actually succeed and England abdicated. Whatever uses they could make of Lord Vaughn, and he was sure Brendan was fooling himself in that regard, he was even more sure that his position would be supplanted by some goose-stepping goon soon enough. He had heard what was happening in Paris. He imagined it would be no better on the isle. America was looking like the only option with any prospect for a future.

For the present, Arthur was glad to see Vaughn acting as a convivial host. He laughed boisterously and seemed to enjoy a little self-deprecating humor as he mocked himself as the Grand Magus. It was just the two of them this evening with no hangers on or leering knaves fondling the merchandise. They played pool, smoked cigars, drank lightly, and enjoyed the company of only two of Arthur's ladies, Maggie and Veronica, a blonde and a redhead. It was all quite normal.

The next evening, however, Brendan Vaughn was nowhere to be found. Arthur checked with James, the head butler, and with a few of the other hands about the house. He even checked with some of his women, Veronica especially, since Vaughn had spent the previous evening in her company. All answered in the negative with shakes of their heads or no from their lips. They were unconcerned. But Arthur knew Brendan Vaughn to always be present in the house at night. Not one for late jaunts was the lord of the manor. Arthur went back to James. Did Lord Vaughn say he was visiting the missus tonight? No. Did he receive any phone calls? Not that he was aware of, sir. Arthur waited. It was maddening if only for the thought that repeatedly needled at his brain: Malcolm Schreck. Vaughn had been playing at ease the previous night. And now he had gone up to the barn. Arthur raided the bar for a much-needed drink.

Just as he was about to grab a coat and head to the stable Schreck and his man were occupying, heavy horse hooves pounded outside the window and suddenly halted. A moment later, the main door opened, and Brendan Vaughn staggered in, a great arm pulling the door closed behind him and the horse and carriage thereafter leaving with a much more controlled haste.

Vaughn said nothing as Arthur looked at him from some distance down the hallway. He steadied himself with one arm on the banister of the stairs, the other clasping a hand to his forehead. He was pale, sweaty. *Either drunk or very ill*, Arthur thought as he hurried toward him. "Brendan?" he said. "Brendan!"

Vaughn turned toward the steps and, with an exertion that seemed propelled more by force of will than strength, flung himself up the staircase. Arthur went up behind him but was still many steps behind as Vaughn rushed with fevered steps down the hall toward his room. As Arthur turned the corner himself, Vaughn's door slammed shut. Arthur went to it and pounded. He turned the handle, but it was locked from the inside. He looked down as the sliver of light that shone on his black shoes went dark.

"Brendan!" Arthur shouted through the door. "Lord Vaughn, are you all right?" No answer came. Arthur pounded on the door, and soon, others in the house—James, a few of Arthur's women—all came out in their nightgowns and robes, all gathering behind Arthur. Arthur called out again. "Brendan! If you don't answer me, I'll break this door down!"

"Fine" came a voice similar but not entirely recognizable as Brendan Vaughn. "I'm fine. Just need to sleep. Please . . . God . . . let me sleep."

A few moments passed. The group at the door all looked at one another with the same worried expressions on their faces. Finally, Arthur nodded grimly, looked at James, and said, "I want a breakfast brought to this room first thing in the morning. Make it a light one. But if he doesn't answer this door, you come get me straightaway. Understood?"

"Yes, sir," James said, nodding. "Straightaway. Very good, sir."

"All right, ladies and gentlemen, excitement's over. Go back to bed." The girls huddled together down the hallway to their own rooms as Arthur stood for a few moments longer looking at the door, where behind, Brendan Vaughn was in some obvious distress. Arthur could only fretfully contemplate in what kind of state he was. He shook his head and started slowly for his own room. A silent prayer, and Arthur Drake had never been one to pray, passed through his mind.

Chapter 3

The next day no word came from Brendan Vaughn's room, although there was evidence that he had at least some of his light breakfast of a hard-boiled egg and grapefruit half. The glass of juice was also partially drained with the pulp clinging to one side of the glass. The tray was set none too carefully outside the room, so Vaughn, unless he had allowed someone entry, was at least able to get to the door. *A good enough sign,* Arthur thought, *to risk a knock.* After three light raps, he called through the thick wooden panel. No answer came. No sound or sign of movement. Silence. This scenario repeated through lunch and dinner until Arthur felt he should confer with James regarding the situation.

James looked impassively at Arthur. If the old butler felt any concern, he was careful not to show any to his master's houseguest. He said, "Lord Vaughn seems to be timing the retrieval and disposal of his meals with great care. I have yet to witness him opening the door."

"Yes," Arthur replied. "I've attempted to catch him at it myself. He's suddenly become a very patient man. And very quiet. I can't get a word out of him."

"Tomorrow night is the group's weekly meeting, is it not, Mr. Drake?"

Arthur nodded, holding the thumb of his right hand to his lips. "Yes. And if that doesn't bring him out, James, we'll need to employ more drastic measures."

"Such as?"

Arthur clapped James on the arm. "Leave that to me, old boy. But the show will go on with or without Lord Vaughn."

And so it did. Vaughn's Black Orchid Society arrived complete and on schedule or early for their before-meeting cocktails. All would casually inquire about Lord Vaughn. As the drinks flowed, Arthur made his excuses for the master. "All is well," he told them. Lord Vaughn, the Grand Magus, apologized, but he hoped that the group would make the most of the evening without him. In fact, he looked forward to hearing how the spirits moved his followers. No detail was to be held back. The Black Orchid Society made no mention of Brendan Vaughn's strange guest in the stable. It was as if they feared speaking his name aloud. Despite his talents in the darker arts, the very reason for the Black Orchid Society's existence, his presence was not missed by the group.

To James, Arthur instructed to keep the men well lubricated, with their comfort a top priority for the servants in the house. As to Arthur's girls as he called them, he said the evening would be led by them, meaning that they were to take complete control of the mood, the pace, and the revelry. Lydia, the eldest and, by nature, the most dominant of the dozen or so women, would stand in his stead as hostess for the evening. Her lead, the others would follow, and if any of the men got out of hand, which had not truly been a problem despite the group's exaggerated reputation for debauchery, Lydia would suffer no breach of etiquette. She was a strong woman, very persuasive in her way, not to mention decisive in such instances. Arthur was confident that the men, no matter how riled, would follow her rules. To do otherwise would risk pain, where pleasure was preferred.

But Arthur hastily realized, just to be safe, a second guard may need to be recruited. Arthur pulled the defrocked clergyman, Sheffington, aside. "Listen," he said firmly to the man. "Since you used to be such a good boy, I expect you'll recognize a bad boy when you see one. I'm leaving it to you, mate. You're to keep the rest of this lot under control. The girls will do as you like as always, but if I see a mark on any of them or I hear a weepy story about what 'orrible things you made them do . . . I'll be paying you a visit for recompense. Understand?"

Sheffington appeared shaken by this command, but he managed to blurt "Yes, Arthur. Of course. Of course, I'll do just that."

Arthur smiled at him. "Good. Now then let me take your coat." He slipped Sheffington's dark tweed jacket off his shoulders, gave it a look, and said, "Ey, I like this coat. We're about the same height, right? Think I'll borrow it for a while. You don't mind, do you, mate?"

Sheffington's pasty round face under a mop of brown curls smiled uneasily. "No, no. Of course not, Arthur."

"Oh. Thanks. Nice big pockets it has, don't it? Not to worry, Gerry. I'll bring it back." Arthur whirled the coat around his shoulders and slipped his arms through the sleeves. He put his hands in the pockets. "Yeah, nice big pockets. Go have fun now, Gerry. But remember what I said. Recompense."

"Righto, Arthur," said Gerry Sheffington, former clergyman of the Roman Catholic Church in London. "Recompense."

With that, Arthur left the remnants of the Black Orchid Society to their expected activities and walked down the hall in Sheffington's coat. He met James in the hallway just before the entrance, where Malcolm Schreck had arrived a few weeks before. James, as was decided in their earlier conversation, handed him a revolver, a snub-nosed .38. Arthur dislodged the rolling chambers and spun them, looking to see that the gun was fully loaded. He slipped it into the left pocket of the dark tweed coat and then grasped his hat from James's other hand and popped it on his head.

"Are you sure this is wise, Mr. Drake?" James asked blankly.

"Hell, no, James. In fact, I'm sure it isn't."

"Then perhaps a nip before you are off?" James took a smooth metal flask out of his own inner jacket pocket and handed it to Arthur. Arthur quickly unscrewed the cap and took a substantial swig of bourbon.

"Wheew!" he exclaimed. "Thank you, James! You're a man after my old heart, you are."

Arthur passed the flask back to the butler, but James waved him off. "Keep it, sir," he said. "You may need it again before you reach your destination."

"Hmm," Arthur grunted, nodding. He placed the flask carefully into the left inner coat pocket over his heart. "You may be right, but don't worry, James. I can handle myself. Here now." Arthur pulled on James's sleeve until the butler's ear was near his face and said softly, "If I'm not back by what you might think a reasonable hour, throw the clothes back on those knotheads in there, give them each a flaming stake and a pitchfork, and send them up that hill. Got it?"

"Yes, sir," James replied. "And I'll be with them as well."

"Leading, James, I'm sure of that." Arthur winked at the butler and went out the door into the night. After the door had closed behind him, Arthur patted the flask in his left inner pocket and the revolver in his left outer pocket. They both felt good to him—hard and steady. He looked up and saw that the moon was full and bright with a spattering of fluffy gray clouds passing over it as he had seen many times in his life. That moon made it possible to walk the long kilometer to the old barn without the aid of a lamplight or flash, and Arthur was glad of it. He wanted no notice of his arrival for Schreck to plot some unhappy welcome for him as he must have for Brendan. The moon also made it unlikely that either Schreck or his man could sneak up on him unawares as he walked, although in Schreck's case, that may not be the advantage Arthur would hope. The man seemed to thrive in darkness and could likely move about in it without casual notice for some time until, of course, he was upon you. Schreck, however slight he seemed, had a ruthless face, and Arthur had learned never to judge a man only by his size but also by his face and how he held himself. Schreck seemed permanently bent, coiled like a spring or a serpent. Thinking of it made Arthur eager again for a pull from the flask, but he restrained himself. He would save it for when he got closer.

As the track led upward, the trees became more prominent, though the moon remained clear above his head, its pale light glowing on the path where cars and carts would drive up into the countryside portion of the estate. The manor became hidden behind the thick boughs of oaks, maples, and finally, pines. The leaves crackled under his feet, it being some time since a hard rain had fallen to soften them. He noticed every sound and, like a soldier sneaking toward an enemy encampment, attempted to tread around any area that could give his position away.

As his steps carried him closer to the barn, the long east side became visible in the moonlight, and he heard voices or perhaps a voice. Schreck? It must be since the giant who accompanied him hadn't shown that he was capable of speech. But the language was unrecognizable. The voice was harsh and guttural as if being used in exertion, and Schreck had such an unplaceable accent. It may have even been English he was hearing, but the voice made the words difficult to make out. Arthur set his right hand on the bough of a nearby tree as the voice dissolved behind the west side of the barn. Arthur took the flask from the inside pocket. James had been correct and wise. He would need that drink before proceeding. This time, however, he took a more modest one for fear of exhaling too loudly.

Arthur wiped his mouth with the sleeve of Sheffington's coat and took a few tentative steps out into the clearing. The double doors of the barn were at his left. At some distance from them, a large fire pit had been dug, and a few blackened logs rested in its center, tiny traces of red embers glowing underneath, the last signs of a long extinguished blaze. Arthur saw neither Schreck nor the man he called Warren in sight, even as he craned his neck as far as he could to glimpse around the far corner of the barn. As he took another step, his foot snapped an unseen twig. He looked down suddenly, instantly realized his mistake, and looked up. Malcolm Schreck was standing before him.

The two men stared at each other for a moment, and then Schreck's face fashioned into that strange smile of his. One corner of his pale lip reached up, while the other dragged downward. It was an unpleasant look, but Arthur attempted to match its supposed intent as he returned Schreck's gaze.

"Mr. Drake!" Schreck exclaimed. "We're very pleased to see you." Schreck looked upward into the night sky and pointed to the stars. "I see you waited for the moon to shine full. It speaks highly of your wisdom. Such a rare commodity for one as young as yourself."

Arthur took a quick glance behind him. He could hear Warren shuffling about the west side of the barn, but instinct told him to survey his surroundings nonetheless.

"You are alone," said Schreck. "But you have nothing to fear. As I said before, Mr. Drake, I mean you no harm. Now tell me, young man"—Schreck suddenly dropped all pretense of cordiality—"what is it that brings you?"

Arthur swallowed as mildly as he could. "I came to see about Lord Vaughn. It seems he's taken ill. Right after, as it were, he came to see you."

"See me?" Schreck cupped his right elbow in his left hand and absently ran two long bony fingers with abnormally long nails across his lips. "Lord Vaughn? Came to see me . . . oh yes. Yes! Two evenings ago, I believe. As I recall, he left suddenly, a pained expression on his face. I took it to be a flare-up of gout. Disease of kings they call it. Terribly painful."

"It's not gout, Mr. Schreck."

"No?" Schreck took a step closer. "Well, he afforded me no time to make a proper diagnosis. Matter of fact, he seemed very eager to return to the house. Thus, I had Warren drive him in the carriage. You say he still feels the effects of this mysterious ailment? Pity."

Arthur took his own step closer to Schreck. He placed his left hand in his pocket and allowed the grip of the gun to rest in his palm, his forefinger just on the outside of the trigger guard. "He hasn't left his room," he said slowly. "Nor has he spoken, except for a loud cry to be left alone when he returned."

Schreck poked his head forward. "Interesting. And you believe this relates to his visit?"

"Mr. Schreck, I'm not one for games. What did you do to him?"

"Indulged him," Schreck answered, matching Arthur's stern tone. "Apparently, indulging Lord Vaughn is not entirely to his benefit." Schreck stared at Arthur for another long moment and then allowed the smile to return. He chuckled softly. "I wonder if Lord Vaughn is aware of how fine a friend you are to him, Mr. Drake," he said. "Somehow I rather doubt it."

Silence gathered in the space between them until Schreck's face turned quizzical, and he said in a sly turn, "Or is it your own interest you're here to protect? Yes, that seems to my mind more the likely. Flesh merchant. That must be a stately position in the Black Orchid Society indeed." Schreck spoke the group's name with contempt so absolute that Arthur, for some unknowable reason, felt ashamed.

Schreck turned away from him and said, "Two nights ago, you say?" He turned full about again and raised his arms upward toward the sky demonstrably. "And on the third day, he will rise!" he cried. The enthusiasm drained quickly as Schreck lowered his arms and resumed his contemptuous attitude. "Much as your Lord and Savior did," he said, "so long ago."

He continued. "I assure you, Mr. Drake, no permanent harm has befallen him. He will be his dull, obtuse self in short order." It was then that Arthur noticed Schreck wore a dark leather apron under his black frock coat. It shone in the darkness as yet another veil, an added layer to the ill feeling Schreck exuded. The apron came down to an edge just at the shin of his dark pant leg. If not for the frock coat, which gave him an undertaker's bearing, Schreck would look to be some strange butcher, resting after long hours of cutting meat. "Come, my young friend," he said calmly, "let us sit for a while by the fire, and we can have what you English call a chat."

Arthur looked to the cold pit at his right. "What fire, Mr. Schreck?" he asked. Schreck looked into Arthur's face while he reached into his pocket and quickly flung something small and dark onto the charred wood in the pit. A great blaze immediately sprung out of the cold, darkened wood. It burned intense and strong. Schreck leered proudly at Arthur.

"Nice trick," Arthur said, nodding with a grim smile of his own.

"Trick?" Malcolm Schreck replied. "Yes. More of an art, but I would not think you to know it. And one must understand the basics before claiming a title of master, wouldn't you agree?" Schreck motioned for Arthur to step closer to the blaze. "For yourself, however, only a . . . trick."

Warren stepped out then from the corner of the barn, carrying two wooden chairs, which he placed on either side of the pit as the fire began to ebb. "Mr. Warren will get more kindling to keep the fire going," Schreck said.

Arthur looked at Warren, who went off to do Schreck's bidding without a word. "You've got him well trained," Arthur noted. "You say you met him aboard ship?"

"Yes, yes. Sit, Mr. Drake. This will be a long story, and I, of course, wish to hear yours as well. Let us both be comfortable."

As the two men sat, looking at each other over the fire, Schreck's head lowered to his feet. He began toying with the fire with a long stick, while Arthur took out a cigarette from a metal case and lit it.

What proceeded from Schreck's lips was to Arthur both fascinating and horrifying. By the end of the tale, Arthur's cigarette ash suspended limply from the burned paper, the stub of the cigarette dangled from his lower lip.

Schreck began with his meeting Mr. Warren on one of His Majesty's ships, which, he begged forgiveness, he could not remember the name. Schreck was serving as master-at-arms. Because of a rather oddly defined aptitude in the healing arts and also the ship's doctor being a notorious drunkard, Schreck carried on as physician for the crew as well. Knowledge of gunpowder and metals had bestowed on him this title, master-at-arms, even though it was quite obvious that he was not English bred.

Schreck was a man to keep his own counsel among the crew, and the captain, noting that, had also charged him with doling out the captain's discipline. "The man who carries the lash is one to wish a friend," Schreck said. "But he is not." Dispensing discipline was a frequent task since the crew was an unruly, slovenly lot. Under the master-at-arms, the lash became an almost daily routine, seemingly more of his own volition than the captain. The sound of it cracking the air would carry across all decks and into the holds where others awaited its kiss. Any infraction, however slight, could find a man tied to the crossbeam. Schreck went on to describe in an almost orgasmic pleasure, timing his lash with the downturn of the wave, which allowed it to strike the flesh with all the more authority. Something not unlike the flame of the fire itself burned in his dark eyes as he told his tale. When he had concluded, Arthur could hear the waves and feel the cold air against his face and the unsettling rocking motion of the ship's deck beneath his seat.

Schreck grinned. He feigned surprise when he revealed that his fellow seamen, while on a particularly long voyage toward some tropical wasteland, whose climate they thankfully were still many leagues distant, held a deep resentment toward him. This would also have included Mr. Warren, except the young Warren had, in a rather guileless fashion, become Schreck's sole confidant. The crew could not have known the true reason for this, that Schreck had manipulated Mr. Warren's blindly innocent view of morality and coupled it with the big man's own fear of the lash. For Warren, like many men of size and strength, pain was as frightening as death itself. Much better to be the bringer of pain than it's intended.

The mob, in a coordinated frenzy, took their immediate ferocity out on the captain, his mate, and the other officers by declaring mutiny and summarily executing them. They showed no mercy for anyone who held rank above them. The doctor, drunk, of course, was thrown like garbage over the side. Schreck could not recall what offense, other than dereliction of duty, the poor fool had ever committed. For the master-at-arms and Mr. Warren, however, they sought to prolong the punishment and clamped them in irons below deck. The vagabonds took their turns taunting him and spitting on him, and he watched as they raided the ship's storeroom and, in due course, while in their stupid and self-congratulatory revelry, indulged themselves to drink until not one of them could stand without support as the waves crashed against the hull. It was then that Schreck broke through his and Mr. Warren's bonds with what young Drake would conclude as another simple trick, and as they slipped past the drunken fools, they made their way to a small dingy but not before Schreck had paid each and every man on board with a lesson to remember him by.

"What did you do?" Arthur asked timidly.

"Hmm," Schreck muttered. "My memory of details grows thin, Arthur. Oh, if you will allow my familiarity? There may have been a small explosion, or a large one, and their bones could be sitting on the bottom, deep in the depths. Or they may have merely sailed and sailed, unhindered by any attempt to control the vessel. None of the fools had the foresight to save the ship's navigator, I fear. Thus, they may have run aground or simply floated into some distant port. All hands lost, of course."

"So you murdered them."

Schreck's eyes danced side to side as his brow furrowed. "Mine own preservation is of the utmost concern to me, Mr. Drake," he said coldly, "although the English courts may take a different view. In any event, a ship lost at sea becomes legend after time. The earth revolves, and the waves wash away all." Schreck grinned and looked up to the stars. "As to Mr. Warren, you should have seen him then. Beautiful he was and strong. No man could best him. A complete innocent, however. There are times watching him do some task I've set for him that I do regret corrupting him as I did. He was conscripted, of course, along with many unlucky men of those times. Likely, he fell out of the wrong pub door at the wrong time. Elsewise, we never would have met. But we have been together ever since." Schreck rubbed his thumb back and forth across his lips, in silence as he remembered.

"My soul!" he shouted. "I don't believe I've ever told that to any human body. Is it possible?" He looked at Arthur across the blaze and grinned his crooked grin. "Yes," he said. "You've beguiled even me, Arthur Drake!"

Arthur let the comment pass. He looked back across the fire at Schreck with a furrowed brow. "You spoke of His Majesty's ship. From what little I know of seafaring, I believe the lash has fallen out of favor for some time. Just how old are you, Mr. Schreck?"

Schreck frowned. "Oh, Arthur," he said, "is it the vanity of all youth to believe that the world did not exist before they walked upon it? I know the way of it. You see your tall buildings, your factories belching thick plumes into the air, your motorized vehicles, and your airplanes and you think to yourself, it has always been thus. Is it because you believe yourself aged? I tell you, my boy, I was born at a time when dirt was all there was. Earth and mud and shit. My forebears were little people, serfs truly. Sold me off as one too many mouths to feed. Not uncommon was it then to be passed along as a mere laborer. I shoveled shit and milked goats and ate gruel, sent from master to master, learning whatever I could from each—the hammer, the tongs, the fire—until . . . until finally, I fell under the tutelage of one who knew of much darker doings, arcane and hidden throughout the ages. It was this man who taught me because he saw his ancient time was ending, you see, and yet he did not wish his legacy to end. So it came to me." Schreck was silent for a moment, and then he said, "I have carried its burden for longer than I can describe to one as young as you. You think yourself old, do you?

"Now then," Schreck said, poking the fire with his stick so that the cinders jumped from the logs, "tell me something of yourself."

Arthur pursed his lips and said, "I'd rather not."

"Hmm. Hardly equitable, I say," replied Schreck. "I have told you . . . much! And admit this fact, Arthur Drake. It wasn't just to defend Lord Vaughn that you came here. You came here to satisfy your own curiosity regarding . . . me."

"Perhaps secrecy is something we have in common, Mr. Schreck . . . Malcolm."

"Oh, it is true. You and I have very little in common but for one factor. You have no business being in that house with those fools any more than I. Those men down there orphaned from deeds, orphaned from ambition, offspring of titles and privilege, privilege bestowed by birth alone. What could you have in common with them?"

Arthur turned his head to look over his shoulder at the path to the house. "That lot?" he said casually. "They aren't so bad. They do pay the bill and quite promptly, which is very important to me. Besides, what makes you sure I'm not one of them?"

"Your business, for one," Schreck spat, "though I stipulate that it would not be impossible for someone from the ruling class to take up such an endeavor." Schreck leaned forward. "I presume few have either the imagination or the spirit." He added, "But you, my friend, don't rightly carry yourself as such, do you? No, Drake. You weren't born a man of means. You struggled, you fought, and you rose from a harsher world than they will ever know. You will correct me if I'm mistaken in this."

"All right," Arthur said. "If you must know, I was born in a brothel, probably not far from where the bombs were falling. I've no idea who my father was or my heritage. I've no true idea who my mother was either. There was a woman I called mother, but it could have been any one of those young unfortunate girls there. Or I could have been left on the doorstep. I don't know, and it's never mattered a whit to me. That business is all I have ever known. And Brendan Vaughn has made it a lucrative and comfortable one."

"Blessed art thou among women."

"What?"

"Luke 1:42. The Bible?"

"Never read it. I'm surprised you have though. If you don't mind my saying, you don't look the part."

Schreck smirked. "In my day, the Bible was the beginning and nearly the end of a formal education, that and many beatings, of course. I would not hazard to speculate from which I gained more."

The comment forced a memory upon Arthur. He recalled his one brief encounter with religion—a priest, a priest he knew for a time in America. But he only said, "We went to America."

"Did you, now?" Schreck replied. "I've never been to the New World. I fear I am far too accustomed to the old."

"Yeah," Arthur said as if from a dream. Then he seemed to wake. "Yes, the woman I called mother, and myself, a few other girls. She said we would be a novelty there, be able to raise their price, give them a taste of the Limey. We sailed to New York and then by train to San Francisco in 1913. Took almost a year to get there, get established. Felt like ten to me. Never understood why she kept me along. Wasn't much of the motherly type, the old whore. But I learned enough, I guess. Branched out on my own at seventeen and never looked back. In and out of the pokey till I got myself a rep. Never had a confirmed name or citizenship, so I managed to avoid throwing a uniform on for the big war. Then feeling a little homesick, I got my arse back home to England." Arthur looked at Schreck, who returned his gaze blankly. "Not much of a story, I guess, compared to yours."

Schreck leaned forward with a sly look. "I have noticed, young man, since our first meeting that you are ever on guard against those you deem a threat. It begs the question, have you ever felt compelled to kill?"

Arthur grimaced. "You guessed right, Mr. Schreck. Like you, I come from a harsh world, much harsher than where I find myself now. And I reckon, like you, I got kicked around in it quite a bit. We do have that in common. But that doesn't mean I'm going to make you my confessor."

"That is not much of a denial, my friend."

Just then, a tap behind his left shoulder had Arthur jerking almost clear out of his chair. He violently twisted his head around to see the massive shape of Mr. Warren standing over him. "Jesus!" Arthur exclaimed.

Warren simply thrust his left hand forward, and Arthur could see that it was filled with some kind of brown meat. "Venison?" Warren offered.

"No," Arthur replied. "No, thank you." He shook his head as Mr. Warren unloaded the stack of wood under his right arm on the fire and trudged off silently toward the barn. "He speaks," Arthur said.

"Oh yes," said Schreck with an amused look on his face. "Loquaciousness is not his gift, but he can speak in his own, rather limited way. That is why I am so fortunate you made the trek here, Arthur. I cannot tell you how long it has been since I had an actual conversation with anyone. Of course, I have usually avoided the company of other men. History has shown it to end rather badly. Man is a mundane animal with rather mundane struggles, and I am devoid of sympathy. But you interest me, Arthur Drake. Yes, you surely do."

Arthur shrugged in his chair. "If you're looking for a friend, why don't you just conjure one up?"

"Oh," Schreck replied, "you refer to my demonstration for your little club. I will admit that I have contact with such beings, that they await me in Hell is a certainty. It is my strongest intention to keep them waiting. With that manner of friend, I may as well have stayed in Germany with the Fuhrer."

Arthur sat up at this. "You know Hitler?"

"Did I say so?" Schreck started. "No, Drake. It is difficult to know men like that well." Schreck mused on this a few moments and then said, "I was consulted, much as your Lord Vaughn there consulted me. It seems Mr. Warren was careless, or perhaps it was I. No matter. Whatever the cause, we gathered the attention of one of Herr Hitler's underlings—unfortunate, a bespectacled lickspittle as I recall. The Fuhrer, this miscreant, and a few of his more excitable henchmen confessed an interest in the occult, and they thought I could be of some service in this regard. Any power, no matter how inscrutable to their minds, was an advantage over Germany's enemies, an aid to their plans of conquest. With the Nazi's complete control of the territory, my hands were tied, so to speak."

Schreck continued to poke at the fire with his stick as he spoke, his face twisting in contemptuous disgust at the memory. "I made myself proper, you understand, to be courteous to the Fuhrer, in mine own fashion. Even I, who am accustomed to privacy, knew that standing before me was someone to make the world's foundations tremble! A force of will to be admired was Herr Hitler. But also an impatient man he is, far too easily distracted, strong desire to consume but always the wont for the easy path. He is much like your master in that regard."

Arthur said, "Brendan Vaughn is not my master, Schreck."

Malcolm Schreck gave a knowing look back in reply but let the comment pass. "That is why I do not believe this campaign in England will last," he said. "He will seek out less hardy victims. You English, at least those English more to your class, Arthur, you seem to take strange pleasure in this current plight. You revel in your survival against the reign of hell. I admire it. In any event, I grudgingly took on the role of mentor to the Fuhrer, but as my contact with him grew more frequent, it was not long before I began to hear the murmurings of discontent among his inner circle."

"I can't imagine," Arthur said plainly.

"Yes, invited as I was, it shocked me as well. Suddenly, the name Rasputin seemed to be hovering in my vicinity. That caused some concern, I can tell you. But it was when I heard the word 'Jew' in connection to my name that I felt it in our best interests that Mr. Warren and I take our leave. That is why we risked the crossing to your fair isle. Although I take no responsibility for the bombings, you understand. I tell you, my friend, crawling out from under that structure in London, I thought how easily I could have killed him."

"Too bad you didn't," Arthur offered.

Schreck snorted. "And why should I have done?" He sneered. "The man wants to kill millions and enslave the rest. When you know of mankind as do I, it's a perfectly laudable goal."

The darkness grew heavier then in Arthur's estimation. Only the fire seemed to breathe with the crackling of fresh wood. The stars were barely visible, and the woods behind the barn fell silent. All there was before him was the fire and Malcolm Schreck's strange pale face floating in darkness.

"Well," Arthur said abruptly, "I should get back. I've been gone too long. An enlightening conversation, Mr. Schreck, but I should check on Lord Vaughn and make sure he's on the mend as you said."

Schreck smirked mirthlessly. He leaned forward and said plainly, "You cannot go."

Arthur stood then, keeping his eyes warily on Schreck. "After all, Mr. Drake," Schreck said as he stood and stepped slowly around the fire toward Arthur, "you came at a most fortunate time. We are celebrating. And you have brought combustibles."

Arthur looked quizzically at Schreck, thinking of the gun in his waist pocket. Schreck stepped close to him, raised his long and thin left hand, and patted the right side of Arthur's chest.

"In your breast pocket, Arthur," he said slowly, his black eyes staring into Arthur's own, "I can see the print of it in your coat. A flask. Do not say it is only cider you have there."

"No," Arthur answered nervously. "Bourbon, actually. But I thought you said you didn't drink."

"Forgive me. A small lie. I am not proud of it, but as I said, we are celebrating a victory of no small consequence, one that has taken much time and effort to accomplish, I can tell you. I would like very much to show you this. But first, let us drink to top off the event."

Arthur reached into his pocket. "Of course," he said, handing the flask to Schreck. Schreck grinned, taking it from Arthur's hand. He unscrewed the cap, never taking his eyes off Arthur. "To a long life," he said, placing the top to his lips and pouring back a considerable quantity.

Arthur grimaced. "Tell you what, Mr. Schreck," he said, "you keep it. Now as much as I'd really like to see whatever it is you chaps are celebrating, I do believe I should be going now. The girls, you know. They start to get a little antsy when I'm gone for too long. And Brendan, he could be up and about wondering where I've got off to . . ."

Schreck took another drink. "I have told you," he said through his exhalation, "you cannot go. My young friend, I fear Mr. Warren and I must insist." It was then that Arthur saw at his left Warren come out of the darkness toward him, his size suddenly taking the air out of Arthur's chest, an empty yet determined look on his face.

Chapter 4

"Ay! Schreck! Call 'im off 'ere!" Arthur felt Warren's impossibly heavy hand at the small of his back, pushing him ever forward through the barn door as Schreck himself, in his slightly stooped posture, led the way, sipping at his newfound bourbon. He chuckled low and through closed lips.

"I see you resume your more natural manner of speech, Mr. Drake," he said. "I thought the debonair gentleman a mere facade. Seems I was correct." He turned slightly toward the two behind him as he reached up for a candle standing in an old holder on the wall. "I must warn you, Warren is very strong still. Do not test him. Often, when he sees a light dying, he wants nothing more than to snuff it out completely."

"All right, all right," Arthur said, shrugging away from Warren, who did not appear agitated in the slightest. "I'm here. What do you want to show me? I hope it isn't what you showed Brendan because unlike him, I'm not interested."

"Hmm. Not a believer, eh, Arthur?" Schreck said. "Certainly not in that chicanery Vaughn peddles, eh? Sex Magick, he called it. What is that, I ask you? Are you involved in such depravity? Candles in rectums and the like? Fear not, my friend. We only use candles for their stated purpose here."

Schreck held the candle and rubbed the wick until it lit, and a small flame glowed into his face in the darkness. He held it aloft, and Warren stepped around Arthur to retrieve it. "Have you supposed anything I have told you to be truth? No? Well, let's allow for some more light, shall we?"

As Warren stepped around the perimeter of the barn floor, he lit candle after candle off the original until objects and shapes in the room slowly, faintly became noticeable. Arthur squinted into the light but found most of the shapes foreign to him—bent metal tubes leading in curves and soft angles to a table filled with beakers, one or two held aloft, framed by the bent tubes and dripping a strange murky substance; mason jars filled with misshapen objects surrounded by a cloudy liquid; and twigs melded and twisted with animal fur and small bones to make strange symbols that hung from the rafters of the structure. If not for Schreck's beaver hat, which stood like a stovepipe on one corner of the table, there was little sense that a human hand had been involved in any part of the scene. It looked to Arthur to be a laboratory one might stumble upon in the darkened woods. Nature twisted into the unnatural.

"So," Arthur said as he tried to control his fear. He made a show of looking around casually as he felt once again for the gun in his pocket. "This is what you've been working on, eh?"

"Oh yes," Schreck whispered, pulling from the flask. His words were beginning to slur, and his eyes, thankfully to Arthur, were hidden behind half-closed lids. "This is merely a testing laboratory," he said. "Salvage from our previous location and scraps of your master's supply. He will forgive a slight thievery, I think." Schreck straightened himself and brought his flask-filled hand back to Arthur's shoulder. "Did you bring more?" he asked.

"No."

"Pity." Schreck resumed his normal stooped position. "My one true accomplishment, however . . . my long sought-after victory." Schreck paused. For a moment, it seemed to Arthur that Schreck was having an internal argument. He grimaced, shook his head, and then appeared to acquiesce to some conflict of which only he was aware. He gestured with the flask toward a curtained-off space.

"Yeshh," he said drunkenly. "I allow you entry, Arthur. You are a good man to share a secret with, a good man. That I say with great certainty."

The curtain was as black as if it had been pilfered from a hearse. It hung there with only the dust from the floor coloring its bottom edge with a thin band of white specks. Schreck stared at it, while Warren stood at its corner. Then he looked at Arthur with a smug look of contempt.

"You will see," he said. Without another word, Warren slowly pulled the curtain back. As he did, Schreck took one of the candles and walked toward a table now exposed behind the curtain. Warren's slow steps revealed something on the table. A foot? No, feet, bare and pale, sticking out from gray pant sleeves with a hard black stripe down the side stretching longer and longer as Warren moved on. At the sight of them, Arthur took in a deep breath. A black belt appeared along a thin waist and a bare midriff as pale as the feet. A leather strap secured the body—right hand, arm, no noticeable hair or so light it barely registered to the eyes, a bicep, a shoulder curving up to the side of the neck, and then finally, a face, a boy's face, a young face, with a mop of blond hair, matted with sweat.

Arthur gaped at the sight. He stepped forward as if compelled to see this horror more clearly. As he drew nearer to the table, he saw that tubes were lodged in both of the boy's arms. One dripped a green liquid from a glass beaker above him into his left arm at the large vein in the crook of his forearm; the other drained a reddish fluid to another glass beaker from his right.

"A boy!" Arthur gasped. "He's just a boy. What have you done to him, Schreck?"

Schreck looked confused. "An enemy," he said. "This boy is an enemy of England. Have you no loyalty to the country of your birth, Mr. Drake? He is either pilot or bombardier. I do not recognize military insignia, but he was very willing to talk, I can tell you."

"Does Vaughn know of this?"

"No. Only we three here are privy." Schreck began cackling. The bourbon had taken a fuller effect on him than even he realized. It was a most unpleasant sound. "Perhaps we should inform Mr. Churchill!" he said through his laughter.

Arthur ignored the comment. "How? No German planes have reached this far. How could he have got here?"

"Oh, that would be Mr. Warren. A fine hunter is Mr. Warren. Sometimes I allow him to leave, and he returns with treasure. But this is a coup even I could not have expected. He came upon the enemy near his downed craft somewhere just north of London. The right leg was badly broken at both the tibia and the fibula. I set the fractures as best I could with the tools I had, but it is a long time since I performed such carpentry work. On board ship, my usual treatment for such injuries was . . ." Schreck made a sawing motion and smiled.

Arthur looked down at the leg. It appeared swollen and bruised almost black at the ankle. Crude stitch lines ran vertically on either side of the bony prominences. He looked up and down the boy's length and saw that the poor victim didn't appear to be breathing, or if he was, it was with very shallow, silent breaths.

"Is he alive?" he asked.

Schreck took the last swig and tossed the flask away carelessly. It crashed against the floor with an empty, hollow clang. "Oh yes!" he replied with false scorn. "You question my skill as a physician?" Schreck stumbled toward the boy's head, bent over, and whispered into his right ear. "Wake."

The boy's eyes opened. The whites had a yellowish tinge, and his face looked in agony as if sleep was his only refuge from the pain. He saw Schreck and cried out in fear, and then his eyes found Arthur. His lips moved, but no sound came from them until he finally said, in a hoarse whisper, "Helfen Sie mir, bitte, sir!"

Schreck turned his head to give Arthur a sideways glance. "He pleads for your help."

"Ich sprechen! Ich sage ihnen alles was. Sie wissen wollen."

"Oh," Schreck said as if frustrated, "now he's offering information. Bear with me, Drake. He has already told me this story. No need to hear it twice." Schreck looked down on his patient. "Sei still. Wir wissen alles." The boy quieted, but he began to whimper like a child crying for his mother.

Arthur could not hide his disgust. "What do you have him rigged up to here? What's that fluid you're pumping him with?"

Schreck's eyes looked dead. His face dropped all pretense of drunken foolishness, and he stared at Arthur so intently that Arthur took a step back from him. "You ask many questions, Arthur," he said coldly. "You ask if he lives. Look for yourself, man. Is he living? Or dead?"

Schreck's hand roughly grasped the boy's hair. "Arthur Drake, you shall be witness to this. This is my great victory. This body, as you see it, lies dead, the life's blood spilled and soaked into the soil. Nothing remains but the soul. This . . . human soul is trapped within its own shell. Countless years of searching it has taken, long before your whore of a mother excreted you from her womb. Searching for this crucial combination of chemistry and ancient lore, but finally, I have found it!"

Arthur Drake could hardly look at the sight—the boy, in obvious agony, it's source both pain and horror as if he knew the state he was truly in and yet was helpless to change it. "Damn you, Schreck!" he shouted. "This is an innocent boy! Why torture him like this?"

"Oh, he is a boy," Schreck admitted, "but that is no proof of innocence, Arthur, as you surely are aware. The fate that awaited him in the next realm I cannot say with any authority. Perhaps he was too indulgent, slothful, and greedy or perhaps filled with unholy lust as are you. But he hungers now. Yes, he hungers. He has not as yet been able to give word to it, so I can only speculate. But that is not the true test. The true test requires your participation, your price for being a witness to my work."

Arthur looked around the candlelit barn. Warren circled slowly to his left, closing up his only viable escape. "Why would I help you?" he shouted. "You disgusting ghoul!"

"Still unable to grasp it, are you? I will tell you exactly what you are going to do, Drake. You are going to reach into your pocket and bring out that weapon."

"I don't—"

In a flash, Schreck was upon him. His cold hands gripped Arthur behind his head and under his chin. "Did you come here to kill me, Arthur Drake?" he hissed. "I threaten your precious pocketbook, do I? So you come for me with a cheap gun? To remove me?"

Arthur made a weak attempt at struggling, but Schreck's touch seemed to sap all his strength. The room grew colder, and the frigid air clamped like shackles over his feet. Schreck led him toward the body.

"The weapon," he said as he smoothly transitioned from Arthur's left side to his right, his icy grip sliding across Arthur's face and neck. "Remove it." Arthur felt worms wriggling under his skin as Malcolm Schreck's palm ran across his mouth.

"Hear me, Arthur Drake. You who have no belief, you will believe this: if I so desired, I could have you, your little cabal, Brendan Vaughn, and every other fool in that house on your knees setting in a pool of your own spittle! I could bring that house crashing down on your heads and have you yourselves pull the bricks out one by one until it fell. Do you believe that?"

Arthur nodded as the crooked grin came close enough to brush his cheek. "Good," Schreck said through a low chuckle. "Now put your hand in that pocket and retrieve the weapon."

Arthur obeyed. He could do nothing less as resistance of any kind was answered with the wriggling of the worms in his face. With that wriggling came intense pain. His arm shook as he brought the gun out before him. The room was suddenly dark, the only light a dim shimmering at the table where the boy laid, his head lifted, looking at the two men, one watching with grim pleasure as the other rose his left arm slowly toward the body.

"Good, Arthur," Schreck said. "Good. You know what to do now. You are a killer. I knew this from the moment I saw you step toward me. Do not make me wait any longer. Do it!"

Arthur closed his eyes, hoping the image would disappear from his mind. "DO IT, I SAY!" Schreck commanded.

The gun fired. Once, twice, three times it rang out. All three bullets entered the body at the frail chest, but instead of blood, puffs of air followed by a thick greenish-yellow fluid slowly drained from the wounds. Arthur dropped the gun, and Schreck pushed him aside to let him fall to the floor. Schreck looked at the boy, who looked back at him with a face of wonder and revulsion.

"Bitte," he pleaded. "Bitte." Then the boy's head fell back, and Schreck went over to look down on him. Schreck smiled. "My thanks, Arthur," he said. "The test is a great success. And I owe it all to you, my young friend."

Arthur rose slowly. He saw the gun near Schreck's feet, but his stomach reeled, and he could not foresee any good outcome when he imagined lunging for it. He looked at Warren, who looked impassively back at him. Would the monster try to stop him if he just ran? Then he looked at Schreck, who leaned back against the table, smiling his repulsive smile at him.

"You may go now, Mr. Drake," he said calmly. He snorted out the beginnings of a laugh and then allowed it to come out freely, a cackle that sent chills down Arthur's spine even as he stumbled out of the barn, reaching and lunging for any steady surface or post along the way. The laughter followed him as he staggered. Just as he reached the door, Schreck shouted after him, "Would you like Mr. Warren to drive you?"

Chapter 5

ARTHUR'S memory of his run back to the mansion would come with large blank spaces. All he knew was that throughout his struggle to regain his wind, the very sight of the home was enough to lift his spirit. Dank, towering, old, ivy-hewn stone gave him hope, hope that he was going to survive. After his encounter with Malcolm Schreck, Arthur, like Vaughn before him, wanted nothing more than to be swallowed up into the silence of his room, bury his head into his pillow, and scream.

In fact, both Arthur and Vaughn would be forever changed by the experience of meeting Malcolm Schreck. Some of these changes were quite subtle, so much so that neither man would have admitted them if confronted. And yet others were darker, more noticeable among the people who claimed to know them. Each man drew inward, internally questioning whatever beliefs they had previously held and seemed unsure of where to place their next foot forward. Even Arthur, who prided himself on his ability to remain cool and detached, suddenly became quick to anger. Vaughn, of course, was hysterical.

However frightened and disgusted Arthur may have been on his return, the next morning, around noon, he managed to rise and immediately formulate a plan to deal with the demonic intruder currently residing in the abandoned old horse stable. He would roust the whole house, every able-bodied man, servant and guest alike, including the lord of the manor, Brendan Vaughn, to remove Malcolm Schreck and his giant by force if necessary. Vaughn would have to be his first priority. He had a similar experience to Arthur's with Schreck, and it had unmanned him. Arthur would have to bring him out of it somehow. There were many methods of coercion to sway Brendan Vaughn, his pride being first and foremost. But Arthur had never seen the man in such a state. He doubted even dangling Vaughn's favorite taste among the women gathered there would have much effect on him now unless weeping was the desired effect. That wouldn't do at all.

Arthur found himself perspiring at Vaughn's door. He had dressed lightly in the chill of the drafty halls, and yet still, he felt the cool trickle of sweat running down his cheeks and his back. At his feet were the remains of Brendan's third breakfast in seclusion—a half-eaten boiled egg, the yolk clearly showing the angles of Vaughn's front teeth; a similarly drained cup of coffee; and the crust of white toast. *It seems,* Arthur thought, *Vaughn's spirits are on the mend.* Arthur pounded on the door.

"Brendan," he croaked. "Brendan Vaughn!"

"Go" was the answer. And after an interminable few seconds, "AWAY!"

"It's Arthur, Brendan."

"I am well aware of who it is," Vaughn said meekly. "Go away, Arthur!"

Arthur rubbed his fingers over his forehead. If anything, all he wanted at that moment was to go away and retreat to his own room. Perhaps he'd let one of the girls in and just lay there with her, holding on to someone; nothing more. Perhaps that would allow him to stay afloat and not feel as if he were sinking inch by inch into the cold, hard ground. But this was too important. It wouldn't wait another day, not another hour for that matter. He decided to employ the last weapon in his arsenal, one he hoped to not truly need.

"You've been in that room for three days, Brendan!" he called through the door. "THREE FUCKING DAYS! Do you want me to call your wife?"

"God, no!" came the plaintive reply.

"Then open up this FUCKING DOOR!" A few moments of silence passed before Arthur made out what seemed to sound like the lurching thuds of a stumbling gait, growing louder as they reached the other side of the door, followed by a clumsy grab of the doorknob. A key fished its way into the slot with frantic scratches, and then the door slowly angled inward, and there before him was what was formerly known as Brendan Vaughn.

The shape stepped aside and held his arm out in a half-hearted welcome. Arthur stepped into a room where the utter shambles was only matched by the pathetic appearance of its occupant. Books and papers lay strewn about the floor in all manner of disarray. One could hardly take a step without a paper crumpling under foot, and yet there was a body-shaped clearing near the center, where the richly carpeted floor rug could be discerned from the clutter. It seemed that Vaughn had not been entirely idle in his seclusion, but for what he was searching, Arthur could not begin to guess. As for the man himself, he stood there, shoulders stooped, shrank, and diminished in every way from the Vaughn Arthur knew. He was in an old-fashioned white nightshirt that hung down to his blanched and bony ankles. All that was missing was the pointed stocking cap with the fuzzy ball at the end. He looked at Arthur with reddened, weary eyes, a sad expression, and a crown of newly grown hair, gone shockingly white, sticking out in a half circle around his head. His once-proud beard seemed to have been pulled out in clumps; reddened blotches of skin showed like burn marks on his chin and cheeks. Arthur had not looked in a mirror this morning. He hoped he looked better than he felt, but he was confident he did not look as this calamity did standing before him.

"Brendan," he said as Vaughn shut the door behind him, "what have you been doing here?"

"Looking," Vaughn said shakily, "for something that I thought . . . mattered. It meant so much before . . . but . . . I can't find it now."

Arthur took the man's shoulders in his hands and steadied him. He looked directly into his face and shook him until Vaughn looked back at him. Only days before, Vaughn was a towering presence, but now Arthur saw him as an old man, and a part of him felt responsible. An urge to run coursed through him. Other than the women, Arthur barely troubled himself to feel responsible for anyone, including himself. The women were replaceable, and men were pockets to be pilfered, marks to be targeted, drained, and discarded. That was how he had always operated. Was this a true friendship he contemplated with this English lord? Or had Schreck figured it correct? Was he merely protecting an investment?

"That doesn't matter now, Brendan," he said calmly. "You know what matters most now? Ridding your house of this vermin is all that matters."

"Who, Arthur?" Vaughn said pathetically.

Arthur shook him again, harder this time. "Malcolm Schreck! Damn it all, Brendan. What did he do to you? No! Don't answer that. I don't care." Arthur turned and walked a few steps away from Vaughn and then said forcefully as if trying to convince himself as well as Vaughn, "We are going to get every single man and boy on this estate and arm them with every weapon available, from sabers to shotguns to pitchforks, and we are going to drive him and his silent ape as far away as possible! We may have to kill him, Brendan. We can't escape this. Let's clean you up. We have some very dirty work to do."

Cleaning Brendan Vaughn was something of a Herculean task as despite his withered appearance, he was still quite heavy, especially since he was almost no help in his own care and was much like a large baby whose arms, legs, head, and torso had to be manipulated by other hands. Arthur enlisted the aid of Lydia and Veronica, the woman who had accompanied Vaughn on the last evening he was remotely himself. Arthur was glad of the time it took to clean and shave the man. It gave him something to focus on besides his dread at confronting Schreck again. But a rush would have to be put on the job. There was no time for pampering. "Use cold water," he demanded. He wanted Vaughn and the entire male company of the estate to arrive at the barn before dusk when he felt sure that the darkness would only be an aid to their quarry.

Vaughn arrived, with help from Lydia and Veronica, at the bottom of his steps. He had a fur-lined coat on with a bowler hat covering his bald head. White hair lay down from the edge of the hat in a hurried yet uniform appearance. It was his face that was most shocking. Without the beard, Brendan Vaughn, despite his size, appeared a pallid, frightened, old man. His eyes looked about blankly as if he awaited some instruction and was not at all sure where he was. His face, although clean-shaven, was splotchy with angry red marks where he had torn his own hair out by the roots.

Arthur looked at him. "Brendan?"

"Yes," Vaughn answered softly.

"You on board with this? You know what we're doing, mate?"

"Yes."

Arthur turned to James, who had both Vaughn's cane and his double-barreled shotgun in his hands. "Give him the cane," Arthur said. "I'll take the gun." He reached into Sheffington's coat, looked for the gun, and then remembered he had dropped it in the barn after shooting . . . He put the image out of his mind. *Best not to think of that now.* Just then, Sheffington came up to inquire about his coat. Before a word could leave his lips, Arthur stated flatly, "I'm keeping it."

Sheffington attempted to smile weakly in response, but Arthur was off before he could manage it. The ex-clergyman grabbed a heavy blanket from one of the couches in the sitting room and threw it about his shoulders. Although deprived of his coat, he still did not wish to disappoint the thief.

The men had gathered outside near the vehicles. Brendan Vaughn was poured into the back seat of the first car with two more cars behind it. About twenty men, give or take, from Arthur's count had joined. A couple were quite young, the stableboys. The others, from the groundskeepers to the head cook, to James himself, had all armed themselves as best they could with small rifles, kitchen knives, axes, and even pitchforks. They seemed determined, and the look of them buoyed Arthur. They knew of the visitor in the barn, and while most had never exchanged a word or glance with him, they recognized him as a legitimate threat and were more than happy to oblige his removal.

The men silently waited for Arthur to speak. This was not based on Arthur's standing in the home or upon any perceived quality of leadership. In fact, to most of the men there, Arthur seemed in a little better shape than they witnessed in the master of the house, whom they had just seen feebly enter the lead car; rather, it was the desperation of the moment that drew them together.

It was still light, but the sun was on its downward trajectory westward, the very direction they would be going up the hill toward the barn. "All right, men," Arthur said, "if he's agreeable, we'll allow them to leave on their own."

The men stared solemnly at Arthur. "I know this sounds strange," he said softly. "But this is not an ordinary man. He is a threat to this house, and I'm not sure our numbers will make much difference to him and his brute should they decide to fight. If that happens, I want all the firepower on the big man. He's got to go down first. Then we'll deal with his master." Arthur looked around at the gathered faces.

One of the men chimed in. "He's probably in a bleedin' coffin!" The others laughed at this. Arthur was immediately heartened.

"You must have seen him then," he said. "Be a lot easier that way, wouldn't it? Well, let's be off."

Arthur climbed into the lead car's back seat with Vaughn. As many men as would fit came with them. The same formation gathered in the other two vehicles with the two or three extra men standing on the running boards as the cars slowly made their way up the twin grooves of the path toward the barn.

Vaughn tugged at Arthur's sleeve. "I'm here, Arthur," he said. "I'm here."

"Good, mate," Arthur answered. "We'll need you."

It seemed an interminably long time under the canopy of the trees for the cars to reach the clearing. Then as they entered around the front of the barn, they gave a wide berth to the doorway, and each car snuggled closely to the one ahead in a concerted effort to form a blockade should the door suddenly burst open upon them.

Slowly, the men exited the cars and stepped off the running boards. All was still about the building. The fire that had raged the night before was only evidenced by the burned ash of a few thick logs. Brendan Vaughn was the last man out of the vehicles, and he leaned heavily on his cane as he stepped around the front of the lead car. He said nothing but seemed to shiver in his oversized coat. Arthur looked about, craning his neck to the right and left to check the corners of the barn. But there was nothing to see. A light wheel track led from the door with hoof marks centered in between them, but other than that, it appeared deserted.

Arthur let out a deep breath. He cautiously walked toward the single entryway where he had been accosted the night before, turned the knob, and pushed it open. The men, including Vaughn, all followed silently, the only noise being the light wind in the trees above and the sound of their shuffling feet on the ground. The remaining outside light filtered into the barn in a rectangular shape until Arthur's shadow blocked even that as he stepped through the entryway. He looked around and saw . . . nothing. There was nothing as it was only the previous evening. The table where Arthur had seen the tortured German boy and any sign of the boy himself or the two dark occupants of this makeshift laboratory had all vanished as if the whole nightmare had been just that, the ravings of a feverish dream. Arthur breathed heavily. For some reason, this caused him more fear than the anticipated meeting with Schreck. It was impossible for the two of them to have erased all signs of their presence in that short a time. Or was Malcolm Schreck's will alone enough to make it possible?

The men began to filter through the building, past Arthur as he continued to search for some sign of Malcolm Schreck. Then one spoke up loudly. "Master Vaughn! Mr. Drake! Over here!" One of the younger members of the party was standing before a table at the right side of the building. Arthur hurried over to him with Vaughn behind. There, delicately placed as if it were meant to be a centerpiece, was the gun. Under it was a perfectly folded paper. Arthur picked the gun and slid it back into his pocket. He unfolded the paper. There, in a precise and florid hand, were the words:

MY UNDYING GRATITUDE FOR YOUR HOSPITALITY
Sincerely,
M. S.

Arthur read the words aloud and closed his eyes. "Anyone got a match?" he asked. One of the men stepped forward with a small flame, and Arthur held the paper over it till it caught fire and let it burn until the ash drifted from his hand.

"Good riddance," said Vaughn, and all there agreed. Arthur nodded as well, but something weighed upon him. He would not find relief in this outcome. The man was gone, but the hatred and the evil remained. Maybe only in Arthur's blood, and perhaps Vaughn felt this as well, but it oppressed him. *Better to have had the fight,* he thought. *Better to have seen how many bullets and slashes it took for Schreck and his beast to finally go down. Better to have stamped on his rumpled clothes and buried him deep in the ground.* This felt, to Arthur, incomplete.

Chapter 6

The months passed by without a sign of Malcolm Schreck, at least in the physical sense, for both Arthur and Brendan Vaughn were still afflicted with his presence, especially as night fell. There were moments for each man, turning a corner in a hall, ascending a staircase, or just peering into the distance, where the darkness seemed to take his cruel shape. Neither truly wished to be alone during those hours. The drafts that blew in the mansion seemed to whisper the evil name. As Arthur Drake knew and Brendan Vaughn came to realize, the arrival of Malcolm Schreck had been a portent of disaster for the lord and all his estate.

The unraveling began rather quickly, certainly with the physical state of Brendan Vaughn, which was slow to recover. Soon the cherished routines of the Black Orchid Society became a remote memory as its members failed to show, and the attraction of the debauchery and supposed occult secrets dimmed out of desire to forget the tall shadow that fell across the house those months ago.

There was also a painful reality as creditors called, and Lord Vaughn's assets were determined through his possessions rather than his actual paper holdings. The lordship was in arrears and could no longer sustain the servants, the upkeep, or the rather tawdry recreational pursuits that occupy the idle rich. It was enough to strain the friendship that Arthur and his host had retained since before the war began.

The war also provided a clarion call that life at the Vaughn estate was about to change. As if in a line, following the creditors came the representatives of the British Armed Forces. A lieutenant from Churchill's own underground fortress knocked on the door one afternoon. James allowed him entrance, and without much prelude, the situation was made plain to the master. It would seem, since Lord Vaughn was in such financial straits, it would be rather prudent of him to allow the lads to be bivouacked on the estate for training and such.

Lord Vaughn drew himself up as haughtily as he possibly could at the suggestion. "And if I refuse?" he said to the sharply dressed young lieutenant, whose demeanor belied the struggles the man had endured since Germany attacked the homeland.

"Yes," he answered. "That's been anticipated, sir. Your reputation is well-known. And so this request has been backed by Parliamentary decree, which I just happen to have here." The young man pulled a short stack of papers from a brown attaché case and handed the proper documents to Vaughn, who perused them obstinately until he noted the signatures at the bottom. At which time, his shoulders stooped, and he nodded silently.

"When am I to expect these troops?" Vaughn asked, all the steam let out of him.

"Approximately a fortnight, sir," the officer answered. "Preparations were being made before I left. Of course, the weather requires the officers be stationed inside the house, but I expect we should be setting up tents for the other men as soon as possible."

"How many?"

"Roundabout three hundred, sir. If your servants have any homes to go to, they may wish to set themselves back to them. Any females present in the house, sir? You see, we'll be in training, and fraternizing between the sexes can be a difficult distraction to overcome, if you take my meaning, sir . . ."

"Yes! Yes, I take your meaning, Lieutenant." Vaughn looked despondently around the house as he spoke. "We shall all be making arrangements . . . to leave."

"Not necessary, sir, but as you wish. Very good, sir! The country is in your debt. Well . . . good day to you." The young man held his hand out to Vaughn, which the lord of the house took limply into his own, and muttered goodbye. As he watched the lieutenant walk smartly back to his vehicle, Vaughn felt the helplessness, and the rage that he had carried for the past weeks welled up inside him. He looked aimlessly about the old manor, the home his grandfather's grandfather had built. He had never been much of a son, but having no siblings to fight for supremacy, it had fallen to him with no struggle. All he had to do was maintain enough in the coffers to stand the upkeep; and the servants, of course; and the land, the animals, his wife's dowry, the auto collection, and on and on and on.

Lord Vaughn stood shocked. As if he had fallen into an icy stream, a sudden comprehension came over him. He had lost all of it, with a handshake. Of course, he had lost it long before. His pursuits not being those of a lord and gentleman, his reputation among his peers was no better than that of Wilde's Dorian Gray. The Black Orchid Society had been made up of lesser and ne'er-do-well company, which he now understood to be suited to his own. Their help, their charity would do little for him since it was he who had often been the most charitable to them. Damnable situation, that was what it was, just a damnable situation.

He could appeal to his wife's family, but they had been counseling her to divorce for years, and in fact, their separation had only grown colder over time. His thoughts turned to blame. Schreck, of course, had been the harbinger of this storm of calamities but also Arthur, who had provided the stock for these vainglorious pursuits. But what could either of them do for him now? Schreck, thankfully, was long gone, and Arthur? Arthur would propose restraint, of course, as he always did. For an otherwise common pimp, Arthur was the spirit of rationality. In some ways, that had been a blessing, in others, an irritant. But he trusted Arthur and had taken him in to a point where he became the younger brother Brendan Vaughn had never had. And it seemed reciprocated by Arthur as well since he came from . . . wherever it was he came from. But his trust in his friend was borne out of time and necessity. He needed women, pliable women, to gain the influx of men to his cabal. Arthur supplied them. What else had he done, except use him as a bank, hotel, barkeep, and tailor? These thoughts began to consume him, and his pride swelled to the point of anger. As if on cue, Arthur stepped out of the shadow.

"Hello, Brendan," Arthur said as he walked slowly to him.

"Arthur," Vaughn replied. He looked hard at Arthur for a time until his face suddenly softened, and as if resigned to some silent verdict, he nodded. "It seems we must be leaving, Arthur. The war has finally reached our doorstep."

"Leaving?" Arthur asked plainly as if the information had no effect on him. "Where will you go?"

"You mean we, don't you, Arthur?" Vaughn said. "Where will we go?" Vaughn reached out his arms and took Arthur's own into his hands as he faced him. Then he brought Arthur to his breast and hugged him, something Arthur took for a complete surprise as Brendan Vaughn had never been one to be that familiar.

As he allowed the embrace to weaken, he looked at Arthur. "Arthur," he said, "I have been a terrible fool lately, but I wouldn't be so foolish as to leave you to fend for yourself now. We have . . . opportunities. Friends in America I know who can set us up there for a while until we can establish ourselves, get back on our feet again. We can leave this place to the army. I hear the Americans will be coming here soon. Why not take their place over there, eh?" Vaughn smiled, and Arthur weakly attempted to return it.

"What friends are those?" he asked. "You've never mentioned them before."

"Always the worrier," Vaughn answered. "When the army and other government officials get here, you'll find less reason to disagree. You'll pass for thirty with them and find yourself drafted. Now gather up your belongings and as many of the girls who will join us. We'll leave in a few days. You won't find suitable lodgings anywhere in East London now, will you? Don't argue. Be discreet about it though. We can't take everyone."

Arthur stared at him, slightly dumbfounded. This was happening all too quickly for his liking. But Vaughn was right. To find himself back in London, with all the poor sods who were struggling to clean up after the bombing, was not appealing at all to a man who had been living in luxury. The war would not likely reach America, so the only void to fill would be that of the men off to battle.

That prospect lightened the venture in Arthur's view. The details could be explained to him later. The manor was gone to him already. It held bothersome memories. And was that a little hope he saw in Vaughn's eyes? Yes. America afforded that, a new opportunity that could branch out to anywhere while the war raged in Europe. It wouldn't last forever, of course, but surely America was the better place to weather the storm.

Arthur backed away from Vaughn toward the stairway to his room. "You know, Brendan," he said curiously, "I spent some of my youth there, before the Great War. I've always thought of going back someday. I'd bargain that day is here. All right, mate, one last trip it is before we get too old."

Chapter 7

"It's a big country," Brendan Vaughn said casually as he looked out over a clean sandy beach from his hotel window on the coast of Lake Michigan.

"Yes," replied his companion, Arthur Drake. "Why you chose this particular corner of it, I don't quite understand, but yes, it is a big country. You can't even see across its lakes."

Arthur was smoking a cigarette, gazing out the window at the drab and dreary scene of a mist-filled Michigan afternoon. It had been raining on and off since they arrived in September after a long and bumpy flight to New York City. Why they hadn't stayed there, or rather, why he hadn't and left Brendan to his new "friends" was beyond him. Perhaps it was the fraternal instinct he had discovered in himself for Vaughn, or perhaps it was just cautiousness for his own survival in a country he saw could still prove wild. But stay he had, and at the minimum, he had been able to watch as Brendan Vaughn made a substantial, if not total, recovery from the loss of his fortunes. Arthur suspected this was as much his new friends' doings as Vaughn's own, but he wondered silently what they were getting out of the stout Englishman.

The troop occupied the whole second floor of this beachfront hotel, whose primary business was attained during the summer months when the beach would be filled with families, colorful towels, beach balls, and sailboats bobbing on the big lake's waves. Now the beaches were empty, except for a few brave stragglers unhindered by the constant wet and cool wind. Who paid for this arrangement was not for Arthur's ears apparently as Vaughn would tell him simply not to worry about it. He had met these so-called friends of Vaughn. Italians, they were, and not the respectable kind. They would come into the room and bloody take it over, while Vaughn would say nothing. Arthur knew and had often had the company of low-rent thugs in his prior life as a London pimp. That sort could be cold, vicious, and altogether rough. Arthur could be too, if pressed. But this lot was different. Perhaps it was only a cultural difference, or perhaps Arthur had been too long in the genteel company of Brendan Vaughn and the other low gentry, but these Italian hoods seemed to always be simmering with violence. It was unsettling to be in their company for long.

And it was depressing to Arthur, who had only Vaughn and a couple of his girls to keep him company. Besides that, it was no better than England for weather. Always his thoughts turned to leaving, at least for a warmer climate. Out west, they said it was warm and dry, but Arthur only had his memories of San Francisco to remind him of that, and they seemed farther and farther away as he grew older.

Vaughn turned toward Arthur, holding his glass of bourbon in his hand. He looked well, Arthur had to admit, and if he had any doubts or reservations about their new surroundings, he gave no sign.

"This is a fine country, Arthur," he said, "though I've heard winter months here can be hard. All we must do is weather it. Mr. Tagliani is bringing women, booze, all we can handle, he says, to make us comfortable. You should be more appreciative."

"Women used to be my department," Arthur answered, a tad harsher than he intended. "You said we couldn't bring many, and it was hard enough to convince Brenda and Maggie, but if you'd give me some time to make myself acquainted here, I'm sure I could have more at our disposal soon enough."

"I'm quite sure you could, Arthur," Vaughn said. "Johnny has it all in hand, he assured me. Aside from that, you remember the drive. There didn't seem to be anything we passed that resembled much of city life. I can't imagine where you could find people, much less a woman. Either they left or they just don't have much of a population around here now. These girls are from Chicago."

"Gun molls then," Arthur said.

"Willing companions for cold nights, Arthur."

Arthur shrugged. Of all the things that came to his mind sitting in a lonely hotel room, companionship was the least of his worries. "Might you tell me again why Johnny Tags is concerned with our comfort?" he asked.

Brendan Vaughn pursed his lips tightly and sighed through his nose. He had been glad when Arthur accepted his offer of coming to America, but it seemed that since the man didn't have complete control of the arrangement, he resented it. It was becoming damned annoying. Vaughn had been able to leave England with enough cash on hand to invest in a venture scheme, which was none of Arthur's bloody business. All Arthur was required to be was another Englishman so neither of them would be completely alien against all others in this country. And he couldn't even do that without complaint.

"Mr. Tagliani has done me and, in turn, you, a great favor, Arthur," he said sternly. "He's given me a new identity, a new start in a new country. The old world is dead, or soon will be, once the war is finally over. The least you could do is let go of your old prejudices and help me assimilate to the new one."

That was rich, Arthur thought, *coming from a man who considered it a positive that he may have had to turn his estate over to the Huns. Instead, he had been booted by his own countrymen and now found himself indebted to Italian mobsters.*

"My only prejudice is to our safety, Brendan," Arthur said. "Could you not have found some more legitimate, less dangerous crooks to align yourself with?"

"What are you blathering on about now, Arthur?"

"Tags seems all right," Arthur said. "But he's the boss, the sophisticated one. His men, his soldiers, are cold-blooded killers, Brendan. And if he gives them a simple look, we'll both be finding out how deep this lake is. And it could happen for a lark, I'm telling you."

"You exaggerate again, Arthur." Vaughn drank the last of the bourbon from his glass and quickly refilled it. "I'm going to be just fine. And when my feet are firmly underneath me, I'll depart quietly, and you won't have anything left to worry about."

"You've always been a terrible judge of character," Arthur said.

"You're proof of that, Arthur," Vaughn said. "I thought you had some balls on you."

"I had the balls to stare down Malcolm Schreck," Arthur said firmly.

Vaughn shrank from the remark. "That's a name I prefer not to hear again," he said. "I should think you knew that."

"Yes," Arthur said, "I know. I just want you to remember who I am, especially here. We don't know how things are here. We're at a disadvantage. We need to stick together to survive it."

"Yes," Vaughn replied. "Well, I think you're being overly dramatic, but I take your meaning. Now please get yourself ready and prepare Brenda and Maggie. We need to have our own shiny offerings to present to our new friends. This is a table we can't come to empty-handed now, can we?"

Chapter 8

Arthur did exactly as he was instructed, of course. Whatever issues he had with the arrangement, it was the arrangement he had. Being practical was the only way to bring it to conclusion. He made Brenda and Maggie aware and was given no argument by them. Whores, in general, didn't have much say in how they were required to service, and the girls were well aware of this. Being from London, they had often dealt with a variety of rough characters. These would just be Americans, of a sort, and their hands would grope, and their tongues would try for ears just the same. All the girls needed to do was pretend they were having a wonderful time, and in the pretending, they just might succeed in convincing themselves. They would leave the silent watching to Arthur as they always had. He rarely felt the need to smack them about, and he wasn't stingy with the payment. In fact, they thought themselves lucky as they had both been in the hands of much harder employers in their short but busy careers.

The Italians liked the girls' singsong accents. It amused them to no end having to explain their terminology and to have the Limey version explained back to them. They were loud, boisterous, and already drunk when they arrived. They brought a few of their own women, just so the ratio wouldn't be too much in favor of the men, and all were set upon having a relaxing evening in the semi-deserted Lake Michigan hotel. The thought or fear of police intervention was near to nil as the local sheriff and his deputies had no problem with Chicago money being spent freely in the off-season.

Arthur allowed himself to relax. He took to the company of Johnny Tags, who, when not coldly surveying the room, was actually quite the charming fellow. He was a large man like Brendan Vaughn, who dressed in the latest style, much as any businessmen of the time were wont to do. He did not hide his ethnicity, nor did he parade it. His men, however, felt no compunction to follow his example as very shortly, they were in their white tank top undershirts with the crucifixes and St. Christopher medallions hanging about their necks. Johnny Tags looked at them with a mixture of amusement and pride.

"They need this," he said casually. "They been working hard. It's a hard business, so they got to." Arthur merely nodded. He could guess to which business Tags was referring, but in all cases, he felt silence made information flow more smoothly. And he wanted that information as he could not pry it from Vaughn, not even in the interest of self-preservation.

"How ya like it here, Artie?" Tags asked as one of his own girls draped an arm with a fresh drink about his shoulder. "Thanks, doll," he said and sent her on her way.

"It's a nice hotel," Arthur offered.

"Yeah, nice and quiet, huh?" Tags replied. "Maybe too quiet, but coming from Chicago, quiet is good." He leaned in toward Arthur across the table and gestured toward the party. "You don't go in like your boss, huh?"

"Well, Mr. Tag—" Arthur began to say.

"John," the big man said plainly.

"I've heard your friends call you Johnny," Arthur replied.

"Oh, I got lots of names," Tags said. "Tags, Johnny Tags, Boss. A couple of mooks tried to call me Johnny Toe-tags. I never cared for that name, so I made sure they and everybody else got the message not to call me that again. Those guys never did anyways. I think they call that irony." Tags chuckled at his joke. "And to the cops, I'm Giovanni Tagliani. But ain't none of 'em I call exactly friends of mine. Now you, because I think you're smart, you can call me what my mother called me—John. I ain't saying we're friends though."

Arthur laughed. "Of course not," he said. "Well, to answer your question, John, I don't go in because I'm the supplier. Or I was, back home. I'm finding it difficult to let go of the job. I can't say that my girls aren't mine. I do take a taste now and again. But I take it in private. No need for a show."

Johnny Tags smiled. "So I'm right," he said. "You are smart. Smart guy has a future. Smart guy knows the play before he makes a play." Tags sat back, smiling. A moment later, his smile fell, and a look of deadly seriousness passed over him. "Tell me something, Artie. I give your boss the play. Am I being smart?"

"Difficult to answer," Arthur said, passing a glance at the frolicking Brendan Vaughn, "without at least some of the cards. My preference would be to keep the pressure light, a slow start for a greater finish. Mr. Vaughn hasn't ever been as big as he'd like to think, but he can be satisfied if he thinks he's bigger than he is."

"Hmm," Tags grunted. "Sounds a little iffy. You see, Artie, war's gonna be over soon. This country is coming out of it on top. Means more business. More business means more pressure." He looked around, and then he leaned in toward Arthur again and said in a quieter voice, "Some people don't like it, but I'm thinking we need to diversify our employment opportunities. That's where you and the hoi polloi Limey come in. He may not be smart, but you are. He can be the front for you, and you can be the front for us, *capisce*?"

Arthur held his glass up for an impromptu clink with Johnny Tags. He was a foreigner in a strange land. His business had always been whoring, but now he would take the actual business acumen he had acquired with that role and focus it on a new venture. The idea was vaguely exciting to him. As he watched Brendan Vaughn, now known as Rodger Wentworth, frolicking with the rest of the party, he turned to Johnny Tags. "What do you have in mind?" he said.

Chapter 9

It was a simple arrangement, really. Location was the prime motivator as the little town was dropped almost right in the middle between Chicago to the west across the big lake, where Johnny Tags held court, and Detroit to the east, where various other families operated. The town was called Kalamazoo, and despite the odd name, it was growing. Some of that was because of its central location between the two larger cities, and some was because of its pure Americanism. A desire to grow prompted, not surprisingly, growth. In any direction outside it was a vast expanse of rural land and acres of woods. The town itself had a few banks; a hospital, including a psychiatric facility; a motel or two; a Gibson guitar factory; and some rich investors wanting in on the ground floor of its coming expansion.

Arthur Drake found himself right in the heart of its downtown near one of its largest intersections. The street where the building stood took a lazy curve before it headed east on a one-way, a whole block triangular wedge dividing it from the westerly avenue. The front sign above the doorway of the shop said in large and small block lettering,

Wentworth's Needle & Thread.
Tailoring, Fittings, and Suits for all Occasions.
We Carry Hats!

Although it boasted his new name, Brendan Vaughn rarely ever entered the business himself. He left that for Arthur's handsome face and smooth English tones to occupy. Arthur would greet the customers wearing one of the fine suits on display; take their money for any transactions that they made with the business, such as shortening or lengthening pant legs; and even helped the tailor in residence, Carlo (Charles) Righetti.

Arthur found Charlie to be an easy companionship, much different from the more hotheaded Italians he had dealt with before. And so in time, Arthur learned a thing or two about the tailoring business and was soon assisting Charlie with some measuring, trimming, and other light duties, such as standing back and judging how well a suit fit a customer.

Arthur was somewhat shocked at the casual indifference Carlo had to the other business the tailor shop provided—the transport and exchange of drugs and money. A traveler, sometimes accompanied by other men who stood silently in the background, would come through the side door carrying a briefcase. Arthur would excuse himself, and Carlo would nod without looking his way and simply walk slowly to the opposite side of the shop. There, he would make a modest show of inspecting a suit or studying an order, whatever little business he could make of the few moments for Arthur and the men to go around to the back of the shop.

One day Arthur decided in a quiet moment to press Charlie on the subject. He had no reason to distrust him, but the young Italian would sometimes pass a disappointed or sad glance his way, and Arthur wished to know what the source of it was. Carlo was moving slowly about the shop, whistling a note, not a tune but a simple note as if it came with his exhalation.

"Charlie," Arthur asked, "how is it that you're here? In this place particularly?"

Carlo Righetti's voice was like tires rolling slowly over soft gravel. "I'm a tailor," he said, gesturing around the room. "This is a tailor shop. No?"

Arthur looked at him from his seat behind the counter and shrugged. Carlo gave a knowing nod in reply. "Look, Artie," he said, "all I ever want to be is a tailor. Can't sing, can't dance, and I don't like to go so fast in cars. So I take the needle, the thread, the measuring tape, and the chalk, and I try to be a good tailor. Whatever else goes on in this world, I don't wanna know from it. *Capisce?*"

"Sure," Arthur answered, "I *capisce*. But why do that here? There have to be, uh, more legitimate shops where you can work."

"Yeah?" Carlo said, his full, thick eyebrows jumping on his brow. "They hiring dagos?" Carlo walked over to the counter and rested his right forearm on the register while his left set down on the countertop. "My father was a numbers man, Arthur, you know that?" he said. "Came over here from the old country. Couldn't speak the language, but he could do figures, okay? He get hired by the big mining companies to keep their books. The mining company, to a one, sooner or later, they fall in with the mob. So Pop's at his desk one day, and these big, scary guys, they come through the door. Soon as they do, my pop, he give his notice, packs us up, and off we go to the next Little Italy to the next numbers job for the next company. I tell you, pal, I been all over this country, from the Rockies to the Appalachians. But always, they follow. They like a shadow, Artie. You ever have a shadow following you?"

Arthur sat silently. If he had an answer, he didn't give it, although a certain shadow crossed his mind as Carlo spoke.

"One day, Artie," Carlo said, "that shadow, it catch up with you."

"So that's why you're here?" Arthur asked. "They got something on you?"

Carlo let his face fall into a little frown and shrugged. "I was just about to ask you the same thing. But no, Artie, not so much. We practically *paisan*, they say. I say, sure. They run the old owner out. They say you with the needle, you can stay. I ask no question. I make no trouble. Man's gotta work, no?" Carlo sighed. "I know it's no good. But at least they're Italian. One day maybe they leave it to me."

"Righetti and sons, eh?" Arthur said.

"Oh!" Righetti exclaimed. "I'm outnumbered—two little girls and an Irish wife—fool that I am! I come to work for a little peace and quiet!"

They both laughed at this until the tailor shook his head, waved his hand at his chest as if he was fanning himself, and whistled. Then he quietly shuffled about his business as if nothing more needed to be said. Arthur liked him. They had absolutely nothing in common, and yet he did like the little man. In fact, as time went by, Arthur found himself even enjoying the company of the gangsters who came in to the back of the shop. Most warmed to him immediately and, in the routine of drivers and suppliers, never stayed long enough for an issue to rise. Arthur mainly watched the transactions between parties, making sure all was as arranged for Johnny Tags.

Occasionally, a new man would come through the door, a young tough-looking to make a statement or an older one, ready to prove he could still handle himself. When they saw the tall, thin Englishman, they would inevitably say something along the lines of "Who the fuck is this?"

"I'm Arthur Drake," Arthur would say, keeping his hands in his pocket as he leaned against the wall by the little table set aside for the curriers. "I'm an associate of Mr. Tagliani."

The newcomer would look at him with a mix of confusion and anger. "Tags is hiring Micks now?"

"Limey, actually," Arthur replied.

"Same thing, ain't it?"

"Not to them," Arthur said. "Look, mate, why don't we just finish the business, and we can all be on about our day then, right?"

One day one young tough man wouldn't back down, and Arthur's tone, which was casual at worst, only seemed to set fire to him. The others present who had grown accustomed to Arthur tried to vouch for him, but the young man would have none of it and rose from the table with his face set in a hard stare.

"I ain't your mate, you old fuck," he said.

As the other members of both the Detroit and Chicago factions attempted to calm the younger man, who answered to the name of Freddy, Arthur could only think in terms of what the younger man had called him.

"Old fuck."

Old fuck repeated in his mind like a drum beat. *Old fuck, old fuck, old fuck.* What did he mean old? Arthur looked at the calendar on the wall, the year in big, bold numbers—1945. Arthur had been born in 1900, or so he had been told. Forty-five years old. Did that make him an old fuck? Maybe it did, compared to this lout. But old? As he thought this, he saw young Freddy break free of his cohorts and move toward him. He was broad in the shoulders and clearly outweighed Arthur, but still, Arthur thought only of his youth as he pulled his blade out of his coat pocket, allowed Freddy's weight to come at him, grabbed an arm, and swung him toward the wall with a hard crash. Before Freddy could counter, Arthur's blade was at his throat.

"This is a terrible way to die, Freddy," Arthur said in a whisper. "I have a very sharp blade here. Cut through an old leather shoe like butter it will. So it won't be painful. But the pain ain't the horror, right? The horror is knowing you're gonna die, and there's not a damn thing you can do about it."

Arthur heard the guns clicking behind him. "Hold on, good fellows," he said, still holding the knife to a terrified Freddy's throat. "You might want to think about this. Mr. Tagliani is expecting to hear from me. You may know him better than I, but unsanctioned murder of a fellow employee, even if he is a . . . old fuck, might not sit well with him."

"Just let him go, Mr. Drake," one of the hoodlums said, "and we'll consider it."

Arthur smiled. He let the knife back slowly from his attacker's throat and watched the man's hands come up to make sure his head was still there, and no fluid was leaking. Arthur stepped away from him and straightened his tie. "Old fuck, eh?" he said. "You watch out for old fucks, Freddie. We'll fuck you proper."

He took a few steps away from them and turned back to the small gang. "Gentlemen," he said, "conduct the business and leave. This hasn't been a good day for pleasantries."

Later in the following week, word came back that Mr. Tagliani had not been angered by Arthur's action but had instead given young Freddie something to think about. As to Arthur, Tags had not been surprised. Smart and tough were the very attributes that allowed him to leave his business under Arthur's watchful eye. It was clear he trusted the Englishman's judgment, just as Brendan Vaughn once had. But Vaughn trusted nobody anymore. He would cling to Arthur in his presence, but his life had spiraled down to an endless train of drugs and delusion, fueled with his usual appetites for sex and alcohol. Arthur could barely have a conversation with him that was focused on anything except Vaughn's next cheap escapade. It was one of those conversations some months later that was overheard in the darkened room that Vaughn used as an office on the second floor of the lakeside hotel.

The murmurings that began in the hallway grew louder as Arthur and Brendan Vaughn reached the door. It was not an argument, but there was exasperation in the tones of the men. A female voice, young and with a Midwestern blandness, also interjected as the key scratched at the doorknob. The door opened, and the voices rang out clearly in the dark.

Arthur said, "I just want you to slow down on this junk, is all. Why on earth did you get involved with that? You hate needles."

"It calms me, Arthur," Vaughn replied as he stepped toward the high-backed chair that sat directly in front of the fine mahogany desk. "Pour us a drink, will you?" he said. "You've no objection to a drink, do you?"

Arthur turned on the small green-shaded lamp at the bar in the corner of the room. He began pouring as the young lady leaned against him. Her name was Corrine, and she was a local girl he had enticed with his smooth British accent at one of the local bars. She was very young but had taken a shine to the older man's genteel English act. Arthur poured her bourbon first and handed her the glass. He filled two more and turned toward Vaughn.

"I just think you should start taking it easy, Mr. Wentworth," Arthur said. "You still need to heal. You haven't been yourself since . . . that night."

Vaughn slapped the back of the chair. The room was still dark with only the small light shining down on the bar. "Dammit, Arthur!" he shouted. "I told you before I never want to speak of that again!"

"Yes, yes," Arthur replied calmly. "Hopefully, he's found his way back to whatever corner of hell he crawled out of. It was a long time ago. But you're still running from it. And it's wearing on you."

Vaughn took his drink and stepped around the desk to take a seat in the master chair. He pulled the little brass chain for his own small lamp, and the space around the desk lit with a soft yellow glow. There, exposed to that small light, directly opposite Brendan Vaughn, sat the black shape and white bone face of Malcolm Schreck. Vaughn gasped reflexively at the sight of the man, his hands gripping the arms of his chair as if he were bracing for a high-speed crash.

"I don't believe it!" he blurted.

Malcolm Schreck smiled in that same disgusting fashion he had displayed all those years ago. "Then perhaps you should have changed your name to Thomas, Lord Vaughn," he said in his strangely European accent. He chuckled. The room was silent for a long moment. Arthur had come around the chair to look at the figure, and he too was dumbstruck by what he saw. All he could do was hold the young girl back with an outstretched arm as she attempted to see what had caused the two Englishmen to falter so suddenly.

Schreck looked from one man to the other and frowned. There was not much difference in this look from his smile, but he squinted as if he was troubled. He said, "Perhaps one of you gentlemen could explain how I, who come from a corner of Hell, know the Scripture and you apparently do not." He let the comment sit in silence for a moment, shook his head slightly, and sighed. "A failure in your upbringing, I surmise. Well, no matter. We are all together again, eh? Will you not offer me a drink?" Schreck took his large beaver hat, which had been resting on his lap, and set it directly in front of him on the desk.

"How did you find us?" Vaughn gasped.

Schreck knitted his long, pale fingers together. "A keen sense of smell," he answered coldly. "You, Vaughn, emanate a profound stench of fear. And this one"—Schreck indicated with a turn of his head toward Arthur—"smells of that." Schreck threw his thumb behind his right shoulder.

"A better question would be why," he continued, "since the both of you are such great disappointments." He directed his gaze at Arthur, who was still attempting to caution his young lady friend while he stared back at the shape in the chair. Schreck noticed this and allowed his eyes to twist in his skull toward the back of the room. The contempt on his face was palpable as he returned his gaze to Arthur. Arthur found himself surprised that Schreck still wore the same attire he had when they had met. He wondered if Schreck ever took them off.

"Yes, Schreck," Arthur said, attempting to convey some of the toughness that had so quickly drained out at the sight of this apparition, "how did you get here, especially in that getup?" While it may have passed unnoticed in Old England and Europe, where traditions fell a bit harder, the Americans, Arthur had noticed, were constantly in the present, busily trying to keep up with the new fashions, new trends.

Schreck would have undoubtedly caused quite a stir had he been seen about garbed like a nineteenth-century undertaker.

"That drink, Arthur, please allow me to have it, and I will enlighten you," he said softly. Arthur looked at the bourbon in his hand and, regretfully, as he felt he needed it much more, set the glass on the corner of the table. Vaughn downed his at the opportunity of Schreck's diverted attention. Schreck took the drink, raised the glass, and silently toasted them both. Then he brought the glass to his lips and let the fluid drain into his throat.

"These Americans," he said, "not an especially attentive folk. Perhaps they would find me unsightly if they invested a moment to notice. Of course, I am inclined to be discreet. But they are more enthralled by the lights of their flicker shows or some periodical of some sort. I take it from the plainness of voice that this behind me is a native to this land. Why don't we ask it why that is?" With that, Schreck stood from the chair and turned to face the girl.

Corrine stood there, shocked. Her eyes widened, and all the blood that arose in her cheekbones left her face. She had never in her life seen a creature such as Malcolm Schreck. She somehow managed not to scream.

Schreck grimaced. "Still the flesh merchant, eh, Drake?" He looked the girl up and down with all the excitement of judging the strength of a post. Her blond curly hair, her sweet features, and her fine, shapely body had absolutely no effect on his manhood or, indeed, his humanity. He took an inquisitive step toward her only to judge her reaction. She instinctively took an immediate step back.

"Quite young," he said to Arthur, "for someone of your age. How did you secure it, Arthur? Or did you snatch it from under its mother's petticoats?" Schreck's face grew disgusted. "Tell it to leave," he commanded.

Corrine shivered. "I'm not leaving, Arthur," she blurted shakily, "not while he's here."

Schreck straightened at her defiance and looked sharply at Arthur.

Arthur stared back at him as he stood between the soft light of the two lamps. "It's all right, my dear," he said without glancing at her. "This eccentric gentleman is an old acquaintance of ours, Mr. Wentworth and I. We'll just chat for a bit, and then he'll be leaving."

Won't you, Mr. Schreck?" Schreck smiled in response and turned the leer to the girl.

"He means to hurt you, Arthur," she said.

Schreck's hands violently came up and flashed in front of his face as if to ward her away. He growled something inaudible and said harshly, "Very well, girl! Stay! But be seated! Damn you! And be silent!"

Corrine looked at Arthur, who nodded with a small comforting smile, and she took a seat in the corner near the bar. Schreck watched her, shook his head again, and then turned back toward Arthur and Vaughn.

"Such devotion, Drake," he said as he stepped back toward the chair. "I allow it to be a trick of your own doing."

"Speaking of devoted," Arthur said as he sat in a small chair by the wall, "where is your Mr. Warren?"

"Yes," Vaughn added without much volume. He looked around the room as if he expected the large man to now step out of the shadows. "Where is he?"

Schreck smiled. "Never far, my friends, I can assure you of that," he answered. "Mr. Warren, at least, remains steadfast and true.

"The young man, however," he added, "that you assisted me with, Arthur. You recall the event, do you not?" Arthur's face blanched at the memory. He let himself fall seated in the chair against the room's wall. "He did pass on eventually." Schreck let the comment stand for a moment as he watched Arthur's expression. "Oh," he said, holding a hand up, "not from the wounds you inflicted upon him, Drake. Let that not trouble you."

"What's this?" Vaughn asked. He looked at Arthur, confused.

Schreck looked from one to the other. "You never conveyed this, Arthur?" he said, feigning surprise. "That last evening we had in England? Quite a tale it is, Lord Vaughn. But Drake can give you a more detailed account at his convenience. Sufficeth to say, it took me some time to dispatch the boy, utterly, that is. Life and death being the great mystery, no?"

Arthur sighed in the chair. He felt older suddenly. A pain ran through his body at the memories he had successfully suppressed for so long. He said the only thing he could think of at that moment. "What is it that you want, Schreck?"

Schreck clapped his hands together as he looked at the two of them in the spacious office. He seemed to consider the luxury of it for a moment. Then he said, "Merely the company of old friends. So many years I have spent wandering with only Mr. Warren. Loyal, he is, but not a man for which conversation comes naturally. Being among my fellows as I was with you, I felt the pangs for lost companions. And although, my friends, there is not much in the way of knowledge you could share with me, I, for one, would be glad to impart some of mine own to you." He sat back in the chair and let his arms fall to the rests, his long, bony fingers curled over their bulbous ends. "We could reform your . . . what was it? Oh yes, your Black Orchid Society." There was silence for a long moment. Schreck's gaze fell to Vaughn, who was powerless to mask his terror.

"Yes," Schreck breathed. "Perhaps even these Mediterraneans you've associated with here would desire to know of your . . . other interests."

At that moment, the phone on Vaughn's desk broke the silence, and Schreck jumped at the sound. "Infernal contraptions!" he growled.

"The telephone frightens you?" Arthur asked sternly.

"No!" Schreck barked. He stood suddenly and turned away from the desk. He passed a glance over at the girl who sat on the edge of her chair in the corner, tense and nervously biting her lip. Vaughn let the ringing continue until finally, he answered. It was an older style of device, and Vaughn held the earpiece to his ear and braced the base with his other hand to speak into the mouthpiece.

"Hello?" he said, quivering. "No, Johnny, you're not disturbing us. Nothing important. Yes, yes, of course, Johnny, we'd be very happy to . . . When? Fine, fine. Yes. We'll be expecting you then. Yes, yes . . . Goodbye."

Vaughn set the earpiece down into the receiver and watched Schreck. Schreck turned about slowly and, lifting a finger to his head, said as if it was an afterthought, "Yes," he said. "Yes. Quite a remarkable instrument is this. Hmm . . . Unseen and yet heard. Lord Vaughn, is this device your preferred method of contact? If so, perhaps you would be so kind as to give me your number."

Schreck snickered. "No matter," he said as he removed his hat from the desk and began to walk toward the door. He nodded toward them one at a time and backed up a few steps from the desk. "Gentlemen," he said, "we must gather again and soon. Do not trouble yourselves further. I know exactly where you are. Good evening."

With that, Malcolm Schreck walked out of the room. He paid no attention to the girl by the bar. She lowered her head as he drew near. Entering the hallway, he looked down both ends, placed his hat rather smartly on his head, and disappeared toward the rear of the hotel.

Drake and Vaughn sat in silence, looking at the space Schreck had just moments before occupied. Arthur Drake looked at Brendan Vaughn and said, "Let's have a drink."

Corrine, for her part, immediately began asking a variety of questions regarding the strange figure. Since neither man was much inclined to share details, it began to take the tone of an interrogation. Finally, Arthur took her into his arms and held her tightly. She was very young. She did not resist. There was nothing to worry about, he explained calmly. This funny little man was a performer who had a stage show back in Europe. That was why he wore the strange clothes. He was just putting on a performance for them. It meant nothing. It was just unexpected.

Corrine returned Arthur's embrace. "He looked . . . awful," she said. The word was spoken and aptly described all its connotations in the single utterance.

"Yes," Arthur agreed. Schreck had looked awful. He had always been hideous. But he more resembled the aftereffect of his performance on their first meeting. Whatever sorcery, whatever concoctions he was subjecting himself, they were obviously affecting him. Of course, it may be only his true age finally catching up. His oily black hair had many more wisps of gray, and the lines in his twisted face seemed etched deeper under his eyes and along his narrow cheeks.

The young woman with Arthur could not know or understand the true depths of his malevolence. Fortunately, for most people, they would never encounter a being like Schreck. It was as foreign a concept as a distant planet in the universe. In truth, Arthur could not have expressed it adequately even if he wished to do so, and Corrine, being an American, would never be satisfied with the explanation.

She would be compelled to know every detail. Arthur could only hope that she never discover how lucky she was to be ignorant.

While Brendan Vaughn continued to drink, Arthur silently debated what to do. He could leave, keeping his reasons to himself. He wasn't exactly sure which of them, Brendan or he, had drawn Malcolm Schreck all the way across the ocean to find them. But in all likelihood, it was Arthur, and he knew it. What the possible source of this attraction was, Arthur couldn't fathom. Schreck held great disdain for human contact, and he made that bias quite clear. That fact alone seemed to rule out a sexual motive, to Arthur's relief. But still, he had come.

The man was a mystery to Arthur, and one of Arthur's gifts was the ability to take the measure of people. Perhaps that very feeling was returned by Schreck. Something in Arthur attracted him. Schreck was, in spite of his matching grotesqueness in appearance and character, the most fascinating being Arthur had ever met. How the man held to the past so tightly while the world spun on. It was as if Arthur realized in his presence how much his own life had always been on the periphery, how little he knew of real truth, real knowledge. These thoughts were fleeting when they turned to Schreck the man. How disgusting what havoc that secret knowledge would unleash. To be near Schreck would be to risk becoming like him, a twisted version of humanity. And still, there was a compelling magnetism to it Arthur Drake could not deny. Arthur looked at his own reflection in a small rectangular mirror on the wall. He envisioned himself changing into a warped image of evil, like Malcolm Schreck, all the while still holding the beautiful and largely innocent young girl. He shuddered.

Chapter 10

The months of 1945 were eventful. In April, shortly after his birthday, Adolf Hitler married Eva Braun in the bunker. They took their honeymoon in hell. It is a cruel thought perhaps that the naive young Eva had shared her husband's fate. She had been such a good and happy girl, one who loved dresses and having fun as all girls her age should do. The old man had been kind to her in ways he seemed incapable of showing to others. She had consented to, if not fully embraced, a life with him. And judgment is often cruel.

Months after that, while the locals and the families from Chicago enjoyed the sandy beaches of Lake Michigan in August, America unleashed a weapon that finally ended the war on both fronts. Two cities in Japan, made mainly of flammable paper, were totally destroyed. The result was joyous to the Western Allies, but the destructive force of the weapon would ensure a constant tension between the newly arising great powers for the future of the world.

England retreated to its own primarily to lick the wounds of the war and regain some semblance of normalcy while diminishing as a major world power. America and Russia, however, would settle into a frigid, secretive war for supremacy of Germany, Europe, and a great portion of the globe itself.

Americans knew little of this at the time. VE Day had brought huge and happy crowds into the streets, VJ Day, a heavy sigh of relief. It was finally over. The boys would be coming home from the devastation in Europe and the Pacific. Many would be broken by it, unable to heal from the horror they witnessed. Others would only want to return home to restart whatever life they had left behind. Arthur Drake thought of these men with a mixture of opportunity and dread.

Malcolm Schreck had not shown his face again. Perhaps the sheer thrill of frightening the two Englishmen had been enough for him to go on with whatever secret life he envisioned for himself. Perhaps he had died laughing at the memory of their pitiful helplessness. Arthur could only hope, but Schreck was gone again, and the life Arthur had taken up at the hotel and the tailor shop with Carlo Righetti went on.

The Englishman and the Italian American became fast friends. They didn't socialize together outside the shop, although Righetti's small girls and dowdy Irish wife would sometimes visit at lunchtime. The woman was standoffish and seemed to take more than her share of opportunities to henpeck her husband. The girls, however, would hop up and down to hear their shoes bang on the wood floors, and they always ran toward Arthur as a new and handsome face to look at. He, in turn, would reach into the jar of candy and happily hand them some sweets. Righetti loved baseball and Frank Sinatra, and either could be heard on the radio as the days went by. It was the Pussycats in Detroit or the Cubbies in Chicago, another benefit of being so squarely situated between the two cities. Righetti tried to teach Arthur the game as he was a wizard with the stats and the players. It was as close to a normal life Arthur had ever known and, in some ways, regretted not having himself.

Still, the darker version of business in the tailor shop, Wentworth's, resumed without a hitch as well. Arthur had become a routine and welcome sight to the gangster element that entered the shop through the alley door. He had a calming effect if some of the players came in agitated for any reason. A sharp word or a view of a cop car caused some of the men to pull their hair-trigger tempers. If the words were spoken in Italian, Righetti would occasionally translate for Arthur, usually in a soft whisper. Other than that, he steered well clear of this business.

Even Brendan Vaughn finally relaxed and seemed content. Johnny Tags had needed him, or at least his false identity, to purchase land and build a house somewhere to the east, in some remote area of the thick Michigan forest.

"Where exactly?" Arthur asked, for as glad as he was to see Brendan Vaughn able to legitimately puff himself up, he didn't like the idea of being left out of this deal. Vaughn was still a wild card in Arthur's opinion, and these moments of extreme highs could be replaced just as quickly with damaging lows. He had seen it many times.

Vaughn turned toward him in his smoking jacket. It was four o'clock in the afternoon, and yet Brendan Vaughn looked as if he had been up a mere hour. "How in hell should I know?" he said. "I walk fifty yards to the beach and fifty yards back to the bar. I have no desire to stroll in the forest. Do you?"

Arthur grimaced first and then allowed the grimace to change to a smile. "I'm glad to see you rejoining us, Brendan," he said. "You look much better these days since you've been off the junk." Arthur knew the best way to get information from Vaughn was to compliment him first. The man would not be satisfied with the compliment and so would go to any length to add to it.

"It took no small effort," Vaughn blustered. "I won't lie to you. But I've never felt better in my life. A few glasses of some quality bourbon will do me just fine, thank you. Tags has noticed too, ready to bring me back into the business operation, though I am quite proud of the way you've handled it in my absence, Arthur."

"Thanks," Arthur replied succinctly.

"So," Vaughn continued, "Tags purchased some property in my name, and construction is already underway." Vaughn waved his hand in the general direction of east. "Somewhere out there," he said, "a place for his men to hold up, he said. When the heat is on or when they have to . . . what did he call it? Go to the mattress or something like that. Lie down? Sleep? I can't figure these dagos out, Arthur, but he needed me for some cover, and I agreed. All very hush-hush, you know."

Arthur clapped his hand on the big man's shoulder. "Probably better we don't know, eh?" he said. "But I am glad for you." He looked a long time into Vaughn's face. Seeing nothing but blank contentment, he said, "Well, I should get to my room. Corrine and I are having dinner tonight. Can't disappoint. You know how it is."

"Not anymore, thankfully," Vaughn replied. "Send me a new girl before you go, will you, old chap? The plump one, I think. Yes, the plump one, if she's available. I like these Michigan girls."

"Sure, Brendan," Arthur said, "whatever you want." They smiled at each other, but it felt off to Arthur. Something was different to him in Vaughn's look. The man seemed to be studying him. Arthur nodded again and backed away a few steps and then turned from him. He felt Brendan Vaughn's eyes follow him to his door.

Chapter 11

The last day of Arthur Drake's life began pleasantly enough. It was early October, and at the shop, the '45 World Series could be heard playing on the radio. As it happened, in 1945, the Detroit Tigers faced the Chicago Cubs for the title, something never to be repeated. Since many of Major League Baseball's players had joined the service and were still overseas, the series itself promised to be unremarkable. When asked who he thought would win, Charlie Righetti replied flatly, "Neither." Although Hank Greenberg had returned early enough from the war to play, the majority of both teams' rosters involved a very modest bench. Righetti's obvious disappointments in the play amused Arthur as he watched the Italian grimace, groan, and throw his arms out as if to push the game away from him.

Arthur slept in that last morning with Corrine by his side in the bed. With her, it almost felt like something strange was happening. Arthur had never allowed himself this particular brand of comfort, and there had been moments recently when thinking of leaving her filled him with an emptiness he hadn't ever experienced. This sort of arrangement had always been casual, borne of convenience, nothing more. He supposed this newfound distress he had discovered was what was known as love. It was terrible.

Not being on any specific timetable, Arthur cleaned up in a lazy fashion, getting dressed slowly, looking at Corrine lying in bed as he straightened his tie. Before he left her, he bent down to kiss the girl goodbye. She shuffled restlessly in the bed but didn't wake. She merely mumbled something unintelligible as Arthur slipped out the door. A quick cup of coffee on the porch, watching and listening to the waves of the big lake pour onto the beach and fall away, gave Arthur a feeling of peace and contentment. It was a crisp, beautiful morning in October. As the car with the young driver pulled along the side of the hotel, Arthur quietly thanked his luck that he was there to see it.

The drive into town from the lake took just under an hour. Although the boy, Ralph, drove over the bumpy gravel road a bit fast for Arthur's liking, Arthur still spent most of the time looking out the window at the Michigan countryside. Arthur had never learned to drive himself. He had always lived close to his work and, besides, had never been comfortable at the high speeds of vehicles. He looked over at the boy. Whatever he was doing, it didn't seem to take much concentration, and Arthur grimaced as the car barely slowed even as it entered the more restricted driving of the town. As it pulled into the alleyway entrance to Wentworth's tailor shop, Arthur looked at the boy and held out a ten-dollar bill to him.

"Thanks, Ralph," he said casually.

Ralph took the tip and nodded. "Be seeing ya, Mr. Drake," he said.

"Be seeing ya," Arthur replied. He shut the door, and the car immediately took off from him, although Ralph would be forced to stop not thirty yards away. Arthur took off his hat and stepped through the door. When it slammed behind him, he heard Charlie Righetti's voice call out to him.

"Artie! That you?" the little man said in his usual raspy way.

"It's me, Charlie," Arthur answered. This was a routine that happened every day that Arthur came in to the shop. He smiled at the familiarity of the old joke that was coming.

"Good morning!" Charlie said loudly. "Where you been? Thought you weren't coming in today."

"Sleeping, Charlie," Arthur answered.

"Sleeping?" Charlie shouted in mock surprise. Then Arthur heard the long whistle and, finally, the punch line. "Brother, you sure got the life." Arthur nodded and smiled. "Uh-huh" was all he said.

Righetti stood at a rack of long tweed coats, studying the collars. Each one had the stitched monogram, C. Righetti in the inside collar. Charlie waved Arthur over. "Eh, Artie," he said just above a whisper, although nobody else was in the shop, "come 'ere."

Arthur walked over to him and stood there. Righetti, a much shorter man than Arthur, ran his hands along the collar of Arthur's jacket. "How long you have this coat?" he asked.

Arthur thought back. It was the coat he had essentially stolen from Sheffington years ago, but that fact was as hazy as the time that had passed since. "Don't know, Charlie," Arthur answered. "Three, maybe four years."

"When's your birthday?" Righetti inquired plainly.

"Never had a birthday," Arthur said as his eyes went white, trying to think if any day had ever been set aside special for him to celebrate as a birthday. "I'm told I was born in 1900, so that makes me . . . umm, what are we talking about again?"

"Your birthday," Charlie said. "Marone. Man goes all his life no birthday. It ain't right. What day is it? October 7, no, 8. October 8 is your birthday. Happy birthday. Now take off that old coat you got there."

Arthur rather sheepishly did as he was instructed. He handed it to Righetti, who then threw it casually over a nearby chair. "Try this on," he said, taking one of his new long black coats off the hanger. Again, Arthur did what he was told and slipped his arms through the sleeves as Righetti helped it over his shoulders.

"Yeah!" Righetti exclaimed. "That's a nice, huh? How's the fit?"

Arthur turned in the long coat, holding his arms out to full length. The fit was perfect as far as he could tell. "Fine, Charlie," he said. "Just fine, mate. Thank you."

Charlie waved his hand at him and gave his shoulder a pat. "Don't mention it," he said. "Can't have an assistant walking around in a coat with a frayed collar. How would that look?" The two walked over to the counter, where Righetti had a cup of coffee still steaming. He took a sip as Arthur leaned in.

"Now will you let me do something for you, Charlie?" he said softly.

"Like what?"

"How about a woman?"

Righetti took a shuffling half step and turned toward Arthur. "You ain't married, is ya, Artie?" he said. "And Jeannie, I know how she is, you know? But still, I stand up before her family and my family, and I take an oath to God that I don't do that . . . no more. Sometime she make it hard not to think about it, but I don't do it."

Arthur shrugged. "The offer stands, my friend," he said.

Righetti shook his head. "Okay then, you tell me, smart guy, how I face my girls after? They got some of their mama in their little faces. It be like I betray them too, no? No. No." He sighed and smiled at Arthur. "But thanks anyway, Artie. I appreciate it. I do. You wanna get me something? Get out that coffee cake on the table there. It's still your birthday. I turn on the radio. The Pussycats are gonna be on in just a few."

And so the two men, the Englishman and the Italian, sat with their coffee cake and a cup of coffee, listening to the World Series broadcast over the radio. Righetti, coming up with the players' stats before the announcers, explained what was happening to Arthur. And Arthur was laughing at the little man's fluctuating responses of excitement or disappointment over the plays. No customers came in that day, and the light from the sun made the dust particles glow through the windows from west to east as it began to set.

Then as the top of the seventh inning came on, Arthur heard the side door by the alley slam. He looked around as the three men came in. He recognized two of them, but their faces were set in a way he didn't like. He stood from his seat. Righetti remained in his, silent, only the sound of the game coming out of the radio.

Arthur knew of no delivery today. He only came in to see Righetti, and he was always made aware of shipments the day before at least. He looked the men over. "If you're here to see the tailor, you should have come through the front door," he said.

"Shut up," the one called Freddy said. Freddy had been the hothead Arthur had humiliated months earlier. *Is this about that?* Arthur wondered. But even Freddy had seemed to warm to him in the routine of their transactions. This was something different. To Arthur's trained eye, it seemed it could easily head toward lethal. Arthur's knife was in his old coat, he knew. He put his hand in his pocket just to give Freddy something to consider.

The radio announcer came on. "Top of the seventh, Wilson at the plate. He's had his troubles this season, Jim."

"Boy has he," the second announcer agreed. "He just cannot get that rhythm back, but when he does, watch out, boy."

"You're right there. He's the spark they need right now."

One of the thugs piped in, "He can't hit shit. His average is only 185." Arthur couldn't help thinking, *Do all Italians know about baseball?*

"Here's the pitch. CRACK! Oh, he got all of that one! It's way back! Way back! Gone! A home run, and the Tigers take the lead in the seventh!"

Freddie looked at the other thug. "Shaddup, Mario!" he said. "Turn it off." Mario clicked the knob to the off position, and the only sound was the electricity from the radio slowly dying.

Arthur looked the three over calmly. "What can we do for you, Freddy?" he said. "I didn't hear of a drop today."

Freddy looked back at him with a hard stare. "Yeah?" he said. "Well, maybe you don't know everything then, huh? You're coming with us, Drake."

Charlie stood from his seat and stepped behind Arthur. Arthur said, "Not unless I hear it from Tags himself, I don't go anywhere."

"Who the fuck you think sent us?" Freddy answered. "Okay? So let's go!"

"Be that as it may . . .," Arthur began.

"Be that as it may," said Mario. "Listen to this guy."

"Yeah, he's a smart guy, all right," Freddy said. "You're coming one way or the other, Drake. So go ahead, make it the other." Arthur took a step toward him, and this time Freddy landed a fist under his chin. Arthur fell back against the table as Charlie tried to steady him.

"Hey! Hey!" Charlie cried out. "What he do?" He stepped between Arthur and Freddy. Freddy threw him aside, and Charlie crashed against the wall by the table. Slowly, he got to his feet as Arthur and Freddy grappled about the small space.

"You guys knock it off!" Charlie shouted angrily. "We got a business here!" Freddy had Arthur in a headlock and was punching him in the face as Charlie came toward him.

"Handle that little fuck, will ya?" he said, and the other two, Mario and the one face Arthur didn't recognize, began beating on Righetti. Fists came at the little man, in the abdomen and the face. Arthur, meanwhile, took a foot to his chest, which knocked him back, sitting into a chair.

"Artie!" Charlie screamed. "Artie! Why they do this?" Arthur really didn't know, nor did he have time to answer. Freddy had learned from their last encounter. He was easily getting the better of him. Another hard hit to his cheekbone had Arthur feeling dazed. He saw the other two dragging Righetti over to the cutting table, where Charlie would trim shirts and trousers. A long, sharp blade with a wooden handle projected up from the deck of the board. One of the thugs held Righetti's arm flat on the surface, the first knuckles of his fingers stretched out across the cutting edge. Arthur could only watch as one thug gripped the handle of the blade as Mario held Righetti's arm and hand in place.

Charlie's head shook in pain and fear. He said with as much calm as he could muster, "You know what you do. Why don't you just kill me?"

"Would if I could, you little shit," the thug said. As his arm fell, a black hood went over Arthur's head.

"Charlie!" Arthur tried to say through the black fabric, but it was muffled as the hood covered his mouth. He heard the chop of the blade on the table and Charlie's scream very clear. Then there was only silence.

Chapter 12

A small light flickered in Arthur's eyes. It blurred intensely as his lids fluttered against it in response. His limbs were heavy, and he was unable to bring his hands up to shield himself from that growing light. He had no sense of where he was, except that it was cold, and he thought he could hear the chirp of a thousand crickets.

"Are you awake now, Arthur?" a voice said. It was Vaughn's voice, but it sounded tense and demanding. "Finally?"

Arthur shook his head and let the light slowly clear in front of him. He was sitting at a table. The glare that had hurt his eyes so was merely a candle in the center of that table, and across him sat Brendan Vaughn. Brendan wore one of his old theatrical white gowns and an amulet bound by a heavy gold chain around his neck. It bore a design that seemed to be a symbol of the sun. Arthur had seen it before, back in the day when Brendan Vaughn fashioned himself a master of the occult. A velvet robe covered his shoulders, and he looked as he did when they had been in England, having their Black Orchid Society parties. But Brendan's face, however, was not that of a congenial host. It held no comfort for Arthur. His eyes were set in stone, and his mouth was drawn down in a tight frown. In front of him set a deep metal cup with raised letters and symbols about the rim. Arthur couldn't see what the cup held, but it was giving off an odor that caused his head to instinctively turn away.

Another voice broke out against the chirping crickets. "I want you to know, Artie, this don't come from me." It was Johnny. Giovanni Tagliani stood in an open entryway between where they sat and some other room that was too dark for Arthur to see. They were in a house, but even in Arthur's haze, he could see it was obviously unfinished. There were the makings of domesticity but none of the conveniences, including, it seemed, electricity.

"I don't usually take care of my problems this way." Tags continued with regrettable acceptance. "But Mr. Wentworth here wants this to be his play. And since this is his problem, I'm gonna let him play it. Just so we're clear, this isn't my way."

Arthur's head was still swimming. It was as if he had knocked back three stiff drinks in quick succession. He kept blinking against the candlelight as its circle of flame glowed about the table. It gave a menacing look to Brendan Vaughn as he glared at him.

Arthur said, "What are you talking about, Johnny?" He wanted to rub his jaw, where Freddy had struck him, but his hands were tightly bound with a rope, and raising them, he found that the rope led down to his ankles, also tightly bound.

Tags stood there, partially shrouded in the dark. "You tell me, Arthur," he said plainly. He lit a cigar, and that allowed Arthur to see his face in the red glow. "Why you go and bring that *stregone* into our business?"

"That what?" Arthur said.

"That devil. Whass his name? Schreck? We got him downstairs, in the cellar. What you got to do with him?"

Arthur looked at Vaughn, who answered for Tags. "Schreck, Arthur," he said. "Don't be stupid."

Arthur shook his head in vehement denial. "I got nothing to do with him, Johnny," he said plaintively. "He followed us. Both of us! From England. What was I to do about it?"

Tags sighed. He leaned his big body against the frame of the entry and hung his head. "Killing him," he said, "would have helped." Arthur could not disagree with that, so he remained silent.

"That's the thing, Arthur," Tags said. "You know, in my business, it pays to know who's watching. So I got sources, high up with the Feds. Your name keeps coming up, little bits of info here and there regarding us and our friends in Detroit."

"I wouldn't," Arthur protested.

"Maybe not," Tags concurred. "Then again, maybe so. I can't figure it, Artie. Breaks my heart. Things was so smooth there for a while, and I put that on you. But these other interests you have, they give me pause, you know? So in the best interest of business, I agreed with Mr. Wentworth. Time we parted company."

Arthur couldn't believe what he was hearing. Tags siding with Brendan? Over him? He looked at Johnny Tags hard. He hoped his earnestness would be seen by his employer. "You were convinced," he said plainly as he shot a contemptuous glance at Brendan Vaughn, "by him?"

"No, Artie" came Tags's reply. "By the *stregone* down there. I . . . can't look at him. I don't even wanna know from him, and I sure as hell don't want to talk to him, but just knowing he's there, and you're somehow jammed up with him, is all the convincing I need." Tags walked over and took an empty chair by Arthur. "I like you, Artie. But you ain't Italian. Do you know the shit I had to take to convince my partners that you were solid? And now this? If it were me alone, I'd put a quick bullet in you and be done with it. You earned it with me. But you got no name, you got no number, and this is personal for Wentworth here. Don't know why. Don't want to know. But with his name, I got cover. With you, I got nothing. I wash my hands of it."

Tags stood and turned to walk away. Then he stopped. "You know, Artie, I'm not exactly a religious man. I ain't no good at being a hypocrite. But something else is working this. I just can't figure it."

"Johnny," Arthur said as Tags took another step. It stopped the big man, and he turned one final time toward Arthur. "Charlie?" Arthur said.

Tags nodded. "He'll live," he said. "That made me mad, but I got other priorities than Carlo Righetti. I just wanted him roughed up a little. If they had to. Remind him who he was working for. BUT I DIDN'T WANT HIS GODDAMN FINGERS GONE!" Tags shouted this, so it echoed through the house. "Damn good tailor, that Carlo. But don't worry," he added softly. "I'll take care of him."

"What does that mean?" Arthur said.

"It means he's beyond your concern, Arthur," Tags replied. Then Arthur heard his heavy steps walk away, a creaking door open, and then slam shut, and suddenly, he was alone again with Brendan Vaughn.

They looked at each other. Brendan Vaughn's face took a sly, evil sneer. "Everything will be beyond your concern soon, Arthur," he said.

Arthur shot back, "You know I didn't rat."

"Oh, I know that, Arthur," Vaughn replied. "Schreck was behind it. Apparently, Schreck overcame his anxiousness regarding the telephone. Why, I cannot say. That thing downstairs in the cellar, waiting, Arthur, he is like a moth to your flame. I will never understand it. You know, he never said a word as they beat him. He just looked at me. I knew then it was not I who brought him here. Johnny knows it too. So to be rid of you both . . ." Vaughn leaned forward, resting his arm on the table. "Johnny trusts me now, Arthur. This house isn't much yet. But it's in my name. False name, I know, but still . . . that shows a certain amount of faith in me. Wouldn't you agree?"

Arthur looked around in the darkness. To his eyes, which had finally adjusted to the flickering light of the candle, it looked as if they were in a small kitchen area. An old woodstove stood in the corner with its black tin pipe leading up to an imperfect hole in the ceiling. Sawdust and wood chips surrounded its base. Cabinets had been hastily tacked onto the walls, and a wooden-framed windowpane reflected pale moonlight over a porcelain washtub.

"You like it, Arthur?" Vaughn asked pleasantly. "This is where you're going to stay, at least until we come back to bury your bones."

Arthur said nothing. In some way, he thought it very appropriate. Arthur Drake, the begotten son of a whore, a flesh merchant, a handsome thug, a gentleman killer who knew his way with prostitutes and knives but little else, an opportunist mixed up with a cheap cult. Who was he to argue that this crude end was not his due? He took his only solace in the knowledge that Charlie Righetti still lived. At least Charlie didn't pay too high a price for befriending him.

"Well," he said finally, "why don't you just get it over with then?"

"Oh, a drink first, Arthur," Vaughn said, "one last drink to see you off." Then Arthur heard the clomping of feet, two sets, coming up a flight of stairs. A moment later, he heard the familiar sound of Freddy and Mario talking. Then they themselves appeared into the opening Johnny Tags had just vacated.

"Oooh!" Freddy exclaimed. "What happened to your face? Somebody hit you?" Arthur merely looked at him. Freddy shrugged. "Lip too fat to flap, huh? That's okay. I never liked your society talk anyway." He gestured to Vaughn. "Come on, let's do it if we're doing it."

Without hesitating another moment, Freddy and Mario stepped up behind Arthur and forced his head back. Mario gripped Arthur's forehead with one hand, while his other forced his mouth open.

"Slowly, gentlemen," Vaughn said. "Please."

"Fuck you and get that stinking swill down him!" Freddy commanded. Vaughn was taken aback by the attitude. Hadn't Johnny instructed them to obey?

Freddy helped with Arthur's forehead, while Mario grabbed his chin, pinched his nose closed, and forced his jaws open from the other side. "And don't you spill any of that shit on me!" Freddy said.

"This stuff can't hurt us, can it?" Mario asked.

"Shut up, Mario!" Freddy said. "Get going, Wentworth!"

Vaughn stepped around the table with the cup in his hand. He wanted to savor this moment, but the two Italians were having none of it. Brendan rather carefully poured the thick green fluid into Arthur's open mouth. Arthur tried to move his head, but it was no use. Not even Mario's obvious disgust allowed Arthur a moment of escape. He reflexively swallowed.

"Hold him," Vaughn said. "He must take all of it."

"Hurry up!" both men cried out in unison. They didn't understand the purpose of this action. It had come from the mouth of the creep downstairs. He had bragged about it to the fat Limey, and the fat Limey had brought the plan to Tags. The maniac in the cellar had provided the details to his own execution, said it would make him immortal, said he would show Vaughn what true power he possessed. He hadn't lifted a hand to defend himself when they rushed him.

Ritual sacrifice was not the usual method of dealing death employed by any mafioso. Although both Freddy and Mario had been involved in some rather untidy and undignified disposals, this was completely out of their realm. They were, however, acutely aware of their positions as Tags's soldiers. Freddy and Mario together had decided it better to go along than risk Johnny Tags's wrath. Not that he seemed too keen on it himself. He must have feared the evil eye from the sorcerer. Even being near him, dressed as he was and looking as he did, brought up age-old fears borne out of the old country and its ancient superstitions. It was the only explanation they could think of for Johnny's consent. All in all, it was a bad business from any angle. And the sooner it was done, the sooner it could be forgotten.

When the fluid emptied and the cup was drained, they let Arthur fall forward. His head hit the table as if he was already dead, but a groan from his chest showed him to still be breathing. Arthur felt strangely outside of himself. His mind wavered into a semiconscious haze, and he was sure he would vomit; instead, he floated up out of the chair as Freddy and Mario lifted him at both ends and carried him off. He jerked like a cork in water as they descended the steps to the cellar, all the while complaining of his weight and wondering aloud if the stairs would hold. Then they rather roughly dropped him on his back. Opening his eyes for the first time since being forced to drink that terrible brew, he saw the thin form of Malcolm Schreck, trussed up with a rope, just as Arthur himself was.

Schreck murmured a few unintelligible words at his arrival. Another goblet, similarly drained, set between himself and Arthur on the surface of a wooden table. Arthur caught a whiff of the same excrement he had experienced upstairs and gagged.

"What you say, freak?" Freddy said harshly.

"Head down," Schreck groaned.

"We will get to that, Schreck," Vaughn interjected.

Freddy looked down at Schreck's feet. He tried to focus on those strange buckled shoes Schreck wore. He had no interest in looking at his face.

Arthur's fingers reached out. In the dim candlelight and with the effects of the concoction, he could barely see Schreck, but he knew he was close. He turned slightly so the tips of his fingers brushed Schreck's trouser. He pulled slightly at the fabric. "Warren," he said softly, hardly above a whisper. In his mind, he dreamed of Schreck's giant bursting through the door, roaring down the cellar steps, smashing every head against the damp cement walls of the cellar, freeing both his master and, magnanimously, Arthur as well. Warren was never far from Schreck, and his ability to overpower Freddy and

Mario could not be disputed. It gave Arthur hope to think of the silent gargantuan.

Schreck made no effort to reply to Arthur's query. He merely lay there as Arthur did in a heavy fog.

"Oh yes!" Vaughn said sharply. He had heard Arthur's plea. He walked over and roughly brought Schreck up to a sitting position. "Where is your servant, Schreck? Where is your monster? If only he were somewhere nearby." Vaughn turned to the others who stood in the dark, damp gloom of the cellar. A third man, the man who had taken Carlo's fingers now set as a watch on Schreck, stood with Freddy and Mario.

"Gentlemen," Vaughn said, full of satisfaction, "please bring out Mr. Warren."

Suddenly, a loose gray sack flew into the candlelight to land in Malcolm Schreck's lap. Even through his murky veil, Schreck reflexively steadied the sack. He could tell by the rounded shape and weight in his hands what it contained. He looked up with cold hatred at Vaughn and the Italians. As he slowly undid the bounds of the sack and allowed the opening to fall over the skull, Freddy said, "He was tough. I'll give him that. Took a lotta lead, this guy. He stood there like a bull. But when he knew it was coming . . . he looked . . . relieved."

Schreck stared down at the round head of Mr. Warren. Warren had been with him countless years. There was a slight smile on the lips that was almost angelic. It recalled to Schreck the Warren of early days before Schreck had forced him into service. Arthur could only shut his eyes against the sight. His fleeting hope had been slight to begin with and then dashed in an instant. When he opened his eyes again, he was shocked at Schreck's action. Schreck slipped himself off the corner of the dusty wooden table, cradling the head in his long, thin hands. Then he gently set it to rest between him and Arthur, facing Vaughn. With an almost wistful sadness, he slowly bent down and kissed the top of the skull.

"You know the Bible, Schreck," Vaughn interjected into this moment. "I suppose the Baptist comes to mind. How versed are you in Shakespeare?"

Schreck said nothing. He looked at Vaughn with a pure hatred tempered only by his weakness. The draught of his concoction he had willingly downed was affecting both his limbs and his sight. Arthur noticed Schreck's aged, pained face. He was feeling much the same as he lay on his side on the table. The alkaline fluid had tasted as horribly as it smelled. He could feel whatever it contained as if it was in sheer contrast to the blood pumping through his veins.

"Do something," Arthur whispered. How could it be that Schreck, who had threatened and had indeed shown himself able to unleash hell, had yet allowed himself to be overpowered and subdued by Brendan Vaughn and a few barely competent thugs? Was Warren truly the only escape? Had Schreck left his fate to the strength of one man?

"Faith," Schreck answered. "Faith, my friend."

Freddy was growing impatient. Tags waited in the back of one of the sedans, smoking, and, for all Freddy knew, weeping over the death of the smartass Limey. Neither Freddy nor Mario nor the Detroit representative, whom Freddy neither knew nor cared to know, had any clue as to why Tags had agreed to this cruel, strange ritual. *Shoot them,* Freddy thought, *and be done with it.* But Tags had agreed, and for the moment, they were forced to wait on vain, fat Limey, this blue-blooded asshole who apparently wanted to savor the demon's torture.

The state of Freddy's faith, as with the other hoodlums, was in dispute. Their lives to that point had not been done in service to any lord but only the next higher up in the hierarchy of their chosen field. They did, however, have mothers, and to a one, those mothers had tried to instill in their sons some sense of religious faith, some knowledge of the risen Lord. And in that dark cellar, with the prospect of assisting in some arcane ritual, it was Freddy's mother who chastised him. He apologized silently to her. If there was grace waiting in the life beyond, Freddy knew his own choices had denied it to him. But still, it made him queasy to think of his poor mother looking down on him now, about to do this terrible thing.

"What's next?" he asked Vaughn harshly. "Let's get on with it. I don't like this shit. You like it, Mario?"

Mario shook his head, disgusted.

Freddy looked at the Detroit rep. "You like it?"

Detroit affirmed the negative silently.

"You see, Mr. Wentworth," Freddy said, "we may do the devil's work. But we don't worship no devil."

Schreck chuckled in the dim light. "Your acolytes seem unwilling, Lord Vaughn," he said as he leaned against the table facing them. "Loosen my bonds, and I will make believers of them."

Vaughn bent over and grasped the handle of the large black satchel at his feet, Schreck's own bag containing both the secrets and tools of his trade. Vaughn lifted it to his ample belly. He reached in and brought out Malcolm Schreck's familiar book, the old, dusty tome that the lanky snake had brought to Lord Vaughn's estate upon their first encounter. The book was heavy, almost leaden, and its leather binding, which had odd raised impressions upon the face, was frayed through long years of handling and use. But Vaughn had perused it earlier, soon after Schreck's capture, and he knew the secret it contained.

"I highly doubt it, Schreck," he said in response to Malcolm's request, "since I don't believe it myself." He opened the book and began thumbing through its pages.

"Why did you not mention, Schreck?" Vaughn announced triumphantly. "There's nothing in this bloody book! Page after page! Not a word! Not a letter! There is no ancient knowledge in some dark and forbidden tongue! You charlatan! You common actor! You misshapen, bloody fraud!"

Schreck merely chuckled at this outburst and allowed his body to fall weakly back on the table, a dark reflection of Arthur Drake, their heads almost meeting as the top of a triangle, while the disembodied head of Mr. Warren rested quietly between them. The candlelight from long, thin wax sticks flickered above them, throwing light and dark in a wild dance.

What happened then occurred dreamlike in Arthur's mind. He could hear people speaking, but it was as if from a great distance. He felt a swaying motion overtake him, but there was no pain in the experience. He felt grappled with and jostled about, and his coat and shirt ripped off his shoulders unceremoniously, baring his chest to the cold air. But he had no control over the slightest muscle. Dimly, he was aware of being turned upside down as his blurry vision made out the shape of dark black shoes near his head.

"What, a normal blade won't do it, huh?" Freddy said as he looked over the pair of ornately modeled knives, the blades bent like waves upon the edges.

"Out of respect for the art," Vaughn replied. He handed one to Freddy, handle first. "If you would, please," he said. "Mr. Drake was a friend. I wish it hadn't come to this. If you could . . ."

Freddy looked from Vaughn to the blade. Then he looked at his companions, who waited to see what he would do with quiet tension. He turned his eyes to Drake, who hung by his feet from wooden rafters, his arms still connected by a rope to his ankles. He didn't like the man. He had humiliated Freddy in the tailor's shop. But still, the way this was turning held a special dread for him. He crossed himself and took a step toward the dangling figure.

"In the heart, please," Vaughn said absently. Schreck had given these instructions, albeit with the certainty that Mr. Warren would provide the result. How he was to do that would remain a mystery to Vaughn, but it was a moot point since he had decided that it was all a well-rehearsed farce between master and man. Mr. Warren was undoubtedly supposed to have overpowered Schreck's kidnappers. The ruse had been created merely to buy time. But there was no time left for Schreck, and the ruse would have to be played out for Brendan Vaughn's satisfaction alone. At its core, the act would be Vaughn's final foray into the mysteries of occult knowledge. In essence, however, he looked upon it as revenge, revenge upon Schreck for belittling him and making him feel weak and revenge upon Arthur for being Schreck's chosen acolyte. In reality, it was nothing. It was purely a grotesque play of murder, nothing more.

As the two men stood facing the suspended bodies of their victims, Freddy looked over at the determined face of Brendan Vaughn. Vaughn slipped the collar of Schreck's black frock aside and, with his fingers, searched for the space at the left breast, where Schreck's heart would be. Schreck pliantly moved at Vaughn's touch, swaying as his falling hair brushed the top of the table. As a pupil silently mimicking his instructor, Freddy did the same to Arthur Drake.

"You gotta say anything?" he asked of Vaughn. The two hanging men were as silent as the dead; not a gurgle of resistance came from them.

"No need," Vaughn said and plunged the point of the blade slowly into Schreck's breast. Schreck moved a bit from the force, but his body weight did most of the work for Vaughn as the sharp blade slid effortlessly through his rib cage to the organ those ribs protected.

Freddy did the same to Arthur Drake and immediately sidestepped the blood that spurted from the wound.

Blood flowed out with the removal of the knives and scattered in waves on the damp cement floor. It washed over both men's faces, turning them to a red veil. Both Vaughn and Freddy stepped back from it as every living soul in the dank basement considered the repellant display. They watched as the blood began to quickly pool on the floor, the two men's fluids joining together in one large puddle, small streams of it finding cracks to flow out of the main. They watched until the drips slowed. When it was finally deemed manageable, Mario and the Detroit man walked behind the bodies, stood upon the table, and cut the ropes at the men's ankles. They were careful not to allow the bodies to hit the floor. The soldiers dropped to the floor behind the table, gripping the bound legs of the two victims. They appeared quite dead. Their blood-streaked faces showed no sign of the terrible end they had just met. As peaceful a repose as if they had died content in their beds at the end of a full life instead of as they had in a botched, darkly pagan ritual.

For Arthur, the last thing he felt was the warm, sticky fluid washing down his face. He hadn't known what it was or why it felt so strange, but neither could he think of any of the events that led to it. He remembered the image of Malcolm Schreck momentarily, the ghostly image of a death mask. And he remembered Brendan Vaughn in much the same way. But there was no pain or fear that he understood; there was only darkness. *A rather complete darkness*, he thought. It was only after a long, long time, as the darkness remained, did the fear come.

Interlude

Brendan Vaughn, as Mr. Wentworth, sat on a small charter boat in the big lake, heading from the western coast of Michigan to the eastern coast of Illinois to Chicago. There, he would join Johnny Tags for a new venture and, finally, be somewhere out of the quiet farm country of Michigan. The bustle of the Windy City awaited him. He welcomed it. Though he was plagued every so often with pangs for his old, recently departed friend, Arthur Drake, his own private Judas, life began again. Tags had been very cordial to him following the proceedings. The deaths had been necessary, and Tags, having allowed them to be led by Vaughn, had shown a respect for the English lord that he had always thought missing from the relationship. Arthur had held that position of respect before Schreck had mysteriously arrived. With them both rotting in that tiny cellar space, Brendan Vaughn could finally resume the stature they had stolen from him.

For a reason not fully articulated to Vaughn, Tags had declined to join him in the crossing. And that was where the pangs came into play. Brendan Vaughn found himself on a boat with nothing but Italians much younger than himself and some unnamed captain of the vessel, who had merely nodded in Vaughn's direction when he had stepped on at the dock.

Vaughn was the lone Englishman, and he longed for a fellow Brit's conversation. The Italians, Freddy and Mario, consistently spoke either Italian to each other or some American slang that Brendan could not quite follow. And the respect that Tags had shown seemed remarkably absent from these two. He decided he would have to talk to Johnny about it when they arrived.

Freddy, who was obviously the lead soldier of the two young men, had shown nothing but contempt for the whole idea of disposing of Arthur Drake and Malcolm Schreck, at least in the fashion Brendan Vaughn had insisted upon. The men were dead, of course, which was the primary need, and their bodies disposed of in a small potato cellar in the basement. They were tossed in a corner, and a small metal-framed window above them allowed a slivered rectangle of light into the room. Arthur went in first with Schreck's body dropped limply onto Arthur's chest as if the two were lovers who had died in each other's arms. Detroit had rolled the giant's head in between their legs as an afterthought. Then he shut the half door they had struggled to bend their bodies through as they dragged the dead men in and padlocked the coupling with a small keylock.

As they were leaving, Mario noticed the book and Schreck's bag. They had been meaning to throw it all in together but had somehow forgotten these items. They had even forgotten the two blades, which they had casually thrown nearby. Everyone seemed rushed now that the deed was done. They were ready to be gone from this hole. The plan was to return at some time to dispose of the bodies more permanently.

"Hey, Wentworth," Mario said, "you want any of this shit?"

Vaughn looked down at the bag Mario indicated with his shoe. "No," he answered. "Why would I want it?"

Mario smirked. "I don't know," he said. "I usually keep somethin'. Memento, ya know?"

Vaughn raised his hands in front of his face and shook his head. "No, no, no," he protested. "I need no reminders, thank you."

Freddy's hand then suddenly came up and gave him a hard slap on the shoulder. "Let's get the fuck out of here then!" he barked.

Vaughn was surprised at the abruptness shown to him but followed the command nonetheless. Mario took a candle and extinguished the others, and they stepped up and out of the basement.

And now a few days after, they were on a small boat heading west in the dark. An hour into the trip, the Italians became silent. They went about gathering some kind of supplies as Vaughn sat in the stern. He heard the clanking of heavy metal as it hit the deck in front of him. A long, heavy chain and a couple of cement cinder blocks were positioned at his feet. Vaughn looked up at the two men. Before he could ask a question of what the purpose of these items were, he saw Freddy pointing a revolver at him.

"In case you were wondering, Little Lord Fauntleroy," he said, "this is how you do it."

The gun fired, and Vaughn's body jerked a bit. He heard the beginnings of some minor argument about the gas tank and then a crude comment about his weight. And then as Arthur Drake had warned some century ago, Brendan Vaughn found out just how deep Lake Michigan really was.

Chapter 13

The light was very distant. It was all Arthur could do to even recognize it as a light. It had been pitch dark for an eternity it seemed, and yet there now was the light. He was already beyond panic. That had come instantly when he realized he was in the complete and all-consuming darkness. That panic lasted interminably, the endless screaming. It rang in his ears on and on, echoing, until he finally realized it was his own helpless cries he was hearing. It went on and on until the din of it collapsed from exhaustion, and he dreamed.

Nightmares, visions of Malcolm Schreck clawing at him in the darkness. Schreck's black eyes were frantic; his teeth and nails had grown animalistic and savage, all the while growling some foreign gibberish, where only Arthur's own name was recognizable to him. And then there was Brendan Vaughn floating in the darkness, his arms held up, suspended by nothing visible, the body turning toward him, flesh of Brendan's face hanging in stringlike threads, floating, floating. Brendan's eye sockets were being burrowed out by slick slithering creatures, a sickening, horrific display ever playing, one after another, until Arthur grew almost immune to the terrible repetitive performance.

Then the light came mercifully, yet it held no warmth. But it came upon him, and he looked down suddenly to see his legs walking in it. The light became a sidewalk, and the sidewalk went up and up at a steep incline. On his right was the cobblestoned street, and on his left were the houses and buildings all built perpendicular into the hill. This was familiar to him. He was familiar; his body and this trek up the steep hill were all in his memory. He was himself again but young, much younger, and what was more, he knew where he was going. He had to collect. Collection day had come again. He wished for what seemed the thousandth time his mom was not inclined to give credit to locals. But she always did. She could go soft like that sometimes. They were locals, she said, with no fortunes to be spent elsewhere in this town, and their credit was good. They would pay the young boy with the round, hairless face, and nobody would protest. If they dared, they would find someone bigger and more threatening at their doorstep.

Arthur didn't mind getting out of the dank, smelly house. It was summertime, and the scent of saltwater mixed with fifteen varieties of perfume, sex, and cigar smoke was stifling in the seaside house. At least in the outdoors, that scent was relieved for a brief time. The farther away from the water he got, the more clear the air seemed to be. But the incline was very steep, and he was relieved to see the side of St. Paul's Cathedral at the first crest. It was his first stop, and the hill would go on up another two times before it finally reached its summit. The rest at St. Paul's would be a welcome one.

There were a number of priests at St. Paul's with whom Arthur had become acquainted. There was only one, though, who found himself unable to resist the charms of Arthur's home. He was a regular with irregular needs, at least for one of God's representatives. His mom called him Father Randy, although his actual name was Father Barry. He was a transplanted Irishman, serving the San Francisco community, and he came to the brothel to be serviced in return. It struck nobody there as odd that he would come in with a small suitcase in plain clothes, change into his black gown and white collar in an anteroom, and meet with one of the whores dressed as a nun to take her "confession."

What was beginning to strike Arthur himself as odd was that any man would attempt to deny himself those natural needs to begin with. Arthur at fourteen was already stealing away with one of the younger girls in their downtime to play with budding breasts and allow soft hands to reach into his trousers. How any man could swear off such pleasures for a belief in a great, unseen deity was beyond him. He hadn't even taken a blade to his face yet, and already, he understood the futility of that plan. His first goal, outside collecting the money, that is, was to get to that soft, plush hair between the young girl's thighs. A few more strikes at it and he would succeed. He was sure it was a magnificent heaven there and likely the only bit of heaven he would ever know.

But all such thoughts came to an abrupt halt as he turned the corner and reached the short flight of steps to the church's doors. There, at the front of the massive doors, stood Father Tom. Arthur shuddered. Of all the priests who walked in and out of those doors, Father Tom was the one whom Arthur least wanted to see. It made him suddenly wish that his mother had bothered with the foresight to send some muscle with him on his collection route. Father Tom was not a customer, and though he did not show any outward sign of disapproval toward Arthur, neither did he show any warmth. For a priest, he had a decidedly hard look about him. He was a large man, to young Arthur at least, his age about sixty or so, and his balding head was proportionate to his size. His eyebrows were arched, giving him a menacing look, and his voice had a deep, unaffectionate tone. Arthur could not imagine that his sermons were very comforting, given that unforgiving timbre. His hands were rough as well, thick fingers with a strength and texture belonging more to a carpenter or a sailor than to a man who had spent years gently perusing the pages of the Bible. Arthur attempted to walk toward him as if he was not there at all. It was a show of determination for him alone. He held no fantasy of intimidating Father Tom.

"Hello, Arthur," the priest intoned flatly. If there was an accent to his voice, Arthur didn't recognize it. It came out and stopped like a door slammed shut.

Arthur looked up and smiled weakly. "Oh," he said, "hello, Father. I just came to see Father Ran . . . I mean, Father Barry. He said he wanted to talk to me about something."

Father Tom looked down at him, unimpressed. "I know why you're here, Arthur," he said. "You can't come in."

"Not even for confession?" Arthur asked. Now he really wished his mother had sent some muscle with him. It was usually easy for Arthur since playing tough had been part of his natural upbringing to intimidate these Christian types. Even a boy could muster it against the naive and guileless worshippers of God. But it was Father Tom who did the intimidating here.

Father Tom looked over Arthur's head to the street. It was as if he would not even deign to look at the boy. "You are well past the time for confessing your sins, my son," he said.

Arthur shook his head. "Come on, Father," he said. "I'm only fourteen. God ain't gave me no time to sin that much. Not as much as Father RANDY." He said the name forcefully. Perhaps pushing the issue would succeed where subtlety had not. Father Tom was no fool. Surely he was aware of his brethren's habits. And Arthur had no intention of returning to his mom with a cent less than what was accounted for him to collect.

"Don't know where you are, do you, Arthur?" said the priest.

"Sure I do," Arthur answered.

"I'd say not," the priest answered, brutally short. "In fact, I'd say you haven't a clue. But that's expected."

Then as Arthur looked around, he saw all the surroundings that had brought him to those parish steps disappear until only the priest and the huge doors behind him remained. It took Arthur's breath away, and he looked down to see his boy's hands had become man sized, and the clothes he had worn as a boy became the clothes he had worn as a man. Arthur started to shake. What before had been a dark nothingness was now a great blinding light, obscuring all but the priest and the door behind his large darkly dressed frame.

Father Tom looked down at Arthur from the top of the step. His face was entirely devoid of feeling as was his deep, intractable voice. "Now you remember," he said, "don't you?"

Arthur nodded but was unable to speak. Father Tom's large rough hand came down upon his shoulder, and Arthur looked at it as if the very weight of it would crush him. Father Tom said, "You are well past the time of confession or fear, Arthur Drake." Arthur closed his eyes. He felt tears overcoming him, and he convulsed under the priest's hand.

"But not pain," Father Tom said, and this time the words came not without some empathy. "There is much pain left yet for you to endure. But let your pain go for now, my son," he said. "Like all you've known before, there is nothing more that it can do for you here."

Arthur's heavy breathing finally subsided, and he looked at the face of Father Tom, whose harsh, menacing glare showed a glimmer of understanding. It brought Arthur some hope as memories of his life and death crashed together into his consciousness.

"Who are you?" Arthur asked. "You can't be Father Tom. Father Tom must be long dead."

"No," the priest replied, "I am not Father Tom. Though it serves the purpose, and so we are one." There was a moment of silence between them, and the man said, "Shall we soften the view for a moment, Arthur?"

Arthur looked about and found the scene had changed to a more peaceful setting of a long pier extending endlessly outward, a sandy beach, and waves from some unknown water washing over white sand. Gulls cried out over the sounds of the water. *If this is a dream,* Arthur thought, *it sure as hell beat the visions that had been assailing me moments or years before.*

"All right," Arthur said, "where are we?"

"Nowhere in particular," Father Tom replied. The two of them began to walk along the pier as the white light of a sun came down on their shoulders. Arthur found his feet suddenly bare, and he could feel the warm, damp wood soften under the pressure of his soles.

"Mr. Schreck was quite successful, wasn't he?" the man Arthur saw as Father Tom suddenly ventured. The words came with a mixture of resignation and something like pride, so much so that Arthur looked at him, preparing himself for the priest to change form into Schreck. Whatever this vision was, Arthur still held little trust for it.

"This is no dream, Arthur," the priest said finally, reading Arthur's pensive look clearly. "And have no fear. I am not Malcolm Schreck."

"Where is he?" Arthur asked.

"Mr. Schreck's cup runneth over in its own way, my son," the man answered. "He won't trouble us here."

"If you're not him," Arthur said, "and you're not Father Tom, who are you, sir?"

At that, the man chuckled, and it would have been a warm chuckle had it not come from the voice of Father Tom. "I am the one who has need of you, my son," he said. "Malcolm Schreck is a minor disturbance within the greater plans of the world, yet he is one who requires a final resolution. I require you to bring that resolution, Arthur."

Arthur could barely believe what he was hearing. It seemed unlikely that Malcolm Schreck could pose any more of a threat than he could himself. "Why not leave him where he is?" Arthur asked. "He can't do any harm there, can he?"

"Were that part of the plan, it is where you would remain as well, back to the darkness," Father Tom replied. "Is that your wish?"

Arthur shook his head. The waves continued to crash onto the beach, and the cool breeze from the water brushed over his ankles. "But what can I do?" he protested. "I couldn't do anything about him before. He's a devil, you know? I'm just a man. I can't do a bloody thing about Malcolm Schreck."

"Nevertheless, Arthur," the priest said, "this is what we ask of you. Mr. Schreck has delayed his judgment far too long a time for any one soul. Were it not for the path he chose, he could be admired for the power of his will alone. And in truth, Malcolm Schreck could state a good reason for that path. Nothing is done without reason. But he, like every other human being who walks upon the earth, was given a choice—life or death. His choice was death. So it must be."

Father Tom stopped and faced Arthur. The priest's brown eyes were very sharp and centered on his. "This, my son, does not come to you lightly. You too were imparted with free will as a man, Arthur. The same will be given you again."

Arthur looked at Father Tom, suddenly overcome with anger. He had no wish to face Malcolm Schreck in this life or the next. If he were only to stay here, he could at least be at peace. Why throw him back to some new horror? Wouldn't it only be a damned repetition of what had come before?

"I could stay here with you," Arthur said, tears welling in his eyes. "That would be my choice. Why can't I just stay?"

Father Tom smiled. "The plan, Arthur," he replied. "There is a plan, remember?"

"To hell with your plan!" Arthur said indignantly.

Father Tom's smile remained. "The possibility of that is what we endeavor to avoid. Your part in the plan, Arthur, is not yet finished."

The look in the priest's eyes stifled any further objection from Arthur. It said no argument would move him. Arthur looked about as the scene began to fade. Now a dark pinpoint no larger than the light had been earlier suspended in the distance behind the large man. Arthur saw it and instinctively knew the conversation was soon coming to a close. He looked angrily at the priest.

"I don't suppose you'll give me any more help, will you? As if you ever did before," he said bitterly.

Father Tom reached out and brushed Arthur's hair back with his rough hand. "Yes, Arthur," he said calmly. "But just as before, you will not recognize it."

The darkness returned then and engulfed him. The experience Arthur had just known washed away completely in the black void. Only a memory of the moment remained. And somehow Arthur took comfort in it.

Chapter 14

The year of our Lord 1991 began with a war. In the annals of war, this particular conflict would not amount to much, except perhaps as a minor prelude to more dire consequences. But that would be realized much later. This war was set in the Persian Gulf and so was soon to be remembered as Gulf War I or, as the relatively new concept of the twenty-four-hour news cycle in America referred to it, Operation Desert Storm.

In the summer of the previous year, a rather thuggish dictator of Iraq few in America had heard of named Saddam Hussein made plans to invade his neighboring state of Kuwait. Since the United States and many other Western nations had built up Iraq's defensive capability to aid in its war against another neighbor, Iran, it should have surprised no one that Saddam would then use that capability to invade another territory he considered as his own.

Saddam Hussein had styled himself on another infamous dictator, Adolf Hitler. In ruthless barbarity and relentless drive for power, the imitation could have been seen as flattering to the little son of Austria. Unfortunately for Saddam, unlike the Fuhrer, he was unable to even temporarily convince the rest of the world that he meant no harm. Perhaps this was all because of racial and cultural differences between the West and the Muslim world. Or perhaps it was just that the man seemed to grin much wider when people were in pain, trembling in fear, and suffering. In any event, there was also the fact that Saddam Hussein was a terrible bluffer, and so the American president, George Herbert Walker Bush, in reference to Kuwait, stated formally that "this aggression will not stand."

The war began on January 17, 1991. It arose quickly and brought about the usual fears. The specter of Vietnam, not so distant then, always came into play when such events occurred. Talk of resuming the draft was almost immediate. There was also the not so illogical fear of Armageddon-like destructive force being unleashed since Saddam Hussein gave off a quality of someone who enjoyed pushing buttons. Whether he knew what a particular button would do seemed a rather irrelevant point to him. But Hussein was worthy of neither fear, the draft or the bomb, since in just over a month, his forces were pushed out of Kuwait, and they limped back to Baghdad. Americans could watch it all from the safety of their homes on the television.

President Bush rode a high wave of approval right into summer. American losses were beyond minimal in comparison to other conflicts. Just over a hundred troops were killed. More than a few of these were noncombat related. Though every loss mattered deeply to the country, a collective sigh of relief was soon issued. Fear turned to distinct pride across party lines as reruns played daily, and the incredible technical advancements and proficiency of the military proved to the country that America was still the supreme leader when it came to warfare. Bush's approval ratings hummed at around 90 percent in the summer months as the Democrats jousted for which candidate would challenge him for the highest office in November that following year. Most believed by the end of summer, it wouldn't matter whom they chose. The elder President Bush had firmly put the genie, Saddam Hussein, back in his bottle.

None of this, however, was on the minds of the three young friends driving through the rough and rarely trod Michigan territory on a chilly October afternoon in 1991. Ben Whittinger, sitting in the back seat of his childhood friend's, David Wallace's, Jeep, knew it for fact that George Bush was a milquetoast. He had no deep political convictions himself, but twelve years under Republican rule was more than enough. He had been born into a Union Democrat family, and voting *R* under any circumstance made no sense to him. All that mattered to him now was keeping the seat under him.

"Jesus, Dave!" he shouted over the radio. "What's the rush?"

David Wallace's eyes reflected blurrily in the rearview mirror. A pointless accessory, the rearview mirror only showed a hazy image of Ben bouncing in the back seat. The vinyl top of the Jeep had an opaque plastic back window, which was nearly impossible to see through.

"You want to beat the rain, don't ya?" he called back.

Ben had no answer to that. It wasn't the prospect of rain that was sloshing the beer and pulled pork sandwiches around in his belly; it was Dave's choice of route. Somebody might have driven a vehicle here before, but it was before the maples had grown around the track and all the dips and valleys that had obviously been dug by Mother Nature, not by man. Ben looked at the young woman in the passenger seat, watching her as she laughed and groaned simultaneously. Dave's girlfriend, Sherry Adams, had been introduced to her beau by Ben himself, although it hadn't been Ben's idea. His idea had been more in tune to having Sherry for himself, but as in all things, he had admitted defeat stoically in public and drunkenly in private. She looked back at him and smiled.

"Having fun?" she asked in a high, jerky voice.

Ben merely scrunched his face up at her in a mocking smile and nodded. She giggled in response. Ben felt lucky in these moments as it was just as likely that Sherry could be with some other guy who was not Ben's close friend, and he would never have opportunities to see her laugh. They worked in the same hospital. Although not together, that was where they had met. But luckily, Sherry had taken a day job in the laboratory, and Ben was still making rounds in the transport department on second shift. He no longer had to walk around the place with his heart in his throat, expecting to run into her at every turn. Amazingly, he was much calmer now that she was with David. It took a certain edge off his gut anyway.

Suddenly, the Jeep lurched forward and came to a stop. Ben grunted as he instinctively put his hand on Dave's backrest to stop himself from landing up front. They all looked out the window at the large limb blocking their path.

"Come on," Dave said, "let's get it out of the way."

"How much farther is it?" Sherry asked.

"Not too far," he answered, "I don't think, but farther than I want to walk, especially if it starts pouring."

Ben pushed the back of the seat forward and threw himself out the door. He was only twenty-four years old, but thirty minutes in the back of the Jeep made him feel much older. He leaned his head on his forearm on top of the Jeep cover and breathed heavily. He looked over and saw Dave grabbing the thicker part of the limb and was thankful for that. He stepped to the smaller, lighter end and lifted, while Dave did the heavy work. He took a moment to wave and smile at the girl in the Jeep. Why not?

Haunted houses were all the rage at this time of year, and Dave Wallace had the ingenious idea of going to a real one, uninhabited by people dressed in *Planet of the Apes* and *Dracula* costumes. David worked as an assistant to a real estate agent, working toward his own license, and this previously unknown property was finally going up for sale. The state, apparently, had declined to purchase it as an addition to the twenty million acres of public land it already controlled.

Aerial photographs had plotted out the remote wooded plot in which two and a half acres had been owned by a man named Wentworth. Rumor had it that Mr. Wentworth was merely a false name, and the man had been an English lord during WWII. He had bought the property and built the house as a hideaway for gangsters way back at the end of the war. What had happened to him, nobody could say. But the deed sat in a file for years and years until finally, the company David worked for bought all the deeds from whatever company had previously owned them. David's boss, the agent he assisted, showed him the aerial photos, stating that the house would likely come down soon as it was clearly uninhabitable. David looked at the shoddy two-story structure and saw only the perfect opportunity to scare the hell out of his girlfriend. David had an instinct that secretly, a scare sometimes opened legs easier than flowers did. He had no idea if they could even get into the house, but the look of it was unnatural and so a perfect recipe for a Halloween excursion. Ben, of course, had just happened to be along for the ride.

The two young men got back into the vehicle, and they drove on, continuing to bounce on the uneven terrain. They drove about another five minutes before another tree blocked their way. This, however, they were not going to move as it was the full and thick limb of an oak tree. It didn't matter. Rising above the downed limb was the old, rotted house.

The three friends looked out the windshield and up at the dilapidated structure. After a silent moment of staring, Ben Whittinger exclaimed, "Holy moly!"

"What did I tell you?" said David. It was everything he could have hoped for with the purpose of the excursion. Whoever had built the house had been ambitious; that was clear. It must have been meant to hold quite a few men. But now it stood like a shipwreck in a sea of tall, uncut grass and weeds, listing to the right as they faced it. The windows, if they held any glass at all, were broken and single-paned. The sills and siding were all made of faded gray wood, the years and the seasons warping here and wilting there, the paint hanging piecemeal where it hadn't yet molded completely through. Much of the siding was not flush, and large holes had developed through water damage and wear. Looking at it, it was as if the hand of God had smacked it but failed to knock it down.

Ben noticed first the listing to the right. It was like a drunk stumbling a few steps out of a bar and leaning against a lamppost to keep from falling outright on the ground.

"What the hell is holding it up?" he asked incredulously. The three had stepped out of the Jeep. Dave helped Sherry over the large fallen trunk that lay in front of the box grill, reaching almost to the headlights. Ben followed after and soon found his question answered. Looking up to the shattered roof, he could see another large tree, halved near the top of the building, a huge branch reaching through the sparse shingles like a giant arm diving into a pickle barrel. The limb had obviously come to rest somewhere inside the structure, the weight of the tree both shifting it to the right and simultaneously saving it from falling.

The three friends looked at it quietly from a distance. Sherry rubbed her own arms as a chill went through her body. Thankfully, none of them had been fooled by the early morning sunshine and had brought warmer clothes for the trip. David had dressed much too nice, of course. It was his habit to always look good, no matter the circumstance, and his sense of style was attractive but not necessarily always practical. Ben, on the other hand, wore a weathered green Carhartt imitation he had casually picked up at the supermarket.

He had worn it for years since just after high school, and the coat had taken those years well, but its collar and cuffs had taken the brunt. Loose thread lay on his shoulders and in his hands. He had never been one for fashion. Sherry herself wore one of David's old university sweatshirts, its large letter *W* pushed out by her breasts. In both men's opinion, Sherry could make a bundle of rags look good.

Still watching to see if the old house would fall in the rising wind, Sherry said, "Ben, have you called Lorraine yet?"

Ben shook his head. "No," he said flatly, still staring in awe at the old gangster hideout.

"Why not?" she asked, sharply slapping at his arm. Finally, something was able to draw her attention from the house. Ben looked back at her, merely shaking his head, his face unmoved by either the question or her light slap on his arm. David had walked ahead a bit to examine the corners of the house and look at the rotting door, which, though closed, hung limply on one hinge. Sherry took the opportunity to strike Ben's arm with more force.

"Come on!" she said. "Tell me!"

"Oww!" he said. Ben took his hand and grabbed Sherry's upper sleeve. He pulled her toward him as Dave continued to examine the door. Ben kept his voice to just above a whisper and said, "Well, she's kind of a bitch, ain't she?"

Sherry looked shocked. "What?" she protested. "That's not fair, Ben. She is always asking about you," she said adamantly. "She's very concerned about you."

Ben Whittinger smiled thinly. "Well, I didn't say she was an evil bitch," he said, "just a bitch."

Sherry sighed. "You're terrible, Ben."

Ben nodded his assent. It was likely that he was terrible, for as cute as Lorraine had been, she had truly shown concern for him. She had been concerned about his clothes, his drinking, his marijuana, his musical and movie taste, and his sleeping habits. In the two times he had seen her, Ben had come to a realization. He knew that relationships were often prisons of their own making. He had hoped to one day look up and see that the bars had surrounded him over time and to view them as a pleasant comfort. But he did not bargain to take a very short walk to his own cell willingly. And his fleeting time with Lorraine had been much like that. Perhaps he was being unfair. A good woman like Lorraine might see him as a project. And under the right circumstance, he could allow himself to be fixed. But he hadn't taken to Lorraine's sale pitch. He had once seen his father throw a young salesman out the door with more force than the young man probably deserved. Ben himself hadn't been that harsh but, like his father, had just not wanted to hear the close. He also understood, with a lingering disappointment, that the young woman presently at his side had a significant hold on him, more than he would care to admit.

David Wallace's voice brought them both back to the current situation. It was getting late in the afternoon, and the clouds had grown immense and dark. There was the earthy smell of rain in the air when Dave said, "Come on, you two. Let's go inside and check it out."

Dave's voice was excited as if with a child's enthusiasm for a theme park ride. His two companions were unable to share his feelings, however, and stood there, unmoving.

Sherry looked at him. "Are you crazy?" she said.

"Nooo!" he answered, shaking his head vigorously. "It would be crazy to drive all this way and NOT go in, Sherry."

"Well, I'm for being crazy then," Ben chimed in. "How about you, sweets?"

Sherry giggled. "Uh-huh."

Dave put his hand on the old knob, planted his shoulder to the door, and shoved. Something in the old house groaned in protest, and Ben Whittinger and Sherry Adams stepped back in response. They waited a moment, ready to run if the old house folded like stacked cards. When it didn't, Dave poked his head out from inside.

"Come on then," he said with a mischievous grin. "Door's open."

Chapter 15

Ben ran back suddenly to the Jeep as low, rumbling thunder rolled overhead. It would be getting dark soon, and he thought it prudent to have a flashlight. He grabbed the long black Maglite that rested between the two front seats and caught up with his friends as David was helping Sherry through the open door. He had pushed aside a heavy cobweb with the opening of the door, and Sherry did her best to avoid any of the remnants that clung over the top. The floorboards creaked and bent under their weight, and Sherry grabbed Dave's arm to steady herself as Ben stepped in behind her. The three of them stood inside with the door left half open in case an escape became suddenly necessary. Just as another round of thunder boomed, they heard the patter of rain outside.

"Great timing as usual, Dave," Ben said.

"Yeah," Sherry agreed. "But if I see a spider anywhere, I'm out of here, rain or no rain." Looking about the entryway, it was impossible not to imagine a large furry arachnid or several making their way upon their handiwork. Webs stretched from corner to corner, some places floating in the soft breeze, untethered from wherever they had once been connected. It was possible from the sight that they too had been here for many years, used and reused until they broke, and new highways were built in place of old.

The floor plan was simple. The left entryway led to some kind of galley-size kitchen and dining room just off from it; the corner of a dust and web-covered old table was visible from where they stood. To the right was another opening that led to a living room of some kind. There was a rotting easy chair in the room, sitting in front of an unfinished fireplace, the bricks crumbling off the wall as it reached up and out of the ceiling. Everything, every surface, appeared untouched for what must have been many years. An accumulation of dust and webs covered all. A small iron grate sat in front of the fireplace, empty of wood, just the black maw of the opening behind it. And directly ahead, a flight of steps led upward, webs and dust covering it like white fluffy sand. There was a landing up top that led to the left, two closed doors leading to extra rooms or closets visible from below. Under the landing was a wall that ended with a space for a door, which was partially open. It was either a door to a closet or perhaps steps leading down to a cellar. In either case, none of the three were entirely sure how to go forward as a hole had been dug in the floor, a product of years where rain and snow had fallen from the limb of the tree that had crashed through the roof. The large limb breached the roof and hung there like an elbow in search of a table. Water began to drip off it anew as they watched it run down the limb to the bend of the elbow and land on the soft, rotted wood of the floor.

"Gangster house, huh?" Ben asked as he looked over the plain, relatively unfurnished structure.

"That's the story," David answered, putting his arm around Sherry's shoulder. "Guy named Johnny Toe-tags or something like that. You ever heard of him?" Ben frowned and shook his head and continued to scan the surroundings. He took a cautious step forward, careful of the weak spot in front of him. He hadn't turned the flashlight on yet, but the impending darkness would come quickly as the rain held forth a bit stronger. Thunder continued to accompany it like heavy, leaden music.

"I don't think we should be standing too close together," he said as his foot searched for support on the floor.

Dave looked at Sherry and smiled at the look of anxiety on her pretty face. This was the exact reaction he had hoped for, and he was determined to make the most of it. "Let's spread out," he suggested to Ben. "Since you've got the flashlight, why don't you check downstairs?

We'll go up and see what's up there." He motioned to the steps, which although old and covered with webs, seemed sturdy enough. He was eager to explore.

"I don't think so," Sherry offered. She had no intention of leaving the spot where she stood until the two men were back to leave. It was creepy in the house and dangerous as far as she could tell. If she had any influence on the boys, she would have advised leaving well enough alone. But both of them would want to look, of course. Her only hope was that the rest of the place was as empty as it appeared from this spot. The two of them could look for the bloodstained floors and brain-splattered walls if they wanted; she was staying put where she was.

David kissed her. "Okay," he said, "we'll be quick."

Sherry nodded. "Better be," she said. "Please be careful. Both of you."

Ben plotted a course to the opening to the kitchen and stuck his head inside. The table was old, topped with white Formica, cracking at the edges where it met the metal rim. There were a few old chairs with rusted steel legs that hadn't been totally destroyed over the years with weather-cracked seat pads and backrests. He left the sight and edged his way close to the wall to where the old door stood cracked open. He looked up as Dave too was hugging the wall, knocking down the cobwebs as he stepped gingerly up the steps to the landing. He shot a glance at Sherry, who seemed unable to decide which of her friends to be concerned more for as she looked from one to the other.

Ben waited for her to focus on him. "If anything happens," he said with a light smile, "I'll scream."

"You scream, I scream," she answered.

David Wallace said on cue, "We all scream for ice cream."

The boards creaked under each man's every step, and Dave, at almost the top, began seriously to question the wisdom of continuing. He held a finger to his lips as he looked down at his girlfriend, although for what purpose, he didn't really know. It wouldn't silence the house, of course.

Ben Whittinger turned the Maglight on and aimed it down the steps. There weren't many, perhaps ten. The light showed down a perfect circle into an otherwise blackened pit. He reached for the rail that suspended from the wall. He pressed down on it with about half force to see if it would hold weight and was thankful that it would. The steps themselves were made of wood but appeared no worse for wear as he carefully took the first and waited. Nothing. He gave a quick thumbs-up sign to Sherry and soon was out of her sight, slowly descending the steps toward the damp cement basement. Sherry smiled pensively and waited for the sound of a crash from above or below.

Ben was shocked to see pale light coming in from a window at the north side of the basement. Encased in rust-damaged metal, the glass was still solid, but water had clearly seeped through where the metal met the cement. The place had flooded probably numerous times and now had the omnipresent scent of old, musty water. Once again, someone had seen fit to place a table here, this one wooden and decayed. *For gangsters, this mob had lived pretty low,* Ben thought, *although for a flophouse, I am sure the building had lived up to whatever standards had been necessary at the time.* Wooden posts every ten feet or so held the ceiling above, and each had a candleholder screwed in with rotted, damp, mice-chewed stick candles rising loosely from the settings.

Ben washed the area with light. The cobwebs weren't so prevalent here, the dampness making the air too thick to weave in, but there were still some safe corners where the spiders attempted to make due. On the eastern wall was a half door, which Ben considered must have been put there as a stockroom for potatoes or other pickled vegetables as his father's mother had canned in their out cellar for years. There was a padlock on the door, but the hinge had rusted through with moisture and hung loosely. A small, effortless tug would pull the screws out of the rotted wood. Ben took a step toward it to open it and look inside when his eye caught a short wooden shelf hanging on the wall toward the south end of the basement.

There on the shelf was a huge black top hat, the kind only seen in pictures and old movies. It sat there silently as if it was staring back at him, and he reached up to grab it, dusting it off vigorously with the sleeve of his jacket. He flipped it in his hands, looking closely with the flashlight at the deep inside. There was no writing or identification of any kind, but seeing it made Ben wonder what manner of mobsters had been using the old house and if it hadn't been built much earlier than David had been told. Beside the hat was a large old leather-covered bag with twin black handles closing the top and hanging limply down the front. Ben replaced the hat and pulled the bag down. A large rat scurried from behind it, making him jump. The bag was heavy. It had something in it obviously, but Ben hesitated to open it. Something was making him feel unsure whether he wanted to know what the bag held. He decided to walk it over to the table. In the event the heavy contents were human remains, he could leave it and get back to Sherry and Dave. He looked up to the top of the stairs. The light from the landing was fading but, thankfully, still there. He no longer heard rain or thunder, just a stillness that hung oppressively in the air.

The square light of the window sat like an angled brick on the table. Dust floated in the beam. Ben slowly opened the handles, and air seemed to escape from the bag. He looked back at the hat suddenly. Had it moved? Then he bent his head to the opening. He reached in and brought out two serpentine blades. Old blood was crusted at the soldered gold handles. They were nasty-looking instruments. Ben studied them for markings, and on the handles were quivering lines leading to a silver starlike pattern on both sides of the hilts. He considered calling up but thought better of it. *Dave may be making his own discoveries,* he thought, *and I would be happy to compare mine when we both meet up with Sherry.* Though there wasn't much in the house, he was sure he had come upon its prized possessions.

But something else lay hidden in the bag, something in the dark bottom, he was sure of it. His hand reached in again, this time grasping the thick leather hide of a book. It felt like the scales of a dry snake, and the book had a heft to it that took some effort to get it free from the old bag. Once free, the bag snapped shut, and Ben jumped at the sound.

"Jesus!" he gasped. Ben allowed himself a moment to catch his breath. He looked the book over without opening it. It was ancient as if it belonged encased in glass, maybe from the days of the founding. There was a raised design on the leather, perhaps some symbol of masonry, Ben considered. Other than the design, it had no descriptive language on the front cover, so Ben flipped it over, seeing much the same on the back. It was awkward and heavy to handle with the flashlight gripped tightly in his other hand, and he dropped it hard on the table.

What happened next, Ben would never fully be able to describe as the light from the window moved across the table to the ancient book, and his free hand found a spot on the pages to grip and break the spine backward until the covers rested on the flat surface. There was nothing on the pages.

Nothing . . . and then . . .

His hand moved gently over the blank parchment before him, and suddenly, he became acutely aware of a dizziness in his skull and an acid in his esophagus. The floor . . . something had happened to the floor. The floor had disappeared beneath his feet. He hovered somewhere, in a black sea of blood-red currents, swirling and lapping about him. He gripped the flashlight like a lifeline and closed his eyes tightly. He heard a voice in the distance and thought it eerily similar to his own, but how could that be? His mouth felt muffled with thick cotton and his mind stuck in some heavy clamp. The voice that sounded like his was speaking a language he'd never heard before. It rose and fell with dramatic urgency, and then just as abruptly as it began, it was silent.

After a few moments Ben had no accounting for, he found he was leaning against one of the wooden posts behind him, retching up gaseous blue smoke. It was mixed with a harsh acidic bile that was the most rancid he had ever experienced. Then he felt the floor become solid beneath his feet again, and he heard his name being called in a woman's frightened voice. A desperate fear was in that cry. It was Sherry. She was in trouble, and he knew he should go to her, but he could not stop the violent heaving. Opening his eyes, the noxious bluish smoke surrounded him. Was it really coming out of him? Was he dying? He began to panic but still could not move. Had he been able to stop heaving and turned, he would have seen, only moments before, the thin, decayed figure crawling behind him from the open storage door, clinging to the wall, its face strained in a silent howl as it made its way toward the steps, toward the blinding light that reached down from above.

Chapter 16

The man-shaped thing, appearing as if he was ravaged by some terrible disease, threw itself out of the opening of the basement and fell against the opposite wall. Sherry screamed in fright. It was clothed in dark tatters, shreds of fabric hanging on its arms and legs, its head a threadbare ball of stringy white hair above a skeletal, chalk-white face. It said nothing but groaned in pain.

"David!" Sherry screamed. Her boyfriend, David, ran back toward the steps, the house groaning at every drop of his feet, and made his way to the top. Before he could get down three of the steps, a hole opened up under his weight and swallowed his foot. Somehow he managed to fall back toward the wall and not toward the shabby guardrail that framed the stairs. He cried out more at the shock than the pain as the sharp wood scraped both sides of his ankle. He pulled frantically as the skeletal shape moved slowly toward his girlfriend. Sherry looked up at David, and her feet slid back a few steps toward the door. She wasn't sure what she should do at that moment. The ragged man shuffled forward, almost aimlessly. The head jerked slowly from side to side as if it was trying to keep balanced on a wire. But its forward motion and David's predicament on the steps were causing her heart to race wildly. She didn't want to leave David here alone, but she desperately wanted to flee from the shape coming toward her. Suddenly, she screamed as loud as her voice could raise. "Ben!"

Ben had begun staggering back toward the basement steps when he heard Sherry scream his name. It was a desperate cry, and yet much of his own strength was drained from him. He wiped his mouth with the olive sleeve of his jacket. It left a faint blue residue on the sleeve, which confused him even more, and he stumbled, much as the man had before him, up the steps. He didn't notice at that moment the little door by the table opened, nor did he pause to see the arm that groped at the floor crawling out of it. His only determination was to get to Sherry. As soon as he stepped out of the basement, he saw what had caused Sherry to scream out.

The back of its head was almost bone white. There was skin of some sort, but it was cracked and dry like a weathered rubber ball. A slight moan escaped it as it took another uneasy step forward. Ben stepped quickly around it to get to Sherry's side. She was holding her hands over her mouth in an effort to clamp down on her urge to scream again. He reached her just as Dave was finally able to free his foot from the hole. He limped down the steps toward them.

Ben gave a cursory look at Sherry and then back to the man. "Are you okay?" he asked her as Dave reached them. She nodded and threw her arms around David. David returned her embrace but took his free arm and pointed at the disheveled figure that stood mere feet away from them, shifting from one foot to the other in an obvious effort to stay upright.

"What the fuck are you doing here, buddy?" Dave shouted at him. The man blinked incomprehensibly in response. It was then that Ben got his first look at the man's face. The face had the same pallor as the rest of his body that wasn't covered in the tattered remnants of clothing. Like exposed old fossil bone, the cracks in the skin showed no moisture. Whoever the man was, he was obviously extremely malnourished and dehydrated. The absently confused expression on his face made it unclear whether the thing even understood where he was or how he had come there. Ben noticed that even his eyeballs seemed abnormally dry; only their bright-blue color seemed human. If not for the initial shock and scare, this was a man who could only invoke pity in spite of the nagging questions of how he got to such a state.

David, however, was unimpressed at that moment to such considerations. He felt unmanned by the whole situation. Sherry, his girlfriend, finding him unable to help himself out his own carelessness, had called out Ben's name. And this disgusting thing had scared the hell out of her, while he looked on, pathetically trying to remove his foot from a damn hole in a step. He directed his rage at the man.

"Answer me, you ugly son of a bitch!" he shouted. "What the fuck are you doing here?"

Ben held a hand up to David. "David," he said, "relax. It's okay. He can't hurt anybody." He looked at the man. "You weren't thinking of hurting anybody, were you, mister?"

The man in the tattered clothing with the rubbery white skin looked confused by the question. His brow furrowed, and he clamped his eyes shut and shook his head. His arm reached out toward the three friends, and he took another step toward them until Ben yelled, "Stop!"

The man did as he was told, stopping cold at the spot. Ben looked at him, dumbfounded. "Don't you see that hole you're about to step in?" he asked. The man looked down, but it was unclear whether he could see the wet, rotted floorboard in front of him. He began to shake, and he stumbled backward, his momentum carrying him back, until Ben rushed over and kept him from falling.

"Oh my god!" Ben gagged. The man had an overpowering odor. It wasn't a mere unwashed scent that emanated from his person; it was rather a harsh chemical smell mixed in with a long-term lack of hygiene that nearly dropped Ben to his knees. He turned his head away from it as he led the man back toward the opposite wall. It was then that they heard the shuffling scrape of something coming up the basement steps. An arm came into view, clothed again in dark tattered rags. But this creature was not silent as he made his way from below.

"ARRZA!" it groaned hideously. "ARRZADRAK!"

Sherry turned her head and buried her face in David's chest. David's anger left him as the thing crawled out of the basement, squirming in frozen jerky movements on the dust-covered floor.

"Holy shit!" was all he could think to say.

The man leaning against the wall by Ben turned toward him in distress. His horrible face distorted in fear as the other thing continued to crawl on the floor. Then the crawling thing reached out and raised a thin, bony hand toward him. Pointing a long pale finger, it said again, "Arrza!" It looked with a haggard, pain-ridden face, clearly trying to focus its squinting black specks at the man with Ben. Ben looked back at him. It stared at Ben and then the other man and back again to Ben as if it couldn't distinguish between the two figures before it, and then it dropped in a heap, unmoving.

The last light of sunset began to come through the door and broken windows of the house, an orange-purple hue as the storm moved out, and the darkness of evening began to take over the clearing sky. Everyone in the house at that moment seemed stuck in time. David and Sherry were grasping each other tightly, not wanting to look at the scene in front of them, mere feet from the open door that would lead them to the safety of the Jeep. Ben standing close to the first oddly inhuman reflection of a man, both pressed against the wall as if attempting to disappear into it. And the last, most horrific sight was the crawling darkly dressed snakelike figure, who had groaned in some strange language, lying still as if dead on the floor.

Ben looked at his two friends, huddled together, slowly inching their way back to the half-open door behind them. He let himself gather his breath. He had never been so scared in his life, and a sudden realization came over him.

"Real funny, Dave," he said through his slowing heartbeats. The man at his side still leaned against him, his stench coming off in waves so strong that Ben still felt he might vomit.

David Wallace shook his head, bewildered. His eyes were wide with lingering fright. "You think I had something to do with this?" he said incredulously.

Ben's mind tried to work it out as Sherry finally let her head rise from David's chest. She looked at him with a slight questioning expression as well. Was this part of a joke? Would it surprise either Ben or Sherry if it was? Hire a couple of poor men off the street, clothe them in rags, put on some makeup, fifty bucks a piece? How much would it have cost? The only part of it that nagged Ben as he stood there against the wall that made him consider the possibility that his friend had nothing to do with this event was the men themselves. It was too perfect. Even now, if they were acting, they had not broken character. The man beside him was light as a feather and seemed barely able to stay on his feet. The man on the floor had not moved and, by all appearances, could be dead, his last breath a gasping plea before he succumbed.

David's expression did not change. Ben waited for it to break into a grin, waited for the bellowing laughter, and for David to bend himself over, grasping his gut to contain it. But Dave stood just as he had, favoring the ankle that had gone through the step. The look of shock and dismay never changed. David Wallace was not that good an actor. He hadn't arranged this. The men were here because they were here, and whatever had brought them to this state was not false but real.

"Well," Ben said, his voice hardened by the shock of this realization, "help me get them to the table."

"Fuck that," Dave answered. After the shock of the second man's arrival, anger had started to creep in again. He had meant for a truly scary evening but one in which he had control. What had actually happened was anything but in his control.

"I ain't touching these bums!" he said sharply. He held Sherry closer to him and began leading her toward the door. "Where the fuck did you guys come from, mister?" he added as they stepped backward. If Ben wanted to help these two assholes to their feet, he could do that himself. The evening was ruined as far as he was concerned.

Ben shook his head and grabbed around the man's narrow shoulders. He held the figure away from him as best as he could manage as the man was clearly not able to assist himself. Ben led his shuffling feet around the corner to the nearest chair in the galley kitchen and sat him in it as gently as possible. He did not bother to wipe the table of its inches of dust and webs, and the gaunt, skeletal shape allowed itself to lean forward and rest a free arm on the grime. Ben looked at him. It was getting darker, but the pale white skin seemed to glow like a light in the dim. The head of the man fell forward as if he was going to fall quickly asleep, leaning there against the table.

As Ben walked around back to the entry, he saw that both Dave and Sherry were leaving. Neither had any intention of helping him, and looking at the creature lying motionless on the floor, Ben was very tempted to follow. There was a noticeable difference between the two men who had shambled up from the basement. They both were equally repellent, but the first man had looked at him in a confused, almost innocent way as if he had been dropped there, unaware of how he had arrived at the spot. This other, however, although pitiful in his own right, had a look of menace in his shallow face and a piercing inhuman appearance in his eyes. They shimmered with an undeniable darkness to the thoughts behind them. Even now, lying there silently, it didn't seem entirely safe to go near him. But Ben felt a nagging obligation. He looked at his own hands as if willing them to reach down and touch the thing. It held the same prospect as if he was reaching into a boiling pot of water. But tentatively, he knelt down and searched around the man's neck for a pulse.

The thing groaned or rather growled at his touch. Ben jerked his hand away. The skin did not even feel natural. It had a leathery, dry texture, and it was as cold as the dirt under the earth.

"Unhhnma!" the man grunted.

Ben shook his head. "Well, I can't just leave you here," he said. "Come on." And with that, he grabbed the back of the old black coat that covered this man. It was an old-style coat, one that may have been found in a dumpster behind an old theater. The old hat came to Ben's mind. The coat had ragged tails falling limply at the man's legs. Again, the slight weight of the man shocked Ben. He couldn't have weighed much more than a child. Lifting him was easy. Dealing with his reaction was somewhat more complicated. The old man resisted. He tried to speak, but his words slurred again.

"UNNHNNMAAEE!"

It was obvious from his frustration that Ben's assistance was repellant to him. Ben directed him to the table, opposite the other man. There was no chair there, but there was another seat at the head of the table. The man's arms bent to the table and slid across it until he too could be seated, his legs dangling, almost useless in front of him. He grabbed the edge of the table near his counterpart and swung his thin, stick legs in between the table legs. Ben caught a glimpse of his shoes—dusty black, square-toed, and buckled. Ben shook his head at the sight of them. What in the hell was going on with this guy?

Then the grisly old man seemed to grin, if that was his intention, and looked at the other man sitting at the table. The second man reached out with both arms and let his long clawlike fingers grasp the arm of the first man Ben had assisted. A sly look came over his ravaged face. "Arzah!" he gasped. But the other man would not look at him. He tore away from his grasp, and a whimper escaped him.

Ben looked at the two of them sitting there. Darkness was coming quickly now, and he was not sure what he would do. Obviously, these two were not getting into Dave's Jeep and riding back with them. Also obvious was the fact that they were extremely hungry and malnourished. Ben had never seen the like of them before, except in books and perhaps the AIDS patients he had transported at the hospital. They were wasting away. And yet they had a chance to survive. Their immediate needs came to mind. If he were to do anything, that was all he would be able to meet, and he sincerely doubted David's willingness to help.

"You two assholes are real lucky I came along tonight, you know that?" he said. Both men looked at him weakly, but Ben could only return the first one's glance. The other was too much to bear. "My buddy would have just as soon thrown you both back down those steps and not cared whether you lived through it. You scared us so bad. I doubt I'm gonna get his help, but I'll come back with a couple of cheeseburgers and fries either way, get you something to eat at least. You two need to get to a shelter or a hospital, but we're miles from anywhere."

The two men looked at him. Silence was their only response. They gave absolutely no indication they understood a word.

Ben raised his hands and held them in front of him. "*Capisce?*" he said. The more pleasant of the two seemed taken aback by the word, but then he nodded slightly.

"Okay, good," Ben answered. He took his coat off, walked over behind the second man, and draped his shoulders with it. Luckily, all his keys were in his pants pocket, and his wallet was in the Jeep. "I'm not sure I'm gonna want that back," he said. "But I might want it back." He looked to the other man. "You already got a coat. Sort of."

Ben began walking away. He heard the horn of the Jeep blast outside the house. There was only the sound of chirping crickets breaking the silence. "All right, just stay there," he said. "I'll be back as soon as I can. If you can think of anything else, now's the time to say it."

"Blut," the nasty one who now had Ben's coat draped about his shoulders blurted out.

Ben stopped and turned slowly. He met the man's gaze, and it sickened him a little. "What?" he said.

"Blutt," the old man repeated more forcefully. It came out almost insulting as if Ben was stupid not to know what he meant.

Ben looked at the other more reasonable old man. "Is he kidding?" In response, it looked as if the man would cry, but he merely put his head down in the crook of his arm on the table. The nasty man looked at him a second and then turned his face toward Ben and nodded. "Blutt," he said again.

"Okay then," Ben answered. "Gotta go. I'll be back with the food."

With that, Ben Whittinger left the house and hurried back to the Jeep where his friends waited for him. Blutt, indeed. They probably did need blood, a blood transfusion maybe. But how was he supposed to arrange that?

Chapter 17

As soon as he climbed into the back of the Jeep, the argument ensued. It would be a long trip back, and Ben, trying to be diplomatic, attempted to keep the discussion from escalating. David backed the Jeep around and began traveling back on the rutted path they drove up to arrive at the house. He took it slower this time as the bouncing of the vehicle would only have exacerbated his own foul mood.

"What?" he said to Ben. "You gave them your coat?"

"Yeah," Ben answered. "You saw them. It's cold, isn't it?" He didn't understand why that would make anyone upset. Everyone he knew had been giving him a hard time about that beat-up old jacket for years. They practically begged him to get rid of it. Now that he had, it was a problem. "Thanks for your help back there by the way," he added.

"Those two old fucks looked like they just walked out of the atomic bomb!" David said loudly.

"They were disgusting," Sherry agreed and shivered in her seat.

Ben shook his head and grimaced. "I thought you were in school to be a nurse," he said.

"Yeah," Sherry said, turning to him. "So?"

"So do you think you're going to get to pick and choose which people you take care of as a nurse?"

"Ben, this is different, and you know it!" she said bitterly. Even Sherry, who was normally very pleasant, was letting the evening get the better of her. She wanted to forget the whole ordeal, but she knew the two men with her would be hashing it out for weeks if she let them. Both were stubborn and hotheaded, and both were unwilling to admit wrong. Most of all, Ben had shamed her just then, and she did not want to face him anymore. David would understand; Ben would continue to argue. She felt for him some and knew that part of his issue was her. But she also knew that his first impulse would be to drink. His second would be to pack a bowl. Whatever reality they had just encountered would be washed away in a mellow numbness. It tempered her sympathy for any argument he had.

"Leave her alone," Dave said. "Or I'll throw you right out here in the woods."

"You shut up too!" Sherry threw back at him. "This whole night was your idea to begin with! The next time we go to a haunted house, I want to go to a haunted house where there are regular people!"

There was silence for a moment after that as the Jeep finally made its way to a dirt-crusted road. David and Ben both burst out laughing. Sherry hit David's arm. "I mean it! Both of you!"

The rest of the ride was calm. It was about twenty-five or thirty miles to Ben's place, a poor neighborhood house he had formerly rented with David until Sherry had come along. He still had not found another roommate yet and wasn't sure he wanted one. The house was small, and the rent was manageable, even at his pay. He had decided to wait until a roommate fell into his lap somehow. It was easier being alone for the time being.

As he got out of the Jeep and they prepared to part, Sherry called out to him. "Call Lorraine," she said. "She's up. You need an up person." Ben nodded, not wanting to end the evening on a disagreement. Lorraine was up, all right, uptight. But he said nothing and smiled. He waved one last time as the lights of the Jeep backed out of his driveway. Then he went about grabbing what he'd need for his return to the old house. He quickly gathered a couple of soft, haggard blankets from the old footlocker that passed to him from his dad's family. They smelled musty, but for the two old men, it would be an improvement on the odor that came off them. Candles and candlesticks, his own flashlight, another old coat for himself, and his wallet, which had about twenty bucks folded in it. He was glad he had already bought gas and that David had chosen to drive tonight because the trip would be filled with more stops this time. He had to meet up with his cousin Dale, who just happened to work at the local slaughterhouse.

If, by chance, Dale wasn't working tonight, Ben considered his other options, of which there were few. It was October, which meant bowhunting season. He knew some bowhunters and even had done business with local deer processors in the past. But for that plan to work, he would have to be at the right hunter's place at exactly the right time, just after a kill. Most bowhunters Ben knew were notoriously patient. Unless a big buck had crossed under their stand, it was more than likely they passed on a kill, always figuring that something better would come by later once the rut started in November. Some of them were almost snobby about it. A six-point buck would be heaven-sent to Ben once gun season rolled around, but these bowhunters had too much pride to take a scrawny deer like that. Besides, how would he convince them to give him the blood?

His cousin Dale was his only real hope for a supply of fresh blood. Ben wondered why he was even taking such an action seriously. But still, he drove toward the plant. Perhaps it was the nasty old man's word alone. Blutt, he had said, definitive and succinct. Blood.

But Ben remembered also the other's face and how the word had affected him. He appeared to sink even further into himself, and he didn't register objection, so much as an accepting despair. The nasty one had called him Arzah. Arzah? It must be Arthur. It was this man's look that convinced him. Whatever the truth was, these men believed they needed blood. After that whole experience, Ben couldn't let that just lie.

As he expected, Dale was working. Ben was able to get into the parking lot and walk into the building. Security was lax, the only problem for the slaughterhouse being the occasional PETA protestor throwing a stink bomb through the door, or the occasional disgruntled Mexican employee, angry over being shorted in his check. There was little they could do about it besides be angry. Many of them were illegals.

Ben found a worker and asked if Dale Vickers was working tonight. The man was covered in blood. The staff there wore white for some reason, and the sticky red substance ran over the aprons in a variety of states. Chunks of flesh littered the man's sleeve. He was not lazy, apparently, whoever he was. He was smoking a cigarette, and Ben was surprised to see he didn't remove his bloody glove to either bring the cigarette to his mouth or hold the phone receiver when he took it off the wall and held it to his ear. He asked for Dale and waited. When a voice came thinly over the receiver, he held it out to Ben. Ben waved it off.

"Just tell him I'm here, will ya?" Ben said with a tight, slightly disgusted smile. The man took a puff with his free hand and relayed the message. He placed the receiver back on the phone hook and walked away without another word.

Ben looked around. There were thick cement walls in the hallway, and they muffled the noise, but he could still hear miter saws and circular saws and the slow rhythmic *kachunk!* of the air gun. The slaughterhouse was a constant assembly line of death. Ben congratulated himself for his ingenuity in thinking of the place. It was a bloodbath.

His cousin Dale came out of a door in short order. He too was covered in blood. Ben knew Dale hated his job, and he wished better luck for his cousin, but he was glad the younger man was still working here at the slaughterhouse for the moment. Dale came up, looking worried. Nobody ever visited him at work, and the first time could only be because of bad news.

"Is it Grandpa?" he asked.

"Nope," Ben answered. "He's still with us, far as I know. He's not kicking, but he's still there." Dale nodded in response, and then a natural confusion crossed his face. Ben picked up on it and offered his story. He didn't like lying to family. He really didn't like lying to anybody since unless you were sure you'd never see them again, a lie had to be constantly reinforced, which was a waste of energy in Ben's opinion. But there was no way he could tell Dale or anyone else what his true intentions were.

The lie consisted of a timid man Ben invented. He thought of the man and the story to go with him on the drive there. He was surprised at how logical it sounded to him. A timid man, a pussy really, had a deer invading his backyard and his garden nightly. Even though it was past time to harvest any vegetables, the man had asked Ben his options of keeping the deer away. Ben offered to hunt them out, but the man was far too much the pacifist for that scenario. He would hate to have a yard littered with dead deer as if they would all die in a lineup like cattle at the slaughterhouse. So Ben suggested he could get some blood and pour it around the perimeter of his garden. The deer would smell the blood since scent was their primary defense and become spooked by it. Sooner or later, they would leave the garden alone and find a new route to get their nightly meals.

The story sounded semi-plausible, and Dale, though far from stupid, bought it. He had heard of such a remedy himself, although he wished the pansy would just let them hunt the deer out. "Oh well," he said, "not everybody's a killer like you and me, huh?"

"Right," Ben answered. "Sounds like it wouldn't be much of a challenge though."

Dale looked at him blankly. "Who wants a challenge?" he asked.

"Not me, cuz," Ben said. "So can you help me out?"

"Yeah, sure," Dale said. "Give me a few, and I'll be back with some good stuff, full of chunks and everything. You want two pails of it? How big is the garden?"

"Two oughta do it," Ben answered. "I only got two hands, and he'd faint if he saw it."

Dale soon returned with the two metal pails. They even had lids on them with the half-moon hole to open them. Ben was pleased with the catch. All was going smoothly. Now he'd find out just how much bullshit the two old men at the house were dealing. He hoped it was bullshit anyway. The thought alone repulsed him, and he imagined that if it were true, that would be the end of their arrangement because Ben would be bolting out the door soon after. He thanked his cousin for the blood and set off to leave. Before he did, Dale stopped him.

"Hey," he said, "have you been out to see the old man lately?"

Ben sighed and set the pails down. "No," he answered. "Last time I went out there, they had put some Pollack's pants on him, something Ski. When I asked him about it, he didn't even blink. Didn't say anything. Just looked at me. He's already left, Dale. His body just doesn't know it yet. I did my crying for him then. I can't. I can't see him like that again."

Dale nodded and took his gloved hands and smeared some fresh blood down his apron. "Well," he said, "guess I'd better get out there myself. It's a bummer though." Dale looked down at the two pails at Ben's feet. "Gotta get back to work, cuz," he said. "Good luck with that."

"Thank you, cuz," Ben said, smiling. "I'd shake your hand, but . . . hey, you going out for ducks this year?"

"Shit, yes!" Dale said enthusiastically. "Leaving tomorrow, so if you want any more of that, you're going to have to kill something yourself."

"No problem," Ben answered. Turning, he hurried back to his car, placed the pails in black plastic bags, and tied knots at the tops. Then he braced them with old rag towels he had thrown in and took a couple of bungee cords and secured them in each corner to the arms of the hatch. They seemed stable enough. The pails were fairly heavy with the blood, and the substance was rather thick. He would have to drive slowly, especially once he got on the path to the old house. If they spilled, besides having a huge mess to clean in his trunk, he wouldn't have an answer to the mystery nagging his brain. As he got into the driver's seat, Ben felt something he hadn't felt in quite a while, an irrepressible excitement. It was with effort that that excitement didn't weigh down his foot. But he had a couple more stops to make yet. And it was getting cold.

Chapter 18

The Michigan woods were a beautiful, relaxing sight in the autumn months. In the daytime, if you were lucky enough to be out with the sun shining, the leaves became the backdrop of a great impressionist painting, the colors vividly creating fire in the treetops. Looking out on it, you could become entranced. It was near impossible to ignore.

At night, however, far from the streetlights of major or even minor roads, those same woods became oppressive and foreboding. A man in the forest could feel suddenly as if he was drowning, far from shore, instinctively swimming on and on as exasperation took over his mind at the endless water in front of him. The question became one of direction. Had he turned at the right time? Was the road leading in the same direction he started? Was that a landmark he saw or a false memory of some past landmark? Many landmarks seemed to run together—an old barn, a torn-down sign, a tree, and a run-down double-wide with junk cars and tires out front. All seemed familiar and yet not the same in the dark.

Ben Whittinger cursed himself many times as he made his way slowly back to the old house. He cursed his friend David for bringing him, and he cursed himself for not paying close attention to the drive the way there. He was trying to figure it backward with the house itself being the starting point and in this mass of trees, on an unmarked dirt road, with no sign of human life besides his own. Boiling with frustration, the thought occurred to him to bag the whole idea.

Almost as soon as that thought passed, he saw it: the beaten two-track that led to the house. It was still a far piece, and in a Chevy Cavalier, it would be much slower than in David's Jeep, but it was there, all the same. There would be no turning back. The two old men would be in the ramshackle house, built as a hideaway for gangsters, abandoned and in a malignant state of disrepair, just as the two wraiths themselves were broken shells in the shape of men.

Ben did not feel frightened by them. He had been frightened of getting lost in the woods, and he had felt frightened in the basement when time seemed to go blank, and he found himself retching against a wood post. And he had even had a moment of fright when he heard Sherry scream out his name. But he was not frightened of the men. Sickened perhaps, but in their state, what could they do? A strong wind could blow them over, each weighing under a hundred pounds, he was sure of that. He had carried them himself to the table. Even when the spidery one with the twisted vulture's face had called out for blood, he had not been scared, only curious. The fact that he had not been frightened now frightened him some. He had always felt not quite normal or, at least, an outsider among normal people. He figured that to have been growing pains. He was not a brave man either especially. But no moment in his life had ever really called for much bravery.

Now though as the house fell into the view of his headlights, fear entered. Exciting it was, yes, but also frightening. Like the woods, the house altered in the darkness. Whereas in the light of day it had appeared as a spooky shipwreck, in the dark of night, it grew into a wounded animal, cornered and ready to strike. There was no light, except for the light that fell from the moon and stars where it penetrated the woods in scarce beams. There was no sound either, except for what must have been gigantic crickets, their thick bent stick legs grinding out a horrid and constant tune.

Ben gathered his supplies—flashlight, white bag filled with fast food, a brown bag with a bottle of whiskey, and two more blankets he had gathered from his own house. He turned on the flashlight, another thumper, heavy with the D-cell batteries filling the tube, and stepped over the giant limb in front of the car. The blood he kept in his trunk. The blood he would hold for now. Ben decided he didn't believe the old man. Something in his command had persuaded Ben to keep the option on the table. But he didn't believe it.

Ben kept the light trained down as he made his way to the door. He was less interested in the path than in keeping the light off and away from the house. In some way, he thought the beam might awaken the beast.

The house was silent. The two old men were not talking. They made no sound at all, but Ben was sure he felt their presence even before he saw them. He swung the light about the dark entryway, careful to be aware of the holes and soft, rotted wood beneath his feet. When he reached the small dining area by the galley kitchen, he found the old men where he had left them. They appeared in the beam of his flashlight as two castaways washed on a beach. The vulture-faced man at the head of the table had his balding head with its gray-white stringy web of hair lying down on the surface, one arm outstretched where his long bony fingers had grasped for the other's sleeve. That man remained slightly turned away from the hand in a frozen state of despair. Except for the fact that his coat lay in a heap on the floor by the nasty one, it seemed to Ben in all the hours he had been gone, the two had not moved at all. He wondered if they were, indeed, finally dead. But as the light searched out their faces, both men reached their hands up to block the light from the pits of their eyes.

"I guess you're still alive, huh?" Ben said in the darkness. "Looking at you, I wasn't sure."

The first man, the one Ben could recognize most as a human being, said, gasping, "The light, please. Turn it away."

The other croaked out the obvious. "You returned, boy. Why?"

Ben took the flashlight and set it, beam up, on the tabletop. Then he set the rest of his items—the bag of food, the brown bag bottle of whiskey, and the blankets—on the corner. "I wondered that myself," he said. "But when I see two guys like you, two guys who look like they just walked out of a Nazi death camp, I guess I just think somebody ought to try and help them. You know you guys can't stay here, right? This house is going to come down either by machine or"—Ben looked around, his eyes finding the ceiling where the circle of his flashlight came to rest. It was a mass of webs—"or the hand of God."

He added, "You two need to get to a shelter or a hospital."

"The war," the first one said, "it's still over?"

Ben nodded. "If you want to call that a war, then yeah, of course, it's still over," he said pointedly. "Been over for months now. Hey, wait a minute. This just keeps getting weirder and weirder. You sound British." Ben pointed to the man. Then he moved his finger over to the uglier one. "And this guy is what, German?"

The ugly one raised himself as best he could on the edge of the table. "I am not German, boy," he said. Both their voices were quite weak, but the difference in the accents was stark.

"Yeah, well, whatever," Ben answered. "You're not local, that's for sure. How in the hell did you guys wind up here?"

The ugly one squinted as if in pain. "Did you bring what we asked?" he hissed.

Ben grabbed an empty chair and tested it by slamming his foot down on the seat with a couple of hard stomps. Then he took a sleeve and wiped it down and sat. "The only one who asked for it, mister, was you," he said. "I brought something better." Ben reached into the bag and brought the paper-wrapped burgers and fries out and set them down in the middle of the table. Both of the old men turned their heads away.

"What is this?" the vile one croaked.

"It's called a Happy Meal," Ben answered plainly. "As in you should be happy I brought it. Best I could do."

The old man at the head of the table began to turn his head back and forth. He clenched his bony hands into fists and pounded them on the table. He hissed, "Where is Warren? Mr. Warren! Warren!" His voice grew louder until it sounded like thick sandpaper roughing down a wood rail.

"He's dead!" the English man said. "Don't you remember?" At that, the German, for he hadn't offered any other origin to Ben, crumpled and let his head fall back to the table.

Ben looked from one to the other. Even now he was finding this difficult to believe. But there they were, languishing in obvious distress, making no movement toward the food he had offered. It was perplexing. He thought they would have been scrambling for the burgers as soon as they could smell them.

Finally, Ben said, "Okay." He got up from his chair, took the flashlight off the table, and grabbed his coat from the floor. "You're welcome," he said. Then he began reluctantly walking out to his car. Dismissing all else that was odd about the two men, the question revolved around the one aspect that Ben had withheld from them: blood. If they truly needed the blood and not in any medical sense, then they were—and there was no other word for it he knew—vampires.

Vampires are fantasy, he thought as he slowly went to retrieve the buckets of blood. They were fantasy since their conception, created out of man's imagination to rationalize an irrational world and vent religious hysteria, to represent a tangible evil. They were the devil in confrontational form. But unlike Satan himself, whose defeats were firmly in the hands of God, vampires had inherent weaknesses that could be exploited by man and so were far less indestructible than subconscious evil. One could guard against them with simple garlic. Sunlight was death to them, and being from the devil, the sight of the crucifix repelled them. It was the symbol of Satan's ultimate defeat, or so at least the legends claimed.

As time passed, vampire legends and tales became so commonplace they endured only for their entertainment value. Their reign as objects of real terror, if such a time had ever existed, was now long past with Bela Lugosi and Christopher Lee. And yet still, as a precaution he took almost involuntarily, Ben fumbled at the crucifix he wore around his neck. It was an accessory he thought little about in his daily life, but at that moment, it was reassuring to know that it did not hang on his mirror at home. He kept it beneath his sweatshirt as he took the buckets out of the cooler in his trunk. He reached in the trunk one more time for the two plastic ladles he had bought at the supermarket and wedged them in his back pocket. A moment passed where he thought to leave the two buckets on the ground and drive off. Let the old men fend for themselves. Let them debate whether to drink the blood without him having anything more to do with it. What would he get from the knowledge except a loathing and disgust for even being party to it? That solitary moment passed. Ben took a deep breath and walked back to the house.

Returning to the table, he lit a couple of candles he had also bought and placed them at both ends. At least then he could give his flashlight a rest, but the flickering glow did nothing to diminish the gathering mood in the room, nor did it help with the two old men's appearance. If anything, it only amplified their wretched, inhuman faces.

Ben brought the buckets up off the floor and set them on the table. He pushed one in front of the Englishman, the other in front of the one who had asked for it. Ben exhaled heavily. He looked at the Englishman.

"Arthur?" he said. "Am I right in calling you that?" The man nodded weakly, his head turned slightly away from the bucket. "Well, Arthur," Ben continued, "since you seem to be the sane person here, I'll talk to you."

Ben stepped back and took the scene in. "I don't like this," he said. "Part of me says I should get the hell out of here and leave you both to starve because goddammit, I don't believe it. I don't know what you guys have been through. You look like spoiled milk, you know that? I don't know how you got here. And I don't know why you won't eat a hamburger. That's why I brought the blood. If you are really going to drink this blood, then you have got to be the unluckiest motherfuckers to walk the face of the earth. But there you are."

The man at the head of the table finally raised himself and looked first at the bucket and then at Ben. Ben stepped up to the table, placed his finger in the half-moon opening of the lid, and pried the top off. Taking the cup of the plastic ladle, he silently held the stem toward the man, who took it in his long chalky fingers and slowly pulled it out of Ben's hand. Again, Ben stepped back from the table. In the candlelight, there was no more right or wrong. In the dark, there was no hint of life before or a future to come. There was only this moment, the moment Ben Whittinger would discover whether evil such as this existed. And if it did, could he live with it?

The nameless one looked into the bucket. His dried, pitted eyes examined the blood, and then he looked over the bucket with a crooked sneer at Ben. Taking the ladle and dipping it into the liquid, he stirred it slowly like a soup over a stove top. Then he brought it out, letting some of the blood fall back into the bucket with heavy drops. He looked directly at Ben as he brought it to his mouth and drank. His eyes closed as his body quivered. He appeared like a man coming in from the frigid cold, longing for and receiving the warm embrace of a woman. He sighed, and almost immediately, Ben noticed that his pallor became somewhat less fossilized. He opened his eyes and looked at Ben again.

"Satisfied?" he said softly. "Boy?" Even his voice, though still terrible in its mockery, seemed less strained.

Ben's hand reached up to his chest to feel the imprint of his small crucifix beneath his sweatshirt. "Honestly, pal," he said shakily, "you're not the real test."

"Yes," the man whispered, "of course." He took his hand and grasped the one called Arthur. "Arthur," he said, "come. Do not allow your pride to deny it."

Arthur, the Englishman, convulsed under the pressure. If his eyes had been capable, they would have dripped salty tears to the floor. Ben took the seat at the other head of the table and turned to face the Englishman, waiting.

"If you have to, you have to," he said. Ben's fear was beginning to rise. He wondered if the Englishman would follow his counterpart. Was he the same as this other foul thing, or did his reluctance mean he could be reasonable? Of course, it may be that the blood would only unleash a kindred spirit, and then Ben feared this evening would prove a grave error.

Suddenly, the Englishman turned his head up and looked squarely at Ben. The pained expression became determined with some effort. Again, he tore himself from the other's grasp and faced the bucket. Ben took the lid off for him as well and handed him the ladle. The man closed his eyes and dipped it into the blood. Just as the other had done, he brought the ladle to his lips and drank the liquid. He too seemed to fall into a moment of euphoria. Then he dipped again and drank. And again. And again. Fast, fevered draughts he took, some even filled with tissue, it did not seem to matter.

Ben became more frightened then. If anything, this one was in less control. The other one laughed, and the cackle ripped through the dark like a sudden lightning strike. The first vampire took a sudden drink himself in an effort to keep pace with the Englishman.

But the laugh had not only affected Ben, who inched back in the chair, away from the table, his eyes wide with fear. The Englishman, the one the nameless one called Arthur, stopped drinking at the sound of it. His skin too had gone from ashen to a more natural flesh color with a tint of pink at the cheekbones. He rose out of the chair in rush, and it tipped back violently into the open space behind him. Just as quickly, he was reaching for the wretched man who leered back at him. He lifted him by his weathered lapels in a surprising show of strength and forced him back against the small countertop in the kitchen.

"Bastard!" he shouted. "Evil bastard! What did you do to me?"

Ben watched this flurry of sudden violence in silent awe. He rose slowly from his chair, not sure whether to attempt to run. He feared that could draw unwanted attention to his presence. Then he heard the lecherous shape speak.

"I take it," he said, "you disapprove." His thick accent was still noticeable, but his voice had a smoother quality, and both of the men had grown younger to Ben's eyes in even those few moments. In fact, their sudden vitality was more than enough reason to leave, and as Ben turned, he saw out of the corner of his eye that evil-looking head snap in his direction. That snap of attention was enough to release any pent-up adrenaline Ben had in reserve, and he began running toward the door. He heard a barking grunt in his left ear. He made three steps before the wretched fiend was upon him.

Ben dared not look at his eyes as long fingers gripped the front of his sweatshirt with amazing strength. Hadn't this thing been lying almost prostrate, struggling to move a muscle only moments before? Now it had him, and Ben almost passed out from the fear as he did not know whether he should even touch it to defend himself. Then it spoke.

"Oh," it said, "I can hear your heart beating, boy. Did you hope to return home now, eh? Did you?"

Ben took his free hand and reached down the collar of his sweatshirt. Still not daring to look at the face only inches from his own, he pulled out the crucifix. The hands that held him tightly suddenly loosened, and he felt a glimmer of hope. But the evil bastard, as the Englishman had called him, only snorted.

"That," he hissed, "is a very powerful symbol, boy, very powerful, indeed. Unfortunately for you, it is a power not shared by its bearer. You gain nothing from it, I fear."

With that, the long fingers grasped the crucifix and ripped the small chain that held it from Ben's neck. Casually but with a noticeable aggression, the vampire flung it back and away from himself and Ben into a dusty mass of corner behind him.

"Now then," the vampire said, "I tell you, child. The offering is appreciated. Even while it stank of a lowly animal, still . . . you have my gratitude." The blackbird's eyes narrowed into slits. "But perhaps it holds insult. Do I detect insult, eh? Look at me!"

Ben opened his eyes and slowly turned his head. One of the cold hands clamped down on his face, and Ben felt the wriggling of the veins beneath his skin attempt to flee from it. His mind went hazy, and he felt the urge to vomit, although he dared not allow himself that relief. The vampire raised his other hand, obscuring his grotesque face from Ben's eyes. Standing like a single pale and deformed branch was the forefinger, capped by what seemed to be a long and sharpened blade of a nail. Ben saw then the deadly intent in the thing's dark eyes. He meant to cut him with that razor-edged nail right then and there. A quick slash of that clawed nail and Ben would simply drop as both of the vampires engorged themselves on his blood. This had been a terrible mistake, coming here, and now Ben's young life was finished. He was only to be a donor to these things' unnatural evil need.

Then another hand reached in and placed itself between the razor and Ben's neck. "Malcolm," an English voice intoned. "Malcolm Schreck."

Malcolm Schreck? Ben thought. *Oh God, that's fitting.*

"Malcolm," the Englishman Arthur repeated, "you owe this young man your very existence. Twice over."

Malcolm Schreck's eyes went from Ben to Arthur. The decision hung in the air for a few long silent moments until Schreck growled, "His presence mocks me! And he knows, Arthur!"

With that, Schreck's left hand came down on Ben's right shoulder and squeezed. Ben could feel the pincer sharp fingernails dig into his skin on his chest and shoulder, and he cried out in pain, dropping to his knees before the two vampires. Ben's mind began searching frantically for any possibility of survival until finally, he screamed out, almost involuntarily, "I CAN GET MORE!"

A moment passed before Schreck let him go with a harsh shove. Ben found himself on his back, looking up at two stern faces quizzically staring down at him. "I can," he rasped. "I can get more blood."

Schreck kicked at him. "More of that?" he said contemptuously. "Even begging for his life, he dares to mock us!"

"No, no, no!" Ben protested from the floor. "I work at a hospital. They throw blood away every day. Human blood! I can get it for you."

Malcolm Schreck reached down and pulled Ben up with all the effort of lifting a plastic bag and pressed him against the wall. "You would do this?" he said.

Ben nodded, worried that the wrong word, even in assent, could bring about a quick reversal of attitude. Once again, the one called Arthur stepped forward as if to place himself between them.

"Can we trust you to do this?" he said calmly.

Again, Ben nodded. "You can," he said, keeping his eye on Arthur. "You can." He did not want to look at Malcolm Schreck. Looking at him brought both pain from the memory of his loathsome touch and a confusing sense of shame.

"Understand this, boy," Malcolm said. "Failure to return will not save you, nor will it save your two friends or your family, for with all surety, we will visit upon them first." Schreck said all this coldly with an emphasis on the word "family." Ben understood that the touch of the cold hand had opened him up to Schreck like a book off the shelf. He knew things now, things Ben had never intended to reveal. Ben nodded with a painful grimace.

"Then," Schreck said, freeing his hand from Ben's sweatshirt, "you may go. We will expect your return on the morrow's eve." Arthur Drake took Ben's shoulder and led him toward the door as Schreck turned away. Schreck turned once again and said slowly, "Before you leave, boy, give the date that you find us in."

Ben looked at them each in turn before settling on Malcolm Schreck. "It's October," he said plainly, "1991." Both took the words in silently, and then Malcolm Schreck closed his eyes tightly and turned away.

After what had occurred, Ben did not dispute the idea that they were unaware of the year. Their appearance, their speech patterns, and their needs all pointed to that distinctly outrageous fact. Another fact that presented was that Ben himself, however unwittingly, was responsible for bringing them out of whatever hell they had previously occupied. Not only that, but he had also given them the means to thrive. Doing that had made Ben responsible for their actions from here forward. It was a depressing thought. He had seen their strength, their singularly obsessive determination. What evil would they do if he failed them now?

As he and Arthur reached the door, Arthur Drake seemed to recognize his thoughts. "Thank you . . .," he said, uncertain.

"Ben," the young man offered. "My name is Ben."

"Yes. Thank you, Ben." Arthur leaned in toward him at the door and said quietly, "I am not like . . . him."

"Didn't think so," Ben replied. "But then again, you are, aren't you? Stay here, please. I'll . . . I'll get you . . . what you need." With that, Ben left and headed toward his car. The excitement that brought him back to the old house had waned considerably; the adrenaline that had pushed him along the entire night disappeared. The fall came quickly. The only thing keeping him awake was the residual pain where the vampire, Malcolm Schreck, had touched him on his face and his shoulder. The pincer had broken skin. He was sure of it, though he didn't want to investigate it further. His face was numb, except for the torrent of blood rushing along the veins underneath the skin. He needed sleep. *God,* he thought, *let me sleep.*

Chapter 19

Arthur Drake watched the young man get into his vehicle and start it up and saw the headlight beams strike the large tree limb. *A quiet motor,* Arthur thought. The car had rectangular headlights, not round as Arthur remembered. He accepted immediately that much had obviously changed in the years since he had died. The boy's attitude, speech, clothing, all of it seemed to present at least a subtle change from Arthur's experience. Turning back from the door, he saw that Malcolm had returned to the table, presumably to finish his meal. Arthur looked about the entry and the room by the stairs. He had seen Malcolm throw something away, though he was not sure what it had been. He had not arrived quickly enough, and when he had, his only impulse had been to protect the young man. But it had gleamed as it flew in the air, back to the corner under the steps. The object had clearly gleamed brilliant silver as it passed through the moonlight that penetrated the hole in the roof.

Arthur walked over to the spot he thought it may have landed. There was an inch or two of dust on the old floor. Nobody, besides the spiders and other crawling creatures, had disturbed this house in years. Taking a quick look behind him first, Arthur bent to his knees and ran his hand, his pale but revitalized hand about in the dust. Just as he felt the small metal chain beneath his fingertips, another shoe dropped. It was nearly as dusty as the floor and had a rusty buckle clamped along its side. It covered the remaining portion of the chain and amulet.

"What are you about there, Arthur Drake?" Malcolm said.

Arthur turned his head up toward the pale and pointed face that looked down on him. "If you please," he said.

But Schreck would not lift his foot; instead, he twisted it in a grinding movement, the dust making a clear pattern in the floor where his toe moved side to side. "I never took you to be a man of religious conviction, Drake," he intoned. "You are particularly ill suited to it."

Arthur Drake stood and faced Malcolm Schreck for the first time since they had drank the blood and felt its overwhelming strength. "You never knew me at all, Schreck," he said.

"Truly? Above all others, I chose you to accompany me on this journey. Why should I do that if I was ignorant of who . . . you . . . are?"

Arthur glared at Schreck, disgusted. "Is that what this is then?" he said. "A journey? To where? Hell?"

"Oh! To the contrary, my young friend, we are keeping Hell at bay." Malcolm reached out his hand and grasped Arthur's arm.

"Don't touch me," Arthur said sternly.

"So," Malcolm spat, "you seek the small comfort the boy left behind. His own faith is questionable, but at the least, he has some knowledge of its source. You, you ignorant fool, only hope to gain a pleasant recumbence. How? By pretending to believe in something you've never given a moment's thought."

Arthur stood silent for a moment and then said plainly, "Call it a deathbed conversion."

Schreck lifted his foot and stood aside. He grunted his contempt. "Choke on it," he said.

As Arthur Drake bent to retrieve the crucifix and hold it in his hand, he gently wiped the dust from it and looked at it thoughtfully. He had never held the cross or what it represented with any respect. Father Tom, in his dream, for it had to have been a fevered dream and not the last he would experience in his solitude, had been the only representation of Christianity that had ever appeared to him. Besides the venal hypocrites he had encountered during his years on Earth, this tangible little cross in his hand was the only object of faith to have ever touched him. Small though it was, it seemed to have an enormous significance here and now, especially with the stooped form of Malcolm Schreck nearby.

"I tell you we are gods. Here and now, it is we who are gods," Malcolm said quietly. He faced the door to the outside, which remained cracked slightly, and the breeze came in through it. It gently blew against his ghostly face. "The deity you have adopted gives us free reign, Drake. Call it His wish, if it aids in your accepting the gift I have given you. We shall not suffer for it as long as we keep our heads about us. And believe me, Arthur, should we fail, we will share the same fate, for truly both of us, you and I, surely we have Hell to pay."

Arthur placed the emblem in the pocket of his coat. "This is the same 'gift' you gave that young boy all those years ago, isn't it?"

"Boy?" Malcolm replied, turning back toward Arthur with a scowl. "Ahh, yes, the German soldier. Yes. Hmm, we have been idle for a long time, Arthur. But with the blood, flesh becomes whole again. With the blood, life is renewed. A simple requirement, do you not agree?" Schreck stepped over to face Arthur. He did not move to touch him but looked deeply into his eyes. "We shall suffer no more, Arthur. Hell will taunt me no more. And you, with the blood promised from the boy, Arthur, I tell you now, your youth will be that which you had been only dimly aware. What promise can any god give you to rival that?"

"The boy, Schreck," Arthur said. "We were speaking of your early experiment with the German boy. I recall you saying you had dispatched him. Lucky boy, that one. How did you accomplish it?"

Malcolm Schreck's head cocked at an awkward angle, searching his companion's face for some sign of levity. When none came and Arthur maintained the seriousness with which he asked the question, Schreck merely chuckled. He raised his finger and shook it in front of Drake.

"Arthur Drake," he said, "have we come thus far together that you now take me for a fool?" His mirthless chuckle led him toward the basement door, and he disappeared down the steps, leaving Arthur alone, searching for his own answer. Then Arthur, picking the flat, metallic scent of blood in his nostrils, walked back toward the kitchen to satisfy his depravity in private.

Chapter 20

Lt. Phillip Lewis hated being called into the captain's office. Not out of fear of criticism of his detective work or out of any trepidation regarding his colleagues' appraisal of him personally. It was just that the captain tried so damn hard not to make an issue of his race that it became embarrassing to endure. Lewis had learned early on that being black in a small-town police department had many challenges, not the least of which was rising in the ranks. But it was proving himself in spite of his skin color that cut him deepest. Not that anyone would know that. Lewis maintained a silent dignity in every situation, a control that kept him from becoming what many seemed to need him to be, either an overly sensitive, prideful black man or a simple minstrel clown.

He was not the first black detective on the force, but he was the only black who currently held the position. The first, Joe Adderly, back in the late seventies, early eighties, had allowed himself to fall victim to his own secret releases, becoming a neutered, drunken copy of who he was supposed to be. The second—Lewis forgot his name—his tenure had been so short, simply got caught in flagrante delicto with a hooker. It was an offense many white officers indulged in, but being black, the man was held to a different standard and so was unceremoniously shipped out, feeling lucky enough not to be wearing orange pajamas. Guys like that usually made their way into a security position. Lewis couldn't remember him very well, except as another casualty.

Phil Lewis knew from a lifetime of experience that outside a few exceptions, he was regarded by many in the force one of three ways: nigger, fucking nigger, and goddamn fucking nigger. Only his size kept him from ever hearing it in his presence, but some of the guys wore it on their face as clear as the badges on their uniforms. Whenever he saw it, he had taken to giving the offender a sly wink as if to say "I know what you're thinking." Sometimes Lewis had to remind himself there was a fourth category held by his black brothers in blue, and that was "Who does this nigger think he is?" Lewis had an answer for that as well: "I'm the nigger who passed the detective's exam, the one you ought to be asking to mentor your dumb asses." It amazed him, really. The rigid mind-sets of so many people were amazing. It didn't seem to matter their race, religion, or type. No matter what the Lord may have intended, they almost always fell right to shit.

Now here he was, in the captain's office again, being gestured into taking a chair opposite the captain and next to a fresh-faced kid in a white shirt and tie. Lewis himself was thirty-eight and perhaps only a few years older than the other man, but he tended toward the casual in appearance, whereas this guy seemed to be dressed too perfectly. It made him look eager and young. When the captain gave his name, Jeff Kipner, Lewis instantly recognized it. While the captain made good on his niceties, Lewis remembered why.

Kipner was out of Detroit post suspension. It was probably better for him not to remain there because he had nearly killed a perp in a rage and, in so doing, had almost lost the case for the DA. Apparently, the verdict had gone according to plan, but a sacrifice was always necessary in cases like this. Kipner had been working vice, if memory served, on a child porn ring. The evidence had been discovered in the possession of some highly placed bigwigs in the community. Well, they may have had evidence of their guilt, but they also had money, of course, so they weren't to feel too much pain. The low-level scumbag who produced the shit was a different story. He had to be brought to justice for the community's well-being.

Kipner and his then partner found the guy in some slum apartment building. This was info sweated off one of the bigwigs the community just couldn't live without. So when they tracked the scumbag down, they burst through his apartment door with a warrant. He, of course, attempted to flee the scene, and Kipner caught up with him at the window. Looking around the apartment, there was a cheap corner devoted to his photography—a black felt facade, a four-poster bed, and a fern. It would all have been legitimate if his subjects had reached the age of consent. But this piece of shit was using toddlers. How he acquired them Lewis didn't know, and not being there for himself, the picture wasn't complete for him. In any event, while rounding up the perp, Kipner claimed he had heard a muffled cry coming out of an old hope chest. His partner went over to it and found it was locked. Kipner got a little rough with the perp. Not too bad at that point, but the asshole wouldn't give up the key. He just shrugged and smirked.

Kipner, understandably, decided he had the purview to take it to the next level. He flung the perp hard onto his back, knocking the wind out of him, and then he straddled him and started smacking him with an open hand. The perp started pointing to a desk drawer while he was still attempting to breathe. Kipner's partner found the little key that fit the chest and opened it. Then Kipner looked over to see something terrible, something Lewis, in his long years in the force, had never, thankfully, come across. It was a crying little girl in garish makeup and a flimsy flapper-style outfit. The little girl went straight into his partner's arms. Kipner watched his partner carry the child out of the room. In his statement, he had reported looking down at the asshole's face and seeing a stupid, lustful smile. Then Kipner said he only remembered beating on that stupid smile. Right and left and right and left again and again until that stupid smile was not only gone but also permanently altered. The perp's normally scuzzy appearance began to look like an overripe fruit. Kipner didn't stop hitting until he heard his partner's gun cock in his ear.

Looking at him now, Lewis thought Kipner appeared as timid as a lamb. He seemed nervous but not overly so, just nervous enough that Lewis thought Kipner would have liked to jump into a new set of skin. He shook Lewis's hand firmly, said nice to meet you, and returned his attention to the captain. Lewis wasn't sure he would have handled that scene differently had he seen the child pop out of the chest, but he likely would have. Vice was a tough assignment. It tended to take you down roads that led so far from what ordinary everyday people found normal that it made you suspicious of normal, everyday people. But here he was now, and the captain was ordering them politely to partner up.

"With all due respect, Captain, this town is kind of small to be needing partners," Lewis offered. He was actually saying it to offer Kipner an out as well, but the captain wasn't truly in the market for alternatives.

"Getting bigger every day, Lewis," Captain Farrel replied. "You know that better than most."

Oh god, here it is, the obligatory backslap. Good job, Lewis. I always had faith in you in spite of . . . you know.

Captain Farrel then decided to really step in it. "Kipner," he said, "you got any problem with black people?"

Kipner turned his freshly shaved face toward Lewis. "No," he said blankly. "I like black people. Black people commit normal crimes. They don't go in for this Hannibal Lecter shit, posing people, skinning them, you know, shit like that." Lewis let out a small laugh. The captain didn't find it amusing apparently.

"You're forgetting Wayne Williams," he said. The captain was of the mind that there was no superiority among whites when it came to murder, and he didn't like the implication that there was.

"Anomaly," Kipner replied.

Lewis decided to join in, being the one expert in the room on black murderers. "He's right, Captain. We usually just kill for money, crack, or tennis shoes. Or sometimes 'cause it's just so damn hot out. But not for any peculiar sexual arousal, Wayne Williams notwithstanding."

The two detectives looked at each other passively with just the slightest show of humor between them. Kipner had done the duty of breaking the ice. So be it. Lewis would show him around.

As they walked out of the office together, Lewis turned to Kipner and said, "Just one thing. Don't be expecting any black-guys-do-it-this-way-white-guys-do-it-that-way shit, okay? I don't do comedy routines."

Kipner considered this for a moment, and then he said, "Fair enough."

"Good."

Kipner nodded. "How do black guys do it anyway?"

Later, after Kipner was shown to his desk and had got himself adequately situated, he asked Lewis what was still on the board here. Lewis took him over to the chalkboard and studied it himself for a few moments and then said, "Unsolved? Well, we've got a few cold cases from years back before I got here. More recently? You know, it's damn hard to solve a murder when one isn't even accomplished. What we've had here lately is the summer spree of gang shootings."

Lewis went to his desk and sat, while Kipner took a corner of the same desk and wedged a cheek on its edge. "Being here in the middle of your old beat and Chicago," he continued, "we're just a natural attraction for courier routes and territory disputes between the cities. You got I-94 less than three to four miles away, same for U.S. 131 if you want to head south. These kids drive in here, want to make their bones or just want to cause a little havoc in the hood. But for some reason, they've taken to using .22s and shooting out the back of a moving car. If you're a shit shot with a .22 out a window at 30 mph, best you can hope for is to wing somebody. Or hit an innocent little kid." Lewis watched Kipner's face for a reaction to that, but none came. He merely nodded.

"Yeah," he said. "Had dealings with some of those guys back in Detroit, mainly more of your heavy-hitter types though. They like sending the bench in for this shit."

"Yep," Lewis agreed. "Eager but stupid. They're all named something Dawg too, all members of the Dawg family. But we've got our local families here and, strictly speaking, a few informants among them, but they don't give up too much. No reason to, I guess. Pretty much SSDD around here right now. We're coming into the slow season."

"I hope so," Kipner said. "Easy money spends as well as hard earned. And I don't need any more bullshit in my world. It's taken me a long time to get back."

"I know, Kip," Phil Lewis replied. "Sorry, just natural, you don't mind, do you?" Kipner pursed his lips and shook his head in the negative. "I read about you." Lewis continued. "It's too bad. But you ain't the first cop to get divorced over the job, and you're sure not the first one to take the fall for some scumbag rich guy. But there it is. Let's just try to do some good around here if we can. My advice: keep your expectations low."

"You got it, boss."

The two cops spent the rest of the day driving around the city, giving Kipner a mental diagram of how the town was laid out, its main avenues and some of the intersections where the action occurred. Their car was unmarked but easily identifiable in the hood as a cop car—a dull green Chevy Impala with a black guy driving it and a white guy in a white shirt and tie beside him. What else could it be?

Lewis gave up little about himself, and Kipner remained guarded as well, perhaps figuring Lewis had enough information from whatever reports he had read. Lewis liked the kid, and eventually, a little of their mutual armor wore off during the day. Kipner, he found, was funny without being too bigoted or disrespectful, and he was also insightful, and Lewis found himself in agreement with a lot of his assumptions. Lewis didn't want a partner, certainly hadn't asked for one. *But if I have to have one, Kipner at least has street experience,* he thought. Of course, it was still hard to say until they had something to work. They weren't in Detroit after all.

Chapter 21

Ben Whittinger put on his blue transport smock, his name badge, his dark-blue slacks, and his tennis shoes and drove to work looking as if he had the beginnings of some flu bug. A shower hadn't helped, nor had the noon beer. Looking at himself in the mirror, his brown hair, which was usually unmanageable on a good day, hung down his head around a red bulbous nose and pale cheeks. Ben did his best to make himself presentable, and he was moderately successful. In his job, he saw many good-looking young girls, not to mention some good-looking older ones. He always tried to be friendly, but not overly so like some others on the job. He did have a job to do, and he liked his reputation as a good worker, even if it made some think he was standoffish or shy. Truth was, he was shy. It wasn't something he could help. You never knew what friendly could do for you in a job like this, transporting people and supplies all about the town's one big hospital, but his mood that afternoon was one of self-contempt, and that was a difficult mood for him to hide. So he did his work with as little chatter as possible.

The plan was still to get the blood. He would try to arrange it so he would have it by the end of his shift at eleven. If he could get to it early enough, he might try to get out of work a couple of hours before quitting time. He would make his stops in the lab. Sherry might be there at first. Ben thought about talking to her about the situation, see if she could help him get the bags designated for discard. But how would he explain that? He'd already compromised himself with that damn other story to his cousin Dale. With Sherry, it would have to be the truth, and telling the truth wouldn't be any good to him or her.

This was where the self-contempt came into play. What was it the legends called a thing that procured blood for vampires? A familiar? Essentially, it was a slave, hoping for some crumbs from their master. Renfield. Is that what he was becoming? It was a sickening idea. But the evil one, Malcolm Schreck, had made his threat very clear. Ben didn't know how he would carry out such a threat, but he couldn't leave it to chance that a threat was all that it was. There was something very determined about Malcolm Schreck. And Ben would have thought the whole story complete bullshit had he not seen it with his own eyes. Both of those old men had drunk the blood. Cow blood, animal blood, but it was still blood nonetheless. And with that, they changed before Ben could even register his surprise. They became strong, purposeful, and instantly dangerous. Ben didn't know what Schreck's clammy touch had pried out of his brain, but it was enough for him to see that ignoring it or letting his promise leave his mind like a ten-dollar loan was impossible.

Those thoughts roiled about in his brain, infecting his whole body as he stepped into the lab. More people, more women, and Sherry, of course. *It is four thirty,* he thought. Why the hell hadn't she left yet? This dream girl who had shared some part in a nightmare with him, a part he could not allow to become greater than it was, walked up to him then and smiled.

"Hey," she said. He returned the greeting with a forced, tight-lipped smile. "How are you?" she asked, concern crossing her face. "You don't look so good."

"I'm okay," he said. "Coming down with something maybe. You better keep your distance." Ben really didn't want her studying him like this. It was as if she could read him at times, and this was not a good time for that.

"Well," she said, "I'm glad you're here. I wanted to say thank you."

"For what?"

"For keeping your head last night," Sherry said. "And for trying to help out those guys. You were right when you said that, about being a nurse. I got to thinking, maybe it's not for me."

Ben shook his head at that. "Come on, Sherry," he said. "Don't doubt yourself because of that. That was not a normal situation. I understood how you felt. Dave was right. I was just being an asshole, that's all. You know me."

"Well, it was you who wanted to help those guys."

"Uhh, yeah, I know. Great idea, right? Well, they oughta be in a shelter. Or an asylum."

Sherry reached out and touched his arm. "I was thinking about asking Dave to drive back there and check on them. Maybe we can get them to a shelter. Probably should, don't you think?"

"God, no!" Ben said, a little harder than he meant to. "No, I don't think that." He took a step toward her and put his hands on her arms. "Sherry, don't bring it up to Dave. Don't suggest it. Just put it out of your mind. That whole house is dangerous. We should have never taken you there."

"I know," Sherry said. "But, Ben, what about them?"

"What about 'em? They're two old men. You know what it is about old men? They're a lot tougher than you and me. That's how they got old. So don't worry about them. They probably just moved on by now. Some cop will pick them up for vagrants on the street and give them a meal and a cot. They'll be fine. They're probably very used to living like that."

Sherry came in suddenly and gave him a hug. "It was very good of you to help them anyway. Uggh, the way they looked . . ."

"Hey," he said, gently breaking the embrace, "it takes a long time to get that ugly. I'm telling you they'll be fine. Let's just forget it, okay?"

"Yeah, okay."

"Good." Ben looked at her. She was smiling at him, and it felt like a warm sun was on him. This was why it happened. This was why he loved her, little things about her that just came out naturally for her; she hadn't tried to make him feel the way he did. Now all he could hope to do was protect her. But even then, he decided to take a risk. She was open to him. She believed him about the two vampires. They were just passing vagrants. Now if he just turned his need slightly from the real truth, she would believe him again. All he would have to do is play it out a little further.

"Hey," he said, "I know why I came in here. You guys got any expired blood going down to the incinerator?"

Sherry looked at him, perplexed. She said, "I think so. Expired 1500. Why?"

"'Cause I got to go down there anyway. Seems some idiot in surgery threw away a lady's earrings by mistake. They want me to go through the garbage and linen bags and look for them."

"Why don't they just do it?"

Ben faked a mocking whine. "They're too busy!"

Sherry laughed a bit, still mildly confused about the request. But she went over to the refrigerator and retrieved three bags of expired human blood—O positive, unassigned blood, expired, universal donor. Ben mentally wagered that none of the people who donated blood had any thought to whom it went to, but boy, would they be shocked if they ever found out about this.

When Sherry looked at Ben with an odd expression, he said, "See? Be a nurse. Nurses don't have to go down and pick through garbage."

"I guess not," she said and laughed.

"But they still have to wipe asses." Sherry laughed and waved him off.

Ben left and went down to the incinerator. He took a look around to make sure nobody was there and stuck the blood bags in his pack. When he got a chance, he would take it to his car and drop the blood into his cooler. No sense having it on his cart all night, except maybe if he ran across more. But this would do for the two blood drinkers, he imagined. It would have to until he found a way to kill them.

Chapter 22

The world turned. It had certainly turned many a time since Malcolm Schreck had last walked upon it. And now it was a new world. But how new was a question that Schreck only considered mildly and discarded. It was irrelevant. What little he had gleaned from the boy had been primarily of a personal nature. He gained nothing of any pertinence regarding the makings of his whereabouts or what lay beyond. Schreck made his way slowly down the basement steps when the last darkness of evening began to fade that first morning. It was an instinct he had acquired long before this new creature with his face and body was born, a long-held aversion to harsh sunlight that did not require the condition of vampirism. Even so, before he descended, he took a look about for Arthur Drake and hoped the man would have the sense to follow him. Drake made no indication that he understood. *That would soon change,* he thought.

Malcolm Schreck then took his first good look about the room where he had presumably died. Damp, musty, and water-stained it was; covered in thickened dust and heavy cobwebs, each and every thing present showed only the wear of many brutal years. Forty? No. The boy had said the year was 1991. That made it over forty-five years. *Astounding,* Schreck thought. Quite astounding to have been lying dead, unburied for so many years, and yet now, with the infusion of blood, only his weathered clothing seemed to show any sign of drastic change.

Then Schreck spotted a familiar object—his old leather bag. And beside it on the table were the great book and, of course, his hat. But hold. These things had been touched, he deduced, and recently. Dust had cleared from their surfaces in the form of gripping fingers and thumbs. The boy. *How odd,* Schreck thought. How utterly odd that was. The only other human hands ever to attempt to open the awesome doorway to the dark secrets the book held had been an obtuse fool named Brendan Vaughn. The secrets within its pages had remained just so for that unfortunate waste. But a young boy with neither the knowledge nor the desire had been made privy to the exact incantation to awaken himself and Drake from their entrapment. How could this be? Schreck worked his hand over an empty page, and the book screamed back at him. He snorted a bemused approval and closed it shut.

Mr. Warren. On every night possible since the discovery within those pages, Schreck had trained and retrained, enforced and reinforced the spell upon the meek workings of Mr. Warren's brain. At first, Warren surprisingly had rejected this training. *What was the master doing?* he must have thought. Schreck had never asked such a complicated task of him. His was the physical labor, the strength of body, not of intellect. And oh, Schreck knew it had been so much longer than Warren had ever feared being under the master's watch. Occasionally, the master would give him a sour drink, and Warren must have gathered, weakly, that this sour drink kept him above the sea. The sea was where Warren had always longed to return. Horses and carriages had their purpose, but the waves and the salty breeze were where life began to Warren. And where, to his feeble mind, it should have ended. But Master Schreck, as he often did, had other plans for him.

Warren had succeeded in committing to memory the few words, repeating them and repeating them in the crescendo as had been taught to him by Schreck. The spell should have transpired as proscribed, but then the unthinkable had happened, and Warren found himself dead. Happily dead too, it would seem, if the Mediterranean's account had been accurate. How sad that fact had been to him. Schreck had little experience with sadness. Schreck had actually found himself saddened by the news of Warren's demise, not for himself, although he knew his fate to be now in great question, but for the damnable loss of his friend. And yes, Warren could be named such, if anyone could be. Whether Warren returned the sentiment was another matter of little significance, but to have the feeling at all was a bitter potion for Schreck to swallow.

Schreck found Warren's enormous skull in the place where the cutthroats had left it, in the dank little vegetable cellar where he and Arthur Drake had lay together for all those years. It was altogether cleaned of flesh. It was merely a skull now, a huge skull that had once secured the large moon face of Mr. Warren. Apparently, not being able to feed on the full corporeal bodies of the other occupants of the dank little room, the vermin had gone to work on the one piece of unspoiled flesh. It had likely taken only a year or so before the full meal of Warren's head had been completed. Then they could only scurry about, risking a nibble on the two men's clothing.

Schreck looked up and saw the beginnings of dawn overtake the darkness through the small fractured window above. He sat and leaned his body into the closest corner under it. Placing the head in his lap, facing him, Schreck let his own head fall back against the cool cement.

The boy. His thoughts now centered on the boy. No innocent was this boy. Schreck surmised the boy was likely formulating plans to kill him. Drake, though he shared the same needs as himself, would likely attempt to charm the boy into an alliance. If allowed, Drake would assume the role of a tragic victim of an evil man's plot, innocent himself of any deviltry. Already, he had laid the foundations for this fiction by coercing Schreck to spare the lad.

A flesh merchant who sold females into a cabal of lechers? Innocent?

A blade man, a cold and calculating killer who stole money from the weak and who had sunk many a sliver of metal into flesh to exact punishment for mammon? Innocent? Schreck thought not.

And yet compared to himself, who had held council with the underworld, perhaps Drake was an innocent. But that hunger, that undeniable need for blood had for a few startling moments, overtaken him. If the boy failed to bring his promised gifts and came back with some simple plot to kill them, Arthur's baser instincts would surely prevail. Of this, Schreck was confident.

Of the boy, however, he was less so. The boy was an American. Busy creatures, these Americans were. Even though his time among them was short as his first step had darkened upon their soil, Schreck saw the New World for what it was—a gigantic churning machine filled with the likes of merchants of all manner. Buyers and sellers crowded the streets in great abundance. Schreck had recognized an abundance of greed here as well, far greater than any he had come across in the Old Country. Europe had been filled with naïfs, people only interested in the simple day to day. It was a rather willful blindness that had allowed Hitler to rise among them. They cowered before the strong or the loud aggressor. Americans, whatever else could be faulted them, allowed their greed far more sway.

Schreck had always avoided human contact, excepting for his time in the service of the Royal Navy, where he was able to exact a certain revenge for the inconvenience. Not only did he find humanity a slobbering mass of stupidity, with the sole exception of Mr. Warren, but he could not find any practical use for their company as well. He had always been, and remained most comfortable, in solitude. Avoidance was a simple matter. He was not welcome. Either from their repulsion of him, their great naïveté, or from their insatiable greed, Schreck had shunned them. And now he found himself trapped in the apex of all three calamities. America. It was an unfortunate circumstance.

But it was clear; the boy's assistance would soon come to an end. It would be either through Schreck's own end or the boy's. Of course, he had no fear of the former. Crucifixes and a weakly held ambiguous belief in some higher authority would be of little use. Even a person of strong conviction would find his God inattentive at just the moment he found his need was greatest. It had always been thus. But Schreck understood what his own needs were to be. He would have to acquire an accomplice better suited to them. Warren was an irreplaceable asset, and yet he must have a replacement. As Schreck allowed the first night of his new life to fall away to morning to repose in the vicinity of his former arrangement, his thoughts drifted past the outer limit of his confinement. The ideal man for his wants was his focus, a man of strength and of purpose but one whose will could be easily constrained by Schreck's own, one that would gain him access to new prey.

Chapter 23

The large Dodge truck had slammed into the huge branch that lay adjacent to the old house at a high rate of speed. As Ben pulled up, he saw, even in the dark, that the deep tire tread had ripped the track and ground like a shredder, and the back end of the truck had shifted sideways from impact with the heavy tree limb. Ben stopped the car and looked up at the house. The door had been busted off its hinge, leaving a heavily damaged frame and a dark open space where it had once hung in its crooked fashion. He kept the car running as he processed the scene.

It seems likely there is a dead man in that house, Ben thought. The bloodsuckers couldn't wait for his return and had somehow drawn a victim to them like flies to light. It must have been a bear of a man to have knocked that door down, no matter how weakly it hung on its rusty hinges. The truck itself spoke of brute power and intimidation. It was black, unmarked by anything but its brand and a plain blue Michigan plate, but its tires were grossly oversized, and it had an extended black grill that now pitted into the huge limb. If the driver of such a vehicle was alive in there, Ben wasn't sure how he would be greeted. It was more likely he was dead already as Ben originally considered. The man could be lying on the dust-covered floor with the two hovering over him like carrion birds, draining his life away at this very moment.

Upon entering the space where the door had hung, Ben saw its remains lay on the floor before him, half resting on the opposite wall. Whoever did this had not only knocked the door off its hinges, but he also had pitched it five feet across the entryway. Ben looked right to where the rotted fireplace and dilapidated chair sat. No one was there, but a flicker of candlelight from the old kitchen caught his left eye, and he saw the shape of a man who leaned a heavy shoulder against the entry's right frame. Just as Ben had suspected, he was a large man, much larger than himself, and his body blocked most of the candlelight that came from the room. Ben could only see the red ash from a cigarette glowing about his neck and the smoke that blew heavily after it. The man was obviously not dead, or apparently, did he seem in any danger of becoming so. It was very puzzling for Ben to see him just leaning there as if against a corner lamppost, watching nothing in particular.

"Hey," Ben said warily as he stepped toward him.

The man's head turned for a quick glance over his shoulder, but he remained where he was and did not return the greeting; instead, Ben heard the Englishman, Arthur Drake, call out to him.

"Ben," he said, "in here. It's all right. You can come in."

Ben walked gingerly forward. He had the blood from his cooler in the backpack, and he held it at the top handle, so its straps brushed the floorboards as he stepped. When he reached the man at the entryway, he stopped and looked up at him, for up was the natural way Ben's neck turned to face him. Still, the man said nothing. He looked down at Ben and snorted. Ben saw that the two vampires had resumed their former spots at the table. Except now, on the table, along with the candles, was a black leather bag that Ben vaguely found familiar.

Malcolm Schreck wore a huge top hat that also seemed eerily familiar to Ben. Old and as ratty in appearance as its owner, it towered off his head like a round black stovepipe. Scheck took it off, exposing his oddly shaped cranium and stringy black hair, and set it on the table. "Have you brought what you promised, boy?" he said flatly.

Ben walked forward a few steps toward the table and turned toward the new man. Finally, the stranger removed himself from the doorframe and stood to his full height, his hands in his pocket. He wore a red-and-black plaid coat. His size was so great he seemed to hold all the light from the candle upon his chest, and he raised a large hand to his mouth to remove the cigarette between his thick fingers. He just about filled the entryway standing there, and Ben looked at Arthur as the obvious question crossed his face.

"This," Arthur said morosely, "is Karl. He arrived. Earlier."

Ben looked at Karl. "Why?" he asked plainly.

"In the fucking neighborhood, ya little runt!" Karl replied with low and stern authority. "Why do you think?"

Malcolm stood from the table and interjected, "It was decided, boy, that perhaps we ask too much of you." He stepped around the edge, and his dress, once again, confused Ben. It was out of a time so distant and past. Ben remembered seeing old drawings of people who dressed like this. They drove black carriages with heavy-curtained windows. They drove the carriages to graveyards on misty mornings. How old was this thing?

"Oh?" Ben said. "You think that's smart?" he added with caution in his voice. He looked down at the cracked leather bag with the black handles. "What's in the bag?" he asked.

Schreck's long thin fingers rested gently on the edge of the table as he stepped toward Ben. He glanced down at the bag. "Prized possessions, boy," he whispered. "Cherished memories from an older time." Schreck opened the handles and reached into the bag. The first item he brought out was an old weathered book, a huge thickly bound volume with the binding shorn at its edges and paper wrinkled and starched from what could have been centuries of existence. Ben felt the same vague remembrance that the large hat and the black bag had given him, although once again, he couldn't entirely place it, except for a feeling of being submerged in cold darkness.

The second item Schreck retrieved was an enormous human skull, hairless with a few large teeth missing; in life, its owner could only have rivaled the new stranger in size. The stranger, named Karl apparently, giggled rather girlishly at the sight of it. Ben looked at him in mild surprise at the sound, but Karl only grinned through the red glowing stub of his cigarette.

"You see this skull here, boy?" Schreck continued. Ben looked at the clean but yellowed bone of the huge skull. "This was once a companion of mine. His loss was a bitter one for me. A man of enormous strength and resolve was my Mr. Warren. I have need of such a man again."

Ben looked at Karl. The enormous strength was not in doubt to Ben as he watched Karl bounce back and forth on his feet in a display of nervous energy.

Karl glared back at Ben. "What the fuck are you staring at, bitch?" he growled.

Ben looked at Arthur, who sat morosely at the table, ever so slightly shaking his head and watching silently what was transpiring before him.

"You agreed to this?" Ben asked him, unable to contemplate such a person willing to aid these creatures, even as he himself was in that exact position.

Arthur returned his gaze and opened his mouth to speak. It was moments before he was able to blurt out "Just as you see everything here, Benjamin, I had no part in it or any knowledge of it. I couldn't do anything about it."

Malcolm Schreck snorted his disgust at the comment, and Ben turned his attention back to him to find he was yet another step closer to him. Ben could smell him now, and it was a mix of formaldehyde and damp earth.

"I'm of the belief, boy," Malcolm said, "that you have handled these prized possessions of mine." Schreck said this with a grave menace in his voice, and he stared, unblinking, at Ben with black dead eyes.

Ben attempted to control his breathing. Trapped between this grotesque animal and the hulking stranger, there was no obvious escape, and for the third time, he regretted entering the house at all. "I don't remember touching anything, Mr. Schreck," he said nervously. "But I might have, I don't know. Except the head. I know I never touched . . . the head."

Schreck gestured to Karl, and the huge man stepped forward.

"There have been others, boy," Schreck said, "others who have attempted to decipher the mysteries in this book. All have failed to gain even the slightest wisdom from it. It reveals absolutely nothing to them, even while they believe they walk among its authors. And yet you, who appear before me a bewildered whelp, held sway over its secrets. Have you knowledge that you have hidden from us? Have you eaten forbidden fruit?"

Arthur stood from the table. "Malcolm," he said plainly, "where would we be if not for Ben? After so many years, because of this boy as you call him, we are free of your curse. But since your damn accursedness is never-ending, we have fallen even further into Hell. You're to blame for it! You alone, not him!"

Schreck's head fell. He gritted his teeth, and his sneering mouth grimaced in frustrated anger. "Arthur, once again," he spat, "reminds me of the debt we owe you! For that debt, he thinks to withdraw an oath from me!"

Then Malcolm returned his dead stare back to Ben. "Your gifts," he said.

Ben reached into his backpack, grabbed the three bags of blood, and tossed them onto the table. Malcolm examined them, studying the labels, the plastic packages, searching only for the access needed to be stripped away to get at the fluid.

"Is this all?" he asked.

"It's all I could get. For now."

Malcolm looked disapprovingly at the blood. Arthur said, "It will do, won't it?"

"It must," Schreck replied. "But I fear this boy only wishes to hold your debt over us, Drake, to entrap us here securely in this house like dogs in a pen, awaiting his scraps."

The two vampires stripped the tubes off two of the bags and drank the blood out of the ripped edge. Karl closed his eyes against the sight as the red fluid drained quickly down both of their throats. He opened them again, only to see them squeeze any excess out the bags and let it drip onto their outstretched tongues.

Both of them then looked down at the remaining bag. Three is a difficult number to share among two, and both seemed to realize this at once. But they demurred, for the moment, and allowed the bag to sit on the table, untouched.

Schreck reached into his own leather bag once again, and this time his hand withdrew two serpentine blades. "Recall handling these, boy?" he asked.

Ben took an instinctive step backward and found himself pressed against the bulk of Karl, who immediately threw a large hand into his shoulder and shoved him forward.

Ben turned and looked at Karl. "Why the fuck would you agree to help him?" he said.

Karl took a menacing step toward Ben. The room seemed to get smaller as he entered the space. "Oh yeah," Karl answered. "I agreed, all right." He flicked the remainder of his cigarette at Ben, and it struck sharply against his chest. "This is my idea of a fucking party—me, these two creeps, and a little bitch. If we only had a fucking deck of cards, I could stay here all fucking night!"

Arthur watched Karl loom over Ben and said, "Malcolm, please."

"Karl is like you, boy," Malcolm said. "Here, under my guidance. It seems, however, he does not come meekly as do you. You would keep us as dogs, eh? Allow me to introduce you, boy, to my dog."

At those words, Karl grabbed Ben by the collar and whirled him around, back toward the entryway. Karl took Ben's limp body and ground him back against the frame. The force behind his thrust went right between Ben's shoulder blades and arched his back. Karl took one palm and butted Ben's forehead with it, knocking his skull back against the hard wood. Then Karl's huge hands suddenly clamped around Ben's throat and squeezed. Ben brought his own hands up in an effort to break Karl's grip. He was shocked both by Karl's strength and his apparent willingness to commit murder. Karl giggled his high-pitched snort at Ben as Ben's face began to redden and panic.

"You are just like a little bitch, aintcha?" Karl said through his giggle. "You got little girl hands. Yeah, that's it. Keep trying. Keep trying, you little bitch. Seeing stars yet? Seeing a light?"

As Ben's legs began to falter under him, two other hands reached in and grabbed Karl's forearms. Karl looked angrily over at the owner of those hands. It was the other guy with the faggot voice. But his hands squeezed Karl's arms so strongly that he was forced to release the little bitch. Then an impossibly quick shove pushed Karl to the other side of the frame, and he felt his back arch in pain. A bolt of lightning immediately struck him across his right jaw, and Karl found himself floating. The next he knew, he was lying dazed on his back, having flown past the hole in the floor, his head striking the wall of the steps behind him.

Arthur moved over to the man with a quickness and determination flowing in his body that he had not felt in an agonizing eternity. In fact, he had never felt so strong. It felt wonderful. He watched himself put his dusty shoe on the big man's throat and press down. He saw nothing but fear in the man's widening eyes, heard nothing but the delicious gurgle in his throat. He hardly noticed Malcolm Schreck at his shoulder.

"Oh yes, Arthur!" said Schreck. "At long last, I reunite with an old friend. Oh, I agree with this, Arthur. I agree completely. We shall keep the boy. He has some intelligence. This one is a mere brute. Don't let him die just yet though! Here, take the blade. We will drink his blood while it still flows!"

Arthur Drake looked down at his foot and saw the tongue sticking out through Karl's teeth as the man struggled vainly against his death. The serpentine blade was being offered to his closed fist as Malcolm Schreck tried to gently peel his fingers open from his palm and place it there. Drake looked at him. Schreck's disgusting gleeful sneer was filled with a lust Arthur recognized. He turned his face away and squeezed his eyes shut as if to force it out of his mind. Then his other hand reached up to the faulty banister and gripped it. He screamed out his horror and, removing his foot from Karl's neck, slammed the point of his shoe into the drywall above his head. The plaster showered Karl's face, and he closed his eyes tight to shield them from the debris.

Arthur turned away and stepped back slowly toward the kitchen. Karl, in a coughing fit, turned onto his side, but Schreck kicked his shoulder, and he fell hard again to his back.

"Stay!" Schreck ordered. Karl was much too weak to resist the command. Schreck looked down at him, his hand gripping the handle of the blade, squeezing and releasing, squeezing and releasing. "Disappointing," he muttered and looked over at Arthur, who was bending down to tend to the boy.

Arthur gently smacked Ben's face until the young man looked back at him, still slightly dazed himself.

"Are you all right?" he asked. "Can you stand?"

Ben looked at Arthur and nodded. Taking his hand, he allowed Arthur to help him to his feet, staring at him throughout the process. Drake's face had changed again. Now he appeared only moderately older than himself. It was a handsome face, like something off a magazine cover, and the blue eyes were striking in and of themselves.

It was something entirely lacking in the dull, lifeless eyes of Malcolm Schreck.

Arthur Drake clapped Ben on the shoulder. "Come on, mate," he said. "I think it's high time we left. Don't you agree?" Ben nodded, and like a valet, Arthur guided him to lead the way toward the door. As they passed, Malcolm Schreck stared at them from under his brow. Karl, the stranger, began to scramble to his knees at the same time.

"You motherfuckers!" he shouted. "I'm gonna dream of killing all three of you freaks!"

Ben looked over at Karl as he crawled along the floor, one hand on his bruised right cheek. "Don't chafe yourself, asshole," he said.

"Especially you, you little bitch!"

"Be silent!" Malcolm ordered. Karl whimpered in pain. He fell to his side again and lay there, breathing heavily.

"Arthur," Malcolm said, "you make a grave error. If you leave now, there will be no further understanding between us. I revoke any partnership, any oath. I withhold any assistance. And I will not be forgiving when our paths cross again. And you must know they will."

"I'll take my chances," Arthur replied.

Before they exited, Ben nodded toward Karl. "What about him?" he said.

Arthur put his hand on Ben's shoulder and gently pressed him forward out the empty doorway. "Well," he said, "it's a dog-eat-dog world, isn't it?"

Malcolm Schreck watched them leave in the strange vehicle as he took his first step into the wooded field outside the house. He looked about as the wind picked up, and dying leaves began to float down and drift around him. He heard clearly the rattle as they reached the ground. It was late autumn, and the cool air invigorated him. He saw the red taillights of the vehicle jerk and joggle out of sight among the trees. With Drake's sudden departure came inspiration and also a certain undeniable freedom. Arthur could no longer task him now like some tiresome needling conscience. Nor would he silently berate him, judge him, or blame him. Schreck was liberated from all such constraint. He turned back toward the house.

"Karl!" he barked at the doorway. "Does this machine of yours still function?"

Chapter 24

As Arthur Drake had stepped up to the vehicle, the only light was the sparse white light that managed to sift through the remaining leaves of the trees above. He looked back at the wreck of the house from the passenger side of the car. The house he had never truly seen but which had been the crypt for his body as much as his body had been the cell of his soul. It appeared to him much as he thought he must appear to his young companion—monstrous. There was no other word for it.

So much time had passed. This would be a challenge, being free from the house. How much had changed? How would he navigate it all? The bloody car door didn't even have a bloody handle. He ran his hand about the smooth surface but kept his eyes upon the door of the house, waiting for either Schreck or the new beast he held to come rushing out after them. Ben, seeming to realize his confusion, reached across to the passenger door from the inside and propped it open for him. He sat himself in the plush seat, closed the door, and said nothing.

The young man was still shaken from the violence of Karl's attack. He had expected danger from Malcolm Schreck. There was never doubt of that. But from this strange dude not much older than him? Where could Schreck have found such an animal? The same thoughts briefly crossed Arthur's mind from the moment the beast had busted down the door in pain and fury. After the awful crash of his vehicle into the large limb outside, Karl had flung himself into the house like a blind charging bull, and only when his body finally collapsed in a heap and his pleading whimpers and angry vows of rage broke the dark silence of the house had Arthur any clue to Schreck's intentions. Then it became all too clear. The boy's usefulness had quickly run its course for Malcolm Schreck, so too had Arthur's own use for Schreck since Arthur was adamant in his refusal of all Schreck was and had become. He could not remain there.

As Ben struggled with the car through the shifting path in the woods, bouncing and jostling over the dips and uneven terrain until they reached a far more graded gravel road, Arthur Drake kept a hand on the dash to steady himself. Ben finally, after all his concentration, looked over at him. The man had changed. The lights from his dashboard showed him clearly for the first time. He looked young, at least much younger than he had first appeared when he had looked like a walking corpse. *A handsome fortyish,* Ben thought. He had light-brown hair that remained unkempt but much fuller than that of the old man who had frightened Sherry with his deathly pallor. The blood he had drunk had given him some color in his cheeks, but he was still quite pale. Yes, Arthur had obviously been very handsome in life. If only something could be done about his smell. It was a sweet-and-sour mix of blood and chemicals, only slightly less from his having fed. Ben had smelled something similar while taking bodies to the morgue at the hospital. It made his visits there nearly impossible for him to linger in the dank empty rooms after he had somehow hoisted the bodies from the cart to the table. Now that smell was permeating the small compartment of his car.

Looking at Arthur, he said, "I'm going to roll these windows down a bit, if you don't mind?"

Arthur, realizing the source of the statement, flushed a bit, embarrassed, but nodded his assent. The windows on both doors came down with an electric sound, another obvious change from his memory.

"Well," the young man said as they reached the gravel road, which pointed in the direction away from their current path, "where to, Mr. . . . Drake, right?"

"Yes," Arthur answered. "But please call me Arthur, uhh, Ben."

"Okay, Arthur, where to?"

Arthur swallowed air. "I was thinking your place," he said cautiously, "if it's not too inconvenient."

"Aren't you even going to buy me dinner first?" Ben said and chuckled. Arthur smiled. The boy would be a help to him, he could rest easy about that. And despite all that had happened, he was not panicking, nor had he lost his sense of humor. That was a relief.

"Wish I could, mate," he said. "But I don't have a dollar to spend, I'm afraid."

"Just kidding," Ben answered. "At the very least, we can get you some clean clothes. You're a bit taller than me, but what I have is yours. My gramps left me some coats I think might fit you. I don't know how since he's an inch or two shorter than me. But he had a collection of them, all different sizes. They must have been in the family. I pull one out for kicks every once in a while. Shirts and ties too. They're old style."

"That will be fine, thank you," Arthur said. "I realize how . . ." Arthur trailed off, and he hung his head. If he had been able, he might have cried, but his pain was obvious to Ben. This used to be a man who had a certain style, and being dead for nearly fifty years had been, at the very least, an extreme detriment to that style. But pride was a purely human characteristic, and Ben felt some pity for Arthur for his apparent loss of it.

"It's okay," Ben said quickly. "I gotta say were it not for the dirty clothes, you're looking a helluva lot better than you did. Hanging out with you now, I might get one of your castoffs. We'll just have to go a bit heavy on the cologne, is all."

The rest of the drive, about forty-five minutes or so, consisted of Ben prying into Arthur's origins. How did he get to the house? Who was Malcolm Schreck? How did he get involved with such a character? Who was the big dude? Whose head was that on the table? It was not often you come across the head of a Neanderthal.

Arthur tried to answer without giving up too much. Malcolm Schreck was a shadow that had somehow followed him from Europe after Arthur had fallen into the company of some unsavory people from Chicago—mobsters. He didn't reveal that he had always been in the company of unsavory people, nor did he say that he himself was an unsavory sort. The boy didn't need details. About Schreck, he had little to offer. An occultist of some kind, he claimed to have been alive far longer than possible. Drake thought then it was mostly theatrics, but now Arthur remained vague regarding his own life as well. There was little point in describing his past to this young man. It wouldn't help, and Ben would likely not understand. It was only a fuzzy memory now anyway. Decades in Purgatory would change most men's attitudes. It had forced Arthur to bury his past with his first death. He was now only focused on a single imperative—rid the world of Malcolm Schreck or die in the attempt. He truly hoped that both deeds could be accomplished. If Ben's resourcefulness in acquiring blood remained, he would use it only to achieve this end. Arthur could not have realized that even now, the young man sitting next to him held the exact same goals.

Later, the car pulled into a small gravel driveway, grass and weeds growing thick between the tire tracks. Ben rented a house, he explained. He was sorry, but the maid was on vacation. Arthur assured him that it would be an upgrade, no matter how it was kept. Once inside, it was a very short tour. There were two bedrooms and a basement with one full and one half bathroom. Ben supposed Arthur would rather sleep in the basement during the daytime. He knew that so far, none of the legends seemed to apply to Arthur Drake or Malcolm Schreck, but aversion to sunlight might be a more natural course to follow.

"You live alone?" Arthur asked.

"Oh, no," Ben replied, pulling a much-needed beer out of the refrigerator. "I got TV." He gestured toward the living room, where a couch set parallel to the wall. Across from it was a thirty-two-inch-screen television, atop a box-shaped entertainment center. On shelves were numerous VCR tapes.

"I got a ton of movies, books." He continued, casually snapping the tab on the beer and taking a swig. "Some porno too. Those girls are always ready to lend a hand, so to speak. I ain't alone."

"I see," Arthur replied. It was a pity to see a young man like Ben in such desolate isolation, but it was no concern of his at the moment. Ben's place offered him seclusion and safety, and while he had no plan as of yet to confront Malcolm Schreck, there was at least now the time and opportunity to form one.

Ben offered Arthur a drink. "I don't know if you can," he said. "But let's try and see how it goes."

"Whisky then," Arthur said, "if you have it."

Ben poured a shot, and Arthur downed it on the spot without formality. It was difficult to taste it. It wasn't a half of what he remembered whisky as being. Another effect of Malcolm Schreck's conjuring, he imagined. Ben took his own and chased it with a beer. It was obvious to Arthur that the young man intended to get drunk. He couldn't blame him, considering what he'd been through the past few nights. Arthur doubted he himself would receive any effect from the alcohol. He reached into his coat pocket and felt for the crucifix Malcolm had torn from Ben's neck the previous night. Before the boy could take another shot of whisky, Arthur grabbed his wrist and placed the cross in his hand.

Ben considered it silently. "Thanks," he said finally. "Fucker broke the chain though."

"I would keep it close, Ben," Arthur offered. "If there's one thing Malcolm Schreck can do, it's to cause one to believe in the devil, if not God."

"Maybe I'll need it to ward you off," Ben said, harsher than he intended. "You aren't suppressing any urges, are you? I don't want to wake up with you at my throat."

"No urges, mate," Arthur said. "Don't worry."

Ben allowed himself to fall back on the couch, still clutching the cross in his hand. "Well, if you say so," he said incredulously. If there was one thing he understood about the devil, it was that he was an accomplished liar. And though Arthur Drake had done nothing except help him when he was threatened by both Schreck and the big asshole, Ben remembered how greedily Arthur had first taken his taste of blood. It was a dilemma, but one to which he was growing increasingly too intoxicated to give much thought.

"You mentioned some clean clothes?" Arthur said.

"Oh yeah, yeah," Ben replied and forced himself up off the couch. "Grandpa's stuff. Come on." Ben led Arthur to a larger door in his bedroom that opened on a closet. To the far left side were the coats, pants, shirts, and ties he had spoken of. Arthur glanced at them and stepped into the space to sort them.

"Even got a hat or two of his if you want," Ben offered. "Might be a bit oily. I don't think he ever washed his hair but once a month."

Arthur took out a handful of coats and laid them on the edge of Ben's bed. He opened the collar and looked at the label. Then he opened another and another. He stared in wonder. A cold shudder ran through him as he looked at the inside collars.

"Ben!" he cried as the young man was taking another drink from his beer. "What did you say your grandfather's name was?"

Ben looked at him quizzically. "I didn't say," he said. "But it's Righetti. Charlie Righetti. Why?"

"You're Italian?" Arthur said.

"No, he is."

Arthur faced Ben and grabbed his arms fast in his hands. He looked the young man over in the light for the first time. Yes, it was there, the reason the boy gave off that feeling of familiarity from the moment Arthur's eyes had cleared. It was there, softened perhaps. Mixed with some other heritage, yes, but it was there, Charlie Righetti's face, the face of his last true friend. Arthur's whole body shook as he stared at it.

"What the fuck is wrong with you?" Ben shouted as he tried to free himself. Was that urge for blood finally taking over the Englishman?

Arthur released him and breathed heavily. "Ben! You young fool!" Arthur tore his old coat off and brought the open collar up before Ben's eyes. "What does that tag read?"

"I can barely read it, but I guess it . . . says Righetti . . ." Ben paused and took the coat from Arthur. "It says Righetti," he repeated softly.

Both men stood there in silence, absorbing this new revelation, until Arthur finally said, "Benjamin, I knew your grandfather. He was a great friend of mine."

"How could ya?" Ben said abruptly. "You said you got mixed up with mobsters. My grandpa drove a Hostess Twinkie truck for God's sake!"

"Ben, the Charlie Righetti I knew was a tailor," Arthur answered. "How the hell do you think he came by all these clothes with his own name stitched in them?"

"I figured it was his family's stuff. I don't know. He never said anything about it. Said his fingers got caught in a tailgate, and they had to slice them off. Never said anything about being a tailor, not once. But that still doesn't explain how you knew him. You were in the fucking mob! When Gramps couldn't drive anymore, I had to drive him around. Once a month, I took him to Battle Creek, where he got together with a bunch of other old dagos. They'd sit me down. 'Hey, Geno, get the kid a root beer. You want some cookies? Get the kid a couple of those windmill cookies. Eyy. Eyy.' Then they'd go off to another room and speak Italian. I don't know what they talked about, but I know it wasn't any goddamn Cosa Nostra shit!"

"Ben," Arthur said, "calm down. I'm sorry. I didn't mean to upset you." The boy had a temper to him. That much was evident.

"I'm not upset. Do I look upset?"

"Yes."

Ben held up his hands as if to prove they were empty. "I'm all right," he said evenly. He walked over to the couch and sat again. Arthur followed him and took a seat in the chair opposite.

"I like mob movies," Ben said. "But I'm not dumb enough to think that's all Italians are, a bunch of goombas. Some of these assholes can be proud of it if they want to, but my ma's family wasn't like that. They all earned an honest living. And nobody waved the flag like Grandpa. The American flag. And now you're telling me he was mixed up with the Mafia?"

"Shadows, Ben," Arthur said. "Shadows. That's how Charlie talked about it. They were shadows. It was a long time ago. He knew even a good man like him couldn't run from the shadows forever. They would catch you eventually. I wasn't a good man, Ben. But your grandfather was. Believe me."

Ben nodded, and then the hint of tears welled up in his eyes. "I guess so," he said, nodding. "It's just that now that old man is lying there in that nursing home, just waiting to die. I go there, and he won't even look at me. He doesn't remember me. My dad died when I was a kid. He was the only man in my life after that. They all say I'm just like him, just a grumpy old man. And now he's going to die, Mr. Drake. Then I guess I'll be alone."

Arthur stood. "Come on, Ben," he said. "I'll change into those clothes. Spray some cologne on me arse. Then you and me, mate, we're going to see your grandfather."

"Like I said, Mr. Drake, he doesn't even know he's alive, let alone you or me. Besides that, it's a little late to go see anybody, don't you think? And I ain't driving—"

Arthur cut him off. "Ben, didn't Carlo Righetti teach you any respect for your elders? I'm over ninety years old. You won't find much older than that. Get up! Come on! Get up! If I say we're going to see your grandfather, we're going to see your grandfather!"

Chapter 25

While Ben Whittinger and Arthur Drake made their way to the nursing home where Ben's grandfather, Carlo Righetti, was living out his last days, Eli Lundquist stood in an alleyway of the downtown business district, smoking his last remaining cigarette. He resisted the temptation to take long, deep drags for the stick to burn slower and stepped deeper between the two buildings to block the wind from taking its own toll on the paper. Down at the corner of the building was Barney, or Barney Wheels, since he was sitting in an old discarded hospital wheelchair, his useless legs meekly bent in the standard lifeless pose. There was no muscle supporting them; only gravity placed his feet on the foot pegs below. Barney had the wheels set over a grate as he watched for whatever action might be happening in the street. The grate sent up warm steam from the sewers below that warmed his ass. *You have to take what pleasures you could in a life like this,* Eli thought. There was no action tonight, however, and little pleasure to be had, except for the last cigarette burning between his lips.

Eli had always been unlucky. He had been unlucky in school, where his lanky awkwardness and acne-covered face had not endeared him to the opposite sex. He had been unlucky in parents, whose cold Dutch Reformed religion seemed to offer only rebuke to Eli and little affection. He had been unlucky that his draft number had been called and unlucky enough to carry a gun in Vietnam. He had been unlucky once he returned and got the harsh looks and cold shoulder from his countrymen for doing what his country asked him to do. They were all a viscous gauntlet to endure, and if they had had sticks in their hands, he had been sure they would beat him within an inch of his life. Well, maybe not all of them, but the power of the hateful looks far outweighed any compassionate faces he encountered. In fact, Vietnam was the only place Eli had ever been lucky. He hadn't got a scratch.

Eli's father had offered some assistance to him in his stern and terse way. But it wasn't long before the stifling air in his boyhood home became too much for him, and he left it to face the open city. He felt better in the grimy street than the dust-wiped family home, although it was getting on the third week in October, and the air had more bite than his old army jacket could break. He was thinking of joining Barney at the grate before they both decided to spend the rest of the morning in the homeless shelter to get a cup of oatmeal and maybe a cot to lie down upon. That was when Eli saw the stranger walk up and bow his lanky frame down toward Barney Wheels.

Just my luck, Eli thought. *A man in black. A preacher man?* he wondered. *Making late rounds on the despairing unfortunates like me and Barn?* He took a step closer as the stranger replaced a huge hat on his head. "A costume? Little early for Halloween, isn't it?" Eli found himself speaking this thought out loud as he approached the end of the alley. The stranger turned toward him, and as Eli saw his face, it stopped him cold. It was not only the costume but also the way the man seemed to hang there in the air above Barney. It was more than merely odd. He looked less like a man than a coiled snake, a predator. Then the man spoke.

"Beg pardon?" the stranger said. The voice had an accent. German? European of some kind; it had that slither sound to it. Then the stranger grinned.

Eli kept still, so did Barney, although his weathered hands reached slowly down to the rails of his wheels. *He felt it too,* Eli thought. *Something's not right.*

Eli took a breath. "I said it's a little early for Halloween, mister." If Eli had learned anything in country, it was to tamp down anxiety in the face of the enemy. Not that this weird stranger was an enemy.

He didn't know. But he didn't like the way he stood there. That was a direct feeling he couldn't ignore.

"All Hallow's Eve!" the stranger replied. "Yes! The Feast of Samhain! Yes. Yes. You comment on my attire. No, my friend, I fear that I am not in a celebratory humor. I am simply, how you say, old fashioned."

Eli looked incredulously at the man. Old fashioned? Old fashioned was short-sleeved starched white shirts. Old fashioned was bell-bottomed blue jeans.

"You look like a preacher," he said. "Or a hearse driver. What is it you want, mister?"

"Oh, as I stated," the stranger replied, "I may not be in a celebratory humor, but that is not a deterrent from celebrating, my friend." The stranger snapped his fingers, and a large arm came into view, holding a brown bag with a bottleneck coming out of it.

"Now you're talking," Eli said.

"Gimme." Barney joined in. Whatever his feelings for the stranger had just been, they seemed to have subsided.

"Gentlemen," the stranger said, leering, "there is more where this came from, much more. To our maimed friend first." He handed the bottle to Barney, who took a large swig. "Come, come," he admonished him, "save some for your companions."

The stranger took his bone-white fingers and removed the bottle from Barney's hand. Barney, like a baby getting his milk taken mid-drink, grasped at it with waving arms. Without a backward glance, the stranger closed the gap between himself and Eli.

"Your name, friend?" the strange man asked.

"Eli," he answered. "And I hope that's all you need 'cause that's all I got. I still say it's too early for Halloween."

"On my honor, Elijah, despite the coverings you see upon my person, I stand before you quite naked in spirit. You see, like yourself, I wear the scars of a long and very difficult existence."

Eli took a drink. "Is that a fact?" he said blankly. This was beginning to sound like a sermon. Preachers usually didn't ply their listeners' ears with cheap bourbon, but it still sounded like a sermon coming nonetheless. He made to give the man his bottle back, but just as the long pale hand reached for it, he pulled it back and brought it up to his mouth again. If he were going to listen, the preacher would have to pay.

The crazy grin reappeared. This time the claw came up and grabbed the bottle quickly, and the stranger took his own drink. At this rate, there wouldn't be much time to listen to a sermon. The bottle would be gone, and so too would the attraction.

"You talk funny too," Eli replied. "If you want to get a crowd for your speech, mister, you can come down to the shelter. They might have a newer set of duds for you while you sing for your supper."

"Eli," the stranger said, "I have no Bible to quote for you. I find God a cruel taskmaster. Is He not? I see on your face the same suffering. And where, may I ask, is our God in this? I . . . I am an ugly face to gaze upon, that I know. But is He not here, in my ugliness? His beauty and design? Is He not in every scar? Is He not in the scars you carry? Those seen and unseen? No. It cannot be that He is only to be found in this drink we share."

"Hey," Barney called out, "save some for me!"

"Shut up, you old fuck!" someone growled from out of sight. The owner of the arm, Eli gathered. "Shut up, or I'll see how low you can sit in that wheelchair!"

Eli looked anxiously away toward the street. "Don't be alarmed, Eli," the preacher said. "Your friend will come to no harm. I WILL NOT ALLOW IT!" This last statement was loud with an overt threat attached to it.

The bottle was once again under Eli's chin. He took it and drank.

"For centuries, Elijah," the stranger continued in a much more mellow tone, "men have bowed in prayer to an unmoved deity. They have bowed low and lower, all to show humility they need not have practiced. Perhaps that is the fault in our judgment? For if God exists, and He surely does, would He not wish us to look up to Him? Not downward, no . . . no. Head up and aiming high is where we should be looking! How else would we see His wondrous works? How else shall we view the heavens?"

Eli looked at the stranger. The man's pale neck stretched out as he gazed upward. *It is impossible to see much up there,* he thought, *just the darkness.* The streetlight glare blanched out any stars that might have been in the sky. But still, the stranger, in his crude Victorian dress, his huge top hat, and his black oily hair, looked silently upward. And

Eli, despite his misgivings, despite his urge to take one last drink, to have one more puff from his cigarette, followed his gaze and looked up to the nothing above.

There was no pain, only a jolt of shock and a clammy, sticky warmth. He was being attacked, and he was being held there, unable to move, unable to give much struggle at all. Eli Lundquist, who had survived Vietnam, was finally discovering what so many had discovered before him back in country. He was discovering what death was like. And to his final disappointment, to his last bit of bad luck, it was like all things, over, just as he realized it.

Eli didn't hear the stranger in the odd clothing bark out the name Karl. And he didn't feel himself being casually tossed into the dumpster some yards away from where he took his last breath. He was completely unaware in those final moments that he was not Malcolm Schreck's first murder. Schreck had since youth viewed his fellow members of humanity with a casual disdain. And if a body met a body, whatever use came from that was all the inspection it required. No, Eli's only distinction from any other victim was in the use of his body, the flowing of his lifeblood directly into the vessel existing under the name of Malcolm Schreck. And now that Schreck's need had been fulfilled, Eli Lundquist was of no more importance than an oil-soaked rag. And Eli wouldn't ever know that Barney Wheels, although he had kept his chair facing the street and had not dared to glance back at the scene, was desperately trying to wheel himself away, hoping for perhaps the first time in his life that a cop would drive by. Eli's pattern of bad luck had just followed him to his last breath.

Schreck was satiated and elated with the rush of Eli's life feeding his own. He shook with convulsive energy, even as he ordered Karl to open the lid of the large trash receptacle and tossed Eli effortlessly into it. The blood in the cold bags the boy had offered hadn't the vitality of this . . . human. Yes, yes, Schreck had become something other than human long ago while in the tutelage of his old master. But this new being was more than that man ever was. The body in the receptacle had been a pathway to discovery. For a brief moment, Schreck considered that the unfortunate fellow deserved a more dignified resting place. But the thought was fleeting, and he allowed the lid to close down with a soft clang.

Karl looked frightened. Agitated was more like it. He should have made the connection when Schreck had ordered him to stop some distance from the two men in the alley. Malcolm was slightly surprised by this. Mr. Warren, although not endowed with great intelligence and being more than hampered by the superstitions of his day, had still always been keen to his master's needs. This one, although young and strong, would need more training than Warren had ever required. The source of his fear was the situation before him, not yet of Schreck himself. Schreck was his situation now; could he not see this for truth? Of course, Warren had a child's belief in warding off evil through equally childish superstitions. But this was obviously a much different time from that had been. These men today thought of rationality, not superstition. Schreck had felt it in the boy. Even with the crucifix in hand, the boy thought it impossible that a man like Schreck could exist. But Schreck had convinced him. This Karl had dispensed with all belief not of his own simple senses. But Schreck would convince him as well as he eventually convinced anyone who crossed his path. If Karl Angstrom was to be of any use at all, he must be convinced.

Karl looked around frantically. They had to leave! He would leave this nightmare in an instant if the fucking freak didn't continually take a one-inch fucking drill bit to his brain every time he looked in the wrong direction. *He had killed the guy. Of course, he had killed the guy, Karl, you stupid fuck! What did you think he would do? Suck his dick? No, he sucked his blood. His blood! Oh god! Goddammit! Hardly spilled a drop of it either, which, in a way, was good. Wasn't it? Got to get out of here,* he thought. *Away, anywhere! Away!*

"Karl," Malcolm said, "bring that half man back to me. Now."

Karl looked and grimaced at the spot where the cripple had been. He growled something inaudible but did as he was told, running to the end of the alley and looking both directions. He spotted the chair and the frantic arms of the cripple pushing on its rungs. He ran and easily caught the man. Karl grabbed the handles of Barney's chair with a sudden ferocity, quickly spinning him about and running the man and his chair back toward the tall, bent stranger. Barney was helpless as a young child in his father's arms and too frightened to scream as the dark shape came closer. His graying beard blew back against his open mouth. Barney, like Eli, had never had any luck either, not even in Vietnam, where a bullet had hit the unluckiest spot on his spine. Not where it would kill him unfortunately. That would have been lucky, especially right now. Barney remembered that moment when the bullet hit. A few inches to the left and the damn thing would have gone through the lung, the lung he had done his best to blacken and make useless with cigarette butts and cheap alcohol. A few inches up from that and it would have burst through his heart, an instant death for the organ that had been nothing but a half-assed pump for his poisoned blood. But it hadn't happened that way. The bullet hit just where it would render his legs into useless tubes that would not resist, or allow him to resist, any act of anyone who wanted to manipulate him. He had thought of how death would be welcome since that day and the countless others that had followed. And yet for some reason, perhaps only in the manner of his impending doom, Barney suddenly found a very strong desire within himself, to live.

But the strange man merely bent over toward him and spoke to him again with that strange inflection. "Do you know the name of the man I was just speaking with?" the stranger asked.

Barney lied. He knew Eli very well, at least as well as either of them had allowed, considering their circumstances. "No," he said.

"Hmm," the stranger muttered. "This is good. Would you like to have more libations?"

Libation means alcohol, Barney thought. He wasn't sure, but that was what he thought. "Yes, please," he said as innocently as he could muster.

"Then you must forget, half man, what has occurred this night," the stranger said, "much as you have suddenly forgotten your friend's name. You must do this, if you wish to survive. You understand?"

Barney silently nodded and attempted to sell his acceptance with a modest smile. A new bottle was handed to him, and Barney quickly opened it and began drinking as if his life depended on it, which it did. But the stranger wasn't done yet. His long hand pulled down on Barney's arm, and Barney watched the bottle pull away from his lips.

"If you believe you have suffered torture in your life," the strange and oddly dressed man continued, "and it is evident that you have, I tell you now, half man, if I were you, I would not wish to see me again. You understand? Yes?"

"Yessir."

"Good," the man said, straightening. "Then we take our leave of you."

Barney did exactly as he was told. He was a good soldier. He knew following orders saved lives. He kept drinking, and except for the minor, dark, nagging spot in the back of his mind, he forgot.

Chapter 26

Death is a constant visitor, one that never requires and rarely receives an invitation. It is not bigoted, nor does it concern itself with the class status of its host. Sometimes it's expected, and by some, it might even be welcomed until it actually arrives. For Ben Whittinger, death was a member of the family, entirely unwelcome, and a far too lingering guest, unable to ever completely be shown the door. He had first met the specter of death when his father passed. His father had been very young. Before long, if Ben managed to survive, he himself would be as old in age as his father had reached. And like a parent who loses a child, a child who loses a parent to death, if that parent is beloved, will often find death a near-constant companion, a lingering tap on the shoulder, a whisper in the ear.

And now Ben Whittinger had death sitting next to him in his car in the form of an Englishman named Arthur Drake. Drake now appeared to be only in his mid-thirties to possibly forty, a far cry from their first meeting, where he had barely appeared human at all. Ben could not forget this, even as his resistance to the vampire's smooth charm dulled and, ultimately, fell away. Still, he wondered how long the blood Arthur had consumed would satisfy him and how he could weasel some more out of his work without being caught.

The drive to the nursing home where Carlo Righetti now resided, waiting for his visit from death, was not very long. It was a drive time of about forty minutes with traffic lights that only flashed yellow because of the lateness of the hour. The two men took the opportunity to talk in the car. Arthur was interested in the world today as Ben saw it. This included music and movies, cultural influences, and of course, war. There had been a war on when Arthur had last walked the earth, and he had heard Ben reference a war upon his awakening. It must not have been a continuation of WWII, or the country could not possibly look so peaceful.

No, Ben explained. There had been numerous wars and skirmishes since Arthur had gone into hibernation or whatever state he had been. Korea, Vietnam, a Cold War that saw many people killed but no battles to speak of, all while Arthur Drake had lain in a dank, musty potato cellar. And now America and her allies had just gone over to fight a short desert war, where its enemy had proved impossibly outmanned and outgunned. The damn thing had barely lasted a couple of months, and the casualties were so few in comparison to other conflicts that all America had really suffered for it was a sense of invincibility. The topic was a depressing one to Arthur and, like Malcolm Schreck, one he regretted having begun. Both men in the car consciously avoided speaking of the monster named Malcolm Schreck.

As to the rest, Ben chided Arthur for having missed the best music and movies that time had to offer. "You missed it, pal," Ben said frankly. "Welcome back to the shit." Arthur was lucky that Ben had found him, he said, not somebody who worked at the Gap, whatever that was. Ben liked old music and old movies. He avoided most of the new culture. MTV had destroyed both music, and video for that matter, in his opinion, and the best one could hope for is that a decent movie would occasionally find release. Arthur could peruse his library once they returned home. He would see VCR tapes and albums that were more in tune or, at least, not so jarringly different from what he may have been accustomed to in his time. Sinatra was still alive somehow, and Ben had been smart enough to take some of his recordings out of his grandfather's house before the old man was placed in the nursing home. Arthur could listen to those and feel like maybe the world hadn't changed quite so much. But now music was mostly just a bunch of shithead brats all pissed off that they got everything they ever wanted.

Arthur took all this in with a sly amusement. Ben was sarcastically humorous in his descriptions. Perhaps a bit too negative in his attitude for Arthur's tastes, but he still wished to protect Ben. He needed the lad, but now with what he had just discovered about Ben's heritage, Arthur was also conscious of how fate had turned so tightly against any plan he might conjure that wouldn't involve the grandson of Carlo Righetti. So Arthur allowed Ben to bring him rather crudely up to date without much interruption. He had another reason to keep Ben talking throughout the drive. He was subtly studying his manipulation of the vehicle. Arthur had never driven a car. Driving had never occurred to him in England, and motor cars had been still very new in his youth in San Francisco. If he wanted a lift, somebody was always available to give him one, and if not, he merely waited at the pub till someone was. But now he watched Ben's right foot press on the accelerator pedal and lift and then press on the higher brake pedal. That seemed easy enough, although it wouldn't be as natural for him as it was for the young man next to him. Arthur studied the lazy way Ben gripped the steering wheel. Again, he doubted he would be so adept. His nerves would overcome him in the attempt, and he would likely grip the wheel with the force one grips a fire escape on the way out a window. But he had to keep Ben talking. The boy had seen him looking and wondered whether Arthur was just nervous about the speed, something he understood from driving his grandfather around.

"Don't worry, Mr. Drake," he said. "We'll get there."

"I'm not worried, Ben," Arthur answered. "And you can call me Arthur, if you please. Mr. Drake sounds like a very old man. You're grandfather used to call me . . . Artie. I don't recall anyone else ever calling me that. But I didn't mind being Artie to someone."

"You don't look like an Artie to me," Ben said. "But I have seen you drink blood. That could be it."

"The less we talk about that, the better."

"Okay, Arthur," Ben replied as they pulled into a darkened parking lot. "Well, we're here." He was not sure how they would enter the building. The main doors would likely be locked at this hour. The only hope would be a kind, understanding nurse or nurse assistant maybe. And that was a slim hope. Nurses tended to be very rule-oriented. And night-shift nurses, depending on their age and length of service, were often an implacable force to be reckoned with. The day and evening shifts didn't agree with them. Dealing with all the numerous attitudes and lackadaisical work force, buffered by their numbers alone, was disheartening to the night manager. And bringing any issues of the incompleteness of the previous shift's duties was met with a casual shrug. Late at night was when the night manager could reign sovereign. Late at night was when order came to the institution. Ben looked for a propped door, where someone who didn't feel as strongly as the manager might have left ajar to go out and have a smoke. Not to his surprise, he saw one thirty yards away from the main door and the smoke from the two employees drafting around the corner. They waited for the smoke to clear and the red butts hit the pavement by the door. The two workers left to take a walk around the building's perimeter. Ben and Arthur watched as they passed in front of the main entrance and kept walking, lighting another pair of cigarettes.

"Come on," Ben said. "We'll have to be quick."

Sneaking into the building was not a problem. The two employees left the stone in the jam. Ben and Arthur quietly squeezed through the opening, just enough to let them in. For good measure, Ben kicked the rock out from the door jam and let the door softly close. That would lessen the traffic for a minute or two and likely just give a good excuse for an extended break for the smokers. Ben knew where his grandfather's room was located. This service entrance would lead to a long main hallway, where they would then turn left. The unfortunate aspect was that they would have to cross in front of a main greeting desk, where the charge nurse or someone else would be sitting, munching on potato chips, and going over charts.

The hallway was dark and silent, but the light at the main desk was yellow, glaring, and bright. The two men walked the hall like thieves, close to the wall. Shit! Of course, she was there. Of course, she was old. And of course, they would be caught.

"Ben," Arthur whispered behind him, "let's act casual now. I have a plan. If it doesn't work, we'll come back at a more appropriate time. But I must see him."

Arthur leading, they stepped into the light. "Ahh, good evening, ma'am," he said cheerfully.

The charge nurse stood, surprised. She had on a nursing uniform with a collar and buttons that strained against her ample abdomen. Nursing caps, like men's hats, had gone out of style, but she still wore hers. To Ben, this was a bad sign.

"What are you two gentlemen doing here at this hour?" she asked, an even tension in her voice. A young girl, approximately Ben's age, sat behind the desk as well and smiled brightly as Arthur approached.

"Beg pardon, ma'am," Arthur said. "I'm an old friend of Carlo Righetti. And this is his grandson."

The nurse was unmoved. "Visiting hours are well past over, sir." She emphasized the words as if they were either deaf or didn't speak the language.

"Yes, ma'am," Arthur said, trying to soften his tones as much as possible. "We're very sorry for the time, but I only just learned that Carlo was still with us and—"

"Carlo?"

"Charles Righetti," Ben stated succinctly. This old broad was going to be a problem. One Arthur's good looks and charm were not going to overcome easily.

"Young man," the nurse replied from behind the desk, "it is half past one o'clock in the morning—"

"Lady, I don't care if it's half past a monkey's ass and quarter—"

Arthur stepped in front of him. "Ben! Ben!" he interrupted. "There's no need for argument, dear lady. We realize we're in the wrong here."

"Yes, you are."

The nursing assistant looked down at her lap. She was suddenly embarrassed by this exchange. Arthur noted it and said, "Don't worry, dear. We won't be any trouble." He resumed his attention to the charge nurse.

"I'm returning to London this very morning. A few hours of sleep and I'm on a ship home."

"You're taking a ship?" the nurse asked, incredulous.

"He's flying," Ben said. "This guy is from England. He calls a plane a ship." Ben attempted a Cockney English accent. "He says a lo of tings I don righly unnerstan."

"Is that how you think I sound?"

"Sorry," Ben replied. "Now can we please see my grandpa?"

"Gentlemen," the nurse replied, "the residents of this facility need their rest. I'm not sure you're aware, but people of this age are easily confused and agitated, especially during the night hours. It's called sundowners syndrome, and it can be quite difficult to get them settled after it occurs. Now I am unfamiliar with your grandfather's case, but I believe his name has been mentioned in that regard."

Ben's temper began to flare at this. "Probably because the last time I was here, you had him dressed in someone else's clothes. Someone with a Polish name I think it was. Righetti is Italian, in case you didn't know."

"Young man," the manager stressed, "older men of a certain generation often dress in a similar fashion—"

"Well, apart from being Polish, he was also about three hundred pounds from the look of it, and my grandpa obviously is not."

Just then, the two other employees appeared—a man and a woman in bright pajama-like scrubs. They stepped into the light, taking all this in with quiet surprise. Arthur saw them and returned his attention to the charge nurse. He said, quite calm, in spite of the pressure in his chest, "Ma'am, I'm only here to pay my respects. Once I leave, I'm afraid I won't be able to return for a funeral. I promise you, we won't be disruptive. If he's asleep, we won't wake him. If I could just see him . . ."

"I'll watch them, Mrs. Ferguson." It was the young girl behind the desk. "I'll make sure nothing happens," she said.

Mrs. Ferguson considered this. The harsh look never left her face, but in the silence, she considered. "Five minutes," she said blankly. She looked at the man who had just arrived. "You be nearby too." The man pursed his lips and nodded. The way she said it, he knew he was already in hot water.

The young nurse's aide stepped from behind the desk. She had long dark hair brought back into a ponytail, and despite the less than complimentary scrub outfit she wore, she was petite and attractive. She led them a few steps ahead, out from under the light and into the darkened hallway to Charlie's room.

As they walked, Arthur whispered, "Half past a monkey's ass?"

Ben looked up at him. "You think I want to see my grandpa dying in here?" he said. "Nobody should die in here."

At the door, the girl stopped, looked at Arthur a second, and said to Ben, "I think I've seen you here before. Your grandpa hasn't said anything in a long time, at least as far as I know. I'm sorry about the clothes. I'll keep an eye on it when I can."

Ben looked at her a moment. She looked very pretty just standing there. His eyes dropped, and he said quickly, "It's all right. Thank you."

Arthur smiled at her. "Yes, thank you very much. We won't be long, I promise." They left her at the door, Ben taking one last look behind as they entered the darkened room. The girl stood there a moment and then took a step and disappeared to the side of the entry. The room was dark, but the shape of the bed was clear, and a light from the bathroom showed upon the bedsheets. Ben's grandfather, Carlo Righetti, lay there, asleep. As Arthur stepped to the foot of the bed, his hand suddenly reached for Ben's shoulder, stopping both of them. The fingers gripped and clutched at the coat so tightly that Ben whispered, "What? What's wrong?"

Something came over the Englishman. He looked as if he might burst into tears. Ben wondered if that was even possible. "Oh, Ben!" he said as quietly as the tension in his voice would allow. "Oh my god!"

Arthur found himself hyperventilating. The young man at his side had a familiar face, but that face had not done it. The car had been sleek and strange, but that had not troubled him much. The whole bizarre appearance of Karl Angstrom had not made him aware of anything peculiar. But here, with his old friend Charlie Righetti lying on a bed, with his face, his ancient face, like the withered bark of an old tree, the passage of time came full on his consciousness.

Arthur Drake looked at Ben in agonizing pain. He said, as if in plea for it to be not so, "I've been gone a very long time, haven't I?"

"Yeah," Ben answered. "Yeah, I guess so. Here, take a seat," he offered, directing Arthur to the chair by the bed. Ben took the one opposite, on the other side of his grandfather. "It's all right," he said softly. "He doesn't know we're here. He's sleeping now. So it's okay."

They both studied the old man for a moment in silence. Then Arthur reached his hand out and placed it gently on the shrunken chest, allowing it to rise and fall with the breathing. "Charlie," he said in the darkness.

Just then, the old man's rheumy eyes opened and stared straight up to the ceiling as if waiting for it to open up for him. Arthur slid his hand off and sat back in the chair. The eyes darted slowly to one side and then the other. They tried to focus on Ben, but what Carlo Righetti was seeing wasn't clear.

"Geno," he said. "Geno, be careful . . . over there. Watch . . . out . . . over . . ."

"Grandpa," Ben said, leaning in close and taking the frail right hand of his grandfather, the hand with the fingertips missing. "Grandpa, it's not Geno. It's Ben, your grandson. Ben, Grandpa."

The old eyes seemed to shake as they focused harder on the face before them. "Benny? Hey, Pasquale, why you here? Why you not in school?"

The voice was raspy as Arthur remembered it, but age had taken much of the force and life out of it. It was like sandpaper rubbed half-heartedly on wet wood.

"No school, Grandpa. It's late. We're sorry we woke you up. I brought an old friend to see you."

Ben gestured to the other side of the bed, and the old man followed the gesture over slowly and looked at the other man. His maimed hand came up and rubbed at his eyes. He could not sit up, but it was obvious that was his intent as he shook with the effort. Giving up with a heavy exhale, he said, "Dead. Dead. I must be dead." A look of intense fear came over Charlie Righetti, and he tried to inch away from the face and the man who owned it.

Arthur smiled. "No, Charlie," he said softly, "we're not dead yet, either of us. I'm sorry to come to you like this, my old friend. But you're not dead, I assure you."

"How?" the old man said, looking back to Ben. "Geno? How?" Then as soon as he said the name, he looked back at what to him appeared to be a spirit from the other world, and he said, "Artie. Artie. How can this be?" Then he slumped back to his pillow and stared at Arthur. "I'm sorry, Artie. I'm sorry. I wanted to . . . help you. I was so scared . . . so scared for you." He held up his right hand. The stumps of his fingers came to an abrupt but rounded end at his first knuckle. His eyes began to weep. "They do this to me. Beat me some more and left with you. I couldn't . . . couldn't . . ."

"It's all right, mate," Arthur said, hoping his old friend would accept his story. "They just ran me off, is all. Ran me off. They couldn't kill me either. Boss wouldn't let them. Here now, Charlie, give me your hand." Arthur took the wounded hand in his, clasping it and holding it up so they both could see their hands together. "You see?" he said. "We're not dead, mate. Not yet."

They sat there like that, looking at each other. Arthur could see that Charlie was frightened, trying to figure how the man before him could be the same man he knew so long ago. Yet he hadn't really changed, had he? Charlie was an old man waiting for the hand of death to come reach out to him; instead, he held the hand of Arthur Drake, who, by any reasonable account, should be among the dead. If not by violence as Charlie believed, then by age itself. But Arthur Drake could have walked out of the past just as Charlie remembered him. He hadn't aged at all. Was this how death was coming to him? With the young face from the distant past? Or was he just growing senile like his family had said while he sat there silent. Somewhere in his mind, Charlie Righetti was glad to see the face either way.

"Your grandson, Charlie," Arthur said, breaking the quiet moment, "has been helping me."

Charlie broke his gaze from Arthur and looked back to Ben. "Hey, Pasquale," he said, "you got trouble?"

"No, no, Grandpa," he lied. "No trouble. Just ran into this guy who said he knew ya, that's all." Ben looked to Arthur. "I guess he wasn't lying."

"Yeah," Righetti said. "I know this guy from long time ago. You a lot alike, you two. You both . . . like to sleep all day." He blew out a weak attempt at a whistle and, with his free hand, made a waving gesture. "You got the life, buddy. You got the life." His eyes closed then, and his breathing steadied. The two men looked at each other, and Arthur let the hand rest gently on the chest. Ben kissed the tips of his fingers and touched them to the old man's forehead. "Love you, Grandpa," he said.

They stood and quietly walked out. Ben's eyes were red and painful. He modestly tried to hide them from the girl as she waited for them outside the room. Arthur thanked her and began walking the way they had come, but the girl stopped them.

"Go straight this way and then left," she said. "There's a door you can exit without going by the desk. I told Jerry to let you out. He's waiting for you." Ben nodded, and she touched his sleeve. "I'm glad you came. He's been so quiet. I wasn't eavesdropping, but I could hear him talking just now a lot of times that means . . . well, you know."

"Yeah," Ben said. "Thank you." He did know what it could mean—a last bit of energy, a last time to say your piece, a last goodbye. It didn't always happen that way, but it was a noted occurrence for the old and sick. He nodded again, and the two men walked down the hall. Jerry was there at the expected door and hit a button that silenced the alarm, and they walked out into the cool early morning dark. Ben quickened his pace as they reached the lot, and Arthur stepped faster to reach him.

"Thank you, Ben," he said. "Thank you."

"Just shut up, will you?" Ben said harshly.

"What's the matter?" Arthur asked.

"You made my grandpa cry, you son of a bitch."

Arthur smiled and, grabbing Ben by the shoulders as they walked, gave them an affectionate squeeze.

Chapter 27

Death, it appeared, had been no easier on Eli Lundquist than life had been. His face showed the shock of its arrival with widened, upturned eyes and a slightly gaped mouth. His arms were crooked as if in the attempt to ward it off, and gravity at this time in the morning had no effect on them. Soon, the rigor in his limbs would settle, and he would become lax again. But for now, he was stiff and clearly not serene, lying supine in the garbage dumpster.

The two detectives, Lewis and Kipner, looked down on the body. It had been discovered by a young cook from the small greasy spoon restaurant after the first breakfast rush. He came out with a garbage bag and a cigarette to light hanging from his mouth. Before he could hoist the bag completely into the dumpster and allow the eggshells, half-eaten pancakes, and grease-soaked paper towels to obscure Eli's body, he had suddenly stopped himself short. The cigarette was pasted to his lower lip by just the right amount of moisture. It too refused to fall next to the horrible sight of a dead man in the dumpster. The cook ran inside, and in the usual half-asleep, half-awake motion of the early morning, the police had come and cordoned off the alley. If there was one fortunate happenstance for this occurrence, it was that the manager had also had the foresight to stop the city garbage truck from backing in and hauling the dumpster's contents away before the police arrived. Had he not accomplished this small act, Eli

Lundquist and all would have been unceremoniously tossed into the back of the truck, thereby allowing every piece of stinking, rotting, and disgusting litter to lie on top of the dead man, the formerly destitute and, previous to that, honorably discharged veteran of the U.S. Armed Services.

When the captain had sent them out on this run, Kipner had exclaimed, "Thank Christ!" How anyone could thank the Lord for a murder victim was beyond Lewis, but he merely shrugged and shook his head. Apparently, the younger man had grown weary of talking to would-be criminals and would-be informants about would-be murders that might have occurred had the perps not been teenagers shooting .22s into the fleshy backsides of other teenagers while driving by at speed. Lewis supposed he could understand that. The small town had become a training ground for the bigger cities east and west, and most of these shooters had merely taken the easiest access to the highway and gone about their merry business, seemingly not to know or care if their shots had found their mark. Whooping it up, over the adrenaline rush.

But here, however, was a man truly dead, and unless he was particularly gifted and at the same time severely self-loathing, the cause was foul play. The face and neck were ashen white, and there appeared to be a laceration at or near the left carotid artery. The lac was dry, except for a small trickle of red blood that had dried brown over time. If the event had taken place nearby, there should be a shower of red wash on the street, the dumpster, everywhere. Kipner stepped away and took a tour of the area, looking for any sign, while Lewis set about speaking to the cook.

"You found him?" Lewis asked. He towered over the young man in the greasy apron and hairnet. The kid was finally getting his smoke break. The smell of his cigarette was a welcome mask for the acrid smell of old lettuce and tomato, festering in the alley dumpster.

"Yessir," the cook said quickly. He was nervous. The discovery of the body, coupled with the fact that most guys his age thought cops were clairvoyant to their personal activities, caused him to rush his responses. Lewis held still and smiled at him.

"Take it easy," he said. "You're not in trouble. What time was it this morning?"

"Eight, eight fifteen. I'm not exactly sure. We open at six for the bus drivers and train station crew. They had all left, and I went out with the garbage to drop it before the garbageman came. There he was. Just like that there."

"Okay," Lewis said, writing the pertinent info on his pad. "You ever see this guy before?"

"I didn't take a real good look at him," the cook admitted.

"Think you could now?"

The cook closed his eyes and nodded silently. He stepped over with Lewis to the open dumpster and looked again at the corpse, its position unchanged, its dead eyes unclosed.

"Might have seen him around a couple of times," the cook said, looking back to the open alley as quickly and steadily as he could. "Probably from the Stegman House. Those guys don't wander too far from there. They like to hang out by the grate in this alley. He might've been one of them I've seen before. Never talk to them. You talk to them, their hands out right away—cig, money, your ear, it don't matter. I don't have enough of my own to give them."

"Hey, you don't need to apologize," Lewis offered. "Thanks. Just give your name and number to that uniform over there. We'll get back to you if we need anything."

The young cook nodded, took his last draw on his cigarette, did as he was told, and then disappeared back through the side door to the restaurant. Lewis went over to where Kipner was crouching. He was placing a cardboard marker at a spot near the edge of the wall.

"What do you got?" he asked, bending his large frame over to peer at the spot.

"Not much," Kipner said, "for a slit throat. Possible he bled out in the dumpster?"

"Not much there that I could see either," Lewis said. "Not even on his collar. Kind of odd. We'll have to get him down to the coroner's, see if he has any other injuries. Maybe he got it somewhere else, and somebody just dumped him here."

"Lots of dew on the street, of course," Kipner added. "Not enough to wash away anything like this, but all I see is a couple of splotches could be from our boy. Looks like a pattern formed as they dropped over something. Shoe maybe." Kipner stood. "Just tell me I don't have to go into that dumpster. I know I'm new. I know I'm junior here, but—"

"Don't worry, Kip," Lewis said with a grin. "I don't see any real need. Looks like a dump job to me."

"Could be a serial," the younger man said. "Better check all directions, see if anyone else has had a drop like this."

Lewis looked puzzled. "You're going to take one dead and make a serial out of it? A serial killer? Really?"

"It's not the stiff, Phil," Kipner answered. "It's how he was handled. Like garbage. Anyone does that, if it's not personal, probably thinks just about everybody's garbage, don't you think? Whoever it is, he isn't a virgin. I'm just saying."

"Right," Lewis said, nodding. "Okay, well, let's not get ahead of ourselves. Let's just take the one body we have and figure it out from what he tells us." Lewis took a quick Polaroid of the victim and, as the copy slid out from the feed, signaled to the uniform nearby that they were done. The body, which would be identified by the dog tag that hung beneath his shirt as Eli Lundquist, would be taken to the county morgue, where the coroner could work him up and see if there was anything else it could reveal. For now, the two detectives would see if he was known at the Stegman House, the local homeless shelter.

Kipner tapped Lewis's arm as they walked back to the car. "Can we assume something else for the moment?" he said. "At least until we find out different?"

"What's that?" Lewis asked.

"Our boy is white," Kipner said firmly. "Too weird to be anything but a white guy."

Lewis laughed. "Okay," he said, "works for me. White guy it is."

The cook was correct. The Stegman House was only four blocks from the scene. During the day, the disheveled inhabitants took to the outside. The sun had come out, and they all seemed to look up at it as if it had healing properties long withheld from them. Mostly men, but a few women straggled about in a directionless habitual gathering. Lewis and Kipner decided without speaking of it to bypass the street dwellers and speak to someone in charge. Conversations with the homeless could be as pointless as a car without gas. It would go nowhere. Besides, one of these people could be the perpetrator. As remote as that idea was, the possibility still remained. The victim could have been murdered elsewhere, accounting for the lack of blood in the area, and one, perhaps two of his fellow travelers could have deposited him in the dumpster, only to return to the shelter later. The picture Lewis held would help make the ID. The victim was obviously dead, but he had not been visibly beaten. If he were known here, the mere fact of his death would send a ripple of panic with the residents. And if the perp **was** among them, a warning. Lewis thought it better to keep this between the manager and themselves.

The young manager, Dennis Farley, had a small office in the back of the spacious room where the cots had been neatly arranged. The cots themselves were in various states of disarray with blankets and sleeping bags draped over their edges, some touching the floor, and others rolled into a neat cylinder at the ends of the cots. Small nightstands stood between a few near the back of the room, obviously for those who had earned some extra accommodation. These were kept cleaner than the others, some sense of pride still evident despite the circumstance.

Farley looked at the picture as he took a seat behind his desk. Lewis watched him, waiting for the look of recognition to cross his thin, bearded face. He was probably Kipner's age but had decided to go native. His hair was very long, pulled back into a ponytail. Here was a humanist, Lewis gathered, rebelling against the conformity that the straight society demanded. *Kipner may have looked like this in vice,* Lewis thought. *Probably not as soft though.*

"You recognize him, Mr. Farley?" Lewis asked. Kipner looked around the office, silently checking the artwork and the framed photos so Farley would only feel the large black man's attention as he loomed over the opposite side of the desk.

"Yeah," Farley answered in a soft murmur. "It's Eli. Looks like him anyway. What happened?"

"Other than he was murdered, we don't really know. And we'd like you to keep this under wraps for now. If anyone out there knows he's missing or why, we don't want them making off to the next town. Eli got a last name?"

"They have to register here, but I don't know it off the top of my head I'm sorry to say."

Kipner stepped up next to Lewis. "He ever cause any trouble?" he asked. "Make some enemies among the residents?"

"Not to my knowledge," Farley answered. "He wasn't a problem. Of course, I'm here during the day. If there's any trouble, it's usually after dark. The only mark against Eli that I'm aware of is he allowed one of our promiscuous residents into his cot one night. He was reprimanded for it, and she, thankfully, is no longer here. I never saw the point in making an issue out of human nature, but our director has other ideas. I can't imagine that leading to this."

"No jealousy angle then?" Lewis offered.

Farley blew out a dismissal. "Not unless someone else wanted a disease she carried. No, I don't think so. Eli mainly followed the rules, and when he decided he couldn't do that, he wasn't around. Like most of these poor people."

"Anyone here he hung around then? Anyone who might miss him?"

Farley pushed his large rimmed glasses back up the thin bridge of his nose. His brow furrowed as he thought of the many people in and out of the Stegman House and who cliqued with whom. "Barney," he said hurriedly. "Barney Wheels, they call him. Because he's in a wheelchair. Clever, huh? I don't know if they were together last night. I presume if they were, we'd be talking about two victims, wouldn't you? They're both veterans. Not of this latest disaster, of course. The previous one. You know what I'm saying?"

Lewis looked blankly at him. "I do," he said flatly. "Thank you, Mr. Farley. We'll be in touch. For now, let's keep this conversation between us. If you can get us a proper head count, that would be helpful. Just call the station with it, if you don't mind. Here's my card."

Farley took the card from Lewis. "Is that it? Do you think we're in any imminent danger here? I mean, we have a lot of residents. And our staff . . ."

Kipner smiled. "You'll see an increase in the police presence, Mr. Farley. We take murder seriously. But I wouldn't worry. Like you said, trouble usually happens after dark. Of course, whoever did it could be here. But that's not our first thought. Have a good day now."

Chapter 28

Eli Lundquist's naked body lay on the rollers of the steel table in the precinct morgue. It was now 7:00 p.m., and darkness was falling outside. The large round lights suspended from the ceiling glowed yellow on his pale skin and seemed to wash the cool stone walls with that same languid tone. His eyes were mercifully closed. His belongings were held in an opaque plastic bag—clothes, comb, wallet, dog tags—neatly tucked away and sitting nearby on a counter. His life, as his body had been, was wrapped up in a single bag. His wallet had given some idea of his identity—his name, twice verified by his tags, and his VA card. Years active, 1971–1974.

There was no thought in the coroner's mind of this body reviving. The limbs were cool to the touch. It could be felt through the pale plastic gloves he wore as he examined the arms and legs of the victim. A peripheral examination to see if there were any other markings with which to draw some conclusion of the victim's last breaths found only old bruises on the right shin as if he had bumped into a bed board in the dark. They were days old and healing at the time of death. Eli himself gave no resistance to this last indignity. Whatever form Eli's life took at death, if any, it would not resume occupancy in the physical one he had known before meeting Malcolm Schreck. If Schreck had the slightest inclination of that as a possibility, he would have removed any chance of it on the spot. Malcolm Schreck and

Arthur Drake were two of a kind. And that was exactly how it would stand.

But Schreck had left a piece of himself, unknowingly, with Eli. As the blade had came up to Eli's neck, so had Eli's hand. His fingernails, while no match for the razor-like edges of Schreck's own, were still long and in dire need of trimming. A movement, almost as quick as the one that had drawn the life out of him, had managed to strike Malcolm Schreck's pale cheek. The smallest fraction of skin had stuck to the underside of Eli's long nail. It was the tiniest amount of skin, so tiny that the action would have seemed like a quick breeze of air to Schreck as he clamped his mouth down on the outstretched neck. If Schreck had not been in such a state of exuberance, he might have noticed. If the flesh hadn't closed on his cheek so quickly, he might have seen the evidence of the scratch. But if Malcolm Schreck hadn't noticed his skin in the dead man's fingernail, the coroner did. He held up the pale arm and examined it closely. Then he took a pair of small forceps and tugged gently at the tissue beneath the fingernails, two small fragments of what could be skin. No blood on the tissue. No evidence of what manner of tissue it was. Could be the skin of a cantaloupe, the under rind of an orange, or any number of things the victim had dug into with the first and second fingernails of his right hand. The intriguing question was whether these pieces of tissue were human.

By the time Lewis and Kipner arrived, Dr. Ernest Sherman had completed that evaluation and was casually eating a ham sandwich at the desk opposite the body. Eli remained stretched out naked on metal rollers set over the top of the welled table. The table was welled so that after Dr. Sherman was done examining the body, Eli's excess tissue could be washed down with a hose to a collection sink at the end of the table. There were three other like tables waiting to be used for these purposes in the dank and clammy room, each ending with a deep metal sink and gray hoses attached to the spigots. Eli's body had been eviscerated with precision and delicacy with far more attention and care than Malcolm Schreck had applied, and yet the result, to the two detectives, was just as grisly. The morgue was not a welcoming place for the living. And yet there, Dr. Sherman sat, perfectly content, chewing on his lunch that was spread out next to the microscopes and tissue slides.

"Hello, Phillip," Dr. Sherman said between his swallows of sandwich.

"Ernie," Lewis replied.

"Who's this?" Sherman asked, indicating the shorter white man Lewis had in tow.

"Kipner," the younger man said. "Jeff Kipner, new partner, out of Detwah."

Sherman held out his hand to Kipner, but Kipner merely looked at it. Sherman wiped it down his lab coat a couple of times and re-extended it.

"Show a little respect, young man," he said. "One day you might visit me when you can't shake my hand."

Kipner took the grasp. "Sorry," he said. "Not used to the atmosphere, I guess. By the way, aren't you a little worried about evidence contamination?"

"No," Sherman replied. "You can stand anywhere you want."

Lewis laughed. He had grown fond of Sherman since he first met him a few years back. He was funny but seriously competent. And he seemed to take the fact of Lewis's race without any of the implied controversy it held upstairs in the department. Men like that were hard to find. To find one in a morgue only proved the fact.

"I think he means the lunch, Ern," Lewis said, holding his mirth in check.

"I pride myself on my neatness, Detective Kipner," Ernie said. "Besides, there's at least a foot and a half between the grapes and the sandwich."

Kipner smiled sarcastically and nodded. "Okay."

"What do you got, Ernie?" Lewis said.

Sherman stepped away from the table to the body. He took a pen out of his lab coat pocket and pointed at the victim's neck. Lewis was relieved to see that someone, probably Sherman, had the good sense to close the victim's eyes. Even in the morgue, those open eyes would have transmitted a contagion of fear.

"What do these look like to you, Phil?" Sherman took the end of his pen and indicated the small wound at the left side of the neck, near the Adam's apple. At each end of the laceration were small purplish-gray rashes. "Here and here." The point of the pen nearly touched each rash.

"Not sure," Lewis said.

"Hickeys," Kipner interjected plainly.

Sherman looked at Kipner. "One might think so, if one were so inclined," he said.

"But one wouldn't make much sense, if one did," said Lewis.

The three men stood in silence around the body for a moment. Then Sherman said, "Your report indicated not much blood at the scene. I'll let you be the detectives, but I can tell you that cause of death was severe loss of blood because of a very well-placed laceration to the carotid artery. My sense is the attacker was facing his victim at the time. It's a left-to-right laceration done in a downward sweep, indicating it was performed with the left hand, coming across like this." Sherman demonstrated the motion on Lewis as he stood in front of him.

"That should mean that the attacker would be covered immediately in blood." Sherman continued. "But what if the suspect covered the wound instantly? That first spray hits him, and then he's over it."

"Hold on," Lewis said. "What are you saying? He drank the blood?"

Sherman shrugged. Lewis looked at Kipner, who had his eyes firmly engaged on the wound. "Would explain why we didn't see much of any at the scene, I suppose," Kipner said.

"I thought 'dump job' was a possible explanation," Lewis said. "Ernie, couldn't those rashes be caused by the entry and exit of the blade?"

"Doubt it," Sherman answered. "This was a very sharp blade. And I'll tell you another thing that's unusual. The lac has the hallmarks of an oddly shaped instrument. It begins at a depth of two centimeters. As it comes down, it increases to six centimeters where it tagged the carotid artery and then returns to two centimeters upon exit, all in the space of an inch and a quarter."

"So what does that mean?"

"It means the blade was likely shaped like this." Sherman held his finger in the air and made a wavy motion.

Kipner stood from the wound. "Who uses a knife like that?"

"My thought exactly," Sherman said.

As a youngster, Lewis had never been overly frightened by monster movies or campfire tales. Up to now, only man's ability to kill had ever really made him uneasy. He had experiences of man's willingness to torture and mutilate one another in war, but never had he seen anything so unnatural as one human being drinking another's blood.

"Wouldn't your body reject that?" Lewis said finally. "Wouldn't attempting that, if what you're implying is what you're actually implying, wouldn't it just make you sick, especially in the volume we're talking about here?"

"Yes," Sherman said, "normally. But come here, you two. That's not all. Come over here to my picnic table." The three of them walked together toward the table, where the microscope sat mere feet away from Sherman's lunch bag.

"Our vic here, an Eli Lundquist by the way, all his clothes and personal items are bagged and ready. It seems Mr. Lundquist managed to put up a token struggle against his assailant. He had some nice long fingernails at the time of his demise. Found something under a couple that weren't just dirt and boogers."

"Yeah?" Lewis said, shifting his trousers. "Like what?"

Sherman raised a petri dish with two small samples resting in the gel, two grayish tags of something that neither Lewis nor Kipner had any clue to identify.

"What is it?" Kipner asked expectantly.

"It's skin," Sherman said. "But it's as dead as he is. Dead a lot longer too, I'd guess."

"Now what are you trying to say?" Lewis asked, irritated.

"I'm informing the detectives that this is dead skin. When it got under Lundquist's nails, it was dead skin. How long it's been dead, I haven't any idea, but from what I can tell looking through the microscope, you'd have to say a very long time."

Both men stared at Sherman mutely. "Okay," he said, "let me give you a moment to digest that."

"You're sure that's skin? It couldn't be something else?"

"It's human tissue. Skin. No mistake."

"Ernie, you're a joy to be around, you know that?"

"Yeah," Sherman replied. "Tell it to my wife."

"Okay," said Kipner, "which drawer is she in?"

Sherman smiled. "Hey, I like that," he said. "Funny guy. We could use a funny guy around here. Now why don't you two get out of here and get back to work?"

"Well, Ernie," Lewis said as they walked back toward the large steel door that had let them in the morgue, "we've already established that he's white." Lewis glanced at Kipner as he said this. "Now we just have to deal with the fact that he's dead."

"Just want to let you know," Sherman said, "we're all counting on you."

Chapter 29

Malcolm Schreck stood in the basement of the old house near the spot where his body had been so casually left to rot. He was waiting for the afternoon sun to set in the western sky, contemplating the multitude of rapidly changing circumstances that brought him to this particular time and place. All the while, a pounding went on interminably above his head as his new man, Karl, set about the task of fixing the floorboards that had rotted away with the years of abuse, much as his body had. Karl did this on Schreck's order as he had the door that he had broken through. Obedience was not the issue with Karl. The man knew instinctively the pain Schreck could reap on him should he become intransigent. The issue, ultimately, was that he held no real fear of Schreck, not like Mr. Warren. There was little respect to be had from Karl Angstrom. He did the duties set before him but with such relentless hostility that Schreck could do no less than consider taking his blood when his next hunger arose.

And there was the other niggling factor that had given him little respite since he had taken the man, Eli, in the alley of this small American town. Schreck had been overcome in that moment. Never in his terminally long existence had he ever allowed himself such proximity with other . . . people. And yet he had placed his mouth over the gushing wound at the man's neck. His lips had clamped down on the man's neck. And there was a release in it, a purging of himself into the moment, an animalistic, human, and hateful joy. It was the only recourse for this new Malcolm Schreck to survive. And it repulsed him.

He had touched others briefly certainly to show his power, to exert control, and to cause fear. But now it would seem he would have to touch and enter into a space of human intercourse he had never imagined to exist. The thought pounded in his head with the same steady clash that Karl's hammer flattened the nailheads into the boards above. He wondered how Arthur was faring. Arthur Drake, the man who was, in his original plan, a companion. If Arthur had consented, they were to assist each other through this transition. But the Englishman had rejected him outright. And now he did not even have the familiarity of his man, Warren, to rely upon. A miserable existence was this and yet, when placed against the certain fate that would come with true death, much more preferable.

Malcolm Schreck had his own purgatory to dwell in while he awaited the resourceful boy, the adaptable boy, the one chosen to unravel the dread book. A dire and dangerous world itself, purgatory to him had been at the gateway to the netherworld. And beyond the constant screams of agony and despair were the nagging taunts, the seeds of doubts, and the stares of a million unblinking eyes. Minor demons sent to beset him with the terrors of his ultimate fate. They spoke many languages and tongues unheard of on Earth, and their breath was scalding ash and burning ice. A very long time he had them alone as his companions. And yet they could not completely reach him, could they? In his most despairing moments, he returned their taunts. He stood proudly, defiantly.

"BEHOLD YOUR BETTER!" he called out to the countless staring eyes. "YOU SEE ME? DO WITH ME AS YOU WILL, SPAWN OF HELL! I AM HERE!" Schreck laughed out loud. "Can it be that you are powerless before me? Even your Master dare not. NAY, CANNOT REACH ME! CRY OUT TO ME! TAUNT ME! YOU FEED MY STRENGTH WITH YOUR THREATS OF DAMNATION! I WILL NEVER BE YOURS! You made me strong. Too strong! Where I walk, I reign. And you . . . will always . . . serve me."

The response came as a steaming hiss. And then the legion spoke. "This one has a bitter lesson before it. This one has a head too large and a tongue too long. How will it feel to have a spike through that tongue? How will it feel to have that head heave forward under its own weight until the chain attached to the spike through the long lapping tongue pulls the head off, and this one tumbles down to meet his servants . . . CLOSE?!"

Thus had ended the taunts, at least for a time, though they still rang in Malcolm Schreck's ears as a reminder of judgments delayed and denied. And what was his victory? Alone and with the necessity of blood, human blood, to keep his demons at bay. What a distressing price to pay for a mere semblance of living.

Schreck noted the light in the small window fading. The sun, which he had always demurred against, now held new pains should he expose himself to it. But it was falling. He reached for his bag and his hat and hoped his appearance to Karl would at least stifle the hammering. It was a hope for which he put little stock. Karl was unique, he knew. The young man's boiling rage had called to Schreck like a beacon at sea. What could he do without Warren to assist him but answer with a beacon of his own making, one that had brought Karl crashing like a high tide against a cliff wall, crashing into the house to be at Schreck's service? But unlike Warren, it was not fear that stayed Karl in his position but a tendency toward violence. Schreck saw in Karl's eyes a feverish dream of dealing death to his new master. Schreck could unleash that dream on anyone, and Karl would willingly comply. Arthur, the boy, even Schreck himself, Karl only wanted to feel someone helpless under his pummeling fists. It was clear to be read on the grimacing face and the tight smile of wicked pleasure for some other's misfortune.

The hammering continued even as he stepped into the room. The man did not even deign to look up from his work, which was near to being complete. The hole had vanished, the edges of it cut away to the stronger wood, and new boards lay near perfectly in place. Karl did fine work, even if it was done against his true will, and quickly, for he had also fixed the door as ordered and had even taken an ax to the large bough that he had crashed against with his motor vehicle. The man was a wellspring of constant movement and energy. Unleash him, indeed. With the sun's exit, he had lit the candles in the hallway. They glowed brightly about his sweat-dampened face. And still he pounded nail after nail into the boards.

"Karl," Schreck intoned casually between hammer strokes. Karl stopped mid swing and waited. He did not look up from the boards, but his face held fast to his grim exertion. When no further word came, he said harshly, "What!?"

"You have done fine work," the vampire said in what to Karl was a strange Kraut-like accent. "A respite from your labor and to my ears, if you would."

Karl looked over to the creature. He was stooped to one side as he stood there, ancient old bag dangling from one hand, starched stovepipe hat on his head, leering that greasy smile that was as sideways and crooked as the thing itself.

"Fine!" he barked. He dropped the hammer from his hand and stood to his full height. Immediately, the energy he had expelled on the nails returned to his body, and he began to fidget, throwing the kinks out of his forearms and his knees. The sight was rather comical to Malcolm Schreck, who was looking for anything to warm to in his new assistant.

"Let us sit for a moment, Karl," he said. "You brought yourself some spirits, I assume?"

Karl reached into his heavy coat pocket for the pint of whiskey. He took a swig as he sat across the table from Schreck. Then he pulled a beer can out of another pocket and snapped the tab. Three or four gulps later, he set it down and belched. He offered nothing to the vampire. And if the creep had given even a look of annoyance or disappointment, Karl would have considered it a personal victory and silently rejoiced.

Schreck merely pulled the handles of his bag apart and leaned forward across the table.

"Karl," he said, "have you had opportunity to examine my satchel?"

Karl leaned back in his chair. He fished for a cigarette out of his shirt pocket. "Fuck, no," he said. "Why would I?"

Schreck reached into the bag. "If you had," he said, pulling a heavy object out of the opening, "you would have found a dear companion of mine." Schreck set the head face forward on the table, wispy remnants of its flesh still clinging to the skull.

Karl looked at the huge skull and sneered. "That's what you do to your friends, huh? I guess I got his job, is that it? You ever do me like that, don't carry me around in your fucking bag, all right. Ya fucking creep."

"If I did not need you, Karl, believe me, I could live off your blood for a full month. Of that, I'm quite sure. For now, you would do better to tend to my favor."

Schreck reached into the bag again. This time he lifted out an old weathered book. He laid it on the table next to the skull. "You will never replace Mr. Warren. That I know. But any partnership we enter from this point forward should benefit both parties. You give me transport and access to prey, and I, I will give you extended life, expansive strength, and also, when it comes time, you have my permission to kill the boy."

Karl looked up at him, past the hoary skull that grinned between them. "I've never killed anybody, you know," he said as he blew out a large puff of smoke.

"Then I advise you do it slowly. Give yourself ample time to savor it." Malcolm almost regretted the words as soon as he had spoken them. He sat back and watched for some reaction from Karl, who was in the process of allowing the thought to settle in his mind.

"Rather kill the fucking snoot," he said absently. "He's the one who gave me the sore jaw. Besides, he's already dead, like you, so it wouldn't be a murder rap on me, would it?"

"You will leave Arthur to me," said Schreck, his eyes drawing down on Karl with an intense dead stare. Again, he thought of the boy, Benjamin. Why should he be saddled with this obtuse brute while Arthur had the boy to assist him? Of course, Arthur was like a child himself, probably suffering from the very knowledge and thought of his new situation. But the boy . . . what a strange boy he was, so perfectly normal and yet . . . If only he had encountered him without others present, without Arthur. Of course, the boy carried the crucifix. He was a believer in the risen Lord. When Schreck had touched him, he had felt the boy cry out to that power and felt his anguish when he realized it had deserted him. And yet this boy had been able to unlock the secrets within the tome Schreck had on the table before him. How many could claim that? Himself, his old master, whoever had handed it to that ancient wizard? And now the boy. Christian, apparently. How odd.

And he had cared for them as well after they had risen, hadn't he? He remembered the boy laying his own coat over Schreck's shoulders to guard him from the chill. The biblical aspect of that act had repulsed him—a Samaritan. Yet there was also anger in this child, darkness in him, one deep enough to gain him access to worlds he should not have been able to imagine. He was a killer, this boy, a Samaritan killer. How he could have used one such as this. A fantasy played in his mind, one of master and pupil as he had been so long ago. *Ahh well,* he mused. *Not to be. Not to be.*

Schreck decided then to perform an experiment. He opened the book, turned it to face Karl, and asked, "What do you see there, Karl?"

Karl gave it a cursory glance. "Nothin'," he said sharply. "What am I supposed to see?"

"Hmm. As I expected."

Karl sneered at him. "Books with words bore me. Books without words are even worse." He took a swig of beer and emptied it, dropping the hollow can down on the table with a dull clang.

"That's your magic book, I guess, huh?" said Karl. "That how you gonna make me like you?"

Schreck chortled. "No, Karl," he said. "But it does hold power, this book. It is a channel, a bridge, between those here who can harness it and forces best kept from this, your physical world."

Karl gave the old vampire a queer look. "Yeah?" he said.

"For instance," Schreck continued, "you find my appearance unseemly, do you not?"

"This a trick question? You gonna hurt me again? Send the bees into my brain like you did to get me here?"

"You may speak freely, my young friend."

Karl leaned forward. "You ever heard that old saying 'you look like something the cat dragged in?'" Karl watched Schreck's face fall and then said with as much emphasis as he could muster, "Well, mister, you look like something the cat fucking puked up! I don't know who you are or where you came from with that Kraut accent of yours, but you ain't natural! If this is what the future's got in store for me, then I'd just as soon you did kill me so I wouldn't have to look at YOUR EVIL FUCKING FACE!"

The sound of that last word echoed in the silent house. Malcolm Schreck and Karl Angstrom sat staring at each other in silence. Karl's expression held the same hard anger of his last word, while Malcolm Schreck's bone-white face twitched and grimaced in the flickering candlelight. Malcolm slowly sat back in his chair, still holding Karl in a stare that sucked the oxygen from the room. Then abruptly, he snickered. The snicker gained force. Karl sat back as well, and a grin crossed his face. He let out a girlishly high giggle that also gained momentum. Then both of them, vampire and man, master and servant, partners in the devil's work, laughed loud enough to raise Hell and crack the sky above.

Chapter 30

Sherry Adams knocked firmly on the door of Ben Whittinger's rented house. It had been at least six months since she had last set foot in the place without her now fiancé, David Wallace, accompanying. The two men had been friends since they were young boys and practically inseparable, that is, until she had become entangled with them both. Firstly, with Ben's awkward advance, and then firmly, on David's arm. She knew it had been difficult for Ben. Had seen his reactions change to her presence, not in hostility but in a more pronounced insecurity as if she had lain bare a scar on him that he would have rather kept hidden. She had tried to be as comforting to him as possible and, in those moments when he was able to be himself, felt herself more easily attracted to him. But the choice had been made, and Sherry knew it was unfair to all three to play one against the other. She loved them both, but one was all she would have.

So when Ben called her at work, she was quite surprised. She went to the phone after the overhead page, thinking it would be David, but Ben's quiet, somewhat melancholy voice came through the receiver. He sounded a bit nervous, but he always did without David acting as a buffer to his emotions. He tried some idle chatter, but the silences between questions made her finally ask if something was wrong. He denied that vigorously, of course. But he did have a question for her.

"You draw blood at the blood drives, right?" he asked as incidentally as he could.

He knew the answer to that already. "You know I do," she answered.

"How would you like to practice on me?" he returned with a slight flirtatiousness in his tone. He was trying to keep the conversation light, but the subject was failing him.

"What's this all about, Benjamin?" When he didn't answer right away, she remembered a few nights earlier when he had seemed eager to dispose of the expired blood. And that was right after . . .

"Sherry," he said, "I can't explain it over the phone. Can you come over after work? Can you bring what you'll need to draw my blood? Enough blood for a donation? A large donation?"

She sighed. "Ben, I don't know," she said. "It doesn't make sense to me."

"Please, Sherry. Please. I need your help."

And so it was his pleading as if pleading for her love, not just her help, that brought her to the door at four thirty on a sunny October evening. The sun was just beginning to tilt westward without a cloud to slow it down. As she walked through the door, her own nerves came to the surface. She was here to draw his blood, but she felt warmth in her abdomen that came from an entirely different source, a strange combination of excitement and fear.

He let her inside, backing away from her while looking at her, leading her into the small kitchen, just inside the side door. The age- and damage-stained carpet was as clean as it could get, the cupboard doors closed, the sink clear of dishes, the adjacent dining room picked up. Everything looked as clean as she had ever seen it, at least since the first time she had entered the house alone on that disastrous date. Her first thought was she was not the only woman who had been here. Ben was not a tidy person.

"You get a new roommate?" she asked, shocked at the sight before her.

Ben shook his head. "No," he said, "not exactly." He held out his hand and grasped her gently under the left elbow. "You brought the stuff?"

She nodded as he led her toward the door that led to his basement. She looked straight into his eyes. He had never seemed so serious. It was as if he was taking her to bed for the first time, but it was a basement, a chilly, damp basement that he led her down the steps toward.

He began talking to her. Did she remember the other night when David had taken them to that old gangster hideout in the woods? Did she remember the two old men who had been there? How terrible they looked? He had gone back to the house. When David and she had waited for him in the Jeep, he had spoken with the men, and they had made an insane claim. He had gone back later to test the claim, and it had been true.

At the bottom of the steps, an old footlocker lay on its back. It had rusted some on the bottom. The two doors were closed, and the small black handles faced each other across the narrow division between the doors. Ben pulled the string that led to the uncovered bulb, the socket screwed into a wooden rafter. The light turned on and glowed over the top of the footlocker. It was old, from the fifties probably. It had been his father's. Winchester and Remington stickers were fading on its surface.

Ben bent over and grasped the nearest handle and pulled it up with him as he stood. Sherry jumped into his free arm and buried her face in his chest with a short gasp. There was a man in the cabinet. His head lay on a pillow, his body on a folded sleeping bag, an old blanket covering him. He was either in a deep sleep or dead. The light from above hit his face, but he made no indication that the change in the basement had any effect on him. It was an older face but not the face of the man who had come toward her in the old house. She peeked at him as she held tightly into Ben's body.

"His name is Arthur," Ben whispered. "He was a friend of my grandpa's. Can you believe that? A friend of my own grandpa's. That's why I couldn't leave him there, Sherry. That's why I need your help."

Sherry Adams finally let herself separate from Ben. She looked down on the man. Was this the one who had shuffled toward her, silent, a horrible plague of a human being? Was this the same man? Could it be? This man was old, yes. But he was also, how else could you put it, handsome. His white hair came back over his head and temples, his face was wrinkled and pale, and his lips were almost blue. But he had obviously been a handsome man at some point.

Sherry then remembered the real horror of that night, the other shape that had crawled on the floor toward them, growling. That one had looked like a devil.

"Where's the other one?" she asked, suddenly looking around the whole of the basement, by the washer and dryer, the hanging racks, the corners.

"Not here," Ben answered. "Thank God."

He bent down and reclosed the door, leaving Arthur Drake as they had found him, and led Sherry toward the steps. "Come on," he said. "He'll be awake in a few hours. Let him sleep for now."

Now she understood why he had been so eager to take the old blood. Not to throw it in the incinerator but to feed it to this . . . vampire. This was where her fear emanated from. This was worth fearing. She wanted to run to her car. She wanted to see David, to tell him what was going on with Ben. But instead, she stayed close to Ben as he led her to the couch, and they both sat to discuss the next thing he wanted her to do. She was scared, but Ben was so calm.

He told her everything, slowly and with patience for her questions. He spoke about this dead man in his basement as if he was talking about a long-lost member of his family, a lost uncle or a lost father. He said that Arthur and the other man whom he refused to name had been in that basement for almost fifty years. He spoke of them drinking the cow blood and how they had each grown younger and stronger in a matter of a few seconds as soon as the blood had touched their lips. And he told her of taking Arthur to see his old Italian grandpa and how the old man had recognized Arthur and spoke to him, even though he had lain there silent for so long, only waiting to die.

Arthur thought he had met Christ and that the Lord had the entire event of his death and his awakening as a part of His plan. Ben had scoffed at this, and Arthur had been hurt by his attitude.

"Arthur," he had said, "if there is a God or a Jesus Christ, then he's long since given a damn about what happens to us. He is the biggest deadbeat Dad there is. And if this is part of His plan, He must be doing it for laughs. I mean, look what He did. He put you with the most evil motherfucker on the planet. This guy is a demon walking the earth. Then He has you killed so you can return to become a walking, talking bloodsucker, just like the demon. And He throws the book that brings you and that evil fuck back in my face. Me! Why? He has me read from this nasty, evil shit book so you can come back as a vampire. I still have the taste of it in my mouth! No booze, no beer, nothing touches it! And all so you and I can get killed by the demon. Oh! I love this plan. Great plan."

"Ben," Arthur had replied, "I had never been a religious person in my life. I knew or cared to know nothing about God, Christ, or any plan. No person ever instructed me in it, and no person I knew gave me any example to follow. Only Schreck seemed to have any real belief at all. And you have seen him for what he is. Do only devils know God? I? I was, in life, for me alone. That was all there was. But now I have been dead, and now I am this . . . thing. I am told there is a purpose to this, and I must believe it. Or else I will suffer both my past and my present forever. Do you understand?"

"Sure," Ben answered. "I just don't know what the hell we're supposed to do now." Ben raised his hands, palms up, and waved them in front of his face. "So if you get some guidance, don't forget to let me in on it. 'Cause He ain't talking to me!"

The two had left the argument there. And all Ben knew was that Arthur was getting weaker, looking older. He had gone to the basement silent. Ben had gone to work, and Arthur had apparently used the time to clean the house and listen to his grandpa's Sinatra records. Ben had checked on him earlier, lying in the old footlocker Ben had set down for him. Arthur had been repulsed by the idea but had resigned himself to it. Perhaps he laid everything at the feet of God's plan. But Ben knew he had hurt the old man, and that was what inspired him to make amends by giving Arthur his own blood.

Sherry struggled with believing Ben's entire tale. But the evidence for its truth lay downstairs, hiding from the sun. Ben half sat, half lay on the couch as she gathered the supplies: two pint bags, some large bore tubing, an equally impressive needle, a rubber tourniquet, and a few alcohol swabs. She then knelt in front of him, between his legs, and cleaned his right arm at the crook of his elbow. She pulled out the needle and looked it over.

"So," she said as she fastened the tourniquet to his bicep, causing his antecubital vein to bulge, "your friend down there likes blood, huh?"

"No," he answered, watching her prepare the needle. "He likes Sinatra. He just needs the blood.

"That's a helluva needle," he added.

"The better to drain you," she said.

"Well," he returned, "go on. I deserve it."

They both watched as the blood drained from his arm, down the tube, to the bag below, first one, which Sherry then clamped off, and then the other. Ben was getting slightly dizzy as if he was drinking. For all Sherry knew, he had been.

He looked at her and smiled. "You know, I always understood," he said softly, "what happened between us, Sherry. I can think of at least forty reasons why you chose David over me. They're sitting in a bag in the kitchen closet, most of them, waiting to be crushed for ten cents. But the real reason is you love him. I do too. So I'm going to wish you both well and not get in the way. But if you don't mind, I'm going to continue to love you and even be in love with you because of who you are and because I . . . damn well want to. If you don't mind, that is."

Sherry said nothing. She pulled the needle out of Ben's vein, placed a cotton ball on the hole that was left there, and pushed his arm up at the wrist to hold pressure to the wound. She clamped the second bag off and placed it with the other. They were both full.

She looked down at her hands. She remained kneeling before him. "I guess you don't want David knowing any of this," she said. "I won't tell him, I promise." Then she came forward slowly, letting her body rest against his, and placed her lips on his. Ben had a moment of disbelief and then abandoned it and himself to his desire. They kissed as if they were meant to, both gentle and passionate. After what seemed a very long time but infinitely short to Ben, she pulled herself off him. Ben watched her as she gathered her things.

"You are such an idiot, Ben," she said. "Don't get yourself killed."

As she walked toward the door, he lifted himself on the couch. "I've never been very good at much," he said. "I doubt I'll be any good at getting myself killed."

Sherry looked back at him one last time. "You are an idiot. But you're a good kisser."

As she closed the door behind her, Ben sat there, remembering that kiss. "Well," he finally said to himself, "at least there's that."

Chapter 31

The old creep, Schreck, was acting weirder than usual. *That was some trick, considering,* Karl thought as he looked at the wiry, bent spider take a small file to his front teeth. He had his back to Karl at that moment, looking into a cloudy old mirror on the wall as he jiggled the file back and forth across one tooth after the other. Apparently, Schreck had decided to rid himself of the blade. He was going to just bite his victims from here on. Karl saw the black frock coat, the greasy hair, and the balding, pointed crown and thought of burying the ax he had just used on the big bough outside right between those shoulder blades. That would rid him of this shit job he had.

But Malcolm Schreck could read his mind, or so Karl imagined, because just as that nice thought of the ax came in, Schreck turned around and grinned at him. Karl tried to put all such thoughts out of his head. After all, how had he come to be here, but by the vampire sending a hot drill bit through his skull? And all while being miles away from Karl at the time. He claimed he could feel Karl's energy, and he had need of it. What could Karl's strength do against that? He supposed the guy who used to own the head in the bag, the one who used to hold this post, before his head got lopped off, had felt the same way a long time ago. Bad luck is all you could pin it on.

Karl turned his attention to other people he could hurt. *Should've gone back and killed that lame-o with the wheelchair,* he thought. Could talk, that guy. Had got a good look at them too. And one look at Schreck was all it would take. You aren't forgetting him. Not anybody with him either. Should go find that guy again. Tie him to his chair, tight so he can't squirm out. Roll him into the river or a lake. Karl snorted at the thought of the poor sucker going under. Wouldn't be any worry then, would he?

Then there was always the pussy kid with the English fag. Smart-ass thought he was smart. So smart, this little fuck, even Schreck liked him, Karl could tell, a lot more than he liked Karl anyway. Probably one of those pukes who were taught that bullies were really cowards, and all you had to do was face them down. He loved kicking the shit out of those guys. He'd just have to get him clear of the Limey. For a guy who sounded so faggy, he packed a helluva left cross, that English pansy, probably because he was like Schreck. Schreck likely could crush Karl's head in his hands like a ripe melon, he figured. But it wouldn't be much fun to the freak. Rather see him squirm under the drill. That was Schreck's idea of fun. Yeah, this was bad luck, really bad luck.

It was pitch dark by the time they drove off from the house. Karl insisted on that. Having Schreck sitting in the front passenger seat, looking out the windshield, it had better be dark outside. Karl kept the truck's bright lights on whenever a car approached so there was no chance they could see his passenger. Sure, it pissed them off. That was just a bonus. Plus, aside from looking so hideous, Schreck stunk like a sulfur pit. Karl took to smoking the largest, fattest, most aromatic cigars he could buy while he was near Schreck. He fantasized about an errant ash drifting over and laying upon Schreck's lap, setting him off like a Viking funeral blaze. That wouldn't happen, of course. But at least the cigar masked his stink.

Something was different tonight though. Karl could feel it. The thing needed blood again. He was fidgety, chomping his new pointed teeth together incessantly, and then just as suddenly, he would be staring off as if in a trance. He had brought that smelly old bag with the book in it. Karl, as diplomatically as his own frustrations would allow, asked that the head at least remain at the house. He could get caught with a musty old vampire with an empty book, but a decaying human skull would be hard to explain. So now the old creep just sat there staring as they drove, his lips quivering and his hands on the book, unopened and resting on his lap.

"Vi . . . Vi . . .," Schreck muttered. Karl looked over at him, wondering if he was having a stroke or something. That would be fucking great! Throw him right out into the ditch and hardly have to slow down to do it!

"Vittin . . . Vitting . . . Vhittinger! Vhittinger!" The vampire sighed and laughed, and his body finally relaxed. "Benjamin James Vhittinger," he said with that Kraut accent, chuckling.

"Karl!" he snapped, suddenly spinning his body toward his driver.

"What?" Karl growled in response. What the fuck was the old bastard's problem now?

"You have . . . those things . . . you can talk . . . you place it at your ear, and you speak and—"

"A phone?" Karl said, incredulous. How could he not know what a phone was?

"Yes, yes!" Schreck said. "A telephone! Find me a telephone! We're going to pay a call to the boy!"

"Why?" Karl asked him angrily. "Why don't you just call him like you called me, you old son of a . . . ?"

Schreck's brow furrowed. He looked at Karl as if Karl was mad. "I have no wish to hurt him, Karl," he said plainly.

Karl Angstrom snorted, shook his head, and headed the truck toward the nearest, most remote pay phone he could find. He knew that there was a pay phone to be had at about any four-corner gas station in the rural countryside, and that was where he wanted to be, anywhere but in town, where the vampire had his first victim. The truck was known to few, and he wanted to keep it that way. He considered bringing Schreck's victims to the old, abandoned house. He had even offered to do it. Why risk possibly getting caught where the police patrolled? Where they could be seen? Karl knew Schreck had a deep hatred of people. It was something they shared in common. The pukes of the world were at best a pain in Karl's ass. At worst, they brought out his desire for violence. But there was no need for this ancient creep to show himself to them.

Karl couldn't grasp the next question from the vampire's leering mouth. The thing wanted to know where the public dance hall was located, where they served libations, and males and females were together in revelry. He described it with the same understanding he had tried to describe a phone. It would've been funny if Schreck hadn't seemed so determined.

"What the fuck would you want with a place like that?" Karl asked. He couldn't grasp why the hell Schreck wanted to be among the crowd. It made no fucking sense.

Schreck grimaced. "Myself? Nothing. But Arthur, Karl, Arthur, in his life, was something of a paramour. He enjoyed such things, needed them, even more than other men. It is time he is reminded of that pitiful power he once had and could have again. All he need to do is submit. His refusal will mean his destruction and that of the boy's. Perhaps I allow you to torture the boy first, if that is your wish. Then Arthur can watch as I drink his blood."

Schreck said this with a certain hint of sadness. His plans for Arthur, such as they had been before the debacle with Warren, were not to be. But he felt he owed it to the fool, to give him one last opportunity to accept his gift.

As Karl pulled into the small two-tank gas station and eased the front of the truck toward the pay phone under the single light at the side of the building, he said brusquely, "That's all well and good for the fucking pansy, but how the fuck are YOU gonna get anywhere near there?"

"I do not take your meaning, Karl," Schreck replied.

"Oh, I mean they might have a dress code, and that old funeral suit of yours might not get you in. What the fuck do you think I mean? You just were looking in a mirror. You know what I mean." Karl stopped himself. As much as he wanted to really lay into the disgusting, smelly creep, he realized it would be a bad end to find himself in that shark's bite.

"Leave all to me, Karl," Schreck said calmly. "What you see is truth. I am exactly as you see me. I cannot be otherwise. But the eyes of men can be clouded, if one has the use of a proper veil. Do not trouble yourself, my young friend. We will be accepted. Make the call, please."

That call, placed around 9:30 p.m. on the last Friday before Halloween, was as brief as Karl could make it. When Ben Whittinger answered, he was caught off guard.

"Hey, numbnuts," Karl said. "See you were able to pry yourself away from the fag long enough to answer the phone. Good."

"What do you want?" Ben said, matching Karl's menacing tone.

"The old creep here. He wants you and the Limey to meet us tonight. You know where that pit, Glitters, is?"

"Yeah, but—"

"Shut up and listen. We'll be there. You bring your asses pronto. Got it?"

"How the hell . . . ?" But Karl slammed the phone down before Ben could ask the obvious question. Karl looked at the gruesome passenger sitting in his truck, supervising his every move. It was beyond him as well how Schreck could go unnoticed anywhere. Karl shook his head. *Guess they'd both know soon enough,* he thought.

Chapter 32

It had been a few days since the murder of Eli Lundquist. Mercifully, the press was not privy to the details, so the story was printed and released much like an afterthought. Oh, by the way, a homeless man was killed the other night. Shame. But them's the breaks for those kinds of people, isn't it? Let's move on to more important disasters, shall we?

If he were to be completely honest, Phil Lewis may have thought exactly the same way. The homeless and the streetwalkers, since they had very little in the way of benefits, had a much higher risk in their daily existence. Except for the manner in which Lundquist was killed and disposed of and excepting for the fact that he was a fellow vet, Lewis would have written his name on the board and thought himself lucky to accidentally come across the perpetrator of this crime somewhere down the road.

But Eli was murdered in a rather unusual way. His body had been almost completely drained of blood. There had been scant evidence of it at the scene, which should have been awash in it. There was also the "hickeys" at the wound to think of and the dead flesh beneath Eli's fingernails. Was it a ritualistic killing? A sacrifice to some heathen belief? A blood sacrifice? Or was it just a gussied-up version of the same routine? Had Lundquist just been in the wrong place at the wrong time? Had made a careless comment to the wrong person? Had made an enemy of a very bad character?

Jeff Kipner, his new partner from Detroit, was taking the first angle. He began by probing news releases of any underground cult activity in the area and any murders in the past few years that might fit the profile of Lundquist's demise. Lewis didn't believe it would come to anything much. Were there some miscreant weirdos out there, attempting to specialize themselves from common society? Sure. *Mainly,* Lewis thought, *it was an act.* The ever-aging adolescent who had never quite been able to let go of his juvenile rebellion against his parents' God. They usually had little temerity to actually do any of the acts their "faith" called them to do. The appearance itself was enough to shock the grandparents. Always a thrill for some, to mock your creators.

But there had been news accounts of much younger kids doing terrible crimes, who had committed ritual murders of other children, for some pagan faith. Horrifying, these blank-faced kids, charged with the murder of a friend. Their parents look of absolute shock. It was enough to make you check on your own children at night. But Lewis did not see that as a factor in this case. Something about it spoke of acquired skill. *It was too easy for this perp,* Lewis thought. He wondered if Eli had seen it as well when he first looked at the killer. Had his first impulse been to run, but for some reason, he didn't heed it? Could be. *For Eli to just stand there, the perp had to have been offering something,* Lewis thought, *something Eli wanted or needed.* And it was Kipner's understanding that the bodies found in these ritual murders, if they were meant to be sacrifices, were often left in some kind of state of respect, laid out in a gentle repose. This had certainly not been the case with Eli. He had been used and disposed of like garbage. It was beginning to frustrate both detectives. There was nothing solid in either motive or execution, just a dead man handled like a blood bag.

The other cops were often caught looking at them. No offers of any assistance came with the glances. They treated the new guy, Kipner, with the same suspicion they held for Lewis. Probably they thought he could be a plant of some kind, listening in for any insubordination among the ranks. With Lewis, they feared the threat of a civil rights suit, although he had never given them reason to think that. If he was in the captain's office, it was generally just to fill him in on a case he was working on or a lead he had just came across. *It's not a pigment problem, fellas,* he often thought when he saw their eyes on him leaving the office. For Kipner, the aspect for their wariness was probably more basic department policy initiatives. What did the guys think of this proposal? What did the union board leaders know about any possible threat of the blue flu? It was evidence of a deficit in his fellow officers' sense of security, but Lewis had learned to blow that off long ago.

The captain had made it clear that this case was low priority, primarily because of the vic's status. But also, it was because an off-year election was coming up in a couple of weeks. That had the community abuzz with other seemingly more important considerations. Ritual murders or whatever Eli's murder could be labeled, as long as it wasn't repeated among the more fortunate, were not going to take precedent.

Lewis was sick of the eyes. He gathered his coat; tapped Kipner's shoulder, drawing his partner's attention from the book on occult practices he was perusing; and started for the door. They were going to talk to that old guy in the wheelchair, he decided. It was time to see if Barney Wheels had any thoughts on the subject of his friend Eli Lundquist.

The two plainclothes detectives waited for Barney Hansen in Dennis Farley's small office at the Stegman House. When Farley wheeled him in, Hansen didn't look up to their faces. He kept his eyes down, his long, gray, and unkempt hair framed his face in shadow, even under the bright lights of the yellow-walled room. Lewis introduced himself and his partner as they both displayed their badges for the wheelchair-bound man to examine. He didn't move a muscle to do so, nor did he speak. Lewis glanced over at Kipner, who shrugged in response.

"Mr. Hansen," Lewis began calmly, sitting in one of the office chairs, "we'd like to talk to you about the other night when Eli Lundquist was killed. He was a friend of yours. We believe you may have been the last person to see him alive, outside of his killer, that is. Anything you can tell us about that night?"

Barney Hansen shook his head slowly in response.

"We understand he was a friend of yours, a fellow Vietnam vet—"

"I got no friends," Hansen said gruffly. He was actually a year or two younger than Lewis, but from his wrinkled and splotchy face, gray hair, and watery eyes, he appeared about fifteen years older. It was a hard life that made its impact on Hansen's every feature, all the way to his stooped shoulders and leathery hands. This was a man who could die any day now, and who would come to claim his body?

"We have witnesses," Kipner interjected, "who can place you with him that night." That was actually a lie. It was only by Farley's word that they knew he associated with Lundquist. "And Mr. Farley told us you two were friends."

Hansen looked up sharply at Farley, who had taken his seat behind the desk. "Farley knows shit!" he said.

Farley looked perturbed at this but remained silent. He gave the detectives an exasperated glance.

Hansen was at least speaking now, but he was clearly agitated. "So two guys leave this shithole to get some fresh air, and that makes them bosom buds, huh?"

Lewis looked at the tired, old face and said, "So you admit you left with Eli that night?"

"Yeah," Hansen said, "but he went his way, and I went mine. He went to the alley."

"And where did you go?"

"Couple blocks further down. Went to see Queenie, but she wasn't there. Twenty bucks gets us a bottle and a little lap time." Hansen grinned, looked at Farley, and said, "Make you feel like a man again!"

"You had twenty dollars, Barney?" Farley asked smugly.

"Hoping for an advance," Hansen replied. "Worth a shot."

Kipner stood and stepped over in front of Barney until the man had to look up at him. "So you saw nobody else that night? Nobody passes where Eli was?" he asked. They were going to get nothing from this guy. Either he didn't know anything or he was too scared to say. Kipner thought the latter. He could see just from his own proximity Hansen was hiding something. He went from pure bravado to pure jelly in a matter of two steps.

"Mr. Hansen," Lewis said, "don't you want us to catch who did this to Eli? How about some justice for a fellow veteran? I was there myself. Laos. You?"

"Don't remember. Don't remember much anymore. Not yesterday or the day before that. All I know is here and now. And right now, I'm getting hungry."

Kipner stepped back and sat on the edge of Farley's desk. His partner had made an opening. It was an opportunity to watch the older man work. It wasn't the tack he would have taken, but he knew to stay out of the way.

"You know, Barney," Lewis said, "if you're worried, we can protect you."

"Oh," Hansen replied, "you think I'm in this chair 'cause I'm stupid. You think I'm in this place 'cause I'm stupid. Fuck you."

"Barney!" Farley said. "That's enough of that now."

"Fuck you too," Barney said.

"That's okay, Barney," Lewis said as he stood from the chair. "Thought you might want to help a brother, is all. I've given Mr. Farley my card. If you think of anything, you give me a call."

As the two detectives headed toward the office door, the words hit their backs.

"Big. Black. Truck."

The two turned toward Barney. Kipner took a step toward him, clutched the arm of his chair, and turned him to face them. "Make? Model? Year?" he asked.

"What am I, the fucking DMV? I look like a car guy to you? It was big and black. Had big tires."

"See anybody in it?" Lewis asked. "Anybody get out of it?"

Barney shook his head slowly and bit on his lower lip. The twenty-dollar bill showed up under his nose. He took it in one shaky hand.

"Live it up," Lewis said. "Think of anything else, call. Thank you, gentlemen."

As they got back into the car, Kipner couldn't contain his disappointment. "That's it?" he said as he slipped behind the wheel. "Big black truck? We should be giving this guy the treatment back at the station. He knows a helluva lot more than big black truck."

"Probably," Lewis acknowledged. "But you should be happy anyway. It tells us two things. If this is our boy, he's more than likely white like you said before. And with a truck, he probably doesn't live in town."

"Oh, you're right. That really narrows it down."

"Baby steps, Kip," Lewis said. "Baby steps."

Chapter 33

Ben Whittinger could not contain his frustration. The old man, the vampire now sitting next to him in the Glitters parking lot, had plainly rebuked him. And for what? Principle? What principle could dead men afford?

Earlier that night, as the sun went down, a few hours after Sherry had left, with the taste of that kiss still on his lips, the sweet scent of her hair still coming up off his cheek and neck, refreshing his memory, Ben had gone down the steps to his basement and brought the old man out of his sleep. Arthur Drake was looking very weak. His age was beginning to show rather prominently. It was past time for him to feed. Ben had to help him up the steps as he would have done his own grandfather and gently led him to sit on the couch he and Sherry had just recently shared.

Arthur sat there quietly and let his head hang down to his chest as if the mere act of getting to the couch was enough to drain him of all his energy. Ben kicked at his old shoe. Arthur looked up at him, attempting to focus on Ben's face.

"Got something for you," Ben said and strode toward the kitchen. Arthur heard the rubber of the refrigerator door separate, and Ben quickly returned. He stood before Arthur with both elbows bent at his side, each hand holding a small bag of red fluid.

"This," Ben said solemnly, "is my blood. Take it and drink."

The old man only looked away, a look mixed equally with disappointment and disgust on his face. Ben was smiling until he saw that look. Did Arthur not get the joke? Or did he get it and disapprove. For a man who believed he had been contacted by Christ, Arthur was incredibly religiously illiterate. But did he not recognize the quote?

"Seriously, Arthur," he said, "this is my own blood."

"No, Benjamin," Arthur said, "I don't want it."

"Well, if not for me, then for Grandpa," Ben replied. "It's partly his blood too."

"Oh, Ben," Arthur said rather testily. "Your grandfather has already shed enough blood for me. You think I want his grandson to shed his as well?"

"If it's shed willingly, yes. Besides, if you don't drink this, we're both dead, you know? Either you go first or I go first, but we're both dead. Your friend, in case you forgot, has got it in for us. I can feel him. Hell, I can smell him."

"And I will deal with him when that time comes."

Ben became exasperated. This was beyond any argument he thought he would have to make. The logic escaped him entirely.

"How will you do that lying dead at his feet?" he cried. "And what do you think he'll do to me? This is a little bit of my blood, Arthur. He's going to take it all!"

Arthur Drake had no reply to that. Ben stared at him from his standing position, still holding the bags of blood, waiting for some sense of urgency to come to the old man. This was the only answer, Ben was sure of that. Arthur Drake, a strong and vital Arthur Drake, an Arthur Drake who was able to knock Malcolm Schreck and his ape, Karl, into oblivion. But this weak, pathetic creature sitting here on his couch probably didn't have the strength to swat a fly out of the air. And he was content to stay that way. Ben shook his head and plopped down on the couch next to him.

"What's death like, Arthur?" he asked plainly.

Arthur Drake turned his head toward the young man. "It's not as hard as living," he said.

And there they sat silently like two men waiting for their ship to sink with no fight left in them, completely accepting of the fate. It was later, the phone had rang, and Ben Whittinger heard the familiar menacing tone of Karl Angstrom on the other end. It was almost a relief for Ben, someone to whom he could unleash some of his pent-up anger toward, someone who would easily accept it. But Karl, in his abruptness, barely gave him an opportunity.

After explaining the call and who had placed it to Arthur, Ben took one of the bags of blood and cut across the small tube that hung from the bottom. He drained about eight ounces into a glass and put it into Arthur's hand.

"There," he said. "You drink that. It's not much, but we have a date tonight, and I am not going to carry you, you understand, you Limey son of a bitch! You and I are going to face these fuckers down tonight. And then we're going to die."

Arthur had done as he was so gently requested. It felt good, Ben's blood driving its way into his veins and arteries or whatever now passed for them. It was enough to make Arthur feel a more powerful hunger. But he willed himself not to fall prey to it. Ben made the offer of more, but Arthur smiled politely and said no. He would have to convince the young man that this was enough to push him forward. It would have to be. He had drunk his last drink of blood. For good or ill, he had drunk his last.

Ben looked him over. At the very least, the deep etches that crossed Arthur's face had lessened, and some color had invaded his cheeks. His hair was still white, but it was fuller, and the man's impossibly handsome features had returned, if weathered by age. He was not strong enough for Schreck. It was possible he was not strong enough to handle Karl or even Ben himself. But Ben hoped he could fake it long enough for them to think of a way to end Schreck. Then Ben, if he were still alive, would end Arthur Drake. It was what he wanted, wasn't it?

Ben could see the black truck in the lot, way off in a far corner, where the lights and the other cars of the club's patrons hadn't reached. He drove by the truck slowly. It was apparently empty, and once again, Ben wondered how that misshapen old spider had got himself in that club. He mentioned it to Arthur.

Arthur shook his head. "I don't know," he said. "If Malcolm Schreck was human, I might have an answer. All I know is there's very little he's not capable of doing when he sets his mind to it. I expect Hell is full of bastards just like him."

Ben shrugged. "Well," he said, "if Schreck really is in there, Arthur, he thinks he is in Hell."

Ben Whittinger had always avoided Glitters or any place that catered to the kind of youth who clamored for the digitalized pop beats and clangs that passed for music. He was much more of a traditionalist for whom heavy guitars and simple 4/4 time sufficed to move him. Lately, he had been listening to his grandpa's Sinatra albums with Arthur, and those lush orchestrations, along with Old Blue Eye's velvet tones, had been very nice to accompany a drink with an old man in his house. But he knew what they would be stepping into at Glitters. He had thought ahead for it as soon as Karl had hung the phone up in his ear. As unpleasant as it would be for him, for Arthur, it would be a nightmare.

Ben picked a pair of thick sunglasses. "Here," he said. "You're going to want these." He also gave Arthur a pair of orange rubber earplugs. "And these." The old man already had on one of his grandfather's fedora-style hats and his long tweed coat. He was not going to fit in at Glitters. Neither did Ben himself. But at least he could be shielded somewhat from the attack on his senses that was soon to arrive. Ben doubted that Karl had been that dutiful for his companion. It might be an advantage they could exploit.

Ben took one last look around the lot. If there was one thing he didn't want, it was a surprise attack outside the car. Arthur remained calmly examining the door to the club, watching a stray woman or two leave and enter. It had been years since he had even seen a woman. His eyes had not truly seen the woman that night he was revived, just a blur. There had been dreams, of course, or what he took to be dreams. But a flesh-and-blood woman, one he could touch if he got close? He had not seen in a lifetime. For an odd reason he could not explain, it made him nervous. Or was it excitement? Was it them or their blood he wanted? He could not be sure.

"You ready?" Ben asked.

"As I'll ever be," the Englishman responded.

With that, they each opened their door and began their walk toward doom.

Chapter 34

Marc Bilson did not own Glitters. But he may as well have. From the moment he arrived to the moment he left, almost all the attendants, bartenders, waitresses, the entire flock of people in the club, catered to his wishes. It was his family name, which had at least an appendage in every historical deed of every major company in the small town since its inception, that brought Marc the certain power that comes from an assumed title of wealth. Marc himself had done little to earn the praise, although he had, of course, the athletic build and fine features that came from a select breeding. High school quarterback, scion of American gentry, Marc had a great natural ability but no real drive to apply it. Why should he? His family had assured him of success even if all he did was party at night and sleep through the day. What was the rush for assuming the mantle of responsibility? It would be there when he wanted it. And he didn't want it now.

Right now, all he wanted were the two girls on his arms and the two bruisers behind him to watch his back as he made his way to his father's Mercedes in the parking lot. He needed the girls for entertainment, the bodyguards in case someone with a grudge, and there were many possibilities there, decided to take a run at him. He could have stayed longer to see if anything better showed in the female department, but Marc was getting restless. He wanted for other faces to attend to his needs as he knew instinctively would happen at the next club, all as if by order. So as he drew closer to his car, he barely noticed when the black truck pulled up in front of him. That is, until he saw the thing in the passenger seat staring at him. If it was a man, it was like no man Marc had ever seen in his reality or his dreams. And the black eyes of the shockingly ugly thing with its hideous face immediately made Marc bend over and retch.

The girls hovered over him, and his bodyguards ran up to steady him, placing their hands on the shoulders of his white leather coat and calling out his name. Marc could barely hear them through a din that sounded in his head. And then, just as suddenly, it cleared. He looked up, sweaty, confused. The truck was gone and, with it, the thing that looked at him. None of the others with him had noticed. All they had seen was Marc double over in pain. Someone mentioned a diagnosis of appendicitis. The bodyguard had had it, and it sure looked like that was what Marc had. But Marc looked around for the truck. He felt like someone had punched him in the balls. And he would feel that way for the rest of the night. His evening ruined, Marc Bilson would never know how close he had been to Hell for many years to come.

Driving the truck back to their original spot in the lot, far off in a secluded and darkened corner, Karl slammed the gearshift back up into the park position.

"What the fuck was that about?" he shouted. "You want to be seen?"

"Calm yourself," Malcolm said like a tired mother to her restless child. He sat forward in the seat, watching the young people filtering in and out of the club. His eyes wandered over them as a vulture circling the scent of death. *Yes,* he thought, *this is exactly where Arthur Drake would be made to understand what was being offered to him.* Arthur had forgotten his past. All those years in Purgatory had shaken his memories off like ash in the wind. A reminder was all that was required, and the young bodies that flashed their essence in youthful vigor would be quick to bring those memories back to the fore.

"Karl," he said quietly, "that young man I had you drive up to . . ."

"What about him?" Karl grunted. He had wondered why the old freak wanted him to get closer, and after they had driven off, he was still no nearer an answer. Karl had sized him up—blond, perfect hair, perfect clothes, two bitches hanging on him like decoration. Guy was big enough but a pretty boy. He still needed two other dicks to make sure guys like Karl didn't crowd him. Karl hated pretty boys worse than he hated punks like that Whittinger fuck.

Karl's thoughts wandered for a moment. There, he was beating on Ben Whittinger mercilessly until the big blond pretty boy showed up to try and stop him. Karl immediately began beating on him in his daydream as if his size meant nothing. Karl was unstoppable, a raging flurry of fists and kicks with his heavy boots when the man went down, beating and kicking the pretty boy's face into mush. It was great! Fucking great! Karl could not contain his joy, thinking of the terrific and terrible violence he would inflict on both of these shits. A little grin came over his face in the smoky cab of his truck until he looked over at the old freak and saw the big blond pretty boy sitting next to him.

"Jesus!" he cried. Karl began frantically feeling for the door handle. He was prepared to throw himself out of his own truck at the sight of the man he had just been murdering in his mind, but the blond's hand came down upon his own, and it had a damp, familiar chill to it.

"Don't be alarmed, my friend," the blond said in that funny accent Schreck had. "It is I."

Karl looked hard at the blond. It was true. He wasn't as pretty up close. But that could be because he was bent like the old freak would be, and his smile was something that would cross a snake's mouth. It unnerved Karl looking at him, so he looked away, out the driver's side window, breathing heavily.

"You questioned how we would enter, didn't you, Karl?" Schreck said with a chuckle on his lips. "You didn't believe. And now you do, do you not? I am becoming quite accustomed to that reaction. Come, let us prepare for our friends inside."

Karl took a few more heavy breaths through his nostrils. "You sure they'll come? We're still taking a fucking hell of a risk. You may look like that . . . but . . ." Karl looked down at Schreck's hat and book, both sitting on the freak's lap, both a reminder of the face underneath the man who sat beside him.

"That is why I need you, Karl," the blond man replied. "Did you think you were only to serve as my driver? No, you are so much more to me, my friend. It is you who will clear the path and you who will handle any attempts to distract us from the prey. And yes, Arthur and the boy will come. They must, and they know this. They will come. I will have need of both your strength and your cunning, Karl. Prepare yourself."

Karl looked hard at the blond man. If he peered long enough at the face, Malcolm Schreck's image appeared as a shimmering ghost beneath the handsome features. It was both disturbing and exhilarating to Karl what Schreck could do. And this was the first time the old creature had ever paid him anything close to a compliment. He had said he needed Karl. Karl was a dead man, he was sure. But at least he wouldn't die of boredom. He took another heavy deciding breath.

"Okay," he said finally, "let's do this."

Chapter 35

Ben was right, Arthur concluded. The nightclub Glitters would be hell on Malcolm Schreck because it was hell on Arthur. The lights; the blaring, incessant beats; and the metallic clangs bore like knife blades into his senses. If Malcolm were unprotected, unlike Arthur, he should be easy to find, on his knees, screaming. And this was just the entry to the club. The real damage waited beyond the closed doors ahead.

The doorman at the inside entrance looked the two of them over with a pained expression on his face. He was a small middle-aged man, happy to have the job of taking the cover charge for entry. Occasionally, one of the cast-off girls would still be around at closing, needing an assist to get home. Tim, the doorman, never belittled their need, and sometimes the play even worked. But tonight was starting off very strange. Marc Bilson had left with his goons and his girls, and then almost immediately, he had returned with a different, much meaner-looking goon, who was dressed like a yokel from the outskirts in a heavy plaid coat, dirty jeans, and thick, oil-stained boots. He was going to be a sight on the dance floor, this guy. Marc himself looked as if he was terribly ill. Tim attempted to ingratiate himself with Marc as he always tried to do when one of the city's bigwig kids showed, but Marc only looked at him as if Tim had crawled out of the sewer to stand there, watching the door. Tim knew Marc to be a prick, but this look of utter disgust was a new standard Tim hadn't seen before. It was Marc's boy who spoke.

"Leave him alone," he said gruffly through his cigarette. "Can't you see he ain't feeling good?"

Tim looked up at him. At five feet six inches, Tim looked up at just about everybody. "Yeah," he answered, "I can see that." Tim tried to sound tough, and as an act, it was a good performance, but he really wished one of the other guys was around to back him up. He could see Marc's new man had a mean streak that he didn't bother to hide. "Who the hell are you anyway?"

"Old high school buddy," Karl said.

"Well, since he's coming back, he can get in," Tim said. His nerves were starting to wear with both of them. It wasn't agitation; it was something else, just a feeling Marc Bilson himself was giving off. It seemed oddly dangerous. "But it's three bucks to you."

Marc turned his head toward him. He was bent over at the shoulder blades, and a milky pallor covered his skin. The look on his face withered Tim's resolve.

"Okay, Marcus," Tim said, "forget it." He watched the two of them enter through the double doors and saw Marc react as if struck by a blow. The new guy steadied him, and then they were gone. Tim shook his head as other groups started to filter in toward the entrance. *Weird,* he thought.

And now here was another weird occurrence. Twice on the same night, within a half hour of each other, another odd couple was coming toward him, some pink-faced kid dressed like the bruiser before, entirely too unfashionable for this club, with an old, old man covered up like somebody out of an old Bogart movie with dark shades on to boot. *Well,* Tim thought, *there is no dress code. I just take the money.*

Ben looked at Tim standing there in his red polo shirt with the word "Glitters" on his right breast and the popping sparkles of celebratory streamers bursting around the word. Tim was shaking his head, looking slightly overcome.

"Is it old folks' night, and nobody told me?" Tim said to the younger man. "Three bucks a piece, six for the two of you." He thought of saying there were other places the kid could take his grandpa. Bill Knapp's, for instance. But he had been told by management that if anybody needed kicking out, they could be kicked out after they paid, so he said it all in his expression alone. The kid dutifully brought out the bills, and Tim watched as the two of them entered the club. It was going to be some night.

Arthur Drake brought his arm up instantly to shade his covered eyes. The thumping noise penetrated the rubber earpieces like sharp chisels in his head. He took a moment to gather himself. Turning toward Ben, he shouted, "It's not Sinatra, is it?"

"It's not even Men at Work!" Ben shouted back. Arthur, of course, didn't understand. He looked around the club. The mixing scents of strong perfume, cologne, and cigarettes invaded his nostrils. *Perhaps it isn't so different from the past,* he thought. A group of young people dancing on the square floor underneath a glowing glitter ball, the reflections spinning among their bodies. They weren't together though, these dancers. They maintained a distance among themselves, but they were throwing their forms about to some sense of the beat of the music. Watching them, Arthur felt a glimmer of life in his chest. A memory perhaps? Or just a wish?

"There's Karl," Ben said, pointing to the other side of the dance floor. Karl was sitting with his large forearm resting on the top rung of a double-rung guardrail slightly above the floor. He was easy to spot for his attire alone, but his demeanor identified him even more accurately. He seemed completely disinterested in any of the activity going on around him. There was no sign of Schreck, though Karl was sitting next to another man of approximately his own size.

The music slowed down. A normal song. Spandau Ballet? Some of the dancers closed in together, some filtered off the floor. *Finally,* Arthur thought as he looked at Karl.

"I don't see Schreck," Ben offered.

"He's here, Ben," Arthur answered, "playing another one of his tricks. But he's here. I can feel it."

As they made their way around the walkway above the dance floor, Arthur looked at the women. Some giggled at the sight of him. "How cute," he heard one say. Arthur grimaced. His old life was truly gone. He supposed all old men came to that realization at some point, but all those missed years felt like a dagger in his belly. There was a time when he could have walked into a club like this, and both women and men would rally around him. Even women who weren't in his professional stable had been attracted to him. If he wanted it, they came to offer it. But now he was a sick, wasted, and ancient version of that man. And in those young, supple bodies, the bodies of these women who would now neglect any desire he had, was the blood that would create a false copy of that man. Arthur's hands clenched into fists at the thought as they drew nearer to Malcolm Schreck.

The young blond man next to Karl looked up at them. The face was sharp and beautiful, the face of Marc Bilson. The expression was one of malice and disgust, the face of Malcolm Schreck.

"My friends," the face said with no hint of friendship, "please be seated. We have been given a short reprieve from the clamor in this . . . pit. Let us make good use of it."

Ben sat across Karl, who gave him a dismissive glance before returning his attention to the dance floor. Arthur took a seat across Schreck.

Ben addressed the blond. Schreck was somewhat visible underneath the ruse, but it was the attitude of his posture and his horrible expression that gave him up. "Smart thinking, Mr. Schreck," he said sarcastically. Even Karl could not resist snorting his consent at that. "You know, there are little dark bars we could have met all over this town where they at least play music. You might have been able to slink in unnoticed as yourself. Why come here?"

"This is for Mr. Drake, boy," he said, his hard accent passing his new lips. "Has Arthur told you nothing of his past? There was a time when Arthur surrounded himself with his fellow man, beings just as they are here, and women. Arthur had his choice of women, boy, a power neither you nor I could ever understand."

As if to demonstrate this statement, a young woman rushed up to the table where the four sat, intent upon one another.

"Marc!" she cried. "You came back!" She was in a satin skirt, much too short for the cool fall weather outside, and a pink fuzzy sweater held her ample chest in an innocently provocative manner. Her jewelry about her wrist, neck, and ears reflected the shimmering lights in the club. The other three men watched as she hurriedly bent over to kiss the man she knew as Marc on the cheek. She drew back suddenly as if she had come upon a hornet's nest.

Schreck twisted his head toward Karl. "Karl!" he hissed. "Deal with it!"

Karl looked at the woman, who was now rubbing her perfumed hand over her nose vigorously. "Sure," he said, grabbing her quickly by her free wrist and flinging her forcefully onto his lap.

"Hey!" she said. "Hold on a minute!"

Karl grinned and held her secure. "You want him? Gotta come to me first, baby," he said. The girl looked at Karl, who was attempting to put his most demure face toward her. She struggled a moment longer and then sighed. She had seen Marc make this arrangement before. Since he was the prize, she settled into her assignment with a quiet acceptance.

Arthur spoke up then. "Young lady," he said, "what is your name?"

"Candace," the girl replied, paying closer attention to Karl. She had to admit, he wasn't ugly. And strong too. He smelled like a mixture of cigars and gasoline, but it was better than the whiff that had come from Marc. Where had he been?

"I wonder, dear," Arthur continued, "if you wouldn't mind coming back a bit later. We have a private matter to discuss."

"She stays!" Karl barked. It had been a while for him, and if there was anything that could wash the stench of Malcolm Schreck off him, it was this woman who had fallen into his lap. He would not be giving her up just like that.

"Is this your grandpa, Marc?" she asked. "I didn't know you were English."

The club returned to its nameless dance beats, loud and garish. Candace squealed on Karl's lap. "Ooohh! Let's dance!"

Malcolm Schreck squinted against the onslaught. He waved his hand up in front of the young woman's face. "Sleep," he said. Candace cooed and let herself rest comfortably in Karl's arms. But it was not just Candace who seemed to fall into a restful aura. The whole club slowed, and the banging clatter muffled to a shadow of its former volume.

Ben looked around. The air of the club, the smoke, took on a red tinge. The people still moved, but all was as if in a thick fog, and the figures on the dance floor began to blur. *Hell of a trick*, he thought. He looked at Malcolm Schreck, who now appeared as himself, and nodded to the old wizard, impressed. Schreck returned the nod with smug satisfaction.

Arthur leaned forward. "You seem to have grown stronger, Schreck," he said.

"And you weaker, Arthur," Schreck replied. "Has the boy's resourcefulness been found wanting? Why not return with me? I will make you strong again, young again, beautiful again. Would that not please you, my young friend?"

"I am not the same man as I was, Malcolm. You saw to that. Even with Ben's assistance, I still bear the price you've placed on my soul."

Malcolm sneered. "Your soul was damned before ever I laid eyes upon you, Arthur Drake. I'm offering a permanent deferment of the payment you owe. And it is my final offer. Look about you, Arthur. Have any of these . . . beings gave a solitary thought to their souls? They cry out to you, Drake! And it all could easily be restored. You to your prime again. You know, with me, all things are possible."

"Because you would kill for it," Arthur shot back. "You've already killed. I can read it on you."

Schreck's posture stiffened. He looked at Arthur from under his brow like a disappointed instructor at an errant pupil. "Oh, Arthur," he said softly, "you could follow a trail of bodies back to my own youth, if you so wished. These things are not important. I tell you, my young friend, we could be gods here. We would set ourselves upon a whole new enterprise, a true religion, not as that charlatan Brendan Vaughn purported to be but a true, real dominion over the dark forces."

Schreck visibly shook with an almost religious fervor as he described this to Arthur. "You would be our face, Arthur, our beautiful face. Your beauty, your talents, you would gather these children to us, these lost children whose only wish would be to glory in your presence. Sacrifices, such as we have need, will be infrequent. You have my oath on that. Only as it becomes necessary. And they will be willing, Arthur. Nothing to trouble the mind of a god. You will be a wonder to behold. And I? I will be the power. I shall control the whirlwind. And Benjamin here," Schreck continued, "will not be made to die. I will instruct him. He has an aptitude so few others ever dream to achieve. Karl has his uses, but Benjamin, Benjamin shall join us at the center of power. His smallest wish made reality. His greatest desires made whole at his word. You were quite correct. I owe him that. What would his life have been without us, eh, Arthur? No more than the common drudgery of the common folk."

Arthur looked down at his hands, silent. He could see the hellish red-tinged scene of the youth pouring their energies out as if in desperate pleas. A part of him did want this, some part he thought long dead. Some secret he had kept even from himself, even from God.

Malcolm took the moment's opportunity to turn to Ben. "Come, Benjamin Vhittinger. What say you to that?"

Ben looked at Arthur, his face still downcast, and then to Karl, who sat with the sleeping girl in his arms as if unmoved by the whole occurrence. Then he faced Malcolm Schreck, who waited in delighted anticipation for his answer.

Ben sat forward in his chair, stared intently into Malcolm Schreck's face, and said with all the conviction as he could muster, "What do I say? I say get thee behind me, Satan, for thou knowest not the ways of the Lord."

Malcolm Schreck grimaced in agony as if hot, scalding water had been thrown in his face. "NNNNGAUGH!" he groaned, shaking in rage. In a few moments, he gathered himself just enough to speak and said, glaring at Ben, "I hope you have not grown too attached to this boy, Arthur. His death will not be pleasant for you to see."

"Ben speaks for us both, Schreck," Arthur answered. "If I only had known what to say to you, I would have said it a lifetime ago."

Suddenly, the club returned to its previous state of harsh noise and shooting lights. Schreck stood and appeared again as the ruse he had employed when they had arrived. "You both will die," he said as the blond man named Marc. "I will see to it personally. Come, Karl. Bring the wench."

By this time, the club had gained in patrons enough that movement among the throng was difficult. Malcolm Schreck, even in this more pleasant form, had to force his way through with Karl behind pulling the barely wakened Candace with him.

Ben and Arthur watched from their chairs as Malcolm Schreck attempted to navigate the crowd of young people. Seeing his way blocked by a gathering of idlers in the walkway, Schreck made a path straight for the dance floor. This was an obvious mistake since the dancers, bouncing to the heavy, driving beats, were even less inclined to notice his desire to leave.

"Look at him go," Ben said.

"I think you hit a nerve, Ben," Arthur replied. "Good man. But not good for the girl, I'm afraid. We need to get her away from them."

With that, the two men stood and took as clear a path as they could for the exit, Malcolm Schreck, Karl Angstrom, and the young woman they held struggling through the crowd ahead of them. A strobe light began flashing, and in it, between its flashes, Ben could swear he saw Malcolm Schreck alternating between his disguise and his true face. *He had touched a nerve,* Ben thought, *and it was all Malcolm could do to hold it together.*

As Malcolm burst through the door to the entry, he came face-to-face with Tim, the doorman. Tim had seen Marc upset before. Guys like Marc were always upset if some little snag fouled up their plans or somebody just said no to something he wanted. But he had never seen Marc look like this. Before he could say anything, Marc's hands were on his shirt, and he was quite easily being tossed behind Marc and into the chest of Marc's bodyguard, who took a big hand to the side of Tim's face and threw him aside before he even had a chance to steady himself.

Candace began to take real notice now. Marc and his friend were being a bit rough. "Hey!" she cried. "Was that necessary?"

Karl turned his head to face her as he continued pulling her toward the exit. "You want him?" he asked, jerking his head toward the backside of what appeared to be Marc Bilson.

"Yeah," she said. "But what's going on? And my coat's back there. You're hurting my arm!"

Schreck held the door open to the night. "Karl!" he barked angrily. The need for blood was upon him now. More than a need, this was a passion, a passion fueled by rage. Karl recognized the look as evidence that it would be fed either by the girl or him. Dragging her outside after the old vampire, who still somehow maintained this false image of Marc, he let go of her wrist. *Run, bitch,* he thought. *Run.*

Candace stood between them. The darkness of the evening was complete, and aside from the streetlamps that shone down in rounded beams, there was little light to see. Marc stood silently in a darkened patch of sidewalk. She could see his white coat and his blond hair moving in the breeze, but his face was in shadow, and his eyes, his eyes were round black balls like a crow's eyes. Something was wrong, but she didn't understand what. There was a silence that put all her nerves on the surface of her skin, and she grabbed herself to hold her shivers back.

"Oh God," she said plaintively. "Marc?"

Another voice broke the silence. It had a soft English accent, and it said, "Candace, don't move. My sweet girl, don't take another step."

Marc held his hand out to her, still silent. The arm and hand reached into the light, but the body remained shrouded. Arthur stepped toward the girl and called her name again. He walked right past Karl, who made no effort to stop him. Candace stood between the two men, and if anyone was to guess, they were beginning an old dance routine, the one where the woman was tempted by two men, unsure of which way to turn. They swayed in the darkness to an unheard tune.

"You forgot your coat, Candace," the English voice said. "Remember, it's cold out here, sweet one. It's going to get colder. You might catch your death."

Candace turned toward Arthur. Then she looked back at Marc.

"Come with me," Marc growled, "Candace." His voice sounded almost like an animal. It was like nothing she ever expected to come from Marc, and yet it still compelled her. It was all terribly wrong. Terribly wrong.

Ben yelled out. "Hey! Candace! Look at him! It's not who you think it is!"

Karl stepped toward Ben. If the asshole kept shouting, somebody would hear. Somebody would see. Karl moved quickly, never breaking stride as Whittinger made to shout at the girl again. All of Ben's attention was focused on the woman between Arthur and Schreck; he didn't even see Karl coming toward him.

"LOOK AT HIM! COME ON, CANDACE, JUST LOOK AT—"

Karl's fist ran though his head like a sledgehammer through plaster, turning his torso as his legs remained locked in place. The force of the blow and gravity brought Ben down to the pavement.

Then the girl screamed. She had done as she was told. She looked at Marc and saw something else entirely. A hideous, evil-looking creature stepped into the light toward her. An innate reflex, a thing that originated from man's earliest beginnings, an instinct to survive, overcame Candace, and she ran, faster than her heels would ordinarily have allowed, back toward the club. She bumped past Arthur and barely looked at Ben as he lay, breathing heavily, on the ground.

Tim, the doorman, had recovered himself then, and as Candace ran inside, he reached the outside and saw Ben Whittinger on the ground, the bruiser standing over him, the old man, and where he had expected Marc Bilson to be, something entirely different stood.

"What the fuck?" he said.

Malcolm Schreck bared his teeth like a rabid dog. His eyes raged, and he looked at Tim and saw his fear. Malcolm moved toward him, and Tim, having the same human instinct that had taken control of Candace, hurried back inside the door.

Schreck was still coming. As inhuman as he looked, Karl had to stop him. He couldn't go back. The little doorman was running to call the cops right now. Karl knew it. He stepped in front of Schreck and grabbed him. Schreck looked up at him, a fierce determination on both their faces.

Karl shook him. "IT CAN WAIT!" he yelled into Malcolm's face. Schreck looked past him. A few feet away, Arthur was tending to the boy. He could take him now, and Arthur would be helpless to stop him. He would break Karl's grasp and feed quickly on the boy.

"IT CAN WAIT!" Karl repeated. "We gotta get out of here! Now!" Karl began to push Schreck backward. Amazingly, the vampire allowed him to manhandle him back.

"Your last night, Drake!" Schreck howled. "Your last night on Earth! For you! And the boy! Your last night! Do you hear?"

Arthur glanced toward them and watched as the two made their way between the cars back to the truck waiting in the darkened corner. He heard the engine turn, saw the beams come up, and move in a jerking motion, lighting the way ahead of the truck.

Ben began to moan. Arthur lightly slapped his face. "Ben. Benjamin! Wake up! Come on, Ben! Wake up now!"

Ben's eyes began to focus. It was the old man above him, although the face was rather blurred.

"Hey, buddy," Ben blew out of his mouth, "what the fuck was in that drink?"

"A rather large fist. Come on, Ben. Get up. We've got to get out of here." Arthur draped one of Ben's arms over his shoulder and stood. Ben attempted poorly to get his feet under him.

"Where's the girl?" he slurred.

"Safe," Arthur said. "She's safe."

"Well, bully for her!"

"We're in a bit of a spot though. Try to clear your head, my boy. Come on."

Ben looked at Arthur. He was beginning to step of his own volition, but Arthur could see his mind was not quite in the present.

Ben waved his arms up and down repeatedly. "Danger! Danger, Will Robinson! Danger!"

"Oh God," Arthur said as they reached the car. "Can you drive?"

"Sure," Ben said. "Watch. Ten, nine, eight, five, four, three, two, one. See? Nothing to it."

Arthur opened the driver's door, and Ben poured into the seat. "Are you sure you can drive, Ben?"

Ben Whittinger grabbed under his thighs and pulled his legs inside the car. "I can drive this car, Artie," he said. "This car, I can drive." He looked around the interior. "This is my car, right?"

Arthur looked up into the night sky. There were stars and white clouds rolling under the moon. "Lord," he said, "please help us."

Chapter 36

Officer Steve Lanyon sat quietly reading the newspaper in his patrol car, parked just off Barry Road. Barry Road was the main exit route for the partiers coming out of Glitters Dance Club. Getting toward the end of October, Lanyon hoped to make his monthly quota of driving violations off a conveyor belt of reckless youth. It was still a little early yet, so a few random people speeding on the main drag would do for now. This was a routine for Lanyon. He was beginning to get a rep as the local speed trap cop. He hoped it wouldn't be too obvious that he was around, although many of these kids were often just too far gone to care. Those were usually the closers. They would have to go downtown. Lanyon would call for another car or two to help with those kids when the time came. Let Mom or Dad pick them up. Right now, he was just priming himself for a catch and release.

Lanyon set the paper on the seat and took a sip from his thermos. Then the distinct crackle of a call came through over his radio. "Two vehicles," the female dispatcher said in a nondescript tone. There was a large truck in possible pursuit of a car coming toward his vicinity. Dispatch stated the vehicles had been seen leaving the parking lot of Glitters Dance Club following a confrontation among four men at the scene. The four individuals had apparently split into pairs and taken their confrontation on the road. The dispatcher warned to use extreme caution as no backup was currently available, and the two individuals who left in the truck should be considered possibly armed and dangerous. One male, approximately 6'2" tall, 230 to 250 pounds. Second male, description given as inaudible.

Lanyon grinned at this. He answered the call, giving his direct location and intention to respond. He held his position for about two and a half minutes. This was the logical route that the two vehicles would take. Although there were other possible roads, this one led straight east out of town. Since Glitters was on the eastern outskirts, getting to back roads and off into more secluded drives would take mere minutes. After three minutes, Lanyon began to edge forward from his hunting position behind a billboard when he made visual contact with the two vehicles. The lead vehicle, a Chevy two-door, screamed by the front end of Lanyon's patrol car. Its traveling speed on his readout clocked at ninety-three miles an hour with the huge black truck right on its tail, lunging at the back bumper like a charging rhino. By the time Officer Lanyon called in to report he had spotted the two vehicles and they were definitely in a heated chase, they were already three quarters of a mile ahead of him. Lanyon, being a rather large man himself, was still no fool. He requested backup. Whatever had caused this ruckus, it was easily apparent that this was not the type of situation that should be handled by one lone cop. He wasn't frightened or even uneasy about doing the job. He was being practical. Unfortunately, he couldn't wait for any help to arrive. He had his lights on and siren blaring. He was in pursuit.

By the time the chase had reached top speed, Ben Whittinger had at least regained some of his faculties from the sucker punch Karl had landed on his temple. He could have pushed the Chevy over a hundred, but with the dips and bumps of gradually deteriorating asphalt, he was afraid he might lose control and crash. He kept control of the car, but Karl was clearly reveling in terrorizing his back bumper with his bright lights, invading the window and blinding Ben. Karl was loving this, Ben was sure of that. And some part of Ben was feeling the same exhilaration. Taunting death and basking in the fear that came with it, Ben realized he felt more alive at that moment than he had ever felt before. He was more needed and more cared for, more hated and more despised, and more involved in this than at any time he had ever known. Ben started laughing out loud at himself and at the increasing odds against them. Karl Angstrom and Malcolm

Schreck were really out to kill them. And all Ben Whittinger wanted for was a little luck.

Arthur had never enjoyed being in a fast-moving car. Never learning to drive one himself, he had always been at the mercy of the one behind the wheel. And now that person was half delirious, laughing like a madman and driving faster than Arthur had ever been in his life.

Karl flashed his brights once more, engulfing the interior of Ben's car with blinding light. Ben raised his right hand and flipped him off. Seconds later, they crested a steep hill, followed by a tremendous descent of four hundred yards. At the bottom of the hill, a lonely set of railroad tracks crossed with only a yield sign to warn oncoming motorists.

Descending the slope, Arthur saw the train tracks at the bottom first and, as if by order, the round beam of light that was traveling toward the intersection of their path. Arthur wasn't sure how far it had to travel or how far they had to travel, but he was sure they would not make the crossing before the train. The train blew its warning blasts as it approached, the three blasts sounding desperate, frantic.

"Benjamin," Arthur said as calmly as he could manage, "there is a train coming!"

"Perfect," Ben answered, slamming the pedal to the floor.

"Ben!" Arthur cried. "We'll never make it!"

"Better that way!" Ben returned. The train was incapable of slowing, it seemed. It cried out in fear and panic again and again. In the truck, Karl kept the distance between them steady, but even he saw the futility of trying to make that crossing.

"Arthur!" Ben shouted as the road disappeared under them, and the tracks and train closed in. "I think somebody just let me in on the plan!" The perpendicular space between the car and the train was eaten up by time and speed. Both men screamed.

Chapter 37

"Fuuuuck!" Karl bellowed as he brought the heavy three-ton truck to a sliding halt just before the cars of the train passed in front of them. He could not hear the joyous laughter and screams of victory echoing in the compartment of the small car. But he could see its taillights in the narrow panels of air between the railcars speeding away. And he could hear the animal-like heavy breathing of Malcolm Schreck, his long pale fingers gripping the dashboard in front of him.

Schreck had long been confident in his patience. It was a tool his own master had bequeathed to him all those years ago, a hundred and many more, before he came to this time and place. Patience had served him on board ship when discipline among the crew was lost and in the deep forest where knobby-kneed Puritans sought to run him out. But thrice on this very night, his patience had been thwarted, thwarted by a misguided old fool and a crafty youth. He dug his long nails into the plastic dash, and the squeak of it relenting to his pressure was his only reassurance that he still held power.

Then he noticed the sharp flash of lights, blue, red, and white alternating in the cab of the truck. He turned and squinted against them.

"Shit," Karl hissed. The train rolled along endlessly from the south, its rear shrouded in the trees some distance to the right. The truck was trapped. It couldn't move forward, and he couldn't press back without ramming the patrol car.

"What is this?" Schreck hissed.

"Fucking cop," Karl said, grimacing.

"A constable?"

Karl spat. "Yeah," he said, "a fucking constable."

Malcolm sneered. "Why does he linger there?"

"He's taking down my license, stupid, calling it in and getting my name. That's why." Karl looked over at Schreck, who was looking like a rabid dog in his usual old-time clothes and stinking like spoiled earth. "You better change yourself back into blond or something other than . . . you, or we got no fucking chance."

Karl heard Schreck open his door. "No, no, no!" he hissed. "That's a cop! You can't off a cop!"

Schreck reached in for his beaver hat, placed it on his head, and grinned. "I am hungry," he said, and his eyes would suffer no further retorts.

Officer Lanyon watched the door open as he was getting ready to call in the plate number. "CFH 5 . . . what the hell?" Lanyon quickly exited the car and drew his gun. He hadn't quite seen the man, but he saw the interior light come on and a shape walk in front of the truck. The guy moved slowly but purposefully between the truck and the rolling train.

"Sir!" Lanyon shouted. "Return to the vehicle, sir! Sir! I said get back in the truck! Now!" Then the shape made the turn around the driver's side to face him. "Jesus!" Lanyon said. He couldn't quite process it. Lanyon was a veteran of the force. He had made the acquaintance of more than a few would-be freaks—tattoos from eyelids to toenails, piercings in brows and balls and anywhere else you could stick a pin through. But what this was, he had no name for. Lanyon felt a nervous titter of laughter escape him. Something about this thing in the crazy black getup and milk-shaded skin told him that might have been a mistake. Lanyon pulled his gun up over the doorframe and pointed it at the shape.

"Hold it right there, mister!" Lanyon ordered. He tried to convey every ounce of authority in the command, but the air had gone chill in his mouth, and his voice sounded strange, even to himself.

Schreck stopped for a moment. Karl watched from his side mirror, terrified. How long could this train possibly be? How long before more cops rolled over the hill? Then he heard Schreck say, "Hold it right there . . . mister." It was hardly a whisper, but it echoed in the night air. Schreck took another step.

"I said freeze!"

"Freeze" came the cold response. Schreck took another step. He was at the back of the truck now. Karl could see his arms stiff at his sides, his claws tense and open. And he could see an image of the cop, holding his gun straight at the vampire, and all Karl hoped was that the cop would fire. Why wouldn't he fire the goddamn gun?

Lanyon's gun started shaking in his hand. He had his firing arm firmly resting on his doorframe, his other hand grasping his wrist to further steady his aim. And yet there was a tremor. Slight but there, all the same. He realized he hadn't raised his weapon at anybody in many years. But he had never faced anything that needed to be brought down like this man before him now.

"You stop," Lanyon said. "Or I shoot!" The thing smiled at him, and its teeth were the misshapen maw of a wild beast.

"Fire the weapon," the thing said and took a step toward him.

"What?"

"Fire the weapon!" And then it lunged forward, and the gun cracked once, twice, again, and again, and again.

In the truck, Karl flinched against every shot. Then he turned his head cautiously to the side mirror and saw Schreck standing as if suspended on strings. His clicking shoes clacked on the pavement as he was forced back by the shots. *Die!* Karl thought silently, tensely urging it to be true. *Die, motherfucker!*

But Malcolm Schreck did not fall. Karl watched as in a flash, the black-shaped thing was at the cop's throat like a large dog that had just broken through a heavy knotted rope. The gun's last bullet went off harmlessly in the air, and Karl saw the officer's body fall back into the patrol car, and Malcolm Schreck's hat hit the pavement underneath the door.

Schreck emerged right at the time the last train car rolled by. He came up from the body, covered in the cop's flesh and blood. He looked directly at the side mirror, daring Karl to escape. But Karl merely quivered in his seat. All his strength had left him. All his anger and rage failed him. Malcolm Schreck bent down to pick his hat and calmly stepped back to the truck and climbed in beside him. They watched as the last train car disappeared like a breeze.

The road opened up before them.

"To the house, Karl," Schreck said as his neck seemed to move in a strangely inhuman manner upon his shoulders. "There is much work we must do."

Chapter 38

Ben Whittinger's mood was ebullient, victorious, and hyperactive. As Arthur sat in the basement near his makeshift coffin, the young man joined a cacophony of extremely loud thrashing from the speakers upstairs. Music, that to Arthur, made much the same noise as the train would have made had it impacted their car. The singer was screaming as if he was dying in agony. And Ben was doing his best to match him. Finally, the younger man noticed that Arthur was not joining him, and he opened the basement door to call down to him. Arthur could not quite make out his words, and so with a break from the noise, probably between tunes, he asked forcefully if Ben wouldn't mind turning down the volume. Ben nodded from the top of the stairs, disappeared, and moments later, right after the first crash of strings, the noise was mercifully muted.

When he came down the steps, he had a can of beer in one hand and a bag of blood in the other. His grin was wide and beaming. He tossed the bag at Arthur and snapped the tab off the can of beer.

"Salud!" he said, raising the beer to his lips. Arthur looked at him but did not drink.

"Damn!" Ben continued after gulping down a few swallows. "I sure would have loved to have seen his face when we got by that train! What do you think? Think it looked like this?" Ben went on to make a series of scrunched-up angry faces that Arthur thought were probably fairly close approximations of Malcolm Schreck's reaction to their escape. Then Ben laughed like the devil.

Arthur sat there slightly enjoying this display. Yes, he was sure that Schreck was in a rage over what might appear to be his defeat that night. It was, without a doubt, the best of endings for Arthur and Ben to have eluded Schreck and Karl. It was also, quite obviously, not the end of the war. Schreck now had more reasons than ever before to bring Arthur's fate to a conclusion. Not only his but Ben's fate as well, so intrinsically tied together they had become. Ben had not allowed this fact to enter his celebratory mood, but for Arthur, it had been an almost immediate foreshadowing of that knowledge. Arthur was weak, and he was repulsed by the only source of strength given him. He dreaded the idea of facing Schreck again. Ben seemed to be calling for it. The young man didn't know or didn't care who he was dealing with. He was full of victory and light, while Arthur's thoughts were morose and dark.

"Ben," Arthur said, "you realize that an angry Malcolm Schreck is not a man to scoff at, don't you? In fact, there is no version of the man to be taken lightly. He is an instrument of pure evil. It doesn't matter to him what he has to do or to whom he has to do it. His eternal life on this earth is all that matters to him. For some reason I don't understand, he thought I would join him in this. I can't do that. And so he thinks I've betrayed him over a pact that I never made. This is between him and me, mate, not you."

Ben took a stray empty folding chair, unfolded it, and sat to face Arthur. "What made him think you'd want it?" he asked plainly, the foolhardy expression gone from his face.

"Hard to say exactly," Arthur returned. "Probably the company I kept back then. But more likely, he thought me a fellow traveler, someone who only needed a little prodding to walk his path. Fact is, at that time, he was probably right, if his plans had gone his way. If we had been more immediately revived, I'd have just as well had joined him, stood beside him, being everything he wanted me to be. I was not a good man, Ben. I've really only known two good men in my life. Your grandfather was one."

"Who was the other one?"

Arthur looked incredulously at Ben. "Well," he said, "I can't say he's a very bright young man, but he is still a good man."

Ben leaned forward. "You know what I think? I think you haven't gotten out much in about, say, forty-seven years. Schreck thinks I'm like him. How good a man could I be if that's what he thinks?"

"Ben, he is a liar. You must know this." Arthur looked hard at Ben for a moment, his old weathered face studying the younger one. "Ben," he said, "where is your father?"

Ben sat back and pursed his lips at the old man. He took a deep breath. "Up in Heaven, in the arms of our Lord and Savior," he said in a wry tone. "Or so I've been told. Why?"

"Do you believe that?"

"Have to," Ben answered, taking a quick swig off his beer can. "Otherwise, I won't ever see him again, will I?"

"Oh," Arthur said. "So that's what this is about then? You miss your daddy, eh? You want your daddy. And if dying is the only way to be with him, then so be it. Here, I carried the guilt over your grandfather's fate for decades, and now you would put your death on my shoulders as well. Is that it? Do you think I'm going to allow that?"

"I don't see you got much choice, Arthur. You're kind of a prisoner to your needs, aren't you? And I'm the warden. I've got the keys. So why don't you just drink that blood and forget about what a bastard I am, huh?"

Arthur looked down at the bag that rested in his hand. He shook his head and tossed it back at Ben. "No," he said. "You idiot. I had a thousand fathers. Each of them stuck around for a couple of hours at the most, long enough to stain an already stained mattress sheet. And none of them, not one, were worth a dog's shit in the street. Now you, Benjamin, you had two good fathers. But you just can't be happy with the time you had with them. You'll forgive me for thinking that pathetic. I will go to my own death. I've done it once already. But I refuse to bring you with me. You are a good young man, Ben, no matter what Schreck may believe. Do me the courtesy of becoming a good old man."

"Arthur," Ben said, standing from his chair, the lone uncovered light bulb just above his head. He held his hand, the one that grasped the bag of his own blood, out to Arthur. "I brought you this blood. Now I want you to drink it."

"No," Arthur answered plainly.

"Drink it!"

"Fuck you, Ben."

That was enough for Ben. He said, "That's not very Christian of you, Arthur. Okay then. I'm just going to put this upstairs in the fridge. And when that gnawing urge comes over you, a lot harder than it is gnawing at you right now, you can just crawl your old dead ass up the stairs and get it yourself."

Ben turned abruptly, stepped heavily up the stairway as if every step was intended to stress a point, and upon the landing, slammed the door behind him. Arthur watched him go, and when the light from the kitchen disappeared behind the door, he let his head fall.

It would be a couple more hours before Ben went to bed himself. Arthur heard him pacing, could hear the next beer can snap open, then the television come on, and then the pacing stopped. Arthur remained in the chair. He refused to lie down in the cabinet as if in doing so, he was rejecting the warped version of himself that he was. This was to be his last day as an inhuman reflection, his last day as a creation of Malcolm Schreck. He was going to die as Arthur Drake, the bastard son of a whore, the Limey pimp who flashed a knife when payment was overdue, the hired flesh merchant of false English gentry, the foolishly chosen instrument of God, but not as a vampire. Pride drew a line at that for him. He was weak, ancient, and tired. All the years he had missed growing old as a living, breathing person, all the little pains that had foreshadowed the age of fifty, sixty, seventy, and beyond. Pains that had only softly cried in his joints at forty screamed madly at him now. And the craving. Ben was quite correct about that. It had taken all Arthur's strength to throw that blood back at him. The only advantage he felt in the act was that it had fueled his anger, and he had been able to use that anger to lash out at Ben as he knew he must. Arthur wished for a cigarette. Something, anything to replace this hunger.

As the few remaining hours before dawn passed by, the muffled intonations of the television were replaced by the soft, rhythmic snoring of Ben upstairs, asleep in his bed. Arthur stood after a while of listening to that soft snore. He wanted to go to the boy and tell him how much his friendship had meant to him; how proud he was sure both his father and his grandfather would be, knowing the kind of man they had raised; and how proud he was to have known him. Those were things he thought a dying man should say to someone who had been so influential in his life before he took his last breath. Instead, after a heavy battle with the stairs, Arthur turned toward the refrigerator, used it to brace himself for a moment, and then went to Ben's coat that he had draped over a chair and fished through the pocket for the car keys.

Chapter 39

While Arthur Drake was desperately fighting in Ben Whittinger's car to keep the vehicle moving forward in the right direction, toward the old house that was until quite recently his tomb, Lt. Phillip Lewis's precinct, and indeed, every police precinct in the state of Michigan, was a complete madhouse. Officer Steven Lanyon from the Seventh Precinct in a southern suburb of the town of Kalamazoo had been viciously murdered. His body had been found lying half in the front seat of his cruiser, his feet resting their heels on the pavement of the street not far from the railroad tracks. His throat was ravaged by what could only be thought a wild animal. This murder, unlike the one of the homeless man in town, had been no neat and tidy slit of a carotid artery. It had been a mauling. And the fear on the big man's eyes and face was plain to the officers who found him, freshly dead. It was a contagion being masked by despair, bravado, and relentless activity, but the fear was everywhere.

Jeff Kipner, Lewis's partner, strode up to him quickly. "We've got fourteen vehicles within fifty miles with license tags that match that partial plate number Lanyon got off," he said. "CFH 5. Six of those tags are registered to truck owners. Two of those are women. I think we can eliminate them. The other four range in age from twenty-six to sixty-eight. Eliminating the older dudes, we've got one Randy Wiessner, owns an electrical contracting company, thirty-four years old, married with two children ages four and six, and one Karl Angstrom, twenty-six."

"Any priors?" Lewis asked. The captain was screaming at somebody on the phone in his office. Press corps was running the table on all the precincts as news circulated about the cop killing. They would be on everybody who could give an opinion before any real legwork had been accomplished. If either of these guys was a lead, Lewis wanted to get on it fast before he too was cornered. He hadn't known Lanyon, except by reputation around the force, and the rep was good. A cop killing was atypical, fortunately rare, especially in a town this small. This wasn't Detroit or Chicago. This was a town surrounded by farmland. And to have this, a rage killing that looked like an animal attack, made for even more agitation among the police. Was it a wild dog? A wolf? The others didn't tie it into the previous case Lewis and Kipner were working, but both men remembered the big black truck, that one piece of info that Barney from the Stegman House would give them. And the original call from Glitters described a big black truck. If they weren't related, it was one hell of a coincidence.

Kipner returned with another printout sheet, this one holding all info available on Randy Wiessner and Karl Angstrom. Kipner stood close to Lewis so he could read from the same sheet of paper and also because the flurry of people stepping around obstacles to answer the constantly ringing phones made personal space between them impossible.

"The electrician has a few speeding tickets," Kipner said as he glanced over the two names. "Angstrom, though, he's a beaut. Four dropped charges of aggravated assault since high school. All bar fights. Apparently, he won big. School suspension for assault of the vice principal. No charges filed. No record of him graduating either. Currently employed as a construction worker. Even his license picture looks like a mug shot."

"Okay, okay," Lewis said, "let's cover our bases. Give the older guys to Finch and Palmer. Have them checked as well. You take the family man, and I'll go see about Mr. Angstrom. Give me his file."

"Phil, this is our guy. We don't need to cover our bases. Let me go with you."

Lewis was already grabbing his coat and heading for the door. "You remember Bundy?" Kipner nodded. "Did he look like our guy?

Better if we split up. Find anything. Let me know. Otherwise, we'll touch base in a few hours. Check it out, Kip."

Jeff Kipner nodded, but he watched Lewis's back disappear with an uneasy feeling in his guts. He guessed as the bigger and stronger of the two of them, Lewis figured to have a go at Angstrom, while Kipner wasted his time checking on the family man's doings. A cop killer was a man who crossed a very distinct line. Once crossed though, second thoughts about repeating the offense was unlikely. And now Lewis was splitting them up, going in different directions. It felt very wrong. But the man was lead detective. Kipner was in a hopeless situation. So he did what he was told. He'd have to rely on Phil's good sense, which he didn't doubt, excepting, of course, for the circumstances.

Lewis made his way west on the main road that led from Downtown Kalamazoo all the way to the Lake Michigan beach, not far from where Arthur Drake and Brendan Vaughn had been sequestered by Giovanni Tagliani of the Chicago mob all those many years ago. Between the city and the beach, there was a space, farm and forest, and not much else but one stoplight communities of two taverns, a gas station, and a small market. Aside from the time of the year that brought the fall leaves into the beginnings of a flame-covered thatch reflected in the bright sunlight, there wasn't much color out this way, at least not of Lewis's type. He was assured as he drove into Tinsdale's Construction Company's lot that his presence would be regarded as, at the very least, unusual.

Tinsdale's Construction Company was the last known employment reference for Karl Angstrom. Since he had managed to steer clear of conversations with the police for about two years, it was the first stop to checking his current whereabouts. The next would be his place of residence, approximately ten miles north of here. The lot was unpaved with holes of mud where large truck tires had worn into the dirt and a white double-wide sitting at the edge of a circular turnabout. A sign tacked to the side of the modular stated it functioned as the owner's, Perry Tinsdale, main office. Lewis took a good look around before exiting the Impala. There were plenty of trucks in the lot. None matched the description belonging to Karl Angstrom.

Lewis walked up to the door and let himself in. Four burly men in dirty Carhartt jackets and weathered baseball caps sat in a semicircle around a television set, while Tinsdale himself sat behind a desk, smoking a cigarette. The look on their faces as the large black man strode confidently into their space was a bit priceless to Lewis. He bit back the urge to laugh.

"Don't get up, gentlemen," he said, flipping his badge out and flashing it to the entire room. "Phil Lewis, Kalamazoo Police. I'm just here to ask a few questions." Lewis let that sink in for a moment, and then he turned his attention to the boss.

Tinsdale sat back and let his hand release from the desk drawer he had grabbed upon Lewis's entrance. "What do you need?" he asked. "Officer."

"Need to talk to you about an employee of yours, Mr. Tinsdale. A Karl Angstrom."

One of the men sitting in the makeshift break room chimed in, "Psycho?"

"That's enough!" Tinsdale shouted past Lewis. "You need these idiots?"

"Not necessarily," Lewis replied. "But don't you guys leave the lot. I may have questions for you too." The four stood, and their combined weight shook the modular home as they ambled out into the morning sunlight, muttering to one another. Lewis turned his attention back to Tinsdale, who shook his head as the men left.

"Psycho?" the detective asked pointedly.

Tinsdale grimaced. "Told those guys not to call him that. Pet name for him, I guess. They like to rile him up. Don't know why. He could dust off the lot of them and not break a sweat. They aren't the sharpest tools in the shed. So what's old Karl up to now?"

"You listen to the news this morning?"

"Shit. You're kidding."

Lewis shrugged. He took a step toward the desk and looked down at Tinsdale. "I don't think he did it," Lewis offered, "but we're looking at him as a possible witness, for this and another thing that you probably didn't hear about. Have you seen him?"

"Not for about a week," Tinsdale said. "Fired him a few days ago for no call, no show. Left a couple of messages. Expected him to drive up any time in a fucking rage. That's why I had the boys in here, and that's why when you came in . . ."

"Sure," Lewis said. "Well, if you do hear from him, give me a call." Lewis handed him a card.

"Guess this has got you guys pretty upset if they send you all the way out here."

"Blue is the only color we see right now, Mr. Tinsdale. And red. But you're right. We're pretty upset."

"Yep," Tinsdale returned. "Hey, what if he does show up? What am I supposed to do then?"

Lewis turned back as he reached the door. "Whatever you gotta do," he said. "I only want him as a witness, remember? As tough as he is, I think he's found a friend that's a lot worse. Don't let your guard down. You're not exactly right around the corner out here, are you?"

Lewis donned his sunglasses, stepped out of the modular, nodded toward the four employees who stood in a circle near one of the many mud puddles, and got back into his car. He had made his first stop, which confirmed his feeling that Karl Angstrom had found himself a new hobby, a hobby that had interfered with his normal routine of just being a big asshole. Now all he had was Karl's address. Lewis would make his way there to see if Karl was sleeping off his nightly activity. He still didn't believe Angstrom to be the murderer, not of Lundquist or Officer Lanyon. But he was starting to get a picture of Karl as an accomplice. Willing or not, he wasn't sure. Lewis recalled the theories regarding Jack the Ripper. One of the big questions in that case was how the Ripper had pulled off two murders in one night at such a distance from each other. The obvious answer was that he had a driver, a coachman, driving him from one scene to the other. Angstrom struck Lewis as somebody who may have found himself employed for that purpose, probably under duress. And that thought led to a more frightening conclusion. Because although these two murders had slightly different MOs, they also had two very prominent things in common: one, the black truck, and two, apparently, one very evil motherfucker.

Chapter 40

Ben Whittinger rubbed the flakes out of his eyes as the bright afternoon sun invaded his downturned blinds. He lifted himself out of bed slowly, grabbed his well-used bathrobe, and started out to make a cup of coffee to battle his throbbing skull. It was about 3:30 p.m., and the light outside could not be contained by mere cheap blinds. Ben could see the dust particles floating in the air from the windows in the house. Once in the kitchen, he opened the basement door and looked down the steps. The cabinet rested at the bottom of the steps, undisturbed. Arthur would have sealed himself in for the day, as had been the practice, knowing that sunlight would hit him like a scalding acid bath. Ben opened the refrigerator and saw that Arthur had left the bags of blood untouched. *Stubborn old bastard,* Ben thought. What was he trying to do? Leave Ben to take on Schreck, while he went on a hunger strike? *Yeah, that's a great plan, Arthur. Well, that's fine,* he thought. Ben was sure that by the time night arrived, Arthur wouldn't have the strength to refuse, and so Ben would just force-feed the Limey vampire the heme. Let him be mad about it if that was what he wanted. At least he'd be able to put up a fight if it came to it.

    Then Ben happened to look out the kitchen window to the driveway outside the house. He took a sip from the coffee he had made.

"Son of a bitch," he muttered. He looked toward the basement and repeated, "Son of a bitch." He walked down the steps and opened the cabinet. Arthur, of course, was not in the cabinet. The state of his bedding said he had never been in the cabinet that night. Ben took another sip of his coffee.

"Son of a bitch stole my car," he said calmly as if he should have expected it. Problem was Ben knew for a fact Arthur couldn't drive a car. In fact, Arthur often looked as if he would shit his pants if ever Ben took the car above forty-five miles an hour. And now the old man was attempting, most likely very poorly, to drive his car. Ben pictured the car in a ditch, against a tree, in a head-on with another vehicle, probably within two miles of the house, and poor Arthur frying to a crisp in the driver's seat with a handful of people standing there, watching him smolder, wondering whether they should try to move him.

Ben went back upstairs and made a couple of phone calls. His first call was to his mother, who told him in as reluctant a voice as he could bear to hear that his grandfather had fallen back into a coma and that he was expected to go at any time and if Ben was okay after hearing it. He replied that he was, that he had been to see him just last week, and that he had already mourned his loss. It would be a relief now if he did go, he told his mother. Then he said his goodbye and that he loved her and would talk to her soon.

His next call was to his best friend, David Wallace. After four rings, where the answering machine would soon pick up, Ben was about to hang up when David's voice said hello. Ben kept the conversation as casual as he could, the usual opening banter between the two. They had known each other since childhood. It was a secondhand language that they used. Then David brought Sherry into the conversation, wanting to tell Ben of the news that they would be married in late spring of next year, a date yet to be determined but likely mid-May. Ben congratulated them both. He knew they would be very happy together. The good news just kept pouring in for Ben. Next would be "This just in. Ben Whittinger. You're a dead man." Ben laughed a little as this thought interfered with David's words. It fit the moment so David remained unaware of the laugh's true origin. When David hung up the phone, he turned to Sherry, who was sitting nearby.

"That was Ben," he said to her.

"I know," she said, slightly amused that he felt the need to tell her that. "What did he have to say?"

"He just said he loved us."

Sherry nodded and gave a weak smile in return, and then she let her head fall back to the book she had opened in her lap.

Ben threw some clothes on: a shirt, sweatshirt, jeans, and brown work boots. Then he went to his small coat closet and reached in for a leather jacket he owned. He walked outside into the sun. Not a cloud in the sky. A gorgeous afternoon, warm, mid-sixties, a fall scent in the air. Ben reached the small one-car garage that came with the house. He rarely used it. It was full of boxes of his junk, and it was so narrow that opening the car doors was near impossible when he did. He pulled up the large garage door on its loud, creaky rollers; walked in; and wheeled his motorcycle out into the gravel driveway.

Chapter 41

Fall back time had come early that year. The sun was setting as Arthur Drake half sat, half crouched in the old chair at the decrepit, old monstrosity that had once held gangsters and then two dead men. The fireplace to his right was crumbling, and the room was filthy with grime after years of sitting through rain, snow, wind, and heat. There was a large pile of hastily gathered wood near him. Arthur had no idea how he had got to the chair. How he had made it to the house was something of a haze as well. He remembered the sun and how it felt like flame against his skin and how he had done all he could to protect himself. He pulled up his coat collar around him and Charlie's hat down as far as he could on his head, the sunglasses, the ineffective sun visor, and the black gloves, all of it only the slightest protection against the yellow ball. It had taken an eternity. His feet knew the pedals but not how much pressure to apply to them. His mind remembered the direction but not the exact roads. And yet somehow, after countless bleats from other car horns and angry shouting at him to get his old ass off the road, he had instinctively knew where to turn off the correct dirt road to the correct stamped route to the house. It was Schreck. Schreck was a beacon that called to him. It must have been so for each of them after that encounter on Vaughn's estate. That was how Schreck had found him here in

America. The old wizard had laid hands on him, and he had been forever marked afterward.

Mercifully, the sun's intensity was fading, heading west on a downward trajectory, until it turned red and finally disappeared. Arthur could barely move, but a familiar voice made him jerk involuntarily.

"Arthur Drake," Schreck said softly, "you look unwell."

Arthur looked at the figure, the same bent stature with the same rotting clothes. Schreck was like the earth itself—old, beaten, and abused—but still standing. He wore the earth on him, carried it as a scent. Why would he not just let himself fall to it? Why did he fight the natural way of all things? Arthur knew the answer. He just didn't know what he could do about it now in this terrible and emaciated state. He'd come all this way just to let Schreck finish him, just like Ben said he would. Stupid fool.

Schreck went on, "I had Karl bring you in, my young friend. The boy is nowhere to be seen, so I presume you lifted his vehicle." Schreck laughed as he said it. "That is why I chose you, Arthur. For your strength, your courage, and your determination. It is that you use those qualities to fight me that I cannot understand. All I wanted to give you was . . . your youth, your beauty. You see in me now the way it could be for you. And I am ugly. I must admit, there is a sacrifice for genius. Touching . . . people. I knew that would not affect you so much as it does me." Schreck shuddered at the thought. "But as you must also well know, my preservation comes foremost to my mind."

Schreck moved toward Arthur and crouched before Arthur's limp body. He pulled off the hat Arthur wore and set it in his lap. "Are you cold, my friend?" he asked. Schreck reached into the pocket of his battered frock and pulled out a small black disc.

"You remember?" he said. He tossed the disc into some of the wood and kindling that had been placed in the old hearth. It went up instantly in strong crackling flames. "All those years ago," Schreck said, smiling, "you came up out of that fool Vaughn's estate to face me. We sat about the fire, trading tales we had kept secret for all our lives. I can tell you now you stirred strange feelings in me, Drake. I know you believe I mistreated you but forgive me. I have scant experience with such . . . emotions. Mr. Warren, him I took as little more than a child with a child's thoughts. Ahh! I am trying to tell you everything before you die, Arthur. I suppose, things being as they are, it matters not."

Karl stepped in at that moment. Arthur saw him, blocking the last rays of the sun with his wide shoulders. Schreck stood.

"All is as I wish?" he said, still facing Arthur Drake, who was weakly fit into the corner of the high-backed chair nearest the blaze.

Karl spoke through a thick cigar. "It'll hold," he said.

Schreck nodded. "We must have this accomplished before the boy comes," he said.

"I still don't like it," Karl said in response. Schreck stiffened.

"It is not for you to approve or disapprove," he said coldly. "If I were to allow my druthers, I would have you at my feet now and feed you to my old friend here."

"Well, go ahead and fucking do it then!" Karl shouted. He watched as Schreck twisted himself to snarl at his face. Karl lifted his chin with the cigar still firmly in the corner of his mouth, offering his neck to the vampire. The tops of his hands were in the pockets of his jeans, thumbs twitching violently on the cuffs.

Then the sound of a car door closing broke the moment.

"Too soon!" Schreck hissed. "Karl!"

Angstrom stepped over to the door and looked out as he cracked it open. The dusk was bleeding into the clearing where the man stood. Karl described him—black guy; big, about as big as he was; and dressed like an insurance agent. "He's a fucking cop!" Karl said, giggling his high-pitched chuckle. Karl watched as he stepped past the truck with his gun drawn, going over to check out Whittinger's car. Karl had left the door open and had pulled out the keys to stop the warning ding. The cop stuck his head in the open door and looked around.

"Black, you say?" Schreck said in disgust. "You allow an Afrikaner authority?" Schreck shook his head and spat, "Americans." He took a step toward Karl and looked at the stranger outside. "Idiot! The Negro followed you here."

Karl continued watching as the big man walked about the corner of the house.

"Angstrom!" the man shouted. "Karl Angstrom! This is the police! Come out of the house with your hands up!"

Schreck gave Karl a shove from the door. "Out of sight, fool!" he hissed. Karl backed himself toward the rear of the house past the cellar door, went around a corner, and disappeared. Schreck turned back to Arthur, held a long finger to his lips, and melted into a shadow.

Lewis stepped up to the door. He took a last look at the corners of the house. One strong breeze and it looked to fall. It listed to the west. The large bough from the tree that had crashed through the steeple A-frame roof was likely the only thing holding it up. It did nothing for Lewis's nerves. He pulled his flashlight from his coat pocket and let the beam hit the door. Then he slowly pushed it open. He expected a creaking sound to accompany it, but apparently, the door had had recent work. It opened smoothly.

"Police!" he shouted again before he entered. "Angstrom! Karl Angstrom! You in here? Come on out, Angstrom!" Lewis did not think that only Karl Angstrom was in the house. He was starting to regret not waiting for the backup he had called for once he saw Angstrom's truck leave the road. The whole night had been something of a shock. He had driven out the main road to get to Angstrom's address, and the big black truck had barreled right toward him. It had taken great effort not to spin out and give chase right then, but instead, he had driven to the nearest street, let Angstrom get out of sight, and then turned around to follow at a safer distance until only the faintest image of the truck's rear lights was still visible.

And now he was here, at this forgotten old disaster of a house. He didn't know its origins, nor did he care. He only saw the truck that had been involved in two murders, one of which was a cop from very early that morning. Only now that he was here did his instinct for caution kick in. Angstrom, from his description, was a bad enough character to try to take down. If he was armed, even worse. But it wasn't Angstrom whom Lewis branded the murdering psychopath. It was something he couldn't quite understand, something that hadn't acted even human in its killing frenzy. And this was a sorry time for an experienced cop like him to think of it.

Lewis pointed the flashlight up the steps directly in front of him. The last red light of the sun was becoming very faint, and all Lewis could see was the dusty steps leading up to a landing and the gnarly elbow of the tree bough reaching down from the ceiling. Lewis opted to remain downstairs. The steps looked weak, and he would be too easily trapped upstairs with no viable exit. He was still cursing his foolishness when he noticed the crackling of the fire in the narrow room to his right. He turned toward it slowly.

Lewis's flashlight centered on the figure in the high-backed chair. Whether the man was alive was doubtful the way he was positioned there, but it clearly was not Karl Angstrom. Lewis walked slowly into the room, his heart easily outpacing his movements. He could feel it thump in his chest. Lewis looked at the man. He looked ancient and ill as if his body would collapse into dust but for his eyes, which were open and wide, fearful even, and unblinking. They reflected the red glow of the fire. Then the mouth seemed to move, and Lewis flashed his light into the gray face.

"Sir?" Lewis said. "I'm Phil Lewis. I'm a detective with the Kalamazoo Police Department. I'm looking for Karl Angstrom. Can you tell me where he is? Is he in the house?"

Lewis watched as the old man in the chair moved his lips and furrowed his brow, struggling to speak. The only sound was an "Ahhh. Ahhh."

"Lewis kept the gun trained on the man. He didn't look dangerous. He was obviously too weak to be a threat, but still, Lewis felt threatened by something in the man's eyes.

"Where—" Lewis had barely got the word out when he felt a cold vicelike grip on his gun wrist. The frigid clamp felt like it would break his wrist bones. Instinct or reflex caused him to pull the trigger. The bullet hit the man in the chair as Lewis turned his head to look into the face of a monster. It was a mouthful of pointed teeth that Lewis saw only for an instant as the attacker's other claw slapped against his right temple and pushed his head over to his left shoulder. Then he felt the bite.

Arthur could only watch in horror as Malcolm Schreck and the man who had only moments before been standing before him appeared to dance in the darkness. The man was strong, and Schreck seemed angered by his struggle, but in moments, the stranger dropped to his knees as a gaping open wound in his neck spewed his vital fluid in an indiscriminate spray, and he fell forward, his head at Arthur's feet.

Schreck turned his head over his shoulder and spat out the chunk of flesh he had just torn from his victim. With the blood running down his chin onto his stained white shirt, he said, "It seems the heavens have decided to give you a last opportunity, Arthur. Now drink."

Schreck bent down to a knee and began to feed himself. He jerked his hand up suddenly to Arthur's lapel and flung his weight down to the floor next to the dying man. Arthur fell to his side and looked at the man's outline glowing in the firelight, his blood seeping out to puddle on the dirt-crusted floor. Schreck spun his head from the wound.

"I have brought you this blood, Drake!" he growled. "Drink it!" Arthur clamped his eyes shut in response. The words he had first heard come from Ben were filled with hatred from the mouth of Malcolm Schreck. It filled him with revulsion. *What a fool I am,* he thought. *I should have come here with the strength to kill. What did I think to do with a devil like this? I've failed. Failed!*

When he had finally had his fill, Schreck stood above Arthur, looking down at him with a contemptuous glare. "I thought as much," he said. "Oh, it is not you I hold responsible, Drake. It is I. How utterly I misjudged you. You are not worthy of such a gift. So be it. Come, I have prepared a room for you."

Schreck snatched a handful of Arthur's coat collar at the back of the neck and easily lifted him off the floor. He carried him like a parent would an errant toddler toward the stairs. "It would seem Karl is the only soul on which I can rely," he said as if the thought was a pathetic admittance. "And the boy, of course." Schreck stopped midway up the steps and lifted Arthur to face him. "Oh yes, Arthur, the boy is coming. If you are fortunate, you may last long enough to witness his demise."

Upon reaching the landing, Schreck walked into the darkened shadow of the bough to the first door on his right. He took his buckled shoe and kicked it slightly until the light of a half-dozen candles, three to a wall, broke out into the hallway. Then he stepped into the room and immediately gasped in a mixture of horror and pain. He dropped Arthur roughly to the floor and turned his back to the far wall.

Karl had done his work well, Schreck thought, *too well.* Perhaps the boy had not been so wrong when he had confronted Schreck with the nearly two-thousand-year-old talisman. Schreck had discounted it then. He could not discount it now. Karl had fashioned a crude yet perfect crucifix—thick wood cut to size and fastened securely to the far wall. Schreck covered his eyes with his pale hands. He stepped over Arthur's body and, with the point of his left shoe, kicked Arthur's shoulder over so he lay on his back.

"Look on it, Arthur," he said as if even the words were difficult to utter, "if you are able." Arthur let his head fall to his right, and a whimper left his throat.

"No," he groaned. Schreck's intent was clear. He meant to kill Arthur with his newfound faith, beliefs of which Arthur had no great store of knowledge, only purpose, a faith that had only served to incur upon Arthur a particular wrath from the old warlock.

"Not this," Arthur groaned. "Schreck . . . Malcolm . . . please."

"So now you wish mercy, eh?" he said, still facing away from the crude crucifix. "And how many times did I entreat you? And how did you respond?"

"I don't—" Arthur began, but Schreck silenced him with a harsh wave of his hand.

"Deserve it?" he spat. "No, whoreson, you are far from deserving of such an end. But I do this not to martyr you, Drake. You, in your eternal ignorance, could not understand. But the boy, Benjamin, he will understand. Perhaps you will not expire before bearing witness. That would please me, for, Arthur, this will tear the flesh from his soul before I strip it from his body. You yourself will see to that."

Arthur groaned again and wept from his dry eyes. "Jesus," he gasped. "Lord! Help me!"

Schreck walked toward the door, his heavy shoes clicking on the floorboards. "Have you learned nothing, Drake?" he growled. "You will receive the same response as He. But no, you were not aware of that, were you?" Schreck stepped out into the hall. "Karl!" he called out sharply. "It is time."

Chapter 42

It was dark by the time Ben Whittinger turned off the road to the barely noticeable two-track that led into the thick and foreboding woods. The 500cc Honda Shadow was not a motorcycle made for off-road travel. It was hardly made for the dirt road it had just been directed to pass over. The tires would not grip anything but pure pavement, so the packed gravel had its rear end fishtailing at the slightest provocation. But Ben was determined. He wasn't sure Arthur would be there. He could still be in some unknown ditch or around the corner from Ben's somewhere. After placing the weak battery on a charger to turn the engine over, Ben had grabbed the full bag of blood, hoping to get to Arthur in time to save him with it. The man had to be near death or whatever state he was to have, considering his current form. Ben would force the blood into him if he must. He would need Arthur to defeat Schreck, if that were even possible now.

Ben had driven slowly, of course, half expecting to find his car hanging off a neighborhood porch surrounded by civilians and cops, watching in horror as an old man burned inside. But so far, there had been no sign of his vehicle or any untoward commotion. He may have just missed it, of course. There were many routes to take, none that Arthur could be expected to know. Except he felt sure Arthur had taken the one that called to him as it seemed to call to Ben. Probably the snake, Schreck, had left that impression on him.

He didn't need to know exactitudes. He and Arthur, and probably Karl, were all called from the same source. The bag of blood felt cold against his chest.

As he bobbed and weaved through the dips of tire tracks and downed branches, he flicked his bright headlamp on to give himself a longer viewpoint and kept his legs down to steady the bike over the bumpy terrain. Stopping, he raised his visor and caught the distinct scent of smoke coming from the direction of the old abandoned house. He decided to accelerate a little faster now, believing the smoke to be a sign of impending doom. He was already too late. And then a lone branch, thick enough to stop the bike, found its way into his front wheel spoke and sent him flying over the bars. He landed, thankfully, in a soft spot of loose ground. There was no great pain. He had not been thrown into a tree or impaled on a jutting branch. And yet when he had recovered from the shock and saw the motorcycle lying on its side, its headlight shining aimlessly into the dark forest, he felt the damp, sticky wetness of his own blood. He reached into his leather jacket and pulled out the bag of blood, which now set limply in his hand, only traces of the red blood cells left. The rest bathed his body, from his neck to his crotch.

"Shit!" he cursed, throwing the bag at his feet. He went over and shut the machine down, took his helmet off and threw it casually next to the bike, and began trudging toward the house. He figured another thousand yards up the incline and he would reach the clearing. The path had been worn not only by Karl's truck but also by at least one other vehicle. Karl's tires ran deep into the dirt, and these others had slipped in the damp mud. Ben knew the way to the house, however. He needed no track to guide him.

As he reached the clearing, he saw the source of the scent pouring out a hole in the side of the crumbled chimney. Candlelight and flames flickered between the siding boards and the broken windows. The door to the house was open, and there was no sound other than the crackle from the fire and the nightly music from the crickets and aphids. Ben took in a deep breath, and as he slowly made for the door, he recited softly Psalm 23. Appropriately, he reached the door at the fourth verse.

"Yea, though I walk through the valley of the shadow of death, I will fear no evil: for thou art with me; thy rod and thy staff they comfort me."

Ben stepped through the door and heard a voice coming from the small galley kitchen where he had first confronted and, through his naïveté, attempted to assist Arthur Drake and Malcolm Schreck.

"Thou preparest a table before me in the presence of mine enemies." The voice rang out in its odd accent. "Thou annointest my head with oil; my cup runneth over. Surely goodness and mercy shall follow me all the days of my life: and I will dwell in the house of the Lord forever.

"Come, boy," Schreck said calmly. "Come to my table."

Ben looked over to his right and saw the body of a man he didn't know. The fire lit his face in a grim stare of death. Ben did not go over to him; instead, he did as he was told and walked over to the kitchen.

As he stepped through the entryway, he saw Malcolm Schreck sitting in the spot Ben had dropped him in over a long week ago. He sat as straight as he apparently could, his old clothing a shamble of black grime and dirt and a dark stain of drying red blood. They were mirror images of each other. The dark stains of fresh blood covered Ben from his shirt to his pants. Two candles, one at each end of the table, lit Malcolm's pale face with a ghostly glow, and he leered in the light. Before him were his old satchel bag, his decrepit book, and the grotesque head of his former companion. His dark eyes inspected Ben as he stood there silently.

"You are hurt?" he asked in mock deference.

Ben ignored the question; instead, he asked, "How many people have to die to satisfy you?"

Schreck cocked his head like a mongrel dog and said, "As many as I require." He let the comment sit for a moment, and then he added, "I gather that is no great revelation to you."

"Where is Arthur? I know he's here. Where is he?"

Schreck jerked his head toward the ceiling. "Upstairs," he answered. "Go to him, boy. He waits for you. I assure you, Benjamin, you will not be accosted."

As Ben turned to leave, Schreck's voice once again stopped him. "I hold Arthur dearest to me as well, boy. I took no great joy in this. That I reserve for you and you alone."

Ben Whittinger said nothing. He walked toward the steps, barely noticing the new wood on the floor. Where once there had been nothing but a sodden mush, a clean patchwork contrasted with the rest of the grimy boards. The steps were still weak, however, so he moved gingerly up them, keeping his hands out to grab at either wall or rail in case one gave way under his weight. The darkness was complete now. Only a few candles spaced about the floor kept the house from succumbing to it.

The hallway smelled of the damp oak limb that crashed through the roof. It hung there, mere feet from the landing, reaching down like an arm from the sky. Ben went to the first door and could see the pale light coming from the crack. He knew his next steps were going to be painful, but he could not imagine the stark, cold image that the door hid from him.

Ben opened the door and stepped through. The candles lit up the room like a shrine. Ben kept his head forward and down at his feet. He closed his eyes tight. He knew what was there. He had seen it in the periphery, but he was weak. He didn't want to look at it. Slowly, however, he forced his eyes to open and struggled against himself to turn his head toward Arthur. His hands came up to cover the gasp in his throat.

Arthur hung there on the cross, an almost perfect replica of a thousand such images known to man. His clothes, the clothes that remained on him, hung limply on his torso and waist. The shoes, socks, and coat were rumpled together on the floor below him. His head fell lifeless to his chest. There were stains of a greenish-red-tinged fluid beneath the holes in his hands and his doubled feet. The nails were thick and the heads large and round. There were no words to describe the pain Arthur must have felt having those nails driven into his flesh as there were none to describe the pain Ben felt at the vision of him hanging there.

Ben fell to his knees. He wanted to rip his eyes out. He wanted to pull his hair out at the roots; instead, he let out the most painful agonizing scream, a scream like that which had been waiting since the day of his birth to find release.

Below Ben, at the kitchen table, Schreck looked upward at the sound. Was this the victory he had been planning? Some small part of him doubted. He opened the book, the knowledge the old pages held, knowledge that had passed from his own master to him, incantations and concoctions with the formulas for wisdom and instruction that had sustained him over the two centuries of his life, Malcolm Schreck's own dark Bible. But now looking at the page, Schreck saw nothing. Nothing. He passed his hand over it, looking for it as a blind man reads Braille. But there was nothing. He was as abandoned as Arthur, as alone as the boy. It frightened him. Where was Karl?

Up in the room, Ben raised himself to his feet and stepped up close to Arthur. He took his hand and cupped the old man's face. It was cold. The eyes were closed, and if he had ever breathed since being revived, he gave no sign of effort now.

"Arthur," Ben whispered, "I'm sorry."

A long moment passed, and then a gaspingly weak voice broke the silence. "Ben," Arthur whispered.

Ben reached up and gripped Arthur's face excitedly. He lifted it and stared. Arthur's lips were moving. His eyes remained closed, but his lips moved slightly. He was alive, barely, but alive, all the same. Then he said with grunting effort, "Get . . . me . . . down."

Ben went immediately to grab at the nailhead in Arthur's left palm. He pulled and groaned, placing his foot on the wall for leverage. But the nails were too deeply embedded into the wood and the flesh. They wouldn't budge. "Come on, fucker! Come on!" Ben growled. Then he let it go and said, "I'm going to have to pull you off, Arthur. It's probably gonna hurt. Are you ready?"

Arthur nodded slightly, and Ben grabbed him at the hand and the elbow. Bracing the elbow, he pulled slowly until the flesh of the old gray hand came flush against the rounded head. He knew this was where the greatest pain for Arthur would come, so he gave him no warning and jerked the hand over the nail.

Arthur groaned loudly.

"I'm sorry. I'm sorry," Ben heaved, biting back his emotions. He cradled the loose arm over his shoulder and shimmied his way over to the right arm. He let Arthur dangle as gently as he could allow and went quickly to repeat the process. Arthur groaned again and fell against Ben like a drunken dancer, both his arms dangling limply over Ben's shoulders. Blood or whatever Arthur had for blood dripped lightly from the holes in Arthur's hands to the floor behind Ben.

"Okay, okay, okay." Ben breathed. "This is gonna be the worst of it, Arthur. Then it'll be over, okay?" Arthur groaned in response. It was all he could do in the moment. He hung on both Ben and the crossbeam, his feet now almost flat together as Ben backed away a step from the cross. Arthur was light, no more in weight than a young child, but Ben was breathing heavily nonetheless.

Ben counted off slowly. "One . . . two . . . three!" At three, he pulled back with all his own weight and ripped Arthur's feet off the cross. They both fell into a heap on the floor, and Ben quickly righted himself to lay Arthur's upper torso on his lap.

Arthur looked up at Ben. "Hurts," he said. Ben looked him over, unsure of what to do next. He could carry Arthur out, but he was sure that wasn't going to be allowed by Schreck. Then Arthur said, "Ben, I'm sorry, for what I said."

"Don't worry about that now," Ben answered, his eyes watering as he looked down at the old man. "We gotta get out of here."

"No, Ben," Arthur said, holding Ben's shirt as he spoke. "It's time, past time, to let go."

"But what if you don't die?" Ben protested. "What if it's like before?"

"Better," Arthur answered, "than this. Different though. Different. Hear voices. Calling me. Charlie. Charlie, my old friend. Father Tom. Never told you about . . . Father Tom." Then suddenly, Arthur gripped Ben's shirt with renewed strength. "Ben! Be sure! Be sure, Ben! Burn it down! Burn it . . . downnn."

Arthur's head fell back, his eyes closed, and his mouth hung open loosely. He was gone. Ben was not sure where, but Arthur Drake was gone from this hell. He would suffer no more. Ben let the body slip from his knees to rest gently on the floor.

"I promise," he said. "I promise, Arthur." He stood from the body, made the sign of the cross, and backed away from the wooden crucifix where his friend had been crucified. Then with a last glance down at the old man, he stepped out of the room.

Karl was waiting for him. He stood just to the edge of the doorway, a huge cigar resting in the corner of his mouth, the red ash glow lighting the side of his cheek.

"Karl?" Ben said, but that was all the time he was given. Before he knew to defend himself, Karl Angstrom had thrown one huge hand behind his neck and the other to his front and flung Ben across the hall to the opposite wall. Then Karl took his right hand and pressed Ben's face against the wall, keeping him from dropping just from the pressure of that hand. "You son of a bitch," Ben said through his clenched teeth.

"Yep," Karl responded. He took his hands and placed them on Ben's chest. Then he threw Ben in the opposite direction, slamming his head against the wall behind him. Ben's hands went up too late to protect his head, and he felt himself slide down the wall to sit on the floor. Through numb, blind eyes, he saw Karl towering above him, the cigar burning bright in the darkened hallway, a half-cocked smile crossing his face. Ben saw Karl's leg swing back.

"Wait!" he cried.

"Fuck you!" came the answer as Karl's heavy boot swung forward, connecting squarely with Ben's ribs. If not for the thickness of his jacket, Ben's lung would have punctured from the force of the kick. He landed on his side and began crawling in a futile attempt to get away. Karl removed his cigar from his mouth and blew out a huge plume of smoke, watching him.

Karl slowly followed until Ben reached the hallway rail, where he attempted to pull himself to his feet. Karl was on him, grabbing the back of his collar. At first, in his confused state, Ben thought he might be helping him back up, but Karl hooked a finger in a belt loop and lifted Ben right off the floor until only the tips of his boots helplessly scraped the planks. He felt himself being hefted even higher as Karl reaffirmed his grip.

"You're a fun little toy, aren't you?" Karl muttered behind Ben's ear. "My toys never did last long." Karl giggled in his high chuckle. Then he began to move forward, faster, faster, until the wall at the top of the steps rushed in on Ben, and the overlaying strands of a thick cobweb washed across his face. Ben saw the wall closing in on him. He picked his legs up and slammed his feet against the surface. Then with all the force he could muster, he lifted his body back on Karl's shoulders, toppling them both backward to the floor.

Ben rolled away as Karl's hands angrily grabbed for him. "YOU LITTLE BITCH!" Karl shouted. "Little fucking bitch!"

Ben got slowly to his feet, his right arm curled tightly to protect his pained rib. Breathing heavily, his face a sweaty mix of pain and anger, Ben said, "Karl, don't do this. We can get out of here. We've gotta get out of here."

"You stupid little fuck," Karl said from his knees. "We're all dead already. You, me, your boyfriend, everybody in this house is fucking dead."

Malcolm Schreck's voice broke in at that moment. Hidden by the huge limb, it sang out in the dark. "Karl, are you having some difficulty?" Karl turned his head sharply toward the voice.

"FUCK OFF, ASSHOLE!"

"Karl," Ben said, leaning against the wall, "you don't want to kill me. You want to kill him."

Karl's cigar burned as he sneered around it. "I want to kill you both, just so I won't have to listen to your bullshit. You're both so full of shit. I'll settle for you."

Ben shook his head, confused. "Why?"

Karl inhaled heavily through his nose, lifted himself off his knees, and yelled, "WHY NOT?"

With that, Karl rushed toward Ben. Ben could do nothing now. His ribs were a fire in his side. His last hope had been reason, Karl so clearly outmanned him. But Karl was on his own death march. In his mind, nothing could change the outcome. He may as well die with the satisfaction of beating Ben to a pitiful pulp before he went. He clamped his arms around the smaller man, smashing Ben's arms to his side, sending volts of agony throughout his body. Karl lifted him off the floor until Ben's chest was at the level of Karl's face. Ben threw his head back as he groaned at the overwhelming pain. Karl's grip strengthened behind his back. It was becoming impossible for him to inhale. The air had been forced out of his lungs, and he gasped, trying desperately to suck air inside his chest. Then Karl added a new dimension to his agony. Gently, delicately, Karl began lowering the end of his burning cigar onto Ben's T-shirt. It burned quickly through the thin fabric to Ben's waiting skin. This caused a frantic kicking in Ben, but Karl's grip was relentless, and Ben heard the giggle come as Karl lowered the cigar again to a new spot.

Ben squirmed and twisted. His mind crazily thought of a joke. "Does your rib still hurt?" it asked. In that moment, Karl's grip loosened slightly. So intent on his torture game was Karl that he had slackened his grip. Ben wasted no time losing the advantage and instantly managed to pull both arms out from Karl's vicelike squeeze. Karl's eyes widened with surprise as he watched Ben's arms in motion. He looked on as Ben's right hand pulled the cigar from his mouth, while his left went around Karl's right eye, forcing it open. Ben drove the hot end of Karl's cigar downward into the open eye, extinguishing it as it smoked against the pupil.

It was a moment before Karl realized what had happened. Then he screamed. Bellowing and barking in mad pain, Karl dropped Ben and staggered backward, holding both hands to his burning eye. He kept moving backward until he came dangerously close to the top of the steps, placing his left hand instinctively on the ball of the post to steady himself.

Ben looked at Karl as he stood there, whimpering. Then the burns in his chest caught up with his adrenaline level, and he felt even more those holes of searing pain. The left side of Karl's face was clear. His chin was held up as if Karl was calling him to do it. "Go ahead, you little bitch," Karl's face said. "Do it."

Ben needed no other prodding. He ran full bore at Karl, his right arm cocked as he came forward. As he reached the man, he let it fly, his fist squarely knocking into the underside of Karl's chin. Karl sailed backward down the steps without any resistance. He remained off his feet for five steps, and then his head smacked the wall with a loud thump. His heavy body went down at speed, and Ben watched Karl's legs come over and flip him to his belly. His roll forced him downward like a tree felled at the top of a steep cliff, and his left boot smashed through the old wooden posts that framed the steps. The posts spread his legs apart, and Ben grimaced as Karl's descent was abruptly halted by a final post that did not break. The post was at the point where Karl's legs could no longer part, and he looked up at Ben, his good left eye crossing over to meet his scarred right.

Karl moaned. Somehow he found the strength to twist himself out of the wreckage. Laying his body flat on the steps, he threw himself downward like a crashing plane. Karl slid the few remaining steps to the bottom. He tried after a moment to push himself up off the floor, but Malcolm Schreck, who had watched the entire battle with bemused complacency, placed a careful shoe on his head and forced him back down. Karl lay there motionless, sucking air heavily, and passed out.

Ben stood. The force of his swing had twisted him around, and his weight had brought him down to the floor as Karl went down the steps. Now at the top of the steps, he looked down to see Malcolm Schreck grinning at him like a proud father. Schreck's grin was far too malicious to be afforded any good will. It was false. It could not hide the maggots that scurried from his brain to that evil mouth, that mouth on that face, that face on that head, that head on that body, that body that held a soul so wracked with foulness that to look on it was to risk being infected with its awful disease. But Ben was exhausted. He was a weary driver nearing the end of his journey. He wanted only to rest. He waited. Schreck seemed aware of his want, acknowledged him, and stepped away, allowing Ben to come down the steps unhindered by any fear he may yet have of the old vampire. At the bottom of the steps, Ben walked past Karl and went into the room where the other dead man lay. He reached into the fire and pulled an end of a small branch out of the flames. It burned before him, and he looked down at the man.

"I'm sorry, mister," he said, "whoever you are." Ben tossed the burning branch onto the cushion of the old chair and watched it until its flame attached itself to the fabric. Then he saw the ax resting against a pile of cordwood. *It must be the ax Karl used to chop the wood,* Ben thought. Its base was red, its edge silver, reflecting the orange light of the fire. It was all as if by some grand design. Ben gripped its handle and walked back toward the entryway.

Schreck stood at the entry to the kitchen. His hat sat tall on his head, and his hand grasped the handle of his large satchel, the bag filled with his only belongings: the book, the blades, and the head of his old lost servant. "Well, Benjamin, my young friend," he said, "where shall we go?"

Ben looked at Malcolm Schreck as his hand dragged the handle of the ax behind him, exhausted. "Go?" he said. "We're not going anywhere."

Schreck pointed past Ben to the other room. "That man was a constable of some sort," he said casually. "I am not concerned. But it would be prudent to be gone from this place. Do you not agree?" He held up a set of keys. Karl's keys. "We could take your machine, if you prefer."

Ben stood silent, glaring at Schreck, who said, "Oh, come now, Benjamin. If I wanted you dead, I would not have entrusted Karl to the task. I would have ripped your throat out myself. But you have suffered enough. With Arthur gone, you must come to me now."

Ben took a step forward, the head of the ax dragged across the floor. "Don't you say his name," he ordered.

"The man was a fool," Malcolm Schreck spat. "I merely gave him what he wished. A fool's death. Let us be gone from here, eh? Forget this . . . unfortunate happening."

Ben continued to step toward Schreck. Schreck moved forward himself to meet him. "Ignorance, Benjamin," he said. "Ignorance and self-deceit were what ended him, not I. I am but an instrument of knowledge." As he spoke, Schreck saw Ben's grip on the ax handle loosen. He pressed his advantage. "He refused me, our friend there. You would not make the same error. We are much alike, you and I. Ill winds carry us. Demons possess us, angry demons that rage against our solitude. I felt it the moment I laid hands on you."

With that, Schreck reached out and clasped a chilled palm against Ben's face. The ax handle dropped to the floor with a thud, and Ben's neck moved loosely under Schreck's command. The boy was subdued. Finally.

"What am I to do with you, eh?" Schreck said as he manipulated Ben's head side to side. "Perhaps I drain you just so, maintain your life long enough for you to watch as I pay visits upon that girl you hold so dear and your friend." Schreck considered this a moment, musing absently as he prepared to strike. "Perhaps then your mother."

Ben's eyes focused. Schreck looked at him, puzzled. At that instant, his throat full of saliva as if he had been in a deep sleep, Ben spit the contents of his mouth into Schreck's face.

Schreck staggered back toward the wall. He wiped his hands down his face, revealing a look of pure hatred. Ben took his right arm and, resisting the pain of his ribs, slammed his fist against the protruding nose of Malcolm Schreck. Schreck scuffled backward until his back impacted the wall behind him, sending a plume of dust around his black shape. His body shook with rage as he slowly lowered his hand from his face. His long stringy hair fell over his eyes, and his nose seemed curiously flattened by the blow.

Schreck gnashed his pointed teeth together and hissed, "Fool! I will make you suffer for that! You shall join Arthur in the grave!"

Ben had taken that moment of shock in Malcolm to pick the ax off the floor. He took a purposeful stride toward the old vampire. "Arthur's in Heaven, where he belongs," he said as he swung back with all his might. As his arms came forward, Ben shouted in a harsh growl, "YOU GO TO HELL!"

It was a perfect, clean cut, splitting the center of Malcolm Schreck's prominent Adam's apple. The ax head stuck firmly into the beam behind the wall, and as if through the strength of his will alone, Malcolm Schreck's head rested on the blade of the ax. Ben released the handle, transfixed by the maniacally changing expressions on the vampire's face. Schreck's brow furled in confusion, shock, and outrage, all the while hyperventilating in and out, groaning, and wheezing. And then the rolling eyes fixed on Ben. They stared at Ben with such intensity and hatred he barely noticed that Schreck's body had lurched forward from under the ax. Ben screamed as the cold hands reached his neck and squeezed.

Ben struggled with the body, and a mad dance ensued as he tried to break the clamping grasp on his neck. The head on the ax seemed to bubble, and a thick goo of greenish-yellow fluid tinged with rivers of red slopped thickly on the floor. It oozed out the stump of the neck as Schreck's hands tried to finish the job his head was ordering them to accomplish.

Then the house itself convulsed. The hands on his neck weakened as if shaken off in the heaving motion of the house. The body went to its hands and knees on the floor. The head bobbled and dropped off the ax as Ben staggered away. The earth beneath the floor howled. Then the floor exploded upward. Exactly where Karl had fixed the floorboards, where the drip of years of rain and thawing ice had rotted the old wood, it creaked and bent up. The bough above seemed to reach down completely now, and at its end was formed a gnarled claw. A cold blast came out of the hole, and Ben moved away from it, trying to escape both it and the claw. Then the floor reversed itself and sucked the boards downward like a black hole in space. Everything was cast toward it. Schreck's satchel popped open and lay on its side, the head of Mr. Warren rolled out, and the wretched old book followed after. The bag and its contents made their way into the pit without objection. Schreck's head and hat skid along the floor toward the hole, and as the disembodied head turned toward Ben, he saw the abject fear on the face of Malcolm Schreck. He objected to this. Schreck objected strongly. He had one last order for his corpse before his head disappeared into the hole, however, and like a whip, one of Schreck's hands lunged for Ben's ankle.

Ben screamed as it pulled him down toward the pit. Screams of terror came up from the emptiness to match his own as the body slid down the gaping hole, pulling, pulling at Ben's leg. The ax fell from the wall in the violent shaking, and Ben frantically grabbed for it. He swung it down at the floor like a mountain climber, desperate for it to find some purchase. It did, but the hope it fed was only momentary. Now his hands slid down the handle. He couldn't hold it. He knew what was happening. Schreck was dragging him to Hell, and there was nothing he could do. His feet froze as they entered the hole. The pit screamed. His fingers grabbed the very end of the wooden handle. And then the handle slipped from his hands. He was in the hole. His face froze as he looked down. There was nothing but darkness and Malcolm Schreck's body dangling below him. He kicked the hand away, and the body fell, disappearing into the nothingness. And then Ben followed.

But suddenly, something grabbed his wrist. A strong hand from a massive arm gripped Ben like a warm vice. Ben was oblivious to everything but the freezing darkness and the terrible grip. It pulled against the weight of the pitch-black in a tremendous tug-of-war. Somehow the hand managed to pull Ben out of the pit, and he came out screaming like a madman, clawing and raving. His body was frosted over, and his head and hair was shrouded in ice, his face and eyes wild. He struck blindly at the body under him.

Karl Angstrom yelled, "Get the fuck off me!" He hit Ben with a free arm hard enough to knock him still. Then he pulled them both back to the far wall, struggling against the howling hole's mad hunger as the shaking house went instantly silent, and the hole closed up neatly back into place before them. Fire raged in the other room. The right side of the old house was completely engulfed in it. The intense flames would soon overtake the whole structure. Karl lay his head back against the wall and watched it spread across the wall of the steps. He looked over at Ben with his good left eye as the young man shivered beside him, his eyes mad and wide, groaning and mumbling, incomprehensible, as the police lights flashed outside in the darkness.

The End

Acknowledgements

As Soultrapped is my first attempt to publish, I owe a great deal of thanks to all my friends and family who gave their support. It's a risk, putting your work out into the market, but not one whom I count as close to me ever expressed a doubt. I'm very grateful for that. Success or failure, I hope they enjoy the story.

This story grew out of my love of old horror stories and movies, and fellow aficionados of these will find a few Easter Eggs I've dispersed within its pages. As to actual history, such as the German Blitz and the legend of Spring-Heeled Jack, I found the book, *LONDON: The Biography*, by Peter Ackroyd, to be most enlightening.

Finally, although the characters in the novel are fictitious, I must acknowledge that a few are inspired by real people. One such character would be Karl Angstrom, who was loosely based on a friend of mine whom I'll call Jim. Because that's his name—Jim. Thank you, my friend, for turning that light switch on.

Drew Stockwell
June 29, 2017

Printed in the United States
By Bookmasters